Mama's Comfort Food

To Sharon)
Enjoy !
Phill Dula
2011

Mama's Comfort Food

RHETT DEVANE

Wild Women Writers
An independent publishing company

Mama's Comfort Food

Date of first publication: February 8, 2011

ISBN: 978-0-9829015-2-6
Library of Congress Control Number: TX 7-365-357

Published by Wild Women Writers
Tallahassee, FL
www.wildwomenwriters.com

Logo design by E'Layne Koenigsberg of 3 Hip Chics, Tallahassee, FL
www.3HipChics.com

Cover photo by Rhett DeVane

Author photo by Lance Oliver, www.LanceOliverPhotography.com

Printed in the United States of America

Dedication

- This book is dedicated to all of the healthcare workers who daily provide comfort and the benefits of healing touch and kind words.

- In memory of my mama, Theresa DeVane, a strong Southern woman who understood the link between love and food.

- And in memory of Donna Larson, a dynamic woman and friend who bravely fought the dragon. Twice.

Acknowledgements

Over and over, I see: no one does anything alone.

My heartfelt thank you to all of my loyal friends, family and patients.

To Ann Macmillan, Barbara Mason, and Lois Davidson for sharing their stories.

To all of my friends who joyfully shared memories of their mothers' comfort foods.

To medical experts: Timothy W. Bolek, MD, Radiation Oncology, North Florida Radiation Oncology Associates, TMH Cancer Center; Dawn Bishop, RN, MSN, AOCNS, Director of Oncology Nursing, Archbold Memorial Hospital; Ann Hatcher, RN, BSN, Nurse Manager, Outpatient Oncology Services, TMH Cancer Center; Mary Menard, RN; and Dianne Sutherland, RN.

To John Gandy and Warren Jones of Tallahassee Memorial Hospital.

To proofreaders: Ann Macmillan, Cathy Ricks, Angie Colchiski, and Leigh Ansley.

To editor Paula Kiger, reigning queen of the Big Green Pen.

To editor Donna Meredith of Wild Women Writers Publishing.

To law enforcement experts: Kathy Kennedy, Chris Garrison, Jimmy DeVane, and Kelly Walker.

To the Wild Women Writers Critique Group for encouragement, love and kind direction.

And especially to my readers. Without you, a book is just a random gathering of words.

May we never forget these simple truths: Magic and mystery surround us. Every day we are allowed on this Earth is a gift.

Thank you to God for allowing me to be a messenger.

A note from the author

Each individual diagnosed with breast cancer must make treatment decisions based on doctors' advice, timely research and personal preference. The path the main character follows in this work of fiction is loosely based on a blend of several women's journeys and is not an endorsement for one form of therapy over another.

She was looking deep inside for such a long time
Where head and heart collide
All by herself for far too long
But now she's feeling strong.

The spirit of love is standing by your side
And heaven above will always be your guide.
Wherever you go, don't you know
That love is always on your side.

There is no easy path to follow
But everyone must find a way
To where all hearts must return
When will we ever learn.

The spirit of love is standing by your side
And heaven above will always be your guide.
Wherever you go, don't you know
That love is always on your side.

From "The Spirit of Love"
Hugh McKenna, Mae McKenna
Reprinted by permission.
From the Shore to Shore CD
Mae McKenna 1999

Prelude

Excerpt from audiotape for Karen Fletcher—made by her grandmother, the late Piddie Davis Longman.

"Well, gal. I don't reckon you'll ever get to listen to this tape, what with you all settled in up there in Atlanta, pretendin' to be someone else. It felt odd, not leavin' a tape for you, is all. I made one for everyone else. Maybe, if you come to yourself one day, Evelyn will see fit to give this to you.

"Chattahoochee ain't such a bad little town. You were surely in a bust-a-gut hurry to leave out after you graduated FSU. Nobody really understood why you felt you had to desert us the way you did, but I suppose you had your reasons. It surely hurt your mama and daddy. I pray every day that you'll make it right with them, somehow.

"To call this place a sleepy little town is purely laughable. Maybe it is, to some folks' eyes. But there's a heap going on here. We've had our sweet boy, Jake Witherspoon, beaten up for being a gay feller here a couple of years back. That got us swarmed with reporters and such. Beats all I've ever seen. Then, lo and behold, if one of our prize citizens—Hank Henderson, a lawyer, to boot!—didn't turn out to be a child pornographer. I suppose you heard all of it, you bein' in the TV business and all.

"My point in all this, Karen, is that we've got all kinds of folks, even in such a small place. You gonna have drama anywhere you have human beings. If you ever decide to come back home, you won't be at a loss for entertainment. This place is better than The Young and the Rest of Us! (Laughter) That's what me and my best friend, Elvina Houston, call that 'soda popper,' *The Young and the Restless.*

"I love you, Karen. You was my first grandbaby. I cherished you from the time you was just a twinkle in your mama's eyes. I changed your diapers and wiped your little red behind even before your mama and daddy did. Don't you ever doubt for one minute that you got a family here ready to take you in with open arms. Forgiveness is our nature—comes as easy as breathin' in and out."

"My mama made the best sweet potato biscuits in the whole wide world. I remember standing on a wooden stool when I was just a little bitty youngun, watching her mash the clay-colored dough with her fingers in her favorite robin's-egg-blue pottery bowl. She'd pinch off a handful and roll it around in her flour-dusted hands till it was a perfect ball. Then, she'd mash it gently into a greased pan. When those sweet tater biscuits came out from the oven, the kitchen smelled like heaven on earth. They were light and airy—near to melt in your mouth. My daddy always maintained you could make a meal off a couple of sweet tater biscuits slathered with butter. Yessir, I can catch a whiff of them cooking to this day and get a warm feeling deep inside."

Piddie Davis Longman,
from the audiotape to Karen Fletcher

Chapter One

Anyone watching the woman in the maroon midsize rental car would have thought her behavior suspect. Either she had hit happy hour hard or she couldn't decide whether to head east or west. Every few miles, the car executed a swift U-turn, idled in the paved median, then turned to continue in the original direction.

"I don't know what the bloody hell I was thinking," she said aloud in a polished British accent. Realizing she was alone, she continued in a tone more suitable to the part of North Florida she now covered at twenty miles above the posted limit.

"I must be crazy. Why did I get on the plane and leave Atlanta in the first place? I have no business just showing up."

She shoved a limp hank of hair behind her ear and glanced in the rearview mirror. Good. No cars behind her to wonder if she was some kind of complete nutcase, driving like a maniac and talking to herself.

"And what will I say, exactly? Not like I'm in the neighborhood and just decided to pop by."

Her life could model for a daytime drama. Only, she had yet to see her particular set of dysfunctions in any plot line.

The insistent trill of the doorbell pierced the drone of Evelyn Longman Fletcher's morning shower. Dripping wet and thoroughly aggravated, she twisted the water control hard to the left.

"God knows, I simply don't have time for this," she muttered.

She whipped a thick white towel turban-style around her shoulder-length brown hair and donned a pink chenille robe and matching slippers. Normally, Evelyn welcomed visitors at any hour. Her mother, the late Piddie Davis Longman, had drilled genteel Southern hospitality into her soul at a tender age.

Never close yourself to a front door knock, Piddie had instructed, *you might miss out on the opportunity of a lifetime. Could be Ed McMahon and the prize-awarding team come to hand you a check for a million dollars! And believe you me, he ain't gonna stand out there on your front stoop all day with flowers and balloons and such. Friends come through the back door, but opportunity and blessings from Heaven come to the front.*

Today wasn't such good timing. Evelyn, designer of ELF-Wear, custom clothing for women, children, and infants, was to be featured on the Good Morning Show on Channel Six out of Tallahassee. Two of the ensembles she planned to offer up as proof of her talent were incomplete. The fancy computerized sewing machine that had set her husband Joe back five state retirement paychecks could only do so much. Human hands were required for the intricate finish work.

"I'm a-coming! I'm a-coming!" she yelled loud enough to carry straight through the front door.

She passed by the kitchen long enough to flip on the coffeemaker. No hostess worth her salt would entertain a drop-by visitor without offering food and drink.

"Good. Joe left a couple of fresh sticky buns."

Retired from a thirty-five year stint as staff psychiatrist at the state mental hospital on Chattahoochee's main thoroughfare, Joe Fletcher was the new owner and chef of Borrowed Thyme Bakery and Eatery. Long before his wife arose, he showered and slipped from the house to ready the small main street eatery for breakfast patrons. By the time Evelyn had barely finished her first cup of strong black coffee, Joe was flipping blueberry pancakes and eggs over easy, and buttering tall pyramids of Piddie's famous Cathead biscuits—old-fashioned biscuits made with lard, big as a cat's head. Saturday mornings, he substituted sweet potato biscuits. Before eight-thirty, all six dozen of the russet-colored sugar and cinnamon-dusted breads would disappear.

Evelyn hid slightly behind the door as she opened it a crack. "I'm sorry. You caught me at my morning shower. But if you want to come on in, and can give me just a minute—"

Evelyn stopped speaking when she recognized the caller. Piddie would have told her to shut her mouth, as she'd allow flies to buzz in.

"Mrs. Fletcher?" The thin stately blond woman inquired in a clipped British accent.

Then, in a delicate Southern drawl, she spoke again. "Mama?"

Karen Fletcher, alias Mary Elizabeth Kensington, Evelyn's estranged and deluded forty-six-year-old daughter, offered a weak smile. Balanced like a graceful fashion model, she stood on Evelyn's front porch, framed on either side by a lush Boston fern.

Donald James "D. J." Peterson jerked the wheel of his black Acura NSX hard to the right, narrowly avoiding a Ryder rental van intent on occupying his lane.

"Ya stupid moron!"

He downshifted and maneuvered three lanes of ball-busting Atlanta traffic to the 14th Street exit off I-75. Atlanta drivers had grown surlier in the past years, and for good reason. Not only had the city's population mushroomed, the entire sprawling metropolis had morphed into one contiguous nightmarish construction site.

By leaving his upscale home in Buckhead before five-thirty, D. J. managed to avoid the heavy morning expressway crunch when tow trucks circled like vultures awaiting the inevitable fender benders. A small café two blocks south of his workplace at public television headquarters served fresh pastries and gourmet coffee—by far, a more pleasant start.

His brow wrinkled as he considered his fiancée's brief message. "Curious and extremely odd," he whispered as he sipped a tall caffe latte.

Donald, Mary Elizabeth's voice mail had said, *I'll be out for a couple of days, tops. Family matters which to attend, that sort. Ring you up on my return. Toodles, luv!*

She was one of the few people who could make his given name take on a classy ring. With the killer British accent, Mary Elizabeth could ask him to take out the garbage and sound sexy.

"What family, exactly?" he muttered. "Her mother and father are deceased. She mentioned an elderly relative once. Was it Pity . . . or, maybe Patty? But that woman passed away a few months back. I remember Mary E. wiring flowers to the wake."

D. J. grimaced at a woman behind the service counter who was looking at him in an odd way. "Just talking to myself," he said as he tipped his head and flashed his best lady-killer smile. He really had to break the habit of out-loud pondering. With all the crazies loose on the street, someone was bound to think he was one.

Perhaps Mary Elizabeth's trip had to do with the distant cousins she'd made brief reference to: the ones she'd lived with while attending Florida State University. Still, she'd never seemed particularly tied to them.

In their five-year relationship, D. J. had gleaned a few sketchy details of his fiancée's past. To others, Mary Elizabeth was the epitome of the ice-cold, self-sufficient British female—closed off and emotionally unavailable. His dogged persistence paid off. One by one, her defenses peeled like layers of an onion, revealing a kind, trustworthy core—honest to a fault. He thought about the time a scruffy stray wandered into their path one evening. Both of them were dressed in semi-formal attire for an award function, Mary Elizabeth in pearls and heels. The young terrier-mix, clearly lost, stank of garbage and feces. Probably supported a hundred fleas and an equal number of knotted hair tangles. Mary Elizabeth took one look at its weepy brown eyes and without pause leaned down to scoop it into her arms. She took it to her veterinarian, paid for shots and worming, then kept it in her spare bedroom—separate from the two inquisitive felines—until she could locate a suitable home.

No one at Georgia Metro knew that woman, or the one who kept gift slips for fast food meals in her purse in case some homeless person begged for food or spare change. All the little glimpses of her kindness might have seemed staged—way too smarmy to be believed—except for the fact he had been there and she hadn't used any of the incidents to garner praise from him or anyone else.

He bit into a warm cinnamon roll. Glazed sugar crumbed and stuck in his thick mustache. D. J. frowned as he mulled things over. *And she's been acting so freakin' strange for the last couple of months. Actually, ever since I gave her the engagement ring on Valentine's Day.*

Have I rushed things? Is she getting cold feet? Lord, women are so damn hard to figure.

How many times had he felt like giving up, and what made this particular female so alluring that he'd endure any hardship for an hour of her time? One lesson D. J. had learned the hard way: never push Mary Elizabeth Kensington. She could be a regular hell-cat when cornered. Best to let her gallivant off to God knows where. Eventually, she'd call.

"What a hopeless loser I've become."

D. J. used the soiled napkin to wipe the crumbs from the bistro table and deposited the waste paper in the trash bin on his way out. Crisp spring air greeted him, laced with the delicate scent of flowering plants and damp fertile soil. Unconditional love swelled unbidden in his chest, a down payment on disaster.

"My mama—cook? That would've been the day. If it didn't come from a can or box, we didn't eat it. Still, I can pop one of them Swanson frozen dinners in the oven and think of home. Especially the one with the fried chicken, mashed potatoes, and that cherry dessert."
                                   Wanda Jean Orenstein, hair stylist

Chapter Two

Tiger stripes of morning sun pushed through the mist, casting shining dapples of light across clusters of blooming azalea and bridal veil spirea bushes beneath towering pine trees. The soprano mating calls of songbirds filled the air, with bass undertones provided by an occasional bumblebee harvesting nectar.

Amidst carefully groomed grounds, the Witherspoon mansion sprawled on a small rise—a gracefully aging dowager. A fern-studded porch stretched the length of her façade, providing deep shade for a series of white rocking chairs. Built in the late 1940s by Colonel Bud Witherspoon for his bride, Betsy Lou, the Greek Revival style home sported tall Doric columns spanning two stories: the sort of overdone Southern mansion where Scarlett O'Hara could have stepped out for a breath of fresh air, a crinoline-stiff gown forming a three-foot moat around her.

In 2000, the North Florida grand dame had been resurrected from decline and renovated as the Triple C Day Spa and Salon. Under the meticulous watch of Jake Witherspoon, Betsy Lou's only son and sole heir, the home once again paid tribute to Southern grace and over-the-top fashion.

Directly behind the house, spa reservation specialist and little-ole-lady-hotline president Elvina Houston sat on a wrought iron bench beside a patch of pine straw-thatched ground. By midsummer, the Piddie Davis Longman Memorial Flower Garden would be in full glory. This early in the season, patches of early weeds were the only hints of green amidst the blanket of brown.

Elvina glanced toward the row of windows on the back of the mansion. Mandy Andrews, co-owner and head stylist, darted back and forth readying her workstation for the first patron.

"Jolene Sims—frost, wash and set," Elvina recited, "and for Wanda Orenstein, Takweeta White for one of those fancy braided African-American styles. Melody won't be in from her dental appointment until mid-morning, so no manicures on her schedule till Suzanne Peters at eleven. Stephanie's off for the day, so no massage therapy clients."

She studied the diamond-studded gold watch Piddie had bequeathed in her last will and testament.

"I've got a half-hour, Piddie. I'm moving a bit slow this morning, so I'll have to cut to the chase."

Elvina smoothed a wrinkle from the paisley print cotton dress Piddie's daughter Evelyn had designed and settled into the daily monologue. The grief counselor had strongly recommended venting pent-up emotions, and the routine of chatting with her deceased best friend had become a soothing balm. For forty years, Piddie Longman and Elvina Houston had started every day with a lengthy telephone conversation. That, plus the two had been two-doors-down neighbors. Since Piddie had provided no forwarding number upon death, Elvina figured the daily memorial-side chat was the next best thing.

She glanced toward the heavens. "Hope it's as pretty up there as it is down here. The trees have painted themselves a bright shade of lime green, and the dogwoods are near to busting out in bloom all over town. The azaleas we helped the Ladies' Beautification Committee plant along Main Street are just splendid this year! Some springs are better'n others, it seems."

Her expression grew wistful.

"I can't fathom it's been right at a year since you left us. I miss you as bad now as then. So much has happened."

Elvina chuckled. "Good thing the hospital uptown is more a prison nowadays than a mental institution. If this was back in the fifties and someone caught me sitting here yakking to thin air, they'd lock me up for sure!

"You'd be proud to know that scoundrel Hank Henderson has ended up in the Forensic Unit up there. He's crazy as a bedbug, I hear tell. Doesn't look like he'll ever stand trial for all the bad he did to those younguns, Tameka and Moses Clark. Can you imagine? We had a *gen-u-wine* child pornographer right here amongst us!"

She snorted. "Course, you and me knew it all along, that something stunk to high Heaven about that man. Lordy, if Jake's beating didn't put us on the map, then Hank's dirty philanderings surely did! Both of them, something to be known for. It's a downright crying shame. Chattahoochee'll take a while before it can come up from under it all.

"Let's see . . . Angelina Palazzolo had a skin cancer cut off her temple. It didn't look like a whole lot of nothing, but turns out it was. Mandy spotted it when Angelina was in for a cut and blow dry. Told her to get it checked out. Sure enough, it was cancer. Doctor over in Tallahassee cut on her, took a chunk from her face. He did a good job, though. You can barely see the divot. Mandy said she'll trim some soft fringe there to cover up the spot as soon as the wound clears up."

Elvina swatted the air with one hand.

"Now, everyone for miles is scrambling to Mandy to check for bad spots. She keeps a'telling them she ain't allowed by law to diagnose, but that don't mean a hill a'beans to folks. She just gives them the name of the skin doctor and sends them packing if she suspects anything. So far, she's found four places that had to be removed.

"Hattie was by yesterday with the baby. That youngun is growing like a weed, I'll tell you. She still looks around like she's searching for you. Near to breaks my heart."

Elvina jumped as if she'd been stung by one of the bumblebees servicing the azaleas.

"I almost forgot! Lordy, I'm getting as bad as you were about re-membering things. Evelyn just called here no more than five minutes ago. She was all riled up about something, but I couldn't wedge a word out of her, no matter how hard I tried. She told me to spread an invite to all the gang here and the rest of the family. We're to show up at her house this evening at six-thirty. Must be important if she's called a conference. Said she wouldn't be in a'tall this morning. That, in itself, is odd. She's not finished with the outfits for her TV debut day after tomorrow.

"Any-who, I'll keep you posted on that one. It must be rich, to have gotten your daughter so all het up."

Inside the mansion in the staff kitchen and lounge, Jon "Shug" Presley draped a coat-length lab jacket over a brass hook on the antique hall tree and slipped off his mud-encrusted shoes. "I've really got to remind Jake to call the plumber about the faucet by the back door. I step right in the puddle it's created every dang time."

Wanda Orenstein smiled over the top of a steaming mug of strong black coffee. "It's 'cause you wear nurse-y shoes, doll. White's a magnet for mud. Now, if it's light-colored clothing, it'll attract red sauce. Don't suppose I have a single white shirt without a stain on the front."

Jon pointed toward the coffeemaker. "That fresh?"

"Hawaiian Kona, special dark roast. Just made it myself, so I know it'll do you."

Wanda watched him choose a tall pottery mug and fill it with the spoon-dissolving liquid. His usually military-straight shoulders drooped slightly.

"Jake said you were up and gone this morning long before daybreak."

Jon eased into a ladder-back chair and leaned on the round oak table. "My lady across the river went bad about two-thirty. Family paged me." He took a sip of coffee and moaned. "Gah, this is so what I needed."

"I don't know how you do it, Shug, facing death all the time. And the hours you keep! Are you sure floor nursing at Tallahassee Memorial wasn't better?"

Jon shrugged. "Pros and cons both ways. I like the hands-on care I give with my hospice work. These days, being in a supervisory position like I was at Memorial, means a pile of paperwork. When I was there, I barely got a pee break, much less time to spend with my patients. And they're the whole reason I went into the field to start with. As to the death thing, I don't fear it. Death's just another part of life. Hopefully, I make it a little easier, somehow."

"The lady, did she die?"

He nodded. "About an hour and a half ago. I left when the social workers came in. She has three adult daughters, and they were all there at the end. Great family. Very little bickering amongst themselves."

"Bet you see some doozies."

Jon rolled his eyes. "You wouldn't believe the stuff I've witnessed. Wave a little inheritance in front of some folks, and it's like throwing a pot roast to a pack of pit bulls."

"You off for the day, now?"

"You kidding? I just stopped in for coffee. I have one client in Grand Ridge and another, this side of Marianna. That's just this morning. You have a busy day?"

"Elvina sees to it that we're booked solid, not that I'm complaining. Pays the mortgage."

Jon grinned impishly. "Today a Pinky day? Elvina tells me you've got one heck of an admirer there."

"Elvina needs to learn to keep her trap closed." She laughed. "That'll be the day, now won't it?"

"How many times a week does Pinky Green come in for a trim? I swear he's in there every time I pass the salon."

"He has sideburn issues, or so he says. Every time I turn around, he's in my chair. If he wants to ask me out, I sure hope he'll hurry and get to it. I feel almost bad about taking his money."

"He's shy, Wanda'loo. Maybe you should ask him out. Save the man some bucks."

"Lord, why are we talking about this anyway? I've been married three times already, and thrown every one back. I don't need a man to clutter up my life. It's nice and simple now, just me and the dog."

"Still, a little companionship would be nice."

Wanda shrugged. "I've got you, Shug."

"News flash. Number one, I'm gay. Number two, I'm happily united to Jake. You need someone else in your life besides me, sweetie."

"It's less complicated with you, though." Wanda looked pensive for a moment, then grinned. "Pinky lights up bright red in a half second if he's the least bit put on the spot. It might come in handy, you know, him being that way. It'd be like having a nightlight when I get up to go to the bathroom in the dark."

"You are so bad. Speaking of Elvina, where is the old girl? I thought she'd be bustling around here somewhere. The Oldsmobile's parked out back."

"I'm surprised you didn't see her when you came in. She's out having her morning chat with Piddie."

From her viewpoint, Wanda could see the edge of the memorial flower garden. "Just breaks my heart when I see her out there. She's talked to Piddie every day since she passed. Rain or shine, she hasn't missed a single day."

Jon pushed away from the table and returned his empty cup to the kitchen. "People find all sorts of ways to grieve, Wanda'loo. Take a stroll through any graveyard, and you can see all sorts of earthly mementos left next to headstones."

"Elvina hand-picks the weeds from Piddie's daisy patch." Wanda's eyes watered slightly. "I hope I have a friend like her, one that will watch over me."

Jon rested a hand on her shoulder. "Don't you worry your pretty little head, sugar plum. I'll pick the briars off your plot."

"Homemade vegetable soup. Made with a big beef bone to give it flavor. Try as I may, I can never make my soup taste as good as my mama's. On a cold day, when I would come in the house half-frozen with my nose dripping and fingers numb, Daddy would build a roaring fire. Bobby and I would help him bring in the wood. Then, we would all sit down to bowls of steaming soup, rich with the summer's homegrown vegetables from the freezer and home-canned tomatoes. The warmth would sear down my throat, and pretty soon my whole body thawed from the outside chill."

Hattie Davis Lewis

Chapter Three

Jake Witherspoon, florist extraordinaire, plucked a faded blossom from a miniature azalea bush and returned it to the "Spring in the South" front window display.

"Mind if I ride with you over to Evelyn and Joe's, Sister-girl? The delivery van's packed to the gills with candelabras for the Fillmore wedding."

"Sure." Hattie Davis Lewis gathered several sets of soiled sheets from a wicker hamper by the treatment room and stuffed them into a laundry bag. "Let me set up the massage table for my first client tomorrow morning, and I'll be good to go."

Jake and Hattie's West Washington Street business was a study in diversity. Half of the brick façade building was devoted to Jake's Dragonfly Florist. The remainder housed The Madhatter's Sweet Shop and Massage Parlor. In one lazy afternoon, a patron could receive a relaxation massage from Hattie, a sugary confection with fresh gourmet coffee, and a bouquet of fresh-cut flowers. Small wonder the establishment possessed such a cheerful ambience. Touch, taste, and scent could be satisfied in one stop.

A few minutes later, Hattie parked her Ford Escape SUV on the grass beside Evelyn and Joe Fletcher's ranch style house on Main Street.

"Any idea what this is about?" Jake asked when he spotted the vehicles lining the circular driveway.

"Nope. Elvina left a voicemail message this morning. I haven't had time to call her back. Must be important, though. Last time Evelyn called us all together like this, Bobby and Leigh announced they had gotten married, remember?" She groaned. "You don't suppose Ev's cooking, do you?"

Hattie's cousin was locally famous for her terrible culinary skills. Though her kitchen sported every gadget known to mankind, Evelyn couldn't resist the urge to embellish recipes. The results were predictably disastrous.

Jake shook his head. "Joe's pretty much taken over in that department since Evelyn's started her clothing design business."

"Thank heavens." She laughed. "Remember the casserole she made for you when you first came home from the hospital?"

"How could I forget? Nature doesn't even *make* that shade of green. She told me the recipe came from some cookbook channeled by alien visitors."

Hattie rolled her eyes. "Lord help."

Evelyn's spacious living room was filled to capacity with select family and friends. Hattie settled on the couch by her husband Holston. Her brother Bobby and his wife Leigh sat on the matching loveseat. Mandy, Melody, Stephanie and Wanda had brought extra chairs from the dining room, and Elvina Houston occupied the leather wingback chair by the entertainment unit. Jake and Jon nestled into an oversized chair with matching ottoman. Bobby and Leigh's toddler, Josh Tank Davis, and Hattie and Holston's adopted Chinese baby girl, Sarah Chuntian Lewis, played on a handmade quilt in one corner.

Joe walked in, wiping his hands on a clean dishtowel. "Y'all come on back to the kitchen. I've thrown together some sandwiches."

"You know what this is all about?" Hattie asked.

"Beats the heck out of me, Hattie." He shrugged. "I'm as clueless as you all are. Ev's in the back. Says she'll come out to talk to us after we've had a bite to eat."

"Sounds serious," Mandy said.

Joe dabbed a bead of sweat from his upper lip. "She's been holed up in Piddie's apartment all day. Can't get a peep out of her. One thing I've learned about my wife after all these years: she'll come out when she's good and ready. Now, y'all come on back and fix a plate. The roast beef is hot, and I don't like to leave potato salad sitting out too long."

Well after coffee and Joe's famous eight-layer Slap-Your-Pappy chocolate cake, the door to Piddie's suite opened. The addition contained a small sitting room, bathroom, and bedroom where the beloved family matriarch had lived the last years of her life. Evelyn often took to her mama's rooms when she needed peace of mind.

Evelyn stood in the doorway, twisting her hands together. Her usually perfectly coiffed light brown hair was pulled back in a tight ponytail, and she wore no makeup. Her nose and the rims of her hazel eyes were bright red.

"Thank you all for coming on such short notice." She glanced around the room, taking a moment to rest her eyes briefly on each person.

"I'm going to need all of you." Her lips pinched into a thin line.

"What the devil has got off with you, Evelyn?" Elvina asked, "I've yet to see you at such a loss for words."

"Karen has come back to us," Evelyn said.

Elvina smirked. "After all these years of making your life miserable, she's decided we're worth claiming?"

Evelyn wrung her hands. "My daughter has breast cancer."

"My mother burned everything she touched. My brother Byron and I got used to having a little charcoal in our diets. One thing reminds me of her love, though: plain white Wonder bread spread with butter and sprinkled with sugar. She used to give it to us when we were hungry before meals. Since it didn't require my mother to cook, it was always wonderful. I still have a slice every now and then. Of course, now I eat whole wheat bread and Turbinado sugar—loses a bit in the modern translation."

Karen Fletcher

Chapter Four

Karen Fletcher stood in the Italian-tiled threshold of a richly-appointed Atlanta town home. She glanced around the first floor living quarters. She was an intruder in the cherished home of another woman, one with European style and refined tastes. Her alter ego, Mary Elizabeth Kensington: beautiful, talented, well-spoken, generous with her time and money, and a complete fabrication.

Her deceased grandmother's favorite Shakespearean quote floated in the air: *oh, what a tangled web we weave, when once we practice to deceive.* The woven filaments were unraveling, strand by carefully spun strand.

"How did you come to this, old girl?" she said aloud with the practiced British lilt she had perfected over the years. "Got yourself in a bit of a jam, I'd say."

Taizer, a six-month old rescue kitten, zipped into the room and trilled when he spotted his owner. Karen reached down and ruffled his grey striped coat.

"Where's your big sis?"

Tequila, the three-year-old princess Persian, would not acknowledge Karen's return for at least twenty-four hours. By then, she would be on her way back to Florida for who knows how long.

"You guys are going to have to stay put. I'm pushing my luck just being at mother's myself. Don't think I could show up with two cats in tow."

Taizer skittered toward the food bowls and mewed as if he hadn't been fed for centuries.

"I can see where I'm needed," she said as she filled two bowls with dry kibble. Tequila materialized next to her bowl and picked delicately at the offerings, ignoring her mistress.

"Good of you to make an appearance . . . missed you, too."

She wandered through the kitchen and living room to the covered garden patio. The outdoor room was tastefully decorated with a white wicker cushioned sofa and matching chair. A wicker porch swing piled high with plush blue-striped pillows was suspended from an overhead beam. A thick Swedish ivy vine created a solid wall of green on one end of the porch. Dappled light filtered through the leaves.

Was this how relocated government witnesses felt, stepping into someone else's reality? Just pull on a new identity as if it was a pair of dark sunglasses, change your name, and reinvent your life. Only, she couldn't blame her current state on anyone except herself.

Karen allowed her thoughts to drift to the recurring nightly adventure she had named the cave dream. The first time she experienced the vivid lucid dream had been around Christmastime, two months prior to diagnosis, before the screening mammogram, ultrasound, and needle biopsy. Long before her physician mouthed the dreaded word: *cancer*.

In the dream, she was hiking, an activity she had not enjoyed since college—before her work became her entire world. The forest surrounding the broad trail was open and airy with speckles of light playing across layers of spring green leaves. Steep hills laced with switchbacks every few feet, the pungent aroma of damp fertile earth, and a lack of the omnipresent North Florida humidity led her to believe the path traversed a Carolina mountain glen.

Her mood was light, effervescent: the feeling of shrugging off life's cares. The forest quickly became dense, the trail narrowing severely. Clinging vines grabbed at her calves and ankles.

Then, the cave. She stopped and stood, frozen. The opening beckoned like a gaping maw ready to swallow an intruder in one gulp. Something lived inside: a dark being banished to the underworld for sins unfathomable. The demon slept, his tortured breathing barely audible.

The dreamscape reappeared without warning or predictability. Karen awakened clammy with sweat, heart racing with the jolt of flight-or-fight adrenaline.

Following her diagnosis, the dream increased in richness. The images became more tumbled and dark. Leaves glowed in vibrant emerald and lime hues. The sky was blindingly blue with high cotton ball clouds scudding on invisible wind currents. Her nose detected the faint banana-tropical scent of flowering magnolias. The cave entrance appeared more shrouded and ominous. A foggy green-tinted mist hung in swirls in the stale air, where she stood rooted to the rock-strewn ground.

Karen shook her head to clear the images. Several deep inhalations helped to squelch the knot of fear deep inside.

Crumbling like a house of cards. The phrase popped, unbidden, into her consciousness. If not for the illness and impending struggle ahead, would she be witnessing her self-destruction?

No, it wasn't as simple as that. Her first mistake had been returning to North Florida for her grandmother's birthday party. The documentary on graceful aging she filmed and narrated had won accolades, but with consequences. The family gathering stirred something buried carefully and painstakingly deep; she had not been able to repress the emerging feelings. It was only a matter of time until Karen Fletcher and Mary Elizabeth Kensington would have to come to terms. Which selected reality would be allowed carry her forward?

With one visit to Evelyn Fletcher, her British persona suffered a clean, bloodless death. No time to mourn or look back and wonder. Finally honest with herself for the first time in as long as she could recall, Karen had to admit a desperate need for her family. Two doses of chemotherapy had painted a clear picture; she could not do this alone. The thought of possibly losing her breast kept her from confiding in the one person in the city who could stand by her side—her fiancé. Karen dragged two Louis Vuitton Pullman suitcases from the hall closet and wheeled them toward the master suite.

The Marinated Mushroom Bistro was discreetly tucked between two attorneys' offices. Offering a perfect evening retreat, the intimate Italian eatery provided a respite from downtown Atlanta's frantic pace.

D. J. checked his watch for the fifth time in less than ten minutes. "Typical. If that woman ever got anywhere on time, it would throw the balance of nature."

Karen paused briefly by the maître d' station, gave a small wave, and glided to the table. "Sorry, luv. Time gets away from me." The British accent came automatically. She leaned over and planted a kiss on D. J.'s temple.

He hopped up and helped her into a chair.

"Nice little place." She glanced around the dimly lit room. "Smells wonderfully of roasted garlic."

A waiter appeared and poured two glasses of wine.

"Gerald in marketing told me about it. Highly recommended the vegetable lasagna. Said the red sauce was better than his Grandma Celia's."

Karen took a sip of wine. "Perhaps he'd best not mention that to her."

A warm flush of affection coursed through D. J.'s body and settled uncomfortably in his nether regions. "You look beautiful tonight. A little tired, but beautiful all the same."

"Thank you, Donald. It's probably just the low light. Travel always makes me look positively ghastly."

"So, everything turn out okay?"

"As well as expected, I suppose."

"Anything I can help with?"

The server appeared beside their table. After they placed their orders, Karen took D. J.'s hand. "Actually, there is something you can do for me."

"Name it."

She caressed the back of his hand. "Watch over the kitties for a while. I can't take them with me, and it would be dreadful to board them for so long."

"So you're leaving again."

"Yes, Donald, I'm afraid so."

"I take it you'll not tell me where or how long."

"I'd rather not."

D. J. clenched his teeth to repress a rising sense of frustration. "Don't be cross."

"It's a little odd, don't you think? After all, we are engaged."

Karen's eyes glittered. "And you believe that entitles you to monitor my every move?"

D. J. took a deep breath and released it slowly. "Let's not argue. I don't want to take away from my time with you, Mary E."

Karen's eyes watered slightly at the sound of the nickname.

D. J. reached over and caressed her cheek with the side of one finger. "What's wrong, honey? What is so bad that you can't tell me?"

"So many things, Donald." Her voice broke slightly. "But for right now, no questions. I don't think I can take it."

"Hey, hey." He held her hand. "No more."

D. J. smiled slightly. "Good damn thing I love you like I do. Your cats are little hellions. I can't believe you're going to leave me alone with them. You'll come home to find me brutally murdered and covered up in litter."

Karen laughed. "Oh come, Donald, they can't possibly be that bad."

"Oh, yeah? Last time I spent the night, I had to pitch the Italian loafers your little darlings peed on."

"We'll have to close your shoes snugly in the closet tonight, then won't we?"

D. J. weakened. "I'd walk barefoot through the Royal rose garden for one evening with you."

Karen leaned over and kissed D. J. gently on the lips. How could she bear the loss of this man?

"Pot roast. Cooked in a cast iron deep Dutch oven. Loaded with onions and garlic. Later Mama would add chunks of Irish potatoes and chopped carrots. Sometimes, celery. The vegetables would soak up the mingled flavors of the beef and spices, and the gravy would turn out thick and brown. Sop that up with cornbread or biscuits. Umm! Last few years, I've been leaning toward vegetarianism, but still I remember her pot roast."

Pinky Green

Chapter Five

Pinky Green crushed a clove of garlic for homemade vinaigrette dressing. A mixed spring greens salad chilled in the refrigerator, and organically grown vegetables diced for stir-fry lay in mounds on a pine cutting board. A pot of brown rice simmered on the stove. Finally, Wanda Jean Orenstein was coming for a visit.

Funny thing: she had invited herself to his farm two miles west of tiny Sycamore, Florida. He had been working up to it. Four more sideburn trim appointments and he could've broached the subject, for sure. Wanda had stepped up to the plate and knocked the ball clean out of the park.

Fine with me, he thought, *since words just stick in my throat when I'm around the woman, especially if it's about anything serious.*

Pinky's mind transported him back to the first time the two had met. His regular barber on Washington Street was out following hemorrhoid surgery. On a whim, Pinky walked into the Triple C Day Spa and Salon to set up a time and date for a quick trim.

"C'mon back, hon," a red-haired woman wearing tight hot pink pants said, "I'll squeeze you in right now. I got a deep-heat conditioning treatment under the dryer, and I can't stand to twiddle my thumbs."

Pinky loved the fast-talking New Jersey female from the first second he set eyes on her. There wasn't one single piece of Wanda that wasn't alive. Even standing still, she seemed to vibrate. As she chatted and laughed her way through the best haircut he had experienced in his fifty-five years, Pinky felt himself relax. It was the first time he had let go and enjoyed himself in over eight years, since Alice Jo died.

He could put his finger exactly on the reason Wanda grabbed his attention. She possessed the same lust for life as his only sibling. Even as Alice Jo lay dying, the melanoma spreading its deadly cells to her major organs like dust in the wind, his sister had embraced living with a fierce gusto. Born with a wanderlust he didn't possess, she had traveled the globe from one end to the other, sampling the lifestyles and beliefs of faraway places. When she had joined him on the family farm after their mother passed away, Alice Jo had transferred her enthusiasm to the land.

Pinky smiled. Alice Jo would've loved Wanda: dragging her around the vegetable and herb gardens, pointing out this and that, and working in a lecture on the importance of medicinal herbs and organic farming. Then, the two women would've rocked on the porch with tall glasses of lemongrass tea, speaking on all things female and just plain making the world a place worth visiting.

He heard a cacophony of canine doorbells announcing Wanda's arrival and hurried to the front screened door.

"It's okay to get out." He descended the porch steps. "They sound a whole lot worse than they are."

She rolled her window down a crack and asked, "You sure your dogs will be all right with Scrappy?"

Wanda's mixed-breed black Labrador female danced from one side of the back seat to the other.

Pinky sauntered over to the car. "I have the alpha female, Francis, in her kennel. She can be a little over protective. The rest of these guys and gals are friendly enough. Let Scrappy out so she can run. I'll close the main gate, if you're worried about her taking off."

Wanda eased from the front seat. Pinky admired the simple ensemble of dark blue jeans and white shirt. The highlights in her auburn hair glistened in the afternoon sunlight. A faint aroma of citrus and cinnamon reached his nose.

I'm in big trouble, he thought.

Wanda flashed a smile. "You kidding? My girl's such a wimp, I'll be lucky to take two steps without her tripping me up. Where'd you get all the dogs?"

"They find me. Mostly people drop them off. I'll spot them wandering around the roadside, half-starved, and there'll be another one to take in and feed."

"Your vet bills must be enormous."

"I also have half-a-dozen goats, five turkeys, chickens, one milk cow, and at least ten barn cats."

"Bet you never get lonely."

He shrugged. "Well . . . "

Pinky motioned to the front porch swing and disappeared into the house for a moment. He returned with a carafe of wine, two stemmed glasses, and a hand-thrown pottery plate filled with goat cheese, grapes, and toasted wheat bread squares.

Wanda cocked one eyebrow. "This is a surprise. I would have never pictured you for a wine and cheese type of guy."

Pinky grinned. "Just because I'm from the sticks of Gadsden County doesn't mean I have no class." He settled onto the swing beside her. "Actually, you can thank my sister for trimming off my rough country edges."

"I didn't know you had a sister. Does she live with you?"

His face clouded briefly. "Used to. She passed a few years back."

The lingering sorrow in his voice touched Wanda to the core. She laid a hand on his forearm. "I'm sorry."

Pinky's freckled face flushed. They watched the dogs playing in the grass and sipped in silence.

How unusual, Pinky mused, *to be with someone who doesn't feel the need to fill every second with meaningless chatter.* It wasn't exactly what he had expected, given her professional persona. He studied Wanda's profile.

"Like what you see?" She turned to face him.

"Very much."

Wanda leaned over and kissed him gently on the lips. "There, now we don't have to feel all awkward with each other."

Pinky laughed. "You're something else, Wanda Jean."

"You don't know the half of it." She cocked her head to one side. "Something I been wondering . . . what's your real name?"

Amazed at the unaccustomed ease of the conversation, he replied, "Norman Pinkston Green."

"Lord, hon! You sure don't look like a Norman. And Pinkston? What a hell of a name to push off on a poor innocent baby boy! It's a good thing you picked up a nickname."

"Suits me, too. Besides," he pointed to the clusters of freckles across his pale face, "I couldn't tan if I tried. Mama always said I'd be brown as a berry if I could just connect the dots."

Wanda laughed. "What's for dinner? I'm famished. Elvina left me hardly any time for lunch today, so I just grabbed a handful of peanuts."

"I'm making a vegetarian stir-fry. Hope you like tofu."

"I'll try anything once. If it doesn't kill me, maybe twice."

He stood and held the screened door open. "Grab your wine glass and come on in. You can keep me company while I throw it together. It'll be ready in no time at all."

After lingering over dinner peppered with comfortable conversation, they moved to the porch rocking chairs, and Scrappy took a position at their feet.

Pinky said, "You seem a little sad. I didn't bring you down with all my talk about Alice Jo, did I?"

"Not at all. It's actually refreshing to find a man who can talk about feelings." She rocked gently for a few moments. Obviously, something weighed on her mind. Pinky respected the silence.

Wanda's shoulders drooped. "It's just . . . I found out yesterday that the daughter of one of my friends at the day spa has cancer. She's only a year or two younger than me."

"Seems like it's everywhere, anymore. I don't really buy the explanation that it's because of better detection. There're too many people of all ages with cancer. So many lives touched, so many taken away."

"Like your sister."

"I hope your friend's daughter gathers her family around her and is ready to fight. Cancer will make you get real about things pretty darn fast."

Surrounding the farmhouse, the sounds of animals and the earth settling in for slumber reached the porch.

"Alice Jo did a lot of research on medicinal herbs after she got sick—things for easing the nausea following chemotherapy and boosting the immune system. I still grow and harvest the plants. Alice Jo taught me to make tinctures, infusions, and teas. I've got all of the notes saved on the computer in the study—hours and hours of her careful work. If your friend is open to help, I'd be glad to share the knowledge. I know my sister would lend a hand, if she was here."

"Thanks, Pinky. I'll be sure to pass that along." Wanda spotted an old guitar propped next to a plant stand. "Play me something. You do play, don't you?"

"Most every night, I sit out here and pick awhile. Can't swear I'm much good at it."

"Sing me a song then, Pinky Green."

"You sure you want me to do that? Sometimes it makes the dogs howl."

She boxed his shoulder playfully. "I like most any kind of music. Since I can't carry a tune except in the shower, I won't be a harsh critic."

Pinky swung the old instrument into his arms and plucked the strings one by one into tune. "Hmm, I'll play my sister's favorite song. You'll probably remember this one."

Wanda listened as his rich voice sang James Taylor's "Shower the People." She closed her eyes and rocked in time with the mellow folk tune. The evening air held a slight chill, and the crickets tuned up to accompany the music.

Somewhere, between the homemade vegetarian meal, finger-style guitar picking, and gentle romance that followed, Wanda Jean Orenstein tripped and fell headfirst into love.

"My mother makes the best chocolate pound cake. She uses real butter—the kind that comes in a round waxed paper wrapping. She let me lick the batter from the beaters when I was a little girl. We never worried about getting some weird funk from the raw eggs, not at all. The batter was the best part, but I couldn't eat too much or I'd get a stomach ache. She still makes the same cake now and then, for special occasions. I eat a small sliver. Heavens, I don't need all those calories. I would look just horrible in a swimsuit if I let myself go!"

Ladonna O'Donnell, local beauty queen and model

Chapter Six

The formal waiting area for the Triple C Day Spa and Salon was barren. The only noises came from a trickling waterfall fountain in one corner and the low volume new-age music from a hidden CD player. The locals eschewed the fancy holding pen for the down-home atmosphere of the large treatment room farther back in the restored mansion.

The hair stylist salon was a buzz of activity. Ladonna O'Donnell, local beauty queen and model, perched on Mandy's chair with a flower-printed plastic drape protecting her clothing. Lucille Jackson, wife of Reverend Thurston Jackson of the Morningside AME church, occupied Wanda's station. Two professional dryers were in use, and Melody huddled over the hands of her nail patron, manager and head waitress of the Homeplace Restaurant, Julie Nix.

"My outfit's kindly oriental looking," Ladonna said. "So, I'm thinking I'd like one of your up-do's, Mandy. You know, like the one you did for the Miss Lake Seminole Contest last summer."

"I got just the thing." Mandy picked up a section of Ladonna's bleached blonde hair and experimented with different positions. "I ordered these miniature gold fans that will be perfect. Why don't we go with an asymmetrical look?"

Ladonna smacked her bubblegum. "Fine by me. Just so I look right for Unc' David's retirement party."

"Law, I can't fathom Chief Turnbull's retiring," Lucille said. "What's he gone do with hisself after being a police man all these many years?"

"Says he's gonna catch up with his fishing." Ladonna expanded and popped a large fuchsia bubble and gathered the spent gum with her shell-pink painted lips.

"Who's in line to replace him? You heard yet?" Mandy asked.

"Uh-huh. Rich Burns, only you didn't hear it from me."

Lucille held up one finger and gestured to secure her point. "He's a fine man, too. If he takes care of this little town as good as he does that old '54 Chevy he bought off Piddie, we'll all be able to sleep better at night."

"My J.T. sure likes working with him," Melody added. "He's fair and honest as the day is long."

Mandy winked at the nail specialist. "When you gonna break down and marry that man?"

"Soon as I can tie him down long enough so he can ask me, I reckon."

Lucille studied her favorite stylist in the mirror. "You sure are quiet this morning, Miz Wanda. Cat got your tongue?"

Wanda shrugged. "Just not in a talking mood, I guess."

Mandy smiled. "Wanda Jean's been bitten by the love bug."

Lucille slapped her thigh with one hand. "Yeah? Who's the lucky man?"

Wanda's face glowed slightly. "I'm not one to kiss and tell."

Mandy's head fell backward and she let out a belly laugh. "Since when?"

"Some things are so good; a woman has to savor them awhile before she shares with anyone else." Wanda drew her lips into a thin line.

Mandy jabbed the pointed end of a rattail comb toward her cohort. "Look at you, acting like the cat who swallowed the canary! I'll be dog-goned."

"No use trying to get anything out of her," Lucille said. "I've seen that look before, and she'd bust a gut before she'd let it go."

"Just as well. Hearing about hot romance when I'm not getting any might make me peevish," Mandy said.

"Bull doesn't wine and dine you anymore?" Lucille asked. "Y'all haven't been dating that long to have him giving up the romance already."

Mandy chuffed. "Bull's notion of feeling the magic consists of rubbing his day-old growth of whiskers across my cheek and saying,

'Don't you just love your he-man, little gal?'"

Lucille wiped a bead of sweat from her forehead. "Where's Evelyn this morning? I can usually hear her back there with all those fancy machines a'buzzing away."

"She's over in Tallahassee at the news channel, filming her big interview for the Good Morning Show tomorrow. Don't y'all forget to tune in, now," Mandy said.

"That's right! I'm sure glad you said something. I'd never forgive myself if I missed it." Lucille shook her head. "I heard about Karen and her troubles. She back in town yet?"

"Not so's I've heard," Mandy replied. "Reckon she'll be here soon, though. Evelyn's called over and gotten her an appointment with the cancer doctor in Tallahassee. He was recommended by the fella who did Hattie's surgery a couple of years back."

Ladonna piped up. "There's a nut case for you, that Karen Fletcher. Everybody in town knows she's been off pretending to be something she's not."

"She is pretty confused," Lucille agreed. "Used to weigh heavy on my dear friend Piddie, her going off like that."

"I can't imagine how she can even show her face back in town," Melody added over the drone of the exhaust fan.

Prissy Johns spoke loudly to compensate for the noise of her dryer. "I wonder how many folks'll give her the time of day a'tall."

"I, for one, surely will." Elvina stood at the threshold of the salon, her hands propped on her hips. "And I hope you all will, too. I'm fairly shocked by what I'm hearing."

Mandy rolled her eyes. "Don't be so dang high 'n' mighty, Elvina. You've done your fair share of dissing on Karen Fletcher in the past."

Elvina sniffed. "A fact for which I've spent a lot of time down on my knees here lately, begging the good Lord for forgiveness! Besides, it's Evelyn and Joe we need to support, regardless of how we feel about Karen's doings. I don't think Evelyn's touched a bite of food since Karen dropped the bomb on her."

Elvina turned to leave, and then twirled around. "Lord, help. I'd forget my head if it wasn't tied on! Reason I came back here to start with was to tell you your ten-thirty perm canceled, Wanda. It was Sue Ellen Sales. She has a fierce sinus infection. Said her head was near to blowing up, so she's on the way to the clinic to see about some antibiotics."

"That's okay, 'Vina. I have some busy-work I can do. If you can't fill it, don't stress."

Elvina scuttled back to the reception desk.

Mandy shook her head. "Is it just my imagination, or does that woman act more like Piddie Longman every day? I swear she's channeling the dead."

Lucille smiled. "There can be only one Piddie on this earth, but I do believe Elvina's been around her so many years she's beginning to pick up her ways."

Melody spoke up. "One thing I noticed is her hairdo. She's piling it up in a bun now."

Mandy chuckled. "She's got a lot of height to reach to come up to Piddie's bouffant. Last time I did her hair, it stood a good twelve inches!"

"Long as she doesn't start sticking flowers in it like Piddie did. She does that, we might ought to get her to a shrink," Wanda added.

Mandy pointed. "Or get her a nice padded room up in the Hooch."

"My mother was a fancy cook. Sauces, loads of spices, that sort of thing. My favorite? Blueberry pancakes with maple syrup. I can close my eyes and almost taste them. Joe Fletcher makes them as close to my mother's as I have ever tasted. That's one of the fringe benefits of being married to his wife's cousin. I can get myself invited when he's making a batch."

Holston Lewis

Chapter Seven

The Davis family homestead three miles south of Chattahoochee encompassed one hundred and fifty acres of prime hardwoods and aged longleaf pine. Laced with several springs, the gentle hills and valleys gave the property a mountain retreat ambience. Deep in the woods, Hattie's father, Dan Davis, had created a one-acre catfish pond at the base of a natural depression where three streams converged.

Initially, the farmhouse was a rickety wooden affair riddled with holes big enough for the local vermin. Shortly after her mother and father moved in, reconstruction began, room by room until the completed house bore little resemblance to the original structure. The white wooden one-story home with dark green plantation shutters boasted a wide shady porch across the front. A small in-ground swimming pool had been added in the mid-sixties. Mr. D's workshop and assorted sheds were hidden from view. The farmhouse was perched atop a small rise at the end of a one-lane sandy drive, Bonnie Lane.

Recently, Bobby, Leigh, and baby Josh Davis had moved to the family acreage. Their spacious cypress log home was tucked into the forest out of sight of the farm house on a separate driveway off the main lane. The Davis clan's only nearby neighbors were John and Margie Frasier, old family friends who occupied a modest ranch style dwelling close to the highway.

Hattie Davis Lewis sat in her father's worn rocking chair on the front porch with a strong cup of morning coffee in hand. Sarah and her cousin, Josh, played in a large Kiddie Corral set up in the soft grass beneath an old magnolia tree. Spackle, Hattie's mixed-breed mutt, perked his ears and barked.

"Visitors? This early?" Hattie frowned. Her shoulder length brown hair stuck out at odd angles. She glanced down at her stained sweatshirt and faded jeans. "Whoever it is better take me like I am."

A sleek sports car with Georgia plates pulled shy of the grass, and Karen Fletcher emerged from the driver's side.

"Well well," Hattie muttered, "look who we have here." She called the dog to her, then yelled out, "Don't let Spackle scare you. He's all bark and no bite."

"Good morning!" Karen stepped onto the porch. She motioned toward Hattie's cup. "Any more where that came from?"

Hattie jumped up. "Oh, sure. My apologies. I'm not much of a hostess first thing of a morning. What do you take in yours?"

"Strong and black."

"Must run in the family." Hattie disappeared inside, returning shortly with a tall pottery mug and a plate of cinnamon buns.

"Compliments of your daddy." Hattie offered a fresh sweet roll and napkin.

"Amazing, isn't it? My father with a restaurant? I wish he would have started cooking back when I was growing up."

"You saying your mama's cooking stunted your growth?"

"Hardly." A slight smile played across her features. "I have to admit, my warm memories of home never include wonderful aromas wafting from the kitchen."

"Piddie always said Evelyn's cooking kept her regular."

Both women chuckled, and then rocked in silence for a few minutes watching the children play.

"Your yard looks so nice, Hattie."

"Thank Jake Witherspoon for that. He lived with me for a while before Holston and I married. Then, he moved to the upper story at the mansion. Even though he doesn't live out here anymore, he periodically gets overcome with the need to landscape and takes it out on our property. Course, that has slowed down since he and Jon inherited Aunt Piddie's little frame house on Morgan Avenue."

Hattie pointed to an area at the end of the porch. "My favorite is the butterfly garden. It's not pretty yet, but given a couple of months, it'll be loaded with butterflies and hummingbirds fighting over the blooms. Jake designed the gardens at the mansion, too, with help from a nursery in Tallahassee."

"I haven't seen him since I've been home, but he delivered a bouquet of spring flowers to Mama's the day after I drove in."

"Not that I'm upset by your coming by, but . . . this isn't just a social call. I mean, you didn't come to talk about my yard, I presume."

Karen pushed a loose blonde curl from her face. "Mama thinks I should try to mend fences. I don't know how that's possible, since I didn't leave any standing." She turned to face her cousin. "I do hope to have a second chance to . . . to try to build anew." Karen stared into the distance. "I don't know where, or how, to start."

"By telling me who you really are, and why you decided all of a sudden to act like any of us meant anything to you."

"Fair enough." She took a deep breath. "God, it's all so tangled. I suppose, if I had to pick a point where it all started to go off track, it would be in my first year at Florida State. I was such a freaked-out, mousy little thing, back then. Terribly insecure."

"We all were, Karen."

Karen shook her head vigorously. "You made friends easily, Hattie. Always did. I was so lost in those massive freshman classes. Looking back, I should have started out at the community college."

"So you ran off and became British because you weren't Miss Popularity? Is that what I'm hearing?"

"When you put it that way, it sounds so simple. Like it was one big case of pretend that got way out of hand."

"What I'd like to know, Karen, is how you managed to pull off such a huge deception? It takes balls of steel to do what you've done."

"Not really. Just documentation and a vivid imagination. Remember the drama class I signed up for in our freshman year? I tried to talk you into taking it, too."

"Vaguely. I can barely recall what I ate for dinner yesterday, much less something from over twenty years ago."

"I discovered I had a knack for accents—could pull anything off, especially British. I started pretending I was an exchange student from Liverpool whenever I went out to clubs. I was a magnet for men for the first time in my life. Mary Elizabeth Kensington was born, and when I was her, I was witty and confident."

"All the things you weren't."

Karen studied her cousin for a moment. "Precisely. The fake identity helped immensely in the world of broadcasting and journalism. Karen Fletcher would've been just another Southern female seeking employment, whereas Mary Elizabeth stood out—cool, exotic, and impeccably dressed."

"But how did you get past the legal stuff—your diploma?"

"I changed my name shortly after freshman year. The rest was a piece of cake."

Hattie considered. "That's why you didn't walk with the rest of us on graduation day."

"I couldn't. When they called Mary Elizabeth's name, lowly Karen Fletcher would have claimed the diploma."

"Unreal. Still, wouldn't your employers do some sort of background check on you?"

"My degree was legitimate. I had references lined up who only knew me as Mary Elizabeth, and my invented parents in England were deceased. The only kinship I claimed was with a few distant cousins in Florida whom I stayed with off and on during my first years of college."

"You're a piece of work, Karen. Your story would make a great movie script."

"Except for the ending."

"If not for the cancer, you'd still be living large in Atlanta? Don't you have anyone close up there to help you through everything?"

Karen twirled the coffee mug slowly in her hands. "I have a fiancé—Donald. That is, Mary Elizabeth has a fiancé. It remains to be seen if that's the case when this is all said and done."

"I presume you haven't told this man about your cancer?"

"No."

"So, what—did you have an attack of conscience and come crawling back to your family?"

"It wasn't just the illness that brought me back. I had been considering it for some time. Grandma Piddie's party cinched it for me."

"Your documentary film on aging? You surely didn't act like you even knew any of us when you were here last time."

"Professional distance. Mary Elizabeth was the queen." Tears appeared in the corners of Karen's eyes. "When I saw all of you together—happy, close, obviously loving each other—something came apart inside of me. I . . . " She leaned forward and covered her face with her hands.

Hattie reached over and tentatively touched her shoulder."There's always room for one more, Karen."

She dabbed her eyes with a tissue from her purse. "You think?"

"Aunt Piddie always maintained our family was good at taking in strays—people and animals."

Karen stared into the distance. "When I was first diagnosed in mid-February, all I heard was the word *cancer*. The rest was a blur. I got in my car and drove. I wasn't aware of anything until I reached Lake Lanier, a half hour above Atlanta. Couldn't tell you how I got there or if I ran over anyone on the way. I sat next to the water thinking about what it might say on my epitaph. 'Here lies—well, we're not quite sure—she pretended to be someone else most of her adult life.'"

"Cut yourself some slack. There's not one of us who haven't made mistakes. Granted, yours was a doozy."

"You always could cut straight to the chase, Hattie."

"Sorry." Hattie offered a sheepish smile. "Look at me. It took until my mid-forties to realize what I wanted. I took off like a shot after graduation, too, only I didn't make it past Tallahassee. Now, here I am—husband, baby, and back at being a farm girl. I spent a number of years chasing my tail in a circle."

Karen reached over and grasped her cousin's hand. "Thank you for trying to understand—for giving me a chance. It means the world, honestly."

"I'm not the only one you have on your side. Mandy told me Elvina Houston's taken up your cause. Let me tell you, since Piddie died, Elvina's the heartbeat of this town. You'll be lucky to get a moment's peace once she rounds up the troops."

Karen laughed. "I barely remember her."

"She was Piddie's number one. Elvina still holds court with Piddie's ashes every morning at the Triple C. She swears Piddie told her to look out after you and your mama."

"A little help from the other side will be welcome, too." Karen smiled. "There's something else I wanted to talk to you about."

"Hit me with it. We've made it past the hard part."

Karen squared her shoulders military straight as if preparing for battle. "Mama and I saw the oncologist yesterday. He was gung-ho to set up surgery as soon as possible, but I asked to hold off."

"What the heck for? Don't you want the tumor removed? I did! I couldn't get to the O.R. fast enough after they diagnosed the colon cancer."

Karen fidgeted with a loose wicker strip on the seat of the rocker. "I've done considerable research on it, Hattie. I read everything I could get my hands on. I started chemotherapy with a doctor in Atlanta, was convinced I could go it alone. I wanted to try several sessions of chemo first—to shrink the tumor's size. The oncologist in Tallahassee has agreed to continue treatments for three more sessions before surgery. Also, I'd like to plan Reiki treatments with you. Mama told me you were a practitioner."

"Not that I'm not happy to help out in any way I can, but aren't you taking a hell of a chance, not jumping right on this?"

"There has been a lot of evidence with breast cancer treatment lately, where the doctors use chemo and alternative therapies first, then excise the lump. Especially in Europe, they're not as quick to lop off the entire breast."

"And the doctors agreed with your plan?"

"Reluctantly. My tumor is sizable—four by five centimeters. Both the surgeon in Atlanta and the one in Tallahassee recommended immediate surgery. But I'd more than likely end up losing my entire breast. What I hope to do is shrink the tumor down to a size that can be excised with a lumpectomy. I want to save my breast, Hattie."

"Gosh, Karen. That's a huge tumor! Didn't you notice anything? How about your yearly mammogram? Didn't anything show up on that?"

Karen frowned. "I've been terribly blasé about my health. I didn't actually detect a lump. My nipple started to sink in a bit and the skin took on a strange appearance—like the peel of an orange. Still, I didn't put too much importance on it. I was terribly busy at the station at the time. When I finally went in for a physical, my primary care physician sent me in for a mammogram. The rest is history—ultrasound, needle biopsy. Poof! Your life is on the line. Amazing how quickly things can spin out of control."

Hattie nodded. "That any of us think we are in control in the first place is laughable."

"So, can I hire you as my Reiki therapist?"

"No."

"Still can't forgive me?"

"You can't hire me. I'll do it for free because you're family."

"I'd never expect that, Hattie. Business is business, and it's money for you."

"Listen, Mama and Daddy left Bobby and me well set in that respect. I don't actually have to work. I choose to. I want to do this for you. Otherwise, I'd feel helpless, standing by watching from the sidelines. When do you want to start?"

"Tomorrow too soon?"

"Works for me. I'll double-check my massage schedule, but I believe the morning's free. Why don't we set up here on the porch around ten? I'm worthless before I have a couple of cups of coffee. Since I stopped working full time, I ease into the day. I can have Holston take Sarah to his office at the Triple C so we'll have peace and quiet."

Karen glanced around. "Out here? In the open?"

Hattie chuckled. "Reiki translates to universal life force energy. I've been attuned to the energy, and serve as a conduit. This is accomplished by laying hands on various energy centers of the receiver's body, Karen. You don't need to be undressed. All you'll experience is gentle warmth and an overall sense of well-being. You won't flash the world. Besides, it's spring, the perfect temperature, and the birds are singing up a storm. I think it would be a life-affirming place to do healing work."

"Okay, then." Karen stood. "I'd better shove off. Daddy promised blueberry pancakes for brunch. Want to grab the kids and join me?"

"I'd best not. I look like who-shot-Sam. I haven't even had a shower yet. Motherhood will do that for a girl."

"Still, it seems to agree with you."

Hattie jumped up. "Wait here a minute." She disappeared into the house and returned with a small jewelry case.

"I want you to have this—for good luck."

Karen opened the box to find a delicate daisy lapel pin. "How beautiful!"

"Daisies were Piddie's favorite flower, so this always reminds me of her. It was given to me by Ruth Hornsby, the adopted Chinese daughter of our friends from Tallahassee. It was my talisman during a really hard time in my life."

"I'm touched, Hattie. Thank you."

Hattie embraced her cousin. "I'm right here if you need to talk to someone who understands all the emotions that go along with cancer."

"Some day, you'll have to tell me about your ordeal."

"Sure. But for now, we need to focus on getting you through to the other side."

"Mama says this recipe's been passed around so many times, she doesn't even know who deserves credit. She makes it every family get-together and for the dinners at the church. It is so hard for me to maintain my figure!"

Ladonna O'Donnell, local beauty queen and model

Mama O'Donnell's Chocolate Pound Cake

1 cup butter
½ cup Crisco shortening
3 cups white sugar
5 eggs
½ teaspoon baking powder (sift before measuring)
½ cup cocoa (sift before measuring)
1 ¼ cup milk
1 teaspoon vanilla extract
3 cups cake flour (sift before measuring)

Cream butter, shortening, vanilla and sugar together. Add eggs, one a time, beating well between each. Combine flour, cocoa, and baking powder. Sift three times.

Add dry mixture alternately with milk to creamed butter mixture. Mix well. Pour into a greased and floured 10-inch tube pan.
Bake in a 325° oven for 1 hour and 30 minutes. Do not open oven door during baking time. Cool in pan or on wire rack. When cake has completely cooled, frost if desired.

To make frosting:(optional)
In a saucepan, combine one stick butter or margarine, softened, 6 Tablespoons buttermilk, and 1 Tablespoon cocoa. Bring to a boil, then remove from heat. Stir in one box of powdered sugar (sifted) and 1 teaspoon vanilla extract. Add 1 cup chopped nuts. Beat until desired consistency.

Chapter Eight

"Augh! You little shit!"

D. J. leapt from the couch in his fiancée's townhouse, spilling a tall glass of iced water on the Oriental rug. He hurled a decorative pillow toward the foyer where Taizer hovered over a pair of leather Sperry Topsiders. He raced to the hall—too late.

"That's the second pair in less than a week!" he yelled. "One more and I swear your little striped butt is going back to the shelter!"

The expensive deck shoes rested in a moat of cat urine.

"Why can't you piss in her shoes? She's the one that took off and left us. I feed you, pet you, even sleep over a few times each week to keep you and your fat-ass sister happy, and this is the thanks I get?"

After drying as much moisture as possible from the expensive Oriental rug, D. J. sprayed the shoes and tile with cleaning solution. Enzymatic action against odor the label lied. He knew the brutal truth; nothing short of napalm could extinguish the stench of cat urine. He had three pairs of ruined shoes to prove it. Not only was love deaf, dumb, and blind, it also rendered one's nasal passages inoperative.

The cell phone in his jacket pocket trilled, and he rushed to the living room to retrieve it.

"Hello, luv. How are my babies?" the cool British voice asked.

D. J. pitched the saturated cleaning cloth into a plastic bag and deposited it into the trash compactor. "Why not . . . 'How are you, D. J.? I miss you, D. J.! I'm racing home to you as fast as my little car will take me, D. J.!'"

"Donald. You're yelling."

He huffed. "Sorry, Mary E. You caught me in the middle of choking the life out of your little boy."

"Really, Donald. Can he be as dreadful as all that?"

"Tequila's beginning to tolerate me. She slept on my chest most of last night. But the little hellion, Taizer . . . "

"He's just a baby."

"Right. I'll try to bear that in mind the next time he uses urine warfare. Let's not talk anymore about your cats. They are fine. I am the beleaguered one in this scenario. When are you coming home?"

"That's why I called. Seems it'll be awhile before I can return."

"A week? Two weeks? What?"

"At least a couple of months, maybe more."

"You're kidding me."

"Don't be cross, Donald. If you don't want to care for the cats, I'll arrange to board them."

He clenched his teeth. "No, no. I'll do it, damn it."

"You should call Bonnie for a massage. You sound dreadfully tense."

D. J. closed his eyes. "I miss you Mary E. Don't you miss me at all?" he said, instantly loathing the pitiful teenage-crush tone in his voice.

The line was silent for a moment before she replied. "Of course, darling. Really must go now. Ring you later. Toodles!"

D. J. stared at the compact phone as if it held the answers. "I've got to find out what the hell's going on with her," he muttered.

"Yeowl!" Tequila twirled in circles around his ankles, and he leaned down to scratch behind her ears. "At least you're on my side, oh one of great girth."

The rotund Persian waddled to her bowl and cried piteously until he relinquished and poured out a cup of dry cat food.

"You women are all alike. Show a guy the slightest hint of affection, and here he comes, ready to do your bidding."

Tequila regarded him briefly with large golden eyes before turning full attention to dining.

The editing room at Georgia Metro Public Broadcasting—a dark, cramped labyrinth of computer equipment and insistently blinking monitors—reminded D. J. of a Lear jet cockpit. The primary inhabitants, Jason "Simpy" Simpson and Preston "Perch" Pershing, slipped like trained moles between the assorted workstations.

"Morning, Simpy!" D. J. called from the threshold. Like other Georgia Metro employees, he harbored great respect for the dedicated video crew and hovered just outside the door until granted entrance.

Simpy peered over the black plastic rims of nerdy glasses. "C'mon in, Deej. Coffee's on in the back if you want."

"Whatsup?" Simpy asked as D. J. flopped into a wheeled chair to his left. "Figured you'd taken a little vacation with the queen mum once membership drive week was done."

"Nope. I'm hanging around here. Same old."

"Haven't seen her highness around lately. She blast off for the homeland?"

D. J. shrugged. "Beats me."

"You're telling me you don't know where she is? That bites."

"All she told me is that she's dealing with some family matters."

"Hmm." Simpy stabbed at the computer keyboard.

"You work with Mary Elizabeth a lot, don't you?"

"I usually get the honors, right. She and Perch butt heads till someone comes up bloody. But hey, if you think I've got some inside scoop on the Ice Queen, think again. All business, all the time. No idle chit-chat." Simpy worked as he talked, his hand gliding easily between the computer mouse and keyboard. "Not that I mind it, really. I don't much like getting all caught up in private affairs while I'm taping. Too messy."

D. J. sipped his coffee. "Jeez, how long's this coffee been brewing?"

"Put it on fresh at two this morning. Can't be that bad by now."

"Dunno how you keep the hours you do, Simpy. Do you ever sleep?"

"I can go for a couple of days at a time. Then, I fall out. Been that way since college." Simpy studied D. J. for a moment. "You even heard from the princess?"

"Couple of times since she left."

"Some people don't like Mary Elizabeth. Not me. She may be frosty, but she's a professional to the end." He gestured toward a small Lucite award plaque. "Got her to thank for that."

"For the documentary on aging last year. It was quite good."

"I didn't shoot the first few clips. Perch ended up working on that. I was out with sinus surgery for a couple of weeks. But the missus insisted on taking me along to Florida with her. That was a trip!"

Simpy leaned back and laughed. "You should have seen it, Deej. Tables of food for days! Folks were real friendly. Made sure we ate right alongside them after the majority of the interviews were over."

"It was some kind of family reunion, right?"

"Nope. Hundredth birthday party for the coolest little old lady I've ever met." He shook his head. "The whole thing weirded Mary Elizabeth out, though."

"How so?"

"Dunno how to describe it, actually. She was . . . edgy . . . the whole time we were there, glancing around like she expected something to happen. I've never seen her so ruffled. Then, she insisted we leave early, immediately after we ate. The family had a video presentation, kind of a this-is-your-life thing, planned. Mary Elizabeth was hell-bent for leather that we vacate. I would have liked to have seen it. Amateur videos are a riot."

"Odd."

"Yeah. I asked her about it later, but she never gave me a clear answer. Didn't say more than two words to me in the van coming back, either."

D. J. stood to leave. "Thanks for the delightful coffee, Simpy. Good talking to you."

"Sure thing, Deej. Drop by anytime. I'm always freakin' here."

Executive director Wilton "Will" Cooke's spacious office was a direct contrast to the camera crew's high-tech lair. D. J. often kidded his friend that he could be the male counterpart to Martha Stewart. In the five years he had known Will, D. J. had never seen so much as a paper clip out of place. The compulsively labeled designer bins left no room for competition.

"Morning, Big Will!" D. J. called.

"Five pounds less of Big Will, thank you very much." The director patted his distended stomach. Slovenly housekeeping wasn't his sin, but gluttony was.

"Sugar Busters diet still working for you, then?"

"Yes sah! Fifteen pounds to go before I allow myself even a bite of sugar."

"For your own good, stay out of the staff lounge. Janice brought in a homemade German chocolate cake."

Will closed his eyes briefly. "Oh, no."

D. J. smiled. "Don't fret. I'll eat your share."

"Such a friend I've got. One should be so lucky. By the way, great job on the membership drive. Economy in the can like it's been since nine-eleven, I thought we'd be struggling this spring for sure."

"Might work to our advantage. Folks stay home when times are uncertain—watch TV, read books."

"Hmm. Speaking of not staying home, have you heard from our own little English rose?"

D. J. flopped onto a leather arm chair. "Spoke with her briefly last night. She called to check on the cats and let me know it'll be a couple of months before her return."

"About the same information she relayed to me before she left. Not that she doesn't have tons of leave time. The woman never takes a day off. She out of the country?"

"I don't actually know."

Will grinned. "She's got you by the short hairs, eh?"

"What few I have left she hasn't snatched out."

Will shook his head. "Terrible thing—love."

D. J. fidgeted with his watchband. "You wouldn't happen to have the address and phone numbers for her cousins here in the states, would you?"

Will frowned. "You know me better than to ask that."

"Sorry. Lost my mind for a brief moment."

"I can't divulge an employee's private records. Especially not Mary Elizabeth Kensington's. She'd grind my bones and serve me with high tea!"

"True."

Will's face brightened. "Still, you do have access to the princess's private chambers."

"You suggesting I snoop around her townhouse?"

"Not at all. But if you happen to bump into an address book or the like as you are searching for a pen to jot a note with . . . well . . . "

"Mind if I take a couple of hours away from the office?"

"No skin off my teeth. You pulled so many overtime hours in the last few weeks, I'll be doing good to pay you off by this time next year."

D. J. jumped up and headed for the door. "Thanks for the brilliant suggestion."

"That's why I make the big bucks."

D. J. chuckled. "Yeah. You, me and Dan Rather."

In the parking lot, D. J. ducked behind a broadcast van in a vain attempt to avoid Trisha Truman, office manager for GMPBS.

"There you are!" The stiff-haired blonde rushed to intercept him. "I've been searching high and low for you."

A thick cloying cloud of cologne accosted his nose. The few sensors not terminally damaged by Taizer's urine attacks screamed for relief. "You found me. I'm just heading out."

Not to be easily brushed aside, Trisha oozed into his path. "Haven't seen your beloved around lately. Her leave of absence just seems to stretch to infinity." Her plum-red, collagen-inflated lips reminded D. J. of the butt end of a baboon. "She's out of town on family matters."

"Hmm." She touched a talon fingernail to her chin. "I didn't know she had a family."

D. J. edged away. "Been nice chatting with you, Trisha. I really have to get going."

She stepped closer into his personal space buffer zone than comfortable. "You must be starved for company. Why don't you come over to my condo, and we'll throw some steaks on the grill? Nice bottle of wine. Get to know each other." Trisha swiveled her hips seductively.

"I am engaged—in case you have forgotten."

She threw her hands into the air in an expansive gesture. "Just trying to be friendly with a hard-laboring coworker in a time of need."

"Find another charity, Trisha." D. J. brushed past her.

"Have yourself a good day, sweetie, you hear?" Trisha called out in a throaty voice.

"My mother is an amazing cook. The one thing I associate with comfort is her chocolate chip cookies. I remember this one time when I was, oh, eleven or twelve—Miz Nana Heron's piano recital. I so thoroughly screwed up my recital piece—froze right in the middle, my fingers just hanging there over the keys. Man, was I mortified! All of my friends and their whole families were there to witness my failing. Finally, I got up and ran back to my seat. I didn't cry until I got home. Then, Mama brought out her big bowl and we made cookies together. She was never one to bring junk food home, you see. So cookies were special. And you knew she was making them just for you. She let me lick the bowl after we put the cookie sheet into the oven. By that time, I was so caught up in the delight of warm melted chocolate chip goodness, the agony of my humiliation faded away. Not too long ago, we were all together in my kitchen making that same recipe: me, my mama, and my twin girls. It was one of those times you try to freeze in memory to savor later."

Carol Burns

Chapter Nine

Joe Fletcher wiped his brow with the hem of his Borrowed Thyme chef's jacket, and then refilled the coffee mugs for newly-appointed chief of police Rich Burns and his wife. The Saturday morning sweet potato biscuit rush had subsided.

"This is a treat, Carol," Joe remarked, "I don't often get to see such a pretty face at Rich's table."

"It's a treat for me, too. Rich's been bragging so on your cooking, I had to come try it for myself. He's put on ten pounds because of your biscuits!"

Joe laughed. "Don't blame it all on me. I have it on good authority he spends a good deal of time down at the Madhatter's Sweet Shop, too."

"Squealer." Rich pulled a small note pad and pen from his uniform pocket and poised dramatically. "What was your tag number again, Joe?"

"Facts are facts, officer. Where are the twins this morning?"

"Slumber party at Tuck and Elaine Bradford's house. I'll pick them up in a bit," Carol answered. "They'll crash the rest of the day since, I'm sure, sleep was the last thing that happened last night."

"Those girls are growing up fast, aren't they? Seems like only yesterday when my Karen and Byron were that age."

"How is your daughter holding up?" Carol asked in a soft voice.

Joe wiped flour dust from his hands. "Mind if I grab a cup and join you?" He settled into a chair and took a long noisy sip of coffee. "There's nothing in this world better than a good cup of freshly brewed Colombian. My doctor ever tells me to give this up, and I'm throwing myself straight off the Jim Woodruff Dam."

They watched the ebb and flow of traffic on West Washington Street for a moment.

Joe sighed. "Karen started the chemotherapy injections on Monday. She already had a couple of treatments up in Atlanta, from what she told us. The doctor here's just taking up the reins. Karen held out okay for a day or two until she started having side effects. The nausea's fierce. Doctor told her she may lose part or all of her hair, but it'll grow back after the treatments. Way she told Evelyn, it had already started to get a little thin even before the second round of chemo up there."

"They give her anything to help her?" Rich asked.

"Oh, they have all sorts of drugs for the nausea, but you know what works the best? Plain old ginger. I've made her a couple of batches of gingersnap cookies, and Evelyn bought her some ginger syrup over in Tallahassee at the natural food store. Wanda's friend, Pinky Green, brought some herbal concoction over to soothe her mouth in case she gets sores." Joe's eyes watered slightly. "It's amazing how folks are, when you're facing something like this. Help and support are coming from every which-a-way."

"That's the benefit of living in a small town where you still know your neighbors." Carol smiled. "I heard Elvina Houston's rallied the church prayer groups half the way to Marianna."

Joe grinned. "Yeah, same thing Piddie would've done, had she been around. 'Never hurts to enlist the help of the All-mighty,' she always said. Hattie's helping Karen with Reiki treatments. Can't say I really understand it at all, but it seems to improve Karen's peace of mind. They use visualization, where she imagines her body fighting off the cancer cells. Certainly after all the years I spent as a staff psychologist at the hospital before I retired and opened this little restaurant, I'd be the first one to testify to the power of belief."

"I've been meaning to ask you, Joe. What is the significance of the old blue pottery bowl in the closed glass showcase?" Carol pointed to the wall above the cash register.

"That was Piddie's mama's biscuit mixing bowl. Piddie dragged it around with her for all the years she lived in Alabama, and then moved it with her to Chattahoochee after Evelyn's daddy passed. Evelyn says it was her mama's most prized possession on the earth, besides her, of course."

Carol smiled. "That's sweet, you giving it a place of honor here."

"All my recipes, I owe to my mother-in-law. If you gave her a fire and a pan, the woman could sauté the devil himself and make him worth eating."

Carol laughed. "Where'd you get the idea for the name of the shop?"

"Piddie always maintained she was living on borrowed time once she passed the biblical allowance of three score and five. Thyme is one of my favorite spices, so it just made a catchy name, I guess."

Carol pointed to her empty plate. "If this breakfast was any indication, you'll surely stay busy."

"That's why I only do breakfast and lunch. I reserve evenings for home-time with my wife."

Carol leaned over and rested her hand over Joe's. "You know to let us know if there's anything, and I mean *any little thing,* we can do for y'all. We will come running."

Joe cleared the gathering emotion from his throat. "I know it for a fact, Miz Carol."

Evelyn woke with a start, her maternal instinct nudging her from sleep. She silently slid from the king-sized bed where Joe slept soundly. Sunday mornings had become a cherished time, as they were the only mornings her husband didn't rise before daybreak to leave for Borrowed Thyme. She crept down the hallway on tiptoes, and then stood listening outside of the guest bathroom. The unmistakable sound of retching emanated from the other side of the door.

"Karen, honey?" she asked in a lowered voice.

Her daughter's weak voice: "I'm okay, Mama. Go on back to bed."

"I was awake, anyway," she lied. "I'll go make some of Pinky's special tea."

In the kitchen, Evelyn chose a delicate antique porcelain cup embellished with pink and yellow roses. Somehow, having a warm drink from beautiful china would soothe any problem. She reached to flip the coffeemaker on, and then hesitated.

"No, best not to do that," she muttered. "The smell might make her feel worse."

Evelyn placed a second pottery mug on the counter and positioned a silver infuser ball filled with herbal rosehip and chamomile tea into each cup. Normally, she would have steeped and served in the special pot Joe had given her for their last anniversary, but Pinky had given careful instructions on brewing the soothing concoction one cup at a time to ensure potency.

Karen appeared at the kitchen threshold wrapped in a white chenille robe. Her thinning blonde hair hung in limp damp clumps. Dark circles smudged the skin beneath her eyes.

Evelyn forced a small smile. "C'mon, baby doll. Let's have our tea out on the porch. The birds are up singing, and it's the perfect temperature. You go on out, and I'll go fetch the Sunday paper."

Karen shuffled slowly through the kitchen toward the screened-in garden room. Evelyn ducked her head quickly and busied herself so that her daughter wouldn't see the tears gathering.

If only she had a magic wand to wave and take it all away. Or, to transfer the symptoms to her body. Her memories drifted to Karen as a little girl—feverish with chicken pox, thrashing about on her princess canopy bed. *Mama, make it better,* she'd cry out pitifully. And Mama would, given a few days.

The necessary treatment for cancer was unrelenting with the chemotherapy injections, then days of gradually decreasing agony until the next round of medication. Pinky was correct when he said you have to nearly kill the person to extinguish the evil growing inside.

Evelyn closed her eyes. "If you're up there listening, Mama, and I feel you are, please help me be strong enough to see this through."

After fetching the thick Sunday edition of the *Tallahassee Democrat* from the front steps, she steeled herself, forced her breathing to calm, and placed the two cups, honey, and fresh lemon wedges on a tray.

"Tough time this morning?" Evelyn placed the tea tray on a wrought iron table.

Karen sniffled. "I hate worse than anything in the world to throw up. Even those times where I know it'll make me feel tons better to get rid of whatever's in my stomach, I just can't bring myself to do it. Now, it seems I'm not given a choice. The dry heaves are the absolute worst!"

Evelyn stirred honey into her tea cup. "Morning sickness did that for me—with you and your brother, both. It calmed down after about the fourth month with you, but I was sick every single morning with Byron."

"I'm sorry, Mama."

Evelyn flipped her hand. "Nonsense. Nothing for you to be sorry over. It was worth every second, 'cause look what came from it."

"Speaking of my baby brother, is he coming down?"

"He'll be here for your surgery. I talked to him right after you went to bed last night."

Karen tucked a loose strand of hair behind one ear. "I'm certainly disrupting everyone's lives."

"Now, you stop that thinking, missy. Your grandmamma used to say, 'When times are tough, you can't allow yourself the luxury of negative thoughts.' Being there for each other is what family is all about."

"Under normal circumstances, maybe. But I'm sure Byron resents how I've chosen to live my life up to this point."

"That just isn't so, Karen. He loves you. You're his flesh and blood kin, and no manner of nonsense can erase that fact. He wants to be here to support you. Linda can't come down on account of someone has to take care of the boys. They're not out of school yet. She cares, too. She got on the phone right along with your brother and wanted to hear all about what you're having to endure."

Karen sipped the fragrant tea and watched two squirrels battling over the birdfeeder.

"Is there anyone . . . special . . . up there in Atlanta you need me to call for you?"

"No." Karen hesitated for a moment. "There's only my boss, and I've already spoken with him about taking extended leave."

"All right then. You think you could stand a little breakfast?"

"Any sweet potato biscuits left?"

"I do believe so. I can pop a couple into the oven to warm, if that sounds good to you."

Karen nodded.

"I'll have you something to put in your stomach in a flash, then."
Evelyn jumped up and scurried to the kitchen.

"My mother made homemade Italian bread. We would slice it when it was not yet cool and spread fresh butter on it. More often than not, she would have a big pot of tomato sauce simmering on the stove, and she would take up a small bowl for us to dip the bread in. My own children do the same thing when I make bread. They can smell the aroma from miles away, and all of a sudden, I have them underfoot in my kitchen. I give them a bowl of sauce and a few slices, and they move out of my way. Come to think of it, perhaps that was my mother's trick, too."

Angelina Palazzolo

Chapter Ten

Near midmorning, Elvina Houston settled onto the customary seat by Piddie's memorial flower garden.

"Morning glory!" Elvina called, smiling. "I think that's the funniest way to greet someone, don't you, Piddie? I near to bust a gut every time Jake says it to me. Thought I'd use it on you, in case you need a good chuckle.

"I'm sorry it's been two days me not coming to visit. Reckon if you know-all-see-all from your new perspective up there, you know I've been laid up with a sinus infection. I felt it coming on me fast, so I pranced straight over to the clinic for a round of antibiotics. Lord knows, I do hate to take a handful of pills, but when I get my spring sinus troubles, I'd surely suffocate if I didn't.

"The girls had to do double-duty while I was laid up. I felt so bad; I couldn't make it out of bed to perform my front desk responsibilities. That ain't like me, a'tall, missing a day of work, much less two!

"Not that I'm sad to have all the pollen and what not. The flowers have been incredible. You ought to see your yard over on Morgan Avenue! Jake throwed the fertilizer to the azaleas, and honey hush! They have near to kilt themselves blooming."

Elvina patted her violet-print cotton dress. "Jake's the reason I'm so dressed up today. He's throwing hisself a birthday garden party this afternoon. Jon told me the boy's spent two solid weeks cleaning and gussying up the house. I can't wait to see it!

"He took up the old carpets and had the wood floors refinished. Ain't it funny how we rushed to get wall-to-wall carpeting when it came out 'cause it was the thing to have? Now, if it ain't the rage to have the wood floors back! Beats all I've ever seen, how things are so circular.

"Evelyn's sewing up a storm, as usual. She and I are collaborating on a line of ladies' and little girls' Easter dresses with straw bonnets and purses to match. I'm doing the handbags and bonnets, of course. You'd'a been right proud of Evelyn on the TV spot. She acted like she'd been born in front of a camera. Spoke right up and told all about her business and the joy she'd found so late in life designing clothing. The phones have been a'ringing off the hook with women asking to speak to her."

Elvina laughed. "You ought to see the doggie outfit she made for Elvis for the garden party this afternoon. It's a little blue-striped seersucker jacket with a white bowtie. I swannee, that little Pomeranian has more suits than most men I know! Reckon this one will do him for Easter, too. Jon takes him to the children's services most every Sunday. Those younguns love him to death. He sits real quiet and proper while the youth minister is preaching to the children. Reckon he's making sure he's got a home in dog heaven?"

She grinned. "I'm in just such a good frame of mind, Piddie. I can't help myself. This time of year before the heat of summer sets in makes me feel like a youngun myself.

"What else—oh, Wanda and Pinky Green are getting thick as thieves. She floats around the spa half the time like she don't have good sense. I think she spends near all her time off out at Pinky's farm—you know, about eight, nine miles beyond the Davis homestead.

"Pinky's a real nice fellow, and I'm proud for Wanda. To hear her talk, she ain't had the best luck with men folks. Tended to hook up with no-accounts like she took them on to raise. It's high time she found a good one.

"Stephanie's doing okay. She keeps booked regular with her massage therapy clients. I do my level best to help her out. Someone comes in looking the least bit frazzled, I tell them they need to schedule a massage. Between Hattie up at the Madhatter and Stephanie here at the Triple C, I don't reckon there're too many locals haven't had a massage by now.

"Mandy's busy as a bee in a tar bucket working with the new crop of beauty queens. Little Miss Sneads ain't too far off. Neither is the

Miss Marianna contest. Lord help her, she's a saint. The girls ain't so bad themselves, but the mamas! Some of them can be a hard pill to swallow."

Elvina coughed to clear her throat. "Sorry. I'm still a mite phlegmish. Angelina Palazzolo had the gout in her right big toe, but she's on the mend now. She gets it every time she eats too much pork, she told me. Still, she's like the rest of us; we do things we love even though they might be bad for us. If you're gonna dance to the music, you've got to pay the piper, you always said.

"Karen's having a tough go with this last round of chemo before she goes in for surgery. Her doctor's supposed to do another one of them scans a couple of days before she goes in, to see if they've succeeded in shrinking the tumor down. Evelyn said that'll make all the difference in whether they take the whole breast or just a piece. Karen's coming to the party at Jake and Jon's, though. She told her mama she needed to get out and about a little, just to make her feel alive. Poor thing's hair's so thin, you can see her scalp. Evelyn's sewed up several soft turban head wraps for her to wear, and Mandy's already ordered a couple of wigs. Mandy thought ahead on that one—took a snip of Karen's real hair before it all falls out, and is using it to match the shade for the wigs. She and Jake have been cooking up some kind of fashion show for Karen to style the wigs when they come in the mail.

"So, everyone's doing her or his part. Lucille's rallied the prayer groups down at the Morningside AME church. I think you were on target on one thing, Piddie. Your black friends surely know how to contact the Almighty. I've gotten to where I attend the services down there more often than at the First Baptist. I do so love the singing."

Elvina paused, closed her eyes, and took a deep breath of air.

"The wisteria—oh my! It smells so very sweet to me this year. I do hope you have flowers up there in the by and by. All I know is—if I was God and it was my place, I'd fill it full of blossoms and declare it spring for eternity!"

The simple wooden frame house on Morgan Avenue was bordered by a row of flowering ligustrum and an expansive side yard dotted with azalea-ringed pine trees. The lot sloped sharply to the rear of the house where a set of steep stairs led from the back screened porch down to a sandy clearing shaded by a massive Southern magnolia tree. Beds of maidenhair and holly ferns surrounded the opening, with a narrow walkway leading to a small vegetable garden on the lower terrace.

Under Jake Witherspoon's care, Piddie's former home glowed with a fresh coat of white paint, new burgundy shutters, and an updated kitchen and bathroom. Although the rooms were small by modern standards, Jake had chosen colors and furnishings to avoid a cluttered feel.

Jake and Jon's home was decorated in full spring-garden-party regalia. Potted flowers with pastel blooms lined the driveway, walk, and front porch—showy, but a shade shy of over-the-top. Four white rockers with ivy-printed cushions awaited visitors to the front porch.

In the dining room, Piddie's antique mahogany table held an assortment of sweets and canapés: double fudge chocolate chip brownies, red velvet cake, lemon squares, gingerbread cake, salmon spread on toast points, crab-stuffed mushrooms, peeled boiled shrimp, miniature ham-stuffed sour cream biscuits, sun dried tomato hummus, and fresh vegetables with dipping sauce. A matching side table held iced tea, lemonade, soft drinks, and bottled water.

Jake's creation—a massive arrangement of daffodils, iris, daisies, and fern—held court as the table centerpiece. The claw foot tub in the bathroom held a similar spray of seasonal blooms. Smaller floral touches were scattered throughout the house.

In the garden, the clearing beneath the magnolia was dotted with tall citronella candles. Though the party was planned for daylight hours, the faint citrus scent served to repel the ever-present ravenous mosquitoes.

Keeping with tradition, Elvina Houston provided the first knock on the screened door, thirty minutes ahead of official soiree starting time. According to her friends and adversaries, the underlying reason was her fear of missing even one tidbit of juicy gossip. By being the first to arrive and the last to depart, Elvina provided fewer opportunities to be the subject of conjecture.

"Look at you, Miz 'Vina!" Jake gushed, air-kissing slightly to the right and left of the old woman's heavily rouged cheeks. "Don't you look like one tall cool drink of water on a sultry day?"

Elvina adjusted the silk violet-trimmed white straw sunhat to tip slightly over one eye. "I'm aiming for you to refer to me as a work of art like you did Piddie, but I suppose any compliment I come by at my age is to be valued."

Jake touched the brim of Elvina's sunhat. "Did you create this wonderful thing?"

"Surely did. Evelyn made my dress. Fits to a T. We're collaborating on a line of Easter ensembles for ladies and girls, you know. I'm the walking and breathing advertisement."

Jon appeared beside Jake, a squirming Elvis tucked underneath one arm. "Come on in, Miz Elvina. Make yourself at home. Jake, get her a glass of tea." He dabbed at a trickle of sweat on his brow. "Is it hot to anyone else besides me? Heavens, if I'm this warm now, imagine what I'll be by July!"

Elvina shook her head. "I can't imagine a person tall and thin as you are ever feeling the effects of the heat. Now, Sharalee Jefferson, she's the one's gonna just end up rending down to pure lard one hot summer's day! Have you seen the size of her ankles, here lately?"

"I really have to leave you two to visit," Jon interjected. "I've got to get Elvis into his party outfit, and I haven't changed, myself."

Elvina sniffed. "Am I too early?"

"Oh, of course not," Jake replied. "Jon's always on slow time. Reminds me of an old box turtle at times—dawdling and methodical, but he gets there eventually. C'mon inside and we'll chat until the other guests arrive."

By the time Evelyn, Joe, and Karen arrived in the Lincoln, the house was filled to capacity with revelers. Jake provided a play area in the front bedroom for Sarah and Josh. The blanket-covered floor was strewn with brightly-colored building blocks, dolls, trucks, and stuffed animals. Elvis stood guard to one side, judiciously avoiding an occasional airborne toy.

The party migrated from the living room and dining room to the kitchen and back garden. Jon spotted Karen sitting alone at one of the bistro tables Jake had arranged underneath the magnolia.

Jon flashed a toothy smile. "What's a pretty girl like you doing sitting out here all alone?"

Karen shrugged. "I've been visiting around a bit, but I just wanted to be outside. It's so beautiful out here. It's like I've been cooped up for months."

"I'm so glad you felt up to coming, Karen." He placed two tall glasses of fresh lemonade on the table and offered his hand. "I'm Jon Presley, Jake's partner. I've been meaning to drop by Evelyn and Joe's."

"Mama's told me all about you. All good, of course. And don't apologize for not stopping by. I haven't been up to receiving company." She reached up and adjusted her pale blue turban.

"I recall feeling that terrible. Chemo surely can suck the energy right out of you."

Karen studied him. "You had cancer?"

"When I was a teenager. The experience never leaves you. Not totally."

Karen sipped from the frosted glass. "This is so good. It's the first thing sweet I've had in weeks. Mama's on the warpath against white sugar, believes it's the root of all evil, feeds cancer cells, that sort of thing."

Jon grinned. "Hate to burst your bubble, but this is made with Splenda—kin to sugar, except a little different molecularly. Since it doesn't break down under heat, you can even use it in baking."

"Does that mean I can have a piece of that delectable Red Velvet cake without Mama pitching a fit?"

"Certainly does. I'll be sure to let your mother know it's approved."

Jon studied Karen with his trained nurse's eye. "How are you doing, really?"

She sighed. "The nausea's been pretty rough. I've dropped fifteen pounds already because I just can't eat. Daddy's been cooking up a storm trying to find something I can hold down. Anything with the least bit of spice burned my mouth for a few days after I developed mouth ulcers. Pinky Green, Wanda's friend, bought me some herbal lozenges that really helped. Otherwise, I would've steered clear of this lemonade."

"One day, scientists will figure out a way to use a patient's immune system to battle cancer instead of poisoning with strong drugs. But for now, we have to use what we've got."

"I realize that, on an intellectual level."

"Doesn't help when you're in the thick of it, does it?"

"No."

"I'm right around the corner if you need me for anything, Karen—

moral support, whatever medical knowledge I have that can help you."

Karen smiled warmly. "Thank you, Jon. So, how did you come to be a part of this whole Chattahoochee madness?"

"Luck of the draw. Life is just so bizarre, sometimes. I was Hattie's floor nurse when she had her colon cancer surgery. I met her and Jake then."

"You don't do hospital work anymore?"

"Left that rat race behind. I'm a hospice nurse now. I travel a lot locally, but the work's very fulfilling."

Karen shuddered. "All that death."

Jon looked thoughtful. "That's a part of it, naturally. But more than that, it's about living until the end and leaving with as much dignity as possible."

They heard Jake bellowing Jon's name from inside the house.

"I'd better go see what he needs. Men, they can be so helpless sometimes!"

Karen laughed. A tight knot of anxiety loosened deep inside of her. For the first time in months, she felt alive.

"Remember, you call on me if you need to . . . or just if you want to shoot the shit. Okay?"

Jon leaned down and kissed Karen lightly on the cheek before taking the back steps in two's.

Carol Burns's Mama's
Secret Recipe Chocolate Chip Cookies

½ cup rolled oats, regular or quick
2 ¼ cups all-purpose flour
1 ½ teaspoons baking soda
½ teaspoon salt
¼ teaspoon cinnamon
1 cup (2 sticks) butter, softened
¾ cup firmly packed brown sugar
¾ cup white sugar
2 teaspoons vanilla extract
2 eggs
3 cups semisweet chocolate chips
1 cup chopped pecans or walnuts

Preheat oven to 350°. Mix together oats, flour, baking soda, salt, and cinnamon. In another bowl, cream the butter, sugars, and vanilla. Add eggs one at a time and beat until fluffy. Stir the flour mixture into the egg/butter mixture and blend well. Scoop round balls of dough onto a cookie sheet (I use the non-stick kind), leaving about a two-inch space between the dough balls. Bake until cookies are slightly browned. Cool completely before storing in a sealed container. Cookies will be soft and chewy.

Chapter Eleven

The quest for information leading to the location of Mary Elizabeth Kensington developed into a full-blown obsession for D. J. Peterson. Initially, his efforts were limited to the just-happened-to-be-looking variety. Then, his investigative urge kicked in, and the casual search turned into a full-scale, room-by-room pillage. Rising curiosity squelched the initial guilt over mistrusting his fiancée to the point of snooping through her possessions. She had been gone for almost two months now, and the lack of a hint as to her whereabouts was quickly sending him over the precipice.

D. J. started each segment of the meticulous hunt by snapping several before pictures with a digital camera. Assured items could be replaced in the same way as he had found them, he riffled through boxes of files, holiday decorations, albums of recent photographs, and shelves of books. Nothing was overlooked.

He found no evidence of Mary Elizabeth's life prior to her move to Atlanta, as if she had beamed into the city at the age of twenty-one. No baby pictures, family snapshots, or mementos from childhood came to light. Was her life so terrible prior to the late seventies that she had effectively erased any traces? Niggling doubts nudged his consciousness.

D. J. stood at the threshold of the master bedroom closet. Tequila regarded him with cold yellow eyes and twirled at his feet.

"This is it, fat cat," he said, "last chance for your mother to show her true colors . . . or not."

He clicked several frames with the camera and reviewed the resulting images. Mary Elizabeth was obscenely organized. Any changes to the carefully-scripted lair would be detectable. D. J.'s nose caught the faint scent of her cologne lingering in the row of hanging clothes. He closed his eyes and followed the aroma to a navy wool pea coat and buried his face in the fabric.

"I'm pathetic." He shook his head and began to remove the contents of the shelves. Two hours later, D. J. stood amidst a tower of shoe boxes and labeled plastic storage containers. The cats dashed through the maze of high heel pumps and belts.

"I give up, Mary E.!"

The two places he could not gain access to were her computer files and the contents of a fire-proof safe in the rear of the closet. Unless he hired a techie hacker or a safe-cracking thug named Fingers, D. J. stood no chance to gaining entrance to either.

By the time he carefully replaced the closet contents, he felt dejected and thoroughly confused.

"Maybe she's in the witness protection program. That's it, huh?" He crouched down and ruffled Tequila's thick mane. "Yeah, that's it. Your mama saw some drug lord in action, and now the feds are hiding you all. She's really a farm girl from Kansas."

D. J. retired to the study with a fresh cup of brewed decaf coffee. Though Mary Elizabeth's personal files were protected with a password, he could log on under his name and gain entrance to her computer to check the office email. As usual, ninety percent of the electronic messages were advertisements and forwarded nonsense from coworkers. He took pleasure clicking the delete button.

When he turned the computer off and grabbed the armoire doors, he noticed a small brown cardboard box atop a pile of papers. Stuck to one side, "return" was written on a Post-it note in Mary Elizabeth's ornate script. The sender's address read: Mrs. E.L. Fletcher, Main Street, Chattahoochee, Florida.

D. J. opened the box slowly. Inside, a delicate gold mountain scene pendant rested on a bed of cotton. A folded note was tucked in the lid.

Dear Mary,

I bought this in Alaska for you. I hope you like it. I have one, too. Hope this finds you well. We'd love to hear from you. Call us collect any time.

With love,

Evelyn Fletcher

Trisha Truman stared blankly at the computer monitor screen. A search of the State of Florida Public Records webpage had yielded a fantastic find.

"Oh, my God. This is rich!"

She moved the mouse to locate the printer icon and clicked the left button with her index finger.

"One copy for me, one for the boss, one for safekeeping, and one for lover boy." Trisha's salmon-tinted lips curled.

She patted the stack of copies. "Finally, something to bring the great British bitch down a few pegs."

Trisha oozed into D. J.'s cramped wood-paneled office and draped her body seductively across one corner of the narrow teak desk. "Hi, sweetie. Why don't you take a break and treat a hard-working gal to lunch?"

D. J. replied without looking up, "Can't today, Trisha. I'm getting ready to leave town for a few days."

"Hmm. I thought your desk looked awfully neat and clean. You slipping off to join your precious Mary Elizabeth?" She placed undue emphasis on her rival's name.

D. J. glanced up. "You know, Trisha, Mary E.'s never done a thing to warrant your venom, yet you have had it in for her ever since you started here last year. I'd appreciate it if you'd can the comments. They make you look quite unattractive, really."

"I have certain . . . information . . . that might make you change your tune about your fiancée. Take me to lunch, and we'll discuss it."

D. J. grabbed his worn leather briefcase and stuffed a stack of papers and an electronic personal organizer inside. "I can't fathom you'd say anything I'd want to hear."

He snapped the briefcase shut, walked around the desk, and left the office.

"Is that so?" Trisha picked idly at a chip on one manicured nail as she spoke to herself in the vacant office. "Maybe somebody else will then, mister."

She tipped her head upward and the spray-stiff hair vibrated slightly. An evil idea budded.

"Well, why not? The perfect opportunity for me to show my investigative talents presents itself. Who am I to turn it away?"

Small communities were the same across the nation, regardless of geography. Trisha Truman instinctively knew the perfect place to garner inside information. She tapped lightly on Will Cooke's door.

"Door's open!"

Trisha stepped inside. "Will, I need a couple of days off."

Will Cooke snuffed his irritation. Any of his employees—other than Trisha Truman—could refer to him by his first name and elicit no negative reaction. With her, the casual lack of formality smacked of purposeful insubordination. "I don't believe you have any more annual leave and I know for a fact you don't have any sick leave." *You call in every time you break a fake nail, for the love of Pete,* he thought.

"How about family leave? I haven't used that at all. My favorite aunt in Ocala has taken a bad fall. They think her hip's broken."

"That's too bad. I hate to hear about older folks falling. It always gets them down." Will looked up from his computer monitor. "How long do you need, a week, a few days? It's a little slack right now. I suppose I could spare you if you . . ."

"No, sir. Just tomorrow and Friday will be fine. I'm sure. She has kin down there, too. I just want to show my support." She offered a saccharine smile. "You're the best! I promise I'll find a way to repay your generosity."

"Just contact me if you get to Florida and your family needs you longer."

"You got it! I've got a couple of calls to make, then I'm going to get on the road." She blew a kiss on the way out. Will grimaced.

On Trisha's desk, the results of an Internet Yellow Pages search waited: the phone number for the Triple C Day Spa and Salon in Chattahoochee, Florida.

"My mama was big on eating vegetables, especially during the summer when the yellow squash, beans, peas, corn, okra and tomatoes would come in. Some meals, she didn't bother to cook any meat—just bowls and bowls of homegrown vegetables and a hoecake of cornbread. We had a one-acre garden out behind the house. Gosh, how I hated to pull weeds in the dead of the summer! Sweat would just roll down my face and burn my eyes. Even in the early morning, it was still hot and humid. But come dinnertime, it was all worth it. And we'd can or freeze the extra vegetables to have during the winter. Creamed sweet corn—I'd have to say that was my all-time favorite, if I had to choose."
Melody Kaye Allen, nail care specialist

Chapter Twelve

Pinky Green plucked an inchworm from the edge of a glossy green basil leaf.

"Sorry, little feller," he said as he gently placed the worm on a bush at the periphery of the woods surrounding the herb garden. "You'll have to do your measuring elsewhere. Now, if you could keep from eating my basil, it would be a different story."

Wanda watched him curiously, a cup of hot coffee in her hand. "You talk to bugs, too. What an amazing man you are."

"Wasn't a bug, for your information, Miss Wanda. It was a tiny green worm." Pinky's cheeks flushed. "I reckon I've gotten so used to being out here alone, I'll talk to just about anything. I've been known to carry on a lengthy conversation with a pine tree."

She chuckled and stepped over to ruffle a spike of his red hair. "I talk to my dog. Suppose it's not that different. I'm fixing some biscuits inside. You hungry?"

"You're cooking?"

Wanda propped one hand on her hip. "You have a problem with that? What, you think you're the only one around here who can take a turn in the kitchen?"

"No, not at all. I just didn't think Northerners made biscuits."

"I spent a lot of time down here during the summers when I was growing up. My aunt was a great cook, and I trailed her around the kitchen like a lovesick puppy. Now, grits, that's the one thing I haven't taken a turn at, just yet. I'd much rather have hash browns with my eggs. But biscuits—you can't beat a homemade biscuit for breakfast."

"I'll gather some fresh eggs."

Wanda slipped her arms around Pinky, careful to not spill the coffee. "My own little farmer. Who'd have ever imagined it?"

"You want to be the farmer's wife?"

She drew back and studied him closely. "That sounds suspiciously like a proposal."

"Well?"

Wanda leaned forward and kissed him softly. "You sure you can put up with being married to a Yankee?"

"War's long over, Wanda Jean."

"Depends on which one of my exes you ask. Some would say it was only beginning if you tie up with the likes of me."

Pinky slipped a black velvet box from his pocket and flipped the lid to reveal a small diamond ring. He smiled.

"Good Lord! You're serious! How long have you been carrying this around?"

"Couple of weeks. Reckon I was collecting the courage to ask." He ducked his head. "You haven't answered me. Do I get to stand out here in the middle of our garden looking like a complete fool till the sun beats me down?"

Wanda stuck her left hand forward. "Make it official then, Farmer Green."

"My goodness!" Mandy remarked, picking at the tangled clumps of over-processed hair. "Not that I'm trying to pry, Miss—"

"Anna. Anna Freeman," Trisha Truman provided. "Please, do call me Anna."

"Anna, then. How did you get your hair so matted?"

"I drove from Atlanta with the convertible's top down. The weather's perfect for it, you know. I couldn't resist."

Starting from the bottom, Mandy gently worked a wide-toothed comb through the snarls. "You should wear a scarf. Or maybe, tie it in a ponytail."

Trisha chuckled. "I perplex my stylist in Atlanta, too, Mandy.

He's always saying, 'Anna, dahling, I'm gonna snatch that sports car out from underneath you and plop you in an SUV, and one without so much as a sunroof, at that!'"

Mandy winced. "Sorry if I'm pulling. I've got to get these tangles out before I can do a wash and set."

"I know I ought to wear a cover, but I just love the feel of the wind whipping through my hair. That's why I called ahead yesterday to make sure I could get in here for a touch-up before I go to see my friend. I would never get the mess straightened out by myself." She studied her cuticles. "Besides, I tip well."

Trisha glanced toward the opposite side of the room. "Suppose your nail specialist could see me for a fill on my acrylics?"

Melody leaned over from behind the low wicker partition separating the nail care area from the hair salon. "I think I have a space around eleven if you're finished with her by then, Mandy."

"There you go." Mandy smiled. "How's that for service?" Then, to Melody, "Be sure you tell Elvina you've filled the spot. You know how she gets!"

Mandy turned her attention back to her client. "That's one of the benefits of living in a small town. We can always make time for you. So, you said you were visiting a friend?"

Trisha smiled slightly. This was going to be a cake walk.

"Yes. Karen Fletcher. You know her?"

Mandy's face echoed her shock. "Well, sure. Everyone knows Karen. I just saw her yesterday, as a matter of fact. Why, her mama has a clothing design business here at the spa."

Trisha stiffened slightly. "Is that right?"

"Maybe you saw some of her gowns on the way in. They're hanging from the suspended rods behind the reception desk."

"Now that you mention it, yes."

Mandy spritzed detangling solution onto Trisha's hair. "Evelyn's quite talented. The first lady of Florida has ordered a couple of custom outfits, and Evelyn had a spot on the morning TV show out of Tallahassee, here a few weeks back."

"I'll have to scold Karen for holding out on me. I'll shop a bit before I leave today."

Mandy's brows knit together. "I thought everyone up there in Atlanta called her Mary Elizabeth."

"Everybody but me. I'm the only person who knows her real identity."

"Is that so?"

"Uh-huh. I'm watching the townhouse and feeding her cats while she's away. Karen and I are very close."

Trisha relished the ruse, making up replies as she went along.

"I guess it just tears you apart then, what's happening to her." Mandy frowned. "I mean, we all felt harshly toward Karen for a bit, I'll admit. But no one deserves to have breast cancer."

Trisha's pulse quickened. Now the pieces fit perfectly! The numerous mornings she had caught Mary Elizabeth retching in the staff bathroom, the sallow cast to her skin. Trisha had chalked it up to morning sickness. All this time, the princess wasn't pregnant as she had suspected.

"How is she doing with all of it? I mean, just so I'm prepared when I see her."

Mandy paused and studied her patron's reflection in the oversized mirror. "I'm getting the feeling Karen's not expecting you."

"I wanted to surprise her. I guess it wasn't such a good idea."

"You might want to give it a couple of days. She and Evelyn are over in Tallahassee this morning for Karen's last chemo treatment before they do the surgery on her."

Trisha forced a mask of sadness. "I knew I'd catch her at a bad time if I just showed up. But I was afraid she'd beg me not to come if I said anything in advance."

"Give her a couple of days, hon. She's usually past the worst of it by then. I'll just bet it will do her a world of good to see a friendly face. She can't very well turn you away, now that you've come so far and had your hair all done up special."

"You'd best steel yourself for how she looks," Melody interjected.

"Now, she don't look that bad, Melody," Mandy scolded. "The wig I cut and styled for her looks pretty close to real."

Trisha put a hand to her chest. "She's lost the rest of her beautiful hair?"

"Most of it. It was a sad sight, I'll tell you. She marched right in here and told me to shave it all off. Her head's slick as a baby's behind now. Of course, it makes the wig fit like a second skin, and bald was a sight better than the few stray pieces of fuzz she had left."

"Poor Karen." Trisha itched with the desire to return to Atlanta.

"You should stop in and visit her daddy, Joe. He'll be about finished with the lunch crowd by the time you're done here," Mandy suggested. "He has a little place on the main drag. You probably passed it coming in—the Borrowed Thyme Bakery and Eatery."

"Get him to make you one of his chicken salads with sugared pecans," Melody added. "It is G-double-O-D, good!"

"I just might do that. And I'll heed your advice about giving Karen some time before I stop by. I'm not far from here, over in Tallahassee at the Ramada. I'll just shop and find something to occupy my time." She paused and made careful eye contact with both women. "Don't y'all breathe a word about me being here, now."

"You can count on me," Melody said.

Mandy agreed. "One thing about us: we know how to keep our mouths sealed shut."

Really? Trisha mused.

"There we go. Let's get you washed now, missy!" Mandy reclined the back of the chair over the basin. "I'm famous for my scalp massages, Anna. Just close your eyes, and I'll make you never want to visit one of those pricey Atlanta city salons again."

By one o'clock, a freshly coiffed and manicured Trisha Truman was northbound on the interstate, fortified with sufficient background information on Karen Fletcher. When Trisha completed the exposé on Georgia Metro Public Broadcasting's noted spokeswoman, she could take her rightful place in the world of investigative reporting.

Mary Elizabeth Kensington would be lucky to land a job cleaning toilets at a radio station in Hole-in-the-Road, Idaho.

"A bologna sandwich, believe it or not, reminds me of my mom. She worked full time, so she didn't have unlimited time to cook. Whenever she would come home worn out, we had bologna, that thin-sliced, orange-yellow cheese, and loads of mayo on white bread. She liked pickles on hers—dill. I know it's not fancy, but bologna sandwiches remind me of Saturday lunch in her small kitchen, served at the metal and Formica table with the yellow padded chairs."

Mandy Andrews, hair stylist

Chapter Thirteen

Karen smiled, a blissful expression on her face. "Listen!"

Hattie held her hands suspended over one of the many energy centers on Karen's chest. A pulse of warmth caused her fingertips to tingle at the tips.

"What?"

"Those birds. I remember their calls from when we were little girls out sunning by the edge of the pool."

Hattie strained to hear the high-pitched chirps. "The purple martins? Yeah, they've been here for a couple of weeks. I'm so accustomed to hearing them, I guess the sound has faded into the background."

"They used to make Uncle Dan so mad, remember? He had their apartment houses on poles in the yard near the pool."

Hattie's expression grew wistful. "He loved the birds. It wasn't that he wished them harm. I can't tell you how many times he told Bobby and me how they ate their weight in mosquitoes several times a day. He just didn't like the way they used the pool for drinking water and left messy droppings on the concrete."

Karen laughed. "Your mama—remember when one pooped right on her during one of the many picnics by the pool?"

Hattie grinned. "That wasn't the only time. She swore she had a bull's eye painted on the top of her head. A pigeon nailed her one time coming out of the Cut 'n' Curl, too. She was all dolled up with a fresh hairdo at the time."

They fell silent for a few moments listening to the faint chirps of the purple martins riding the air thermals high above the farmhouse.

"Daddy moved the bird-apartment houses a few years back. Pissed 'em off. Seems they really liked the side yard. A few families returned the first year, but they didn't come back in full force until he conceded and relocated their condos to the original location. The next year, Daddy was so excited when he spotted the first scout bird. A few days later, the whole shebang arrived with their little birdie bags in tow. He didn't mess with nature after that."

"Uncle Dan was a piece of work."

"Uh-huh."

"I'm realizing how much I missed out on things. He and your mama—gone. I never saw them after I left for Atlanta."

"Yeah, I'm sorry for you on that account, Karen. We really do have a great family. I miss them both so much. I do feel closer to them though, living here on the Hill."

"You're so lucky. It's beautiful here. So peaceful. Maybe one day, I'll be able to find a place where I can feel at home again."

"You will."

Karen took a deep breath. "Know what I notice the most now?"

"What's that?"

"Scents. Not the manmade kind. Most of them make me queasy. Natural aromas, like . . . lying here, every now and then the breeze shifts just right, and I smell the honeysuckle vines in bloom in the woods behind your house."

Hattie lifted her nose and sniffed.

"I can't seem to snuffle enough air into my nose. I caught the faint perfume of the native azaleas in the hollow by the highway as I drove out here." Karen took another deep breath. "And wisteria! There's a maze of wisteria vines in the thicket by the Triple C Spa. Wonderful"

Karen opened her eyes and studied the flower garden at the edge of the porch. "As corny as it sounds, this cancer has made me notice . . . things."

"It was food for me. Not during, but after. I was scared to eat anything for a long while. It hurt—a deep pain, awful." Hattie shuddered involuntarily. "But after the surgery, as I recovered, I was ravenous. It all tasted so good!"

"Food is the last thing on my mind right now. I can barely hold rice and toast down."

"It gets better, Karen."

They were silent for a few minutes.

"You know what the Reiki makes it feel like when you hold your hands above the tumor?"

"Hmm?"

"Like . . . when you pour salt on a garden slug and it curls up. Like little fingers are pulling back inward—an octopus dying and its tentacles sucking back toward its body."

"Wow."

"I believe all of this is working, Hattie. I really do. I visualize as you taught me when I'm lying in bed at night. I see the tumor getting smaller and smaller until it's an insignificant dot that blows away on the wind."

"That's perfect, Karen."

"D-Day is coming up after my last chemo, you know. They'll do another scan and measure the tumor before I go in for surgery. I just know it's shrinking. I can feel it."

Shammie, Hattie's aged Persian cat, stretched and regarded them with golden eyes. Karen reached down to the large cat resting on her stomach and stroked her thick fur.

"She's certain her part in this has helped immensely, as well." Hattie said. "Cats are attracted to energy work. They don't want it done to them, but love to hang around and help out."

"I'm glad she's here. Makes me miss my babies a little less."

Hattie shifted her hands slowly over various energy centers on her cousin's body. "Feels warmer over your heart chakra—a lot different than when we started Reiki sessions."

"I wouldn't doubt it. A few more weeks around my family, and I could be almost a human being again."

Hattie worked in silence for a few moments before Karen spoke again.

"How did you feel when you found out about your cancer?"

Hattie hesitated, then said, "I didn't react at first. I was still half sedated from the colonoscopy. I went straight from the Digestive Disease Center to the hospital. It didn't really sink in until my surgeon made rounds later that day. He informed me of the possibility of ending up with a colostomy bag. Before that, I had not even considered disfigurement. Cancer was just something you went in and cut out."

Hattie continued the Reiki treatment as she talked. "Thank God for Jon Presley. He was the floor nurse that night. He happened to come in right after the doctor left. I totally freaked out, lost it. Jon took the time to stay with me and talk it all over—the cancer, my fear. He shared his personal trials with it. I can't discount the rest of the gang, either. They were right there with me, every step of the way."

"Holston?"

"He was in New York when I was diagnosed. Jake was with me, initially. Holston came as soon as he heard."

"I know it was reassuring to have the man you loved by your side."

"Both of the men I loved were by my side. Jake was my rock. As for Holston, I was scared how he would react. We had just become engaged, and there I was in the hospital with a possibility of disfigurement or premature death. I felt like damaged goods."

"Obviously, it wasn't an issue."

"I tried my best to make it into one, until he called me on it." Hattie smiled. "I'm very fortunate. I found out exactly what kind of man I had fallen in love with. He was there with me—all the way."

Karen wiped a tear that had drifted down her cheek.

"Oh, honey. I've upset you. I'm so sorry. Here I am, talking on and on about myself when you're the one going through hell."

"I asked, Hattie. It really does help—hearing from someone who's on the other side of all of this." She dissolved into heaving sobs.

Hattie sat beside the massage table on a low stool, her hands resting gently on her cousin. Years of experience had taught her to simply remain close without trying to staunch the emotions or try to fix the client's problems.

"You miss your fiancé, don't you? Can't you contact him so he can be here with you?"

"I don't have a fiancé. Mary Elizabeth does."

"And you don't trust him enough to be honest?"

"I don't know. I just don't know." She blew her nose on a tissue Hattie provided. "I don't think I could stand any more pain right now."

The Triple C Day Spa and Salon bustled with activity. In addition to the local patrons, customers from out of town filtered in, a result of the First Annual Magnolia and Moonlight Golf Tournament. Stephanie bustled between the massage treatment room and the hydrotherapy room. Both hair stylists' time slots were filled, and Melody complained of a backache from hunching over nail care clients.

"Whew!" Lucille Jackson eased onto Wanda Orenstein's chair. "Y'all are cooking today. I've never seen the front parlor so full."

Wanda whipped the drape to cover the older woman and pressed together the Velcro neck closure. "Golf widows—gotta love 'em!"

"Reckon that means Mister Jake's busy, too."

"I haven't seen hide nor hair of the boy in a few days," Wanda answered.

"He has two weddings, a garden party, and the clubhouse dinner this week," Mandy supplied. She whisked Sue Ellen Sales from the chair to dryer number three and adjusted the controls. "You want a magazine to look at, Miz Sue Ellen?"

Her client nodded, and Mandy selected a home and garden edition. "I got the new *People*, too, as soon as Jocelyn finishes it. She'll most likely be asleep in a few minutes, so you can lean over and get it if you want." She motioned to dryer number two.

"What are we doing, today, Miz Lucille?" Wanda rested her hands on the black woman's shoulders.

"Nothing too fussy. Just trim up the fringe across my forehead. I'm wearing one of Elvina's hats for Easter Sunday, and my hair mashes down into my eyes when I put it on."

"You and the Reverend got special plans for the services this year down at the Morningside AME?"

"We're holding sunrise service down by the lake. Later, we're planning a big dinner on the grounds after the main Easter Sunday service. That's why I need to stop and see Jake after this appointment. I got to make sure he's ordered the lilies for the sanctuary."

Elvina appeared at the salon threshold. "I'm certain he has. Jake's got a memory like a bad mother-in-law."

"You're looking mighty pretty this morning, Elvina," Lucille complimented.

"Thank you, Lucille. Y'all going to have special music on Easter?"

"Sure are. Chiquetta Wilson is going to be the soloist. You remember her? She led the music at Piddie's memorial."

"Y'all best shore up the stained glass windows you just put in." Elvina chuckled. "That woman could break the sound barrier when she hits a high note."

"You coming then?"

"I wouldn't miss it for the world. I'll most likely attend the sunrise meeting with the Baptists, but you can save me a spot by you on the first pew for the eleven o'clock. I'll have to ponder on what I'll cook up."

Karen Fletcher stepped behind Elvina and tapped her lightly on the shoulder.

"Well, look who's here!" Elvina hugged the younger woman. "Melody's all ready for you."

"I really don't know why I'm bothering to get my nails done," Karen said as she settled into the chair opposite the nail specialist. "It's not like the rest of me looks great."

Elvina smiled. "Whatever it takes to make a woman feel better, that's what she should do. Have they scheduled your surgery yet?"

"Soon. My last chemo is coming up. Hopefully, the surgery will follow closely after that, as long as the blood work is okay."

"You always have to not eat or drink anything right before surgery." Mandy frowned. "Not being able to have my morning cup of coffee is what got me when I had my gallbladder removed a couple of years back. I had a screaming headache by the time they finally gave the happy shot. After that, I didn't really give a hoot."

"I can imagine you're ready to get it behind you," Wanda said.

Karen nodded.

"What color would you like today? I have the new spring pinks in." Melody held up a tray of nail enamel bottles.

"Give me harlot red. It drives Mama nuts."

Melody grinned. "Your grandmama always loved her bright red nails, too. She and your mama would go 'round and 'round about it. Evelyn thought ladies of a certain age should wear subdued shades."

"Piddie was anything but subdued," Lucille added.

Mandy propped her hands on her hips. "Karen, I can't stand it no more! Me'n Melody have been dying to hear how the visit with your friend went."

Karen looked over at Mandy and cocked her head. "What friend?"

"The one all the way from Atlanta."

"I haven't had any visitors. Well, take that back. Jon Presley stopped by yesterday for a while."

Melody and Mandy exchanged puzzled glances.

"I can't fathom she changed her mind after driving all that way," Mandy said.

"She?"

"Anna Freeman. She said she was your coworker."

"I don't know anyone named Anna. I'm pretty sure there's no one by that name affiliated with the station, either."

Mandy pursed her lips. "That's weird. She knew all about you. Talked about how she was the only one in Atlanta who knew who you really were, and that y'all were real close."

"She even said she was watching over your cats while you were away," Melody supplied.

Karen felt a chill deep inside. "No, a male friend is taking care of my animals. What did this woman look like?"

"She was short—maybe a couple of inches shy of my height." Mandy held her hand slightly below her eyes.

"And kind of slutty looking," Melody added.

Mandy said, "Her hair was bleached platinum blonde, and not such a good job, I might add. Not that any hairdresser could have done much with it, except shave it off and let her start growing it again from scratch."

"Did you notice what kind of car she drove?"

"It was red," Elvina stated emphatically. "I know, on account of I stepped out to carry the trash to the outside barrel and I saw it. It was exactly like the one Ladonna O'Donnell drives. You know, one of them little bitty things not big enough to scat a cat in. When she gets out of it, Ladonna looks like a praying mantis crawling out of a thimble with those long legs of hers."

Elvina paused. "Where was I? Oh, yeah. I thought—when did Ladonna slip in without me seeing her? Then, I spotted the Georgia tag, and I knew it had to be Mandy's new patron."

"A Mee—otter, that's what it's called," Melody said. "I was trying to remember the name."

Karen felt as if the air had been sucked from the spacious room. "A red Mazda Miata?"

Melody's head bobbed. "That's right. If it's the same as the car Ladonna drives, it is."

Elvina stuck one finger in the air. "There was a parking sticker on the back bumper, too. I don't rightly recall what it said. I wasn't paying it much mind."

The corners of Karen's lips turned down. "And she asked for Mary Elizabeth?"

Mandy shook her head. "No, hon. She called you by your real name. Said she'd come to visit her dear friend, Karen Fletcher."

Karen closed her eyes. "I know exactly who she was, and she's not what I'd ever call a friend. Not by a long shot. If she was here, she was fishing for information."

Mandy propped her hands on her hips. "Lord help us, Melody. We've been had."

Melody grasped Karen's hand. "I hope we haven't caused any trouble for you. I feel so awful. There we were—talking to the woman like we'd known her all our lives."

Karen looked first at Melody, then Mandy. "You would've had no way of knowing. I'm not mad—really."

Mandy snorted. "All I know is—if that floozy causes you any grief, and she shows her face in this town again, I'll personally stomp her in the ground."

"It doesn't take a brainiac to make a good fried egg sandwich. Easy peasy. Heat up a skillet with about a tablespoon of oil or bacon grease. Crack one large egg and splat it in the middle. When the clear part is cooked (it turns white—duh!), flip it over. Prick the yolk until it bursts and continue to cook for a few more seconds. Some people like the yolks wet; I don't. Runny yellow in a fried egg sandwich is just plain creepy.

Toast two pieces of wheat bread. Slather with mayonnaise (none of that low-fat junk) and slap the cooked egg on one side. If you want, you can add a slice of sharp cheddar cheese. Yum. Sometimes I add a couple of cooked pieces of bacon—turkey bacon if I'm on a health kick at the time—or a thick slice of cooked country ham. Close it shut with the other slice of toast and smash it down. Done.

Couldn't be more of a comfort food if it came with a pillow and soft blanket. Honestly!"
Jake Witherspoon, owner of The Dragonfly Florist

Chapter Fourteen

Will Cooke's private line light blinked insistently. He snatched the receiver and spoke. "No! I told you no this morning, and I meant it! You're too young to go see a Dead Elephants or Babies or whatever concert, and especially not on a school night. My answer is final."

A small chuckle sounded on the opposite end. "Will?"

He recognized the British lilt immediately.

"Mary Elizabeth? I'm sorry. I thought you were my daughter. She's called my personal line three times in a row this morning with a new improved reason I should bend on this concert issue. How are you? Does this call mean I can see your smiling face soon?"

"Are you busy? Can we speak privately for a few moments?"

He leaned back in the plush leather chair. "Sure. What's up? Are you okay?"

"Not exactly." Karen hesitated. "This is so difficult to explain over the phone."

"You and I have always been able to talk to each other, Mary Elizabeth. Please—"

"I'm not British."

"Excuse me?"

Karen paused a beat. "You'll be finding out the details soon, if Trisha Truman has anything to do with it."

"I'm completely lost now. Why don't you start from point A and work toward point B?"

"My real name," Karen said, dropping the accent, "is Karen Fletcher. I am from a small town in rural north Florida. That's where I am now—with my parents."

He struggled to equate the soft Southern-tinged speech with the woman he had known for over twenty years. "Is this some kind of joke?"

"No, and I'm sorry I have to tell you this way. I was planning on coming by as soon as I recuperated from the surgery."

Will felt as if he had stumbled into an episode of *The Twilight Zone*. The conversation was becoming more surreal by the second.

"Surgery?"

"I have breast cancer, Will."

"My God."

"I go in after the final chemo for, hopefully, a lumpectomy—perhaps more extensive, depending on what the surgeon finds."

"What can I do?"

"You're not angry? I thought you would hang up as soon as I told you the truth."

"I admit I'm flummoxed about the whole masked identity issue. I would really appreciate a more detailed explanation."

"And you'll get one. That, I promise. As soon as I recover enough to travel, I'll be back to clean out my desk."

"You're leaving us?"

"I figured I wouldn't have a choice. I hope you will leave me on the payroll at least until I'm clear of the majority of medical expenses—the health insurance, you know."

Will fought a wave of sadness. "You and I have seen this station through a world of changes, Mary, um, Karen. I think I owe it to you to at least hear your explanation. Besides, I don't see why you would need to quit."

"Depends on what Trisha Truman is planning on doing with the information she's gathered."

"You've been in contact with Trisha?"

"No. She came into town and duped a couple of people into re-vealing details of my life and illness. She even stopped by my father's restaurant and spoke at length with him—all under the pretense of being my dear concerned friend and coworker."

"Where did she get her information, do you suppose?"

"Probably from public records. Given a social security number, you can get most anything off the Internet."

Will groaned. "Employee records—has to be where she gleaned your social and date of birth." He snapped the pencil he held in two. "Damn her!"

"It had to come out, sooner or later. I just wish I could have had more control in revealing it myself."

"Don't worry about Trisha. I'll take care of her. You just concen-trate on getting well."

There was a pause on the other end. He heard the faint sound of crying.

"Thank you, Will. You are a true friend."

"Karen—boy, calling you by a different name is going to take some practice—I have to tell you, D. J.'s suspicious. He may even have figured things out by now. He came in yesterday and asked for a few days off. I wouldn't be surprised if he shows up there, if he has gained access to your parents' address."

She exhaled. "I planned on talking to him after all was a bit more settled. I appreciate the heads-up."

"I'm afraid I may be responsible for all that. He was pretty up-set about you being off somewhere in some kind of family crisis, so I suggested he look for an address book at your place. I'm sorry. I may have caused you a lot of grief."

"I don't think there's anything at my condo to find, but you never know. If Trisha could locate me, anyone can. It's not your fault, Will. He and I need to talk."

"That man worships the ground you walk on. Try not to worry too much. That can't be good for you right now."

"I suppose not."

"You call me if you need anything, and I mean any little thing.

You hear? Actually, if you'll leave your parents' number, I'd like to check on you in a couple of days." He paused. "If that's okay by you."

"I'd like that very much."

He entered the number she provided into his cell phone's directory. "Godspeed to you, Karen. I'll be thinking of you."

"Goodbye, Will."

In all the years of dealing with people, Will had ceased to be surprised by their behavior. This, however, was one of the most bizarre. He stared at the headset for a few moments before he mumbled aloud. "Well, ain't that some shit?"

Evelyn unloaded the dishwasher. The rattle of plates dropped carelessly atop towering stacks and the clang of silverware left little doubt Karen's mother was annoyed. "What's got you in such a snit, Ev?" Joe paused cautiously at the end of one long counter.

"Who says I'm in a snit?" She swiped the countertops vigorously with a damp rag.

"You're still stewing over Elvina and the Easter service, aren't you?"

She pursed her lips and snorted. "I can't fathom why Elvina Houston is insisting on Karen going down to the Morningside AME for church on Easter Sunday. It's a day for families to be together, Joe. I can't fathom it. I just can't."

He refilled his coffee mug and topped it off with skim milk. "Elvina is just trying to help in her own way, I suppose. She's as big a fool for that little church as your mama was, remember?"

Evelyn's expression softened. "Mama got to where she went with Lucille most every Sunday. She liked the singing, she said."

"Church is church, Evelyn. If Karen wants to go with Elvina, let it be. She's a grown woman."

She exhaled slowly. "I know that, Joe, it's just . . . she's so weak right now."

"Elvina will see to it that Karen's all right. She told me she'd bring her on home early if she got to feeling bad."

"I reckon."

Joe smiled. "There's my girl. I can always trust you to see all sides." He walked over and scooped his wife into a hug and kissed her lightly on the forehead. "I've got an idea." He nuzzled her hair.

Evelyn pushed away. "I'm not up for that this morning, Joe. I've got to get to the shop."

He chuckled. "Not that kind of idea. Although, now that you mention it." He grabbed her rump with one hand.

"Joseph Fletcher! You're turning into a dirty old man!"

"I'm your dirty old man and don't you forget it."

Evelyn blushed like a virgin bride.

"Here's my idea. Why don't you and I go to the sunrise service with the Baptists and then accompany Elvina and Karen to the Morningside AME at eleven?"

Evelyn shrugged. "We could."

"They're having a big dinner on the grounds after the service. I can cook up a pot of Piddie's famous chicken 'n' dumplin's, some fresh greens, a hoecake of cornbread, and maybe an apple pie."

"Other than Maizie Clark's funeral, I've never attended church there before."

"Nor have I. Judging from Elvina and Piddie's experiences, we'd be welcomed in."

Evelyn hesitated. "You think Karen would mind us tagging along?"

"Can't imagine she would, but I'll surely ask."

"It does sound like a workable thing. I'd really like for us all to be together for Easter. Too bad Byron won't be here till Monday."

Joe snuggled close to his wife. "Sure you have to leave early this morning?"

"You have to get on to the restaurant, too, I might remind you."

"Yeah, I guess you're right." He kissed her lightly on the lips. "Maybe you and I can go out on a date this evening."

"And leave Karen alone?"

"She's going over to Jon and Jake's for dinner, remember? It'll do us both good to get out a little. We can ride over to that little Chinese place you like in Marianna. What do you say?"

"You've got yourself a date, Mr. Fletcher. Just don't think I'm the kind of girl you can ply with rice wine and take advantage of."

"Easter—A Time for Reconciliation," the sign in front of the Morningside AME church declared. Karen Fletcher stood in the soft grass beneath the series of cement stairs leading up to the sanctuary on Wire Road. In front of her, Elvina Houston stopped every few feet to visit with a member of the congregation. The gathering had the appearance of a summer garden party. Creamy pastel sherbet hues mingled with bold African prints. Throughout the crowd, hats of assorted styles and adornments bobbed atop ladies' heads.

"Your father's parking the Lincoln," Evelyn leaned over and said in a low voice. "The cars are lined up practically to River Junction crossing. I'm glad we all rode together."

The two women watched the parade of smartly dressed parishioners arrive.

"It's a crying shame white women have gotten away from wearing hats to church," Karen's mother commented. "I can't recollect when I've seen so many fine designs in one place."

"Maybe you and Elvina can stir up some interest with your new coordinating ensembles."

"One can hope."

Lucille Jackson appeared at the threshold of the church and scanned the crowd below before joining them.

"There you are!" she said, reaching for Karen's hand. "I'm so pleased you and your family decided to join us for Easter. The musical worship promises to be wonderful today, what with Chiquetta joining us. I've got a spot next to Elvina that I saved for you, as long as you don't mind sitting up close. The Reverend likes to look down from the pulpit and see me there. I've sat on the first pew for going on forty-five years now."

"Joe's going to run home and bring the food after the service," Evelyn said.

The ribbons on Lucille's pale blue sunbonnet rippled in the morning breeze. "Everybody does the same thing. We won't eat until near one o'clock, by the time church lets out and everyone returns with the food. Of course, the children will hunt eggs in the vacant lot behind the building until midway the afternoon."

"Suppose it makes for a long day for a minister's wife," Evelyn offered.

"I don't mind a'tall." Lucille looped one arm through Evelyn's and the other through Karen's. "Let's go on in and get you two settled, shall we? I'll come back and keep an eye out for your husband. I have to say, Miz Evelyn and Miz Karen, your dresses are a sight to behold. And Miz Elvina's hats! She surely has found her calling, hasn't she?"

"Where is Elvina, by the way?" Karen asked.

"Catching up, I'd say." Lucille smiled. "She's taken up your grandmother's habit of asking around after folks before the service starts. She'll be along. I always save her a seat, and she slips in as Thurston is giving the call to worship." She tilted her head toward Karen. "Your grandmother, Miz Piddie, was my very dear friend. Once a month, regular as the cycles of the moon, I'd pick her up for Sunday services. She would stay for dinner with the Reverend and me. We loved her like she was family. I can't bring her to mind that I don't get a smile on my face. She got to the point, before she passed, that she came most every Sunday."

"Mama surely loved this little church," Evelyn agreed.

"Thurston maintained that Piddie was truly a Sister in Christ. She could see beyond the color of a person's skin clean into their heart of hearts. Takes a spirit-filled person to do that. Surely does."

Lucille led them down the left aisle toward the front of the small sanctuary where they settled onto the first wooden pew to the left. The open room was divided into three sections with a series of long pews in the center and rows of smaller pews to the left and right. Folding gray metal chairs had been added at the rear of the room in anticipation of the Easter Sunday overflow.

Five elongated vertical windows cast morning light into the room, giving it an ethereal glow. Two of the windows closest to the pulpit had been recently replaced with stained glass panels in brilliant hues of purple, green, blue, and gold.

Reverend Jackson's pulpit was centered beneath a crudely carved depiction of Christ on the cross. Directly behind, three rows of wooden benches awaited the choir. Though the church lacked the trappings of the high-end, richly-appointed Baptist sanctuaries Karen had infrequently visited in Atlanta, the ambience was one of peace and reverence. Immediately, she got the impression that the people filing in the open door behind her entered with the sole purpose of worship, not to see and be seen.

"Now, y'all make yourselves feel at home. I'll go look out for Mr.

Joe and see if I can coax Elvina inside before my husband closes the doors."

"This is a pretty little church," Evelyn commented. "They've put in the new windows since Joe and I came for Grandma Maizie's funeral. They raised the money doing all sorts of things—bake sales, car washes, and fish suppers. Joe donated several apple pies for one of their functions last year."

Joe slid into place beside his wife. "Sorry it took me so long. I ran into a fellow who was a psych aide up at the hospital when I was working in the unit. He retired a couple of years before I did."

The organist began to play softly, and the remnants of the congregation still outside on the front lawn filtered in and found seating. Though the room was newly air-conditioned, the press of bodies created heat, and hand-held fans fluttered to provide relief. Suddenly, the organist hit a sole note and the members of the Morningside AME choir paraded into the room clapping and singing in unison as they moved toward the front.

Elvina Houston scampered in the choir's wake and squeezed between Lucille and Evelyn. "I reckon I ought to pay more attention."

"Either that, or you just might have to join the choir, since they come in at the very last moment before Thurston does," Lucille said with a wink.

Elvina sniffed and picked up a church hymnal.

The Honorable Reverend Thurston Jackson broke his usual tradition of entering through a side door close to the pulpit and strode down the right hand aisle immediately behind the choir. He stopped to shake hands and pat backs along the way, a broad smile playing across his face.

"Look at him, will you? Near to seventy years old and still prancing down the aisles like he's a young man," Lucille said.

"Filled with the spirit," Elvina stated emphatically, "It puts a wiggle-bug up his pants."

Lucille regarded the elderly woman with a puzzled nod. "If you say so, Miz 'Vina."

After the congregation stood for the opening musical call to worship, the Reverend invited them to close their eyes and enter a place of peace. He delivered a heart-felt opening prayer that summoned up more than a handful of "amen's." "Good Easter Morning to all of you!" he called out.

Nods and answers of good morning echoed from the assembly.

"What a glorious day of reconciliation God has given unto us!"

Karen grinned. The preacher's voice was rich and full with the ability to call forth laughter or tears. She leaned slightly in her seat to gain a better viewpoint.

"Welcome, welcome, to all visitors. We see you, and we'll be sure to speak to you while you are here with us! We are blessed with your presence and God," he paused and allowed his eyes to roam dramatically across the sea of faces, "God has powerful lessons for all of us today!"

The Reverend descended from his elevated spot behind the wooden pulpit and walked amongst the seated parishioners. "I . . . I am just the messenger," he said, his voice, just a whisper. "God is speaking to you through me."

He whirled around and mounted the stairs and motioned for the choir to stand. The music that ensued left Karen dumbstruck, glued to her seat in the pool of sweat forming beneath her dress. One tall portly woman took the lead, her strong soprano voice echoing in waves through the cramped room. The choir swayed and hummed, breaking into accompanying song.

Soon the entire congregation was standing, clapping and singing out. Voices, young and old, joined in. Lucille grabbed Evelyn and Joe by the hand and urged them to unite with the group. Elvina rose and started to jump in place. Finally, Karen allowed herself to participate. The old song wound around and around, growing louder, building as more and more voices blended in. When it seemed as if the roof would surely fly off toward the heavens, the Reverend signaled. The volume lowered gradually, until just a low hum was audible. A tide of "amen's" and "praise Jesus's" rippled though the room.

Following the announcements of church business and special calls for prayer for community members facing grave illness and hardship, Chiquetta Jones rose and walked to the corner of the choir nook. Without musical accompaniment, she sang all four verses of "Amazing Grace." There were few dry eyes in the congregation when her angelic voice ceased. Reverend Jackson called for the weekly offering. All around her, Karen heard the rustle of bills and change as people delved into pockets and purses for monetary donations.

After the prayer over the offering plates, the congregation settled in for the Reverend's main message. A few coughs scattered around the room. Someone quieted a crying infant. The sound of creaking pews calmed as the church leader opened a worn Bible and cleared his throat.

Karen felt as if Thurston Jackson had looked straight into her heart when he spoke.

"How many of us are in need of reconciliation today?"

"Macaroni and cheese. I could eat my weight in the stuff. Leigh, my wife, makes it almost as good as my mama used to. Not any of that pre-fab boxed crap. No sir-ee. Mama's was made with whole milk, butter, and real cheese. She'd put it all together and bake it with bread crumbs on top. It would be all hot and bubbly and the cheese would hang in thin strings from the serving spoon when I dished up a big clump."

Bobby Davis

Chapter Fifteen

Bobby Davis gathered the chipped blue remains of a half-eaten Easter egg. "Here's the one we're missing." He waved toward the cluster of basket-toting children. "Looks like Spackle had a go at this one."

Hattie's mixed-breed mutt wagged his tail. Pieces of cooked egg white clung to his lower lip. Elvis rose up on his hind legs and danced around the large dog's head attempting to lick the dregs of the pilfered holiday treat.

"Gah! Elvis, don't eat that!" Jake propped his hands on his hips. "Eggs give you such atrocious breath!"

"Not to mention the gas that follows later on," Jon added. He scooped the Pomeranian into his arms. The small dog snarled. "Cut the attitude, mister. There'll be no more eggs for you today!"

"Just look at the stains on his little suit." Jake swatted at the soil and dried grass clinging to the lapel. "I hope it comes out. Evelyn will die a thousand deaths if she sees this."

"That's why they make spot remover, Jake," Hattie said. "Good thing you never had children. They live to eat, breathe, and wear dirt."

Bobby placed several eggs into his son's basket, then leaned over to kiss his wife. "I think I'll go on down and feed the fish. Want to come, Hattie?"

"Sure. Holston, you okay with Sarah?"

Her husband held the toddler securely in one arm. "We're just having a ball hunting eggs. You two go on."

"Want to take the ATV?" Bobby asked.

Hattie shook her head. "Let's walk. After that huge dinner, I can use the exercise."

The five-acre field behind the farmhouse rippled in long harrowed rows awaiting the appearance of the first tender blades of field corn. A one-lane dirt road led to the edge of a thick hardwood forest.

"I love this time of year." Hattie picked a strand of tall grass and chewed one end. "Everything's so dang green. Almost hurts your eyes to look."

They ambled in comfortable silence for a quarter of a mile before reaching a screened gazebo atop a small hill. A series of wooden steps with landings at three levels led down to the edge of a one-acre fish pond.

Bobby used a length of lead pipe to bang loudly on the side of an oil drum turned feed container. The vibration served as a call to lunch for the catfish. He scooped a coffee can of commercial floating food pellets and flung them high into the air. As soon as the feed landed in a wide arc on the surface, the water churned with hungry fish. Hattie and Bobby watched the feeding frenzy. In less than five minutes, every morsel had disappeared and the calm returned.

Hattie smiled. "Still amazes me to watch that, even after all these years."

Bobby nodded. "Want to sit a spell before we head back?"

They climbed back to the gazebo and settled into oak rocking chairs.

"I didn't see Evelyn's brood in church today," Bobby commented.

"They all went with Elvina to the Morningside AME Easter service."

Bobby laughed. "Bet that was a sight—Evelyn in a black church."

"She's not bigoted, Bobby. She's actually pretty cool. She just doesn't like to feel she's intruding on anyone."

The faint scent of honeysuckle drifted in the air. Hattie closed her eyes and lifted her nose to catch the sweet aroma.

"Leigh and I are thinking about having another baby. She tell you?"

"No, not yet. We haven't had a lot of time to talk with all that's going on with Karen." She reached over and grabbed his hand. "I think that's fantastic, Bobby."

"How is Karen?"

Hattie shrugged. "Hanging in there. She's scared, naturally. I think it'll be better when she's past the surgery."

"Leigh and I were talking about that last night. Why don't we keep Sarah so you and Holston can go over and sit with Joe and Evelyn at the hospital?"

"You sure?"

"You're closer to Evelyn than I am, Hattie. I think it would make her feel good knowing you were there. Leigh and I can visit a day or two after Karen's past the worst, when she feels more up to company."

"Won't you both be at work?"

"We put in for leave time. Family comes first."

"I can't believe what I'm hearing—my brother, the work-till-he-drops king!"

Bobby ran a hand through his thinning hair. "I'm staring at sixty, here in no time a'tall, Hattie. All this with Karen has made me do some serious soul searching."

"About . . . "

"Retiring."

"But you love your work, Bobby."

"I do. The world's changed a lot since I went into law enforcement. Years back, I was chasing poachers or checking hunting permits. These days, I come into close contact with drug runners and all manner of unsavory types who'd rather shoot me than look at me. Now that I have a young son—I just want to be able to see him grow up, spend some time with his daddy."

"A child changes your viewpoint. I'll cotton to that."

Bobby stared across the pond for a moment. "I've decided to put in for the deferred retirement program with the state. That'll give me a piece of time before I have to go out."

"Do what you have to do, Bro. Who am I to quibble? I only work, at most, fifteen hours a week doing massage therapy. But I'm happy. I've been able to slow my life down and enjoy it more. When I lived in Tallahassee, it seemed New Year's came every other month. It's so easy to grow old fast when you don't take the time to live every day. Certainly, having cancer taught me that."

"My drinking robbed me of my thirties and most of my forties. It's almost like I woke up, and here I was fifty."

"But aren't you glad for where you are now?"

Bobby grinned. Deep creases formed in the tanned skin around his blue eyes. "I wouldn't trade the life I have for ten pots of gold."

"Mashed potatoes: The one thing Mama didn't try to fix with one of her strange add-ins. Not real mashed potatoes—the boxed kind, from those dry flakes. I had never tasted real mashed potatoes until after Linda and I were married. Hers have the lumps and everything. The ones Mama made were always the same consistency—like paste. But with a generous clump of butter and some salt and pepper, they were edible. You would've had to have been there to understand how good they tasted."

Byron Fletcher

Chapter Sixteen

Though Interstate 10 provided a fast-paced, direct connection between the airport in Tallahassee and his home town, Byron Fletcher opted for State Highway 90. He guided the cramped subcompact rental car into the westbound side and eased into the scant flow of local traffic. The first eighteen-mile stretch of the four-lane route passed through the Quincy town square before narrowing to a two-lane country road. Byron glimpsed the small communities of Gretna and Mt. Pleasant, followed by clusters of modest wood framed houses and expanses of pasture and farm land. Three miles east of Chattahoochee, the terrain changed to gently rolling hills forested with tall pines and hardwoods.

He flipped the switches to lower the windows and breathed deeply. The blended scents of cow and pig manure, rich loamy soil, and the pollen of hundreds of budding plants and trees tickled his nose. His professional meanderings had bounced his small family across the North and finally to Ohio, but Byron still associated home with the muggy, bug-infested, Deep South.

"You're nothing but a swamp rat by birth," his wife Linda often reminded him. "You'd sit and chat with a demure belle underneath a flowering magnolia tree sipping a mint julep if you had half a chance."

Do Southerners actually drink mint juleps? he pondered. One day, he would have to try one.

Byron's thoughts jumped to the last time he visited home for Grandmama Piddie's Purt-Damn-Near-A-Hundred Birthday Party. How he and Linda had laughed over the invitation! At first, he and his wife had wondered if they could attend. Both boys were tied up with science camp. In the end, the pull of home and family won out when Linda insisted he be there. He smiled, remembering his grandmother's daisy-studded beehive hairdo and the matching pale yellow linen outfit. He shook his head. No wonder he and Karen had turned out the way they had. It was genetic.

Piddie's party was his last opportunity to visit with the beloved matriarch and the first time in twenty years to associate with his only sibling. Karen attended, strictly in a professional capacity. Intent on filming an award-winning documentary on aging in America, his estranged sister had kept a careful distance. Byron had studied her from across the crowded community hall at the First Baptist Church. She was a stunningly beautiful woman: stately, graceful, her long blonde hair swinging softly with the slightest movement. She had greeted him, as she had the rest of the family, with a courteous nod. A faint, fleeting glimmer of recognition flickered behind the carefully constructed mask.

"Just like the Prodigal Son in the Bible," he said aloud. "Here am I, the dutiful son who toiled in the fields, watching over the flock, and here comes the long-lost sibling who left for parts unknown. But she comes home, and we greet her with open arms, throw a fancy robe on her back, and kill a fatted calf for a feast. It's a little difficult for me not to be judgmental here."

The Chattahoochee city limit sign appeared, followed by a thirty-five-mile-an-hour speed limit warning. Clumps of budding crape myrtle trees stood by the bird sanctuary plaque. He stopped at the first of the town's two signal lights, then decided to cruise the main drag for old times' sake. Three blocks down, he spotted the Borrowed Thyme Bakery and Eatery sign and whipped the car into a parallel parking spot.

The jangle of a small brass bell announced his entrance. Joe Fletcher glanced up from the hot grill behind the counter. "Son!" He expertly flipped two blueberry pancakes before stepping from behind the workstation, quickly wiping his hands on the edge of a white chef's apron.

"Dad!" Byron grasped his father's offered hand.

The older man pulled his son into a tight embrace and slapped him sharply on the back. "When'd you get into town?"

"Just now. Still have the coffee on?"

Joe pointed to the self-serve aluminum urns. "Just finished brewing. Help yourself. Let me finish up these hotcakes before they burn."

"You hungry?" Joe asked. He removed the pancakes to a carry-out container and added small covered cups of flavored syrup and fresh butter. "I'm just finishing breakfast, but I could whip most anything up for you. Want some French toast, or maybe an omelet? Oh, I know, I have some banana nut muffins. I could warm one up for you."

"Got any catheads?" Byron grinned. The term drove his poor Yankee wife knee-slapping crazy.

"You kidding?" His father reached into a covered container. "I'd get run out of this town on a rail if I sold out of Piddie's biscuits."

Joe placed two biscuits onto a pan and slid them into a warming oven. "You want honey with them?"

"Tupelo?" Byron's mouth watered.

"Naturally. Some of the tourists ask for orange blossom or wildflower, but anyone who has a clue at all knows tupelo's the best. One taste will usually change their minds." He pointed to a stack of amber glass containers at the end of the counter. "Jack Pope keeps me stocked up. I sell at least three or four pints a week, more during the winter when the snowbirds migrate south."

Joe sat the warmed biscuits in front of his son and refilled his coffee cup. "You been by the house yet?"

Byron shook his head. He bit into the buttery honey-coated biscuit and moaned. "Man, I miss this."

"I gave Linda the recipe last time you were home. Can't she make you a batch every now and then?"

Byron rolled his eyes. "She refuses to bring lard into our house."

"Can't make a decent cathead without lard," Joe agreed. "Well, I suppose it gives you a reason to come home every now and again." He smiled. "Your mama's been up half the night cleaning house. She's just beside herself having you and Karen home at the same time. She had so much bleach in the guest bathroom, she was almost overcome with the fumes."

"Like the house is ever dirty to start with."

"She's calmed down a bit since she's had her sewing business. Floors will actually go a day or two without being mopped."

Byron smiled. "That's hard to fathom."

"Everyone can change. Look at me! Who would have ever believed

I could take on a second career so late in life?"

"Dad, it's not like you're a hundred years old."

"Still, most fellows my age retire and play golf all day, or park in front of the television."

"I can't imagine you doing either."

The two men sat in shared silence for a moment.

"So, you haven't seen your sister yet."

Byron shook his head.

"That why you stopped here first? You stalling for time?"

Byron shrugged. "Maybe."

"It's a terrible way to gather your sister back into the fold, but I guess the Lord works in ways mysterious. She's pretty beaten down."

"She strong enough to go through the surgery?"

Joe sipped his coffee before answering. "I questioned her decision to hold off on the surgery until they gave her chemotherapy. I've seen how low a person can get after that. Your sister had it set in her head that was the way she wanted it. She's better today than yesterday, and her blood work turned out okay. I'm glad she's getting this thing behind her soon."

"She still insisting she's British?"

"No. She dropped that pretense like it was last season's fashion."

"Amazing, after all those years living as someone else, she'd even remember who she really is."

Joe sighed. "Don't think she has accomplished that yet. I get the sense she's free-floating. Not really sure who she is and what she's about. At least we can be thankful she came to us in her hour of need."

"Maybe she didn't have any place else to turn."

"Still, she's my daughter, and I'd take her in regardless. I suppose some folks wouldn't understand that. When you have children, you keep right on loving them. Always hoping for the best."

Byron reached over and rested a hand on his father's shoulder. "I understand, Daddy, and I wouldn't expect you or Mom to feel any other way."

"I'm so glad you're here, honey." Evelyn released her son from a suffocating embrace. "Did you have any problems with your flights?"

"One minor glitch in Atlanta, but I've come to expect that. We circled for over forty minutes, and I had to gallop to make the connection."

A concerned expression colored his mother's features. "Be sweet to your sister, now."

"Where is she?"

"On the sun porch where she spends most of her time. I think it must make her feel better being out there with all my plants and flowers." Evelyn rested a hand on his arm. "She's mighty fragile, Byron."

"Mom, do you actually think I'd say anything to upset her?"

Evelyn plucked a stray thread from his shirt sleeve. "No. Still, I realize you may feel a certain resentment toward your sister. Now's not the time to open any can of worms."

"I hear you, Mom, loud and clear. Where do you want my suitcase?"

"Leave it there. I'll take it on back to your grandmother's suite. I put fresh linens on the bed last night, so everything's all ready for you. Go on out and see your sister."

Byron paused atop the stairs leading down to the garden room. Karen huddled on one end of the wicker swing, curled into a small ball with a mug cradled in her hands. He had steeled himself repeatedly on the trip from Ohio, but his sister's appearance shook him deeply. She was no longer the stately, composed woman he had glimpsed on television over the past years. Her body had sunk into itself. Dark purple smudges under her eyes attested to the valiant battle being waged within. Her fine porcelain skin lacked the pink blush of health. Any vestiges of resentment melted away.

He stepped down onto the parquet stone floor. "Sissy?"

Karen turned toward his voice. Her face glowed. "By!"

They rushed toward each other and embraced in the middle of the room. Evelyn appeared at the threshold momentarily, smiled, and returned to the kitchen.

"Nice 'do, Sissy." Byron rubbed his hand playfully across her slick scalp. "Maybe you can charge folks to pat your head for good luck, kind of like a statue of Buddha."

Karen reached up and ran her fingers up and over her ears, a habit learned from years of tucking the long hair away from her face.

"I was going to put my wig on this morning, but it's so hot. It gives me a headache after a little while."

"You look fine to me. Besides, I'm family. We're entitled to seeing each other in our raw states."

"That would describe me perfectly. Raw."

Evelyn poked her head through the door. "You kids want some iced tea? I just made a fresh pitcher with sprigs of spearmint in it, just the way you like it."

"Sure!" they cried out in unison.

Byron settled onto the porch swing, his sister tucked underneath one arm. "Next time I start feeling old, I'm going to come running home. No one else calls me a kid anymore, except Evelyn."

Karen giggled like a school girl. "She hates it when one of us calls her by her real name." She imitated her mother's accent. "Just not proper. I'm your mother, not some stranger off the street. My first name is for other folks to use, I'll thank you kindly."

Byron smiled. "You've been here too long, Sissy. You're starting to sound just like her." He studied his sister for a moment. "You up for surgery?"

Karen pulled the chenille robe close to her throat. "Ready as I'll ever be. One last chemo treatment, thank God. I just want this whole thing to be over."

"Mom told me the entire town has rallied behind you. She said Elvina Houston's got folks praying from here to the Mason-Dixon line."

"Not just that, Elvina went on the Internet and put my name on some international hope list. Not that I mind, but it seems weird that people who don't even know me—much less where Chattahoochee, Florida, is—would take time out of their lives to offer up prayers."

"Hey, I'd offer up live chickens to a lava-spitting volcano god if it would help you get well."

"That's not all. I can't tell you how many times I've been told to 'think positive' in the last two months." She paused. "I must sound like a true whiner, but so help me, if one more person gives me the stay-peppy talk, I'll scream."

"Don't feel too cheerful now, I gather?"

"Guarded optimism—that's the way I'd characterize it. With the chemo and all the side effects, I have to fight to feel much of anything, much less maintain a cheerful, win-one-for-the-home-team attitude. I just don't have the energy."

He squeezed her hand. "You have my permission to be a complete and total bitch towards me, if that's what you need, Sissy. It never bothered me when we were growing up. I'll just ignore you like I did then."

His sister sucker-punched his arm. "I see you haven't changed much."

"Nor have you, underneath it all."

"I can only imagine what you think of me." Karen ducked her head.

Byron reached over and tipped her chin upward. "None of your illustrious past makes a hill of beans difference in the way I feel about you. We can hash it all out one day after you're free and clear of this thing, if that's what you want."

"You can call it what it is, By. C-A-N-C-E-R. The big C. Leveler of all. Lover of none."

"My, aren't you poetic? I can see why you are the journalist of the family."

"Was."

"You're not giving up on your career because of the cancer, are you?"

Karen patted his hand. "Big boy! Saying the cancer word!" She grew serious. "I don't think I'll have a choice. Once my ruse is revealed to the world, I'll be lucky to write a shopping list."

"Did you tell anyone in Atlanta?"

"Only one person—my boss."

"Was that wise? I mean, you could go back to work if . . ."

"I had to tell him. One of the office staff who has had it in for me from the first time she came on board over a year ago has gained access to my secret. There's no telling what she plans to do with it. I wouldn't be surprised if I end up on the front page of the *National Informant*." Karen shrugged. "I was going to tell Will anyway—that's my boss, Will Cooke—but I really wanted to do it on my terms."

"You feel like the shit's hit every fan within a hundred miles, I guess."

"I couldn't have found a better way to put it myself."

"Linda sends her love. She really wanted to be here for you, too, but we had no one to leave the boys with."

"I understand. The whole world doesn't grind to a screeching halt because I'm sick."

Evelyn stepped down the stairs carrying a tray of filled iced tea glasses and a plate of cookies.

"You cooking now, Mom?" Byron grinned impishly.

"Don't get smart with me, mister. I can still turn you over my knee."

Karen and her brother struggled to suppress laughter.

"Your father made these. He's the chef of the family now that I've taken on my sewing business. Try one. They're made with a sugar substitute."

Karen bit into a crisp cookie. "Mama has turned against white sugar, By. It's the root of all evil."

Evelyn smirked. "Say what you want, I do believe what I've read."

"You should see the supplements she has me on."

Evelyn wagged one finger in her direction. "Your body is a temple, young lady. We're going to feed it and make it well while starving out the cancer cells!"

A loud ring sounded from the direction of the kitchen.

"That's your daddy's vegetarian lasagna. I best take it from the oven before the cheese chars on the top. He'd have my hide if I burnt it." Evelyn dashed from the garden room.

"I'd feel right at home if she let it turn to charcoal. It would be like old times. Sometimes, I let my toast burn at home just to reminisce about growing up with Mom's cooking."

"You're so bad." Karen smiled warmly. "And I'm so glad you're here, By."

He leaned over and pecked her lightly on the cheek. "Wouldn't be anywhere else, Sissy."

Leigh Davis's
Baked Macaroni and Cheese Casserole

1 package of elbow macaroni pasta, 8 ounces
2 Tablespoons butter or margarine
¼ cup all-purpose flour
2 cups milk
1 cup shredded sharp cheddar cheese
8 ounces cubed processed cheese food (like Velveeta)
plain bread crumbs

Cook pasta according to package directions until a little chewy (al dente).

Over medium heat, melt butter or margarine. Whisk flour in and stir vigorously. Add milk and cook until thick and bubbly—about five or six minutes. Add in cheeses and stir until completely melted. Remove from heat and mix in the cooked and drained pasta until it is coated with the cheese sauce. Pour into a greased two-quart casserole dish. Lightly dust the top with the plain bread crumbs.

Bake in a preheated 350° oven for 30 minutes. Let stand 10 minutes before serving.

Chapter Seventeen

Joe Fletcher noted the jangle of the miniature brass bell attached to the Borrowed Thyme Bakery and Eatery's front door. He hastily removed a tray of hot biscuits from the oven and grabbed a pot of freshly brewed coffee.

The man who seated himself at the corner table next to the store-front window was unfamiliar—tall with wavy dark brown hair and a neat, trimmed mustache. Joe guessed his age at mid-forties.

"Good morning!" Joe called as he crossed the room. "Coffee?"

"That would be great." D. J. flipped the white pottery mug over in its saucer. "I've been driving since the wee hours."

"Where'd you drive in from, if you don't mind me asking?"

"Atlanta."

"Bet you are tired, then. Menu's on the clip there. I just pulled a rack of fresh biscuits from the oven if that tickles your fancy."

D. J. glanced briefly at the printed menu. "Couple of biscuits will do me. I'm not that hungry, but I guess I need to eat a little something."

Joe returned to the kitchen, appearing shortly with a stoneware plate and a tray of condiments.

"That's real butter in the crock. Margarine's over on the side table by the coffee urn if you'd rather have it instead." Joe gestured to a series of glass jars. "Got your homemade blackberry, strawberry, and mayhaw jelly, or I have three kinds of honey. Tupelo's the best in my estimation."

"These are the biggest biscuits I've ever seen." D. J. sliced the still-hot bread and slathered butter on both halves.

"My late mother-in-law's recipe. We call them catheads on account of them being as big around as a cat's head."

D. J. bit into the soft bread and it dissolved in his mouth. "That's about the best damn biscuit I've ever had."

"I thank you, sir. Can I get you something else to go along with them? Maybe an egg or a slice or two of fresh country ham?"

"Don't think so. By the time I eat all this, I'll be more than satisfied."

Joe retired to the kitchen and shoveled the remaining biscuits into a covered display tray. A niggling thought teased the edge of his consciousness. He grabbed a full cup of coffee and approached the stranger's table.

"Don't mean to seem nosey, but you said you were down from Atlanta?"

D. J. wiped the crumbs from the corners of his mouth with a red-checkered linen napkin. "That's right."

"Just passing through, are you?"

D. J. stuffed the urge to laugh. His first taste of Chattahoochee was quickly becoming a scene from a second-rate western. Pretty soon, the High Sheriff would come strutting in the door, six-shooters in hand, and urge him to mosey on out of town.

"Actually, I'm here to look for my fiancée."

Joe smiled. "Is that right? You must love her terribly to come all this way. Who is the lucky woman? Maybe I know her."

"Mary Elizabeth Kensington. She's not from around here originally, but I believe she has distant relatives who live in town. I'm heading over there as soon as I finish my coffee."

Joe felt the blood rush from his head. "Mind if I join you?"

D. J. had heard of little towns being obnoxiously friendly, but this was fast becoming surreal. "Sure, why not?"

Joe pulled out a chair opposite his customer and settled down with his cup cradled between his hands. "Son, I think you and I need to talk."

"And why would that be?"

"My name is Joe Fletcher. The young woman you're speaking of is my daughter."

D. J. nearly choked on a sip of coffee.

"There are some things you need to know if you're dead set on visiting her today."

Pinky Green released the snap closure on his blue jeans and leaned back on the porch rocker with a loud groan.

"If I keep on eating like that, woman, we'll have to let my pants out a notch or two."

Wanda plopped in the rocker beside his. "Know what you mean. All this bliss and happiness has given me a hell of an appetite."

He reached down and scratched Scrappy behind her ears. "Maybe we ought to buy a couple of bicycles and take a ride every evening now that the days are getting longer. There are plenty of back roads around here that don't see a lot of traffic."

"Good idea. Maybe we can check by one of the bike shops in Tallahassee when we go over to see Karen in the hospital."

"Tomorrow's the big day, right?"

Wanda nodded. "Evelyn's nervous as all get out, too. I think she's worse off than Karen, by far. They're going over to the doctor's this afternoon for the final ultrasound to see if the chemo helped reduce the size of the tumor."

"You planning on going over with the family tomorrow?"

She shrugged. "I've gone back and forth about it. Karen will be out of it for the most part with the anesthesia. Still, Evelyn and Joe will need support."

"Did Byron make it into town?"

Wanda wound a sprig of auburn hair absently around one finger. "Yeah. I called the house earlier and spoke to Evelyn. She said Byron and Karen have been talking ninety to nothing since he got in."

She stretched and yawned. "Any-who, I've already given Elvina the heads-up that I want to be off the day of Karen's surgery. I won't show up over there at the crack of dawn, but I'll probably try to be there before she's out of recovery." Wanda leaned over and ran a hand through Pinky's hair. "That is, if I can get my butt out of your bed."

Pinky smiled slightly. A bright red flush colored his face. "I'll make sure you're up on time. Heck, I'll even ride over there with you."

"You sure? A hospital can be a mighty boring place."

"Nothing's boring when you're around, Wanda Jean."

She hopped up and draped across his lap.

"You are an absolute doll."

A quick kiss developed into a passionate exchange of saliva.

"So, when are we going to tie the knot?" Wanda asked when she caught her breath.

"That's up to you."

Wanda played with the pale hairs on the nape of his neck. "Let's wait until Karen's better, okay? I'd really like for her and the family to be at the ceremony."

"There's no rush. Neither of us is going anywhere, right?"

"Better not." She snuggled into his chest, content.

"Wanda Jean?"

"Hmm?"

"You given any thought on what you're going to do with your place in town once we're married?"

She sat up straight so that she could face him. "I don't want to sell it, if that's what you're getting at."

"Up to you. I just asked, is all."

"That little house isn't much, but it's the only thing I've ever had that I could call my own. Can you understand?"

Pinky stroked her hair, and she settled back into the curve of his arms. "Perfectly. I just hoped you'd want to live out here. I can't cotton much to living cooped up in town, but I reckon I'll manage if that's where you are."

"I want to live out here, too, Pinky. I've never been as happy as I am out here with you. Way I figure, I can always find a renter."

The Day-glow orange Post-it note attached to the front page of the *National Informant* read: *Boss man, I spotted this at the stop-n-rob on the corner when I gassed up the company van. Thought you might like to see it. Simpy.*

Will Cooke punched the intercom button on his phone with such force, the base slid backwards and upended a pottery jar filled with pens and pencils.

"Yes, sir?" his assistant's voice responded.

"Locate Trisha Truman. Ask her to come to my office immediately." He cursed under his breath as he retrieved the pencils that had rolled onto the floor.

Will forced himself to deep breathe. Anger would accomplish little, save sending inordinate amounts of harmful chemicals racing to his overburdened heart muscle.

A tap sounded on the office door, and Trisha Truman's bleached blonde head peeked around the threshold. "You wanted to see me?"

"Sit down."

Trisha cocked her head to one side. "Is that an order or an invitation, Will?"

He swallowed the bile collecting like the pooled grease from yesterday's cheap burger. "Please."

Trisha's scarlet lips eased into a seductive smile. "That's more like it."

She eased into the leather wing back chair in front of his desk, slowly crossed her long legs, and began to swing a sandaled foot in lazy circles.

Will snatched the gossip rag news magazine from his desk, discarded Simpy's note from the color-printed front page, and held the periodical toward Trisha. "Have any comment on this?"

She glanced briefly at the bold headlines and allowed her eyes to rest on the picture underneath. A smug expression of satisfaction played across her features. "Imagine that! The woman in that photo looks amazingly like our own British newsperson. Well, what do you know? It is!"

Will clenched and felt several small grains of enamel give way on the top of one of his molars. Given a few more years and the ensuing stress, his dentist would regard him as easy money in the bank. "You don't have a thing to say about why Mary Elizabeth's picture is splayed all over the front of a trash rag like this?"

Trisha studied her manicure and picked idly at a hangnail. "I saw it earlier. Interesting article. Liars get what's coming to them in the end, I suppose."

"Mary Elizabeth is—"

"Oh, c'mon, Will," she interrupted. "We all know now that she's a fake. Her real name's Karen Fletcher and she's a low-rent redneck from North Florida, for God's sake."

Will felt his ears grow warm with rising anger. "Her life's now fodder for the press, thanks to you."

"Me?" She batted her eyelashes. "Why, Will!"

"I know you went to her hometown and lied to dig up dirt, Trisha. I'm sure you were the one who went public with the knowledge."

"So what if I did? I didn't do a thing wrong—just unearthed her dirty little conniving lies."

Will suppressed the urge to grab the nearest object and hurl it across the desk. "You ferreted the information from somewhere, Trisha. My guess is the confidential employee files."

"Who says where I came by it? Could've been most anywhere. The Internet is a wonderful tool for investigative reporting."

"Is that what you're calling it?"

"I knew you wouldn't appreciate the level of my skill, Will. That's why I chose to go over your head. There will be a piece in the Atlanta paper tomorrow." Her lips pursed together into a tight red knot.

Will pushed back from his desk. "I want you out of here immediately!"

Trisha's expression froze. "Wait . . . you're firing me?"

"Bet your ass I'm firing you! Not only did you use confidential information for personal gain, but—"

"You can't prove that."

He snorted. "I suppose I can't. But let me tell you something— any person who would be so ruthless and full of her own puffed-up importance to do such a dastardly thing to a coworker who has done nothing to warrant such ire—God, you make me sick! Now, thanks to you, she has to deal with the ogre of breast cancer and face the damned press to boot!"

"I didn't invent my life like *she* did." Trisha rose. "You can't fire me. I've done nothing wrong."

He flipped open a thick brown folder. "Oh, I have plenty to back me up. Written complaints from coworkers about—" he referred to the top sheet "—blatant sexual overtures." Will continued, picking documents at random. "Repeated absences from duties without proper, hell, without *any* notice." Another: "Excessive personal computer use on company time."

Trisha offered no reply except a fierce expression.

"Most of the men here have approached me about your behavior. The flipping *men*! That doesn't hold a penlight to what the females think about you: Gossip-mongering. Instigator. Snitch. Petty thief." Will took a deep breath. "Each and every one of these, I have discussed with you, and they're documented. Not that talking it over made a piss-ant's pot of good."

Trisha tilted her head and offered a thin smile that didn't make it past her lips. "All of them are just jealous of my obvious virtues. You of all people should know I deserve to be in front of the cameras, not skulking behind the scenes. Okay, so I'm out sometimes. I have health issues. You fire me and I'll have an attorney here before you can take my name off the payroll. I repeat, you cannot fire me."

Will slammed his hand down on the desk, sending papers flying. "I can and I will! Clean out your desk and get the hell out of my station!" His nostrils flared. "I'm calling security and telling them to expect your keys at the door."

Trisha Truman glared at him, her lips set in a grim line. She shoved the chair across the plank floor, leaving deep gouges in the wood. "You will live to regret this."

"The only thing I regret, Trisha, is ever bringing you on board."

On her way out, she slammed the door so hard, one of the framed leadership awards crashed to the floor and sent glass shards scudding in all directions.

As Will fought to calm his breathing, an idea occurred to him. He laughed out loud, imagining his lips sweeping into curlicues at either end, much like the Grinch in his favorite Christmas video. He flipped his cell phone open and located the number.

He might not be able to ultimately save Karen's career, but there might be a way to keep her on payroll and salvage something in the end.

"I have Piddie Longman's chicken 'n' dumplin' recipe, and I have been known to break down and make it for special occasions. A lady from one of our sister churches over in Tallahassee gave me this easy recipe, and I can whip it up really fast when I get to missing my friend and her cooking. Also, it's easy to prepare for just one person, with a little left over for later. It's fooled many folks into thinking I slaved to make it!"

Elvina Houston

Elvina Houston's
Cheatin' Chicken 'n' Dumplin's

One 14-ounce can of chicken broth
½ cup water
One 10 ¾ oz. can cream of chicken soup, undiluted
Two hard-boiled eggs, diced
Five 10-inch flour tortillas
Salt and pepper to taste
Two to three boneless chicken breasts

In a pot, combine the broth and water. Add chicken breasts and cook until chicken is tender. Remove from pot, cut into cubes, and return to pot. Bring broth back to a boil. Cut tortillas, first into halves, then into long two-inch strips. Drop strips into the boiling broth and allow them to cook on high for about three or four minutes. Reduce heat to simmer. Add in the can of cream of chicken soup and the diced eggs. Add a little salt and pepper to taste.

Cover pot and allow it to simmer on very low heat for about twenty minutes, or until most of the moisture has been absorbed by the tortilla strips. Serve warm.

Note: frozen, diced chicken can be used to save time. Just add to broth at the beginning so it can thaw as the broth heats.

Chapter Eighteen

D. J. Peterson parked in the paved circular drive in front of the brick ranch-style house and double-checked the address. He sat in silence for a moment to collect his wildly racing thoughts. He owned no frame of reference for interaction with a fiancée who he knew under a false identity, not to mention one who was facing down breast cancer.

"What the hell." He snatched the keys from the ignition.

A petite middle-aged woman with shoulder-length brown hair answered the door after the first ring. D. J. stood face to face with a shorter, dark-haired, more mature version of his beloved Mary Elizabeth Kensington.

"You must be Donald. My husband called and said you were on your way." Evelyn extended her hand. "I'm her mother, Evelyn Fletcher. I know this must be a bit much to take in all at once."

"Yes."

"I realize you must have many questions for my daughter." Evelyn hesitated. "I can't begin to imagine how you must feel right now. But Karen's quite ill, and she's fighting with all she has. Please, please, don't be too harsh on her. I'm sure there will come a time later on when the two of you can hash things out."

"Is Mary—Karen—expecting me?"

"Yes. She's in the garden room with her brother Byron. He's down from Ohio."

Evelyn touched his arm. "She's having the surgery soon. We're all trying our level best to stay positive for her sake, Donald."

"I understand. May I see her now?"

She escorted him through the kitchen to the porch. Byron stood when D. J. and his mother entered the room.

"Donald, this is my son, Byron Fletcher. Byron, this is Donald Peterson from Atlanta."

The two men shook hands. D. J. allowed his eyes to rest on his fiancée. The pale, winsome creature huddled on the porch swing bore little resemblance to the vibrant woman he had made love with two months prior.

"Byron, let's you and I go in the kitchen and leave them to visit."

"You okay, Sissy?" Byron touched her shoulder gently.

She nodded to her brother, then offered a weak smile to D. J. "Hello, Donald."

"May I?" He motioned to the wicker arm chair adjacent to the swing.

"Please." Her gaze followed his movements.

"At least you didn't mock me by donning the fake accent," he said with a wry smile.

Karen pulled on a stray strand of wig hair. "That would seem a bit unnecessary since you know who I really am."

"Hmm."

Entire epistles of words tumbled around inside awaiting exit, and D. J. struggled to whip them into some semblance of order.

Karen studied her hands. "Did Trisha Truman tell you about me?"

"No, your father did."

"So, how did you . . . ?"

"Find you? Wasn't easy. You didn't leave behind a wealth of clues." He slipped a hand into his jacket pocket, extracted a folded piece of stationery, and handed it to her. "I got the address off this. It was next to your computer." He purposely failed to admit to the month-long meticulous room-by-room search of her condominium.

"Oh. I meant to send this back. There was a gold pendant with it from my mother."

"I left it behind in the box."

"I see."

D. J. snapped the band on his watch. The silence hung like wet drapery between them.

"How are things at Georgia Metro?"

D. J. shrugged. "Same ole. Folks are beginning to wonder where you are."

"Suppose so."

"The kitties?"

"Fine. They miss you. Brat boy has finally stopped trying to ruin every pair of shoes I own, and as to the fat cat, she loves me because

I can operate the can opener."

Karen offered a slight smile. "You know I appreciate you taking such good care of them."

"Mary E—Karen—Jeez, I don't even know what I should call you."

D. J. ducked his head and ran his fingers through his thick brown hair. "I thought of a million things to say to you on the way over here. Now, I just can't come up with any. I guess I'm about as dumbfounded as a man could ever be."

"I can see why you would feel that way."

D. J. turned slightly to face her. "I am truly sorry for what you're going through."

"The cancer?" Karen gave a slight laugh. "It's nothing compared to watching my life fall to ruins."

He leaned forward with his elbows propped on his knees. "Just answer one thing for me, please. How long have you known?"

"I found out the day before Valentine's."

"So, it wasn't just my proposal that upset you that night."

She started to reach out to touch his face, then drew back. "No. That was a pleasant and wonderful surprise. One I shall never forget."

His lips drew into a thin line. "Why didn't you tell me?"

Karen slowly exhaled. "It's complicated, Donald. It has to do with fear and a whole gamut of emotions I haven't even figured out as yet. I just couldn't."

He sat back and crossed his arms. "But you could return home to a family you ditched years ago? What about this makes any sense at all?"

"I don't expect you to understand. It had to do with facing all the lies in my life. I needed to come home if I was going to stand a chance of healing myself. I'm so screwed up, Donald."

"So . . . you and I? Guess it didn't mean a thing to you."

Karen closed her eyes to stem the flood of threatening tears. "I've loved you from the start. This isn't about us." She worked the diamond engagement ring from her finger. "Here."

"Don't want it anymore?"

Moisture welled in her eyes. "That's really not for me to say."

He studied the play of light within the facets of the brilliant gemstone a moment before handing it back to her. "Keep it."

Karen's mouth parted slightly.

D. J. glanced away. "I'm not sure of anything at this moment. I need to mull things over for a bit."

A single tear slipped from her eyes and she brushed it aside.

He released a heavy sigh. "How are you, really?"

She shrugged. "Tired. Nauseated. Depressed. Bald. That about sums it up."

"Surgery's when?"

"After my final chemo treatment. If all checks out with my blood work, Dr. Keegan will do a lumpectomy . . . if he can."

"And afterwards?"

Karen frowned. "Radiation, for sure. Maybe two more rounds of chemo. All depends on the lymph nodes. If they're clear, more chemo won't be necessary."

"I see."

The rhythmic sound of an antique wall clock peppered the silence, ticking off seconds of borrowed time.

D. J. drummed his fingers on his knee. "You planning on returning to Atlanta?"

"I don't know, Donald."

D.J swallowed the lump of sadness threatening to strangle him. "I guess . . . I should be going."

He rose, turned toward the door, then spun slowly around and leaned down to place a soft kiss on her forehead. "Don't worry about the kitties. I'll take care of things at home."

D. J. slipped quietly through the house to the front entrance. His composure hovered dangerously close to shattering. The last thing he needed was interaction with the family. He forced his mind to go blank for a couple of hours until he left the secondary roads for the interstate heading north.

As soon as the cruise control engaged and the engine settled into an even hum, D. J. Peterson sobbed as if his soul had cracked in two.

"My mother-in-law made these biscuits for 'special occasions' and Piddie Davis Longman could come up with more reasons for a special occasion than you could imagine. The original recipe called for lard. I have modified this for modern tastes and use vegetable shortening instead. I make these every week. They are bestsellers."

Joe Fletcher,
owner and chef,
Borrowed Thyme Bakery and Eatery

The Davis Family Sweet Potato Biscuits

1 cup all-purpose flour
3 teaspoons baking powder
2 teaspoons white sugar
1 teaspoon salt
2 Tablespoons shortening
¾ cup mashed sweet potatoes, mixed with 1 Tablespoon of brown sugar and ¼ teaspoon cinnamon.
¼ cup milk
1 teaspoon cinnamon and 2 Tablespoons white sugar. Mixed together.

Preheat oven to 400°.

In a medium bowl, stir together the flour, baking powder, 2 teaspoons of sugar, and salt. Cut in the shortening until the pieces of shortening are the size of a pea, or smaller. Mix in the mashed sweet potatoes and milk to make a soft dough.

Turn out the dough onto a floured surface. Roll or pat out to a ½ inch thickness. Using a biscuit cutter or drinking glass, cut into circles. Place the biscuits 1 inch apart on a greased baking sheet. Dust the tops lightly with the cinnamon/sugar mixture.

Bake for 12 to 15 minutes until golden brown.

Note: you can use either cooked sweet potatoes or canned sweet potatoes for this recipe. If you use the canned, be sure to drain the syrup thoroughly. Reduce the brown sugar to 1 teaspoon. This will keep the biscuits from being overly sweet.

Chapter Nineteen

Karen sat at the kitchen bistro table sipping warm herbal tea. A stealthy movement in the dim light caught her attention. "Mom?"

Joe Fletcher shuffled into the kitchen, his squinted eyes adjusting to the light. "You okay, baby?"

She smiled at the sight of her father in bold tropical print summer pajamas.

"Yeah. I couldn't sleep."

"Me either. Your mother is sawing logs, so I thought I'd get up and have a cup of warm milk and maybe read for a bit."

"Byron's snoring, too. I could hear him clean through the wall in my bedroom. Nice pajamas, by the way."

Joe glanced down. "Bright, aren't they? Your mother tried branching out into men's lounge wear last summer. Didn't quite fly. She has this newfound passion for wild color combinations. I suggested sleepwear ought to be in calming tones. Well . . . "

He threw his hands into the air. "It's a good thing I don't sleep with a night light on, or this outfit would keep me awake for sure." Joe slid a mug of milk into the microwave for a few seconds, then joined his daughter at the table with his cup and a plate of gingersnap cookies.

"This reminds me of back in school when you and I used to sneak midnight snacks," she said.

"We're the night owls of the family, eh?" Joe's expression grew solemn. "You know, your old man was a pretty good counselor in his day. If you need to talk, he can surely listen."

Karen eased the porcelain tea cup into the matching saucer. "I spoke with my boss today."

"Hmm."

"He's come up with a rather novel idea—a way to justify keeping me on Georgia Metro's payroll. I'm unsure about going along with it."

Joe took a sip from his mug. "Why?"

"He wants to film my cancer treatments—the final chemo, surgery, and radiation. We would make a documentary to release in October for National Breast Cancer Awareness Month."

"And you don't feel right about it?"

Karen shrugged. "I've always been the one behind the camera—exposing other people's lives, prodding for information."

"You do such a good job of interviewing on camera, Karen."

The porcelain cup trembled slightly in her hands. "That's altogether different. I'm drawing them out. This would be me on film. My emotions, my pain . . . my family's reactions."

"I see."

"So, there's more than me to consider."

"I would be all right with it if you are, honey. I'm sure your mother will feel the same if it helps you in some way. We can ask her."

"I will." Karen blew out a long exhalation.

"Is that all that's eating at you, baby?"

"No. Will also called to give me a heads-up. Trisha Truman, one of my coworkers, sold the story of my little deception to a national gossip magazine. Also, an article is due out today in the Atlanta paper."

Joe frowned. "Oh, my."

"Right. It will ruin me professionally. Any credentials I've struggled for, my achievements—all will pale in the light of the ugly truth. I've lied to the public for years about my identity."

"I don't understand why this woman would do such a thing."

"Trisha's had it in for me since the first week she started at Georgia Metro. Jealous of my position—whatever. And she has the hots for D.J." Karen shrugged. "Of course, that makes little difference now. She's won. He's free game now that I'm out of the picture."

Joe reached over and rested his hand on her shoulder. "Now, honey. You don't know that for a fact."

"You should have seen the look on his face, Daddy. He was devastated. I don't know if I can ever forgive myself for the pain I've caused him. He didn't deserve it. He's done nothing but love me with complete abandon and cater to my every whim."

Joe felt the heaviness of shared grief. "I'd love to be able to wave my hands and take all of this away from you, baby girl."

Karen placed her hand over his. "I know, Daddy."

"Would you think about seeing a counselor, besides me?" He

hesitated. "As much as I want to help, I'm not very objective when it comes to my only daughter."

"Maybe it wouldn't be such a bad idea. Sometimes, I think I am truly going nuts."

"About the mixed identity issue?"

Karen shook her head. "No. I know it's difficult for you, or anyone else for that matter, to grasp. But I never really believed I was British. Mary Elizabeth was a persona I put on every morning—like an outfit or a fancy pair of shoes. I always knew I was plain old Karen Fletcher underneath."

"That must have been hard for you."

She shrugged. "Not really. It became just another thing to do each morning—shower, eat breakfast, brush my teeth, and become Mary Elizabeth Kensington. It didn't get overwhelming until I allowed Donald to get close."

"And you couldn't drop the disguise at the end of a day."

"Exactly."

"Sounds exhausting."

"If I tell you something, will you think I'm a true lunatic?"

"Sugar plum, you forget where your dear old dad worked for nearly forty years. My patients at the hospital were clearly delusional—not to mention the times I counseled patients in the Forensic Unit. They were mentally ill and had perpetrated heinous crimes such as rape and murder."

"I dim in comparison. Is that what you're saying?"

Joe smiled. "Unless you come after me or your mother with a butcher knife, I'd have to say that. Yes."

Karen hesitated for a moment. "It's like . . . the cancer . . . getting it was almost a relief."

Joe sipped his milk and waited patiently for his daughter to continue.

"My life was spinning more and more out of control. Work was hectic, the pace of Atlanta was insane, and I was moving toward permanence with Donald."

Karen twisted the paper napkin in her hands into a sweaty tube. "I longed for you guys, missed home so terribly. But how could I return? I had slammed and dead-bolted every door behind me."

"And like Dorothy in *The Wizard of Oz,* you had the power to come home all along," her father stated.

"I see that now. It took the cancer to provide a reason strong enough to justify leaving everything behind."

"You regret it?"

She looked thoughtful. "No. That's the crazy part. The most awful things have happened. I've lost everything. And I'm lighter and happier in some ways than I've been in longer than I can recall."

"The feelings you expressed are not that unusual, Karen. Elvina Houston brought a library book by for me to read—on dragon boating. Ever heard of such?"

"No."

"Neither had I. The book, *How to Ride a Dragon,* tells the stories of twenty-two breast cancer survivors from Canada. These dragon boats are long row boats from China that are fashioned to resemble a dragon—head at one end, tail at the other. They are crewed by twenty-two women—one sitting in the bow beating out a rhythm on a drum and a steersperson who stands on the back, with the remainder at the paddles. The book explains the legend behind the sport. Throughout the narrative, the women share their stories of diagnosis, treatment, their emotions and physical pain, and how they came to participate in dragon boat racing. It's all very symbolic of facing down and defeating the dragon of cancer."

Joe took a long sip of milk. "The thing that struck me: a number of women expressed the same feelings as you just did, almost to the word. Some of the women saw cancer as this awful interruption to their busy lives. But the others, like you, perceived the diagnosis and ensuing treatment and surgery as a gift of sorts. They, too, had lives that were difficult and terribly off-kilter. It's a fascinating book. You may read it if you'd like."

Karen dipped her head. "When you're the one with the disease invading your body, it's hard to fathom you're not alone."

"It's personal to you. But there are many more who are battling cancer all over the world."

They shared the silence, each lost in private thoughts.

"How about your young man?" Joe asked in a soft voice.

"Donald is the one thing I'd keep about my old life if I could."

She turned the engagement ring around on her finger. "That's left up to fate now."

"Sometimes, my precious girl, true freedom comes from relinquishing control."

Byron stumbled into the dimly-lit kitchen, narrowly missing a collision with a wheeled butcher block cutting table. "Somebody throw a party and forget to invite me?"

Joe reached over and pushed a chair away from the table. "Here, we saved a spot for you."

Byron yawned and scratched his stomach. "I want popcorn. Anybody else want popcorn?"

Joe glanced at the oak clock on the far end of the counter. "At four o'clock in the morning?"

"Why not?" Byron rooted around in the pantry and emerged victorious with a bag of microwaveable kettle corn.

A few minutes later, he plopped a large pottery bowl brimming with the hot popped kernels in the center of the table. The three Fletchers fell into an easy discussion of local affairs that ended up focusing on Florida State University Seminole football. Rabid fans since the time they were toddlers, Byron and Karen speculated about the upcoming season.

"They should never let the players graduate," Byron stated emphatically. "There we were in the late '90s, national champions, and now, we're practically starting over!"

"I haven't kept up with the roster since your grandmother passed away," Joe said. "Piddie was such a dyed-in-the-wool Seminole fan. She knew every player by name, number, and position. She and Elvina used to nearly come to blows during football season."

"Elvina must have rooted for the Florida Gators," Byron said.

"Didn't stop them from watching the games together on Elvina's big screen. They got along all right until the two rival teams played each other. Those two ladies wouldn't be on speaking terms for a good week after that game every year."

Evelyn appeared at the end of the kitchen counter. "Have mercy! Has my family gone mad? I could hear y'all carrying on over the sound of my Enviroescape White Noise Dream Machine. From the looks of it, I'm the only one in the house who was intent on sleeping!"

The chastised Fletchers exchanged sheepish glances. Byron and Karen said, "Sorry, Mom."

Joe patted the seat on the chair next to him. "Sorry, hon. There's another chair here if you'll join us."

Evelyn frowned at the nearly empty bowl in the middle of the table. "Popcorn? At this ungodly hour?"

Byron raised his hand like a guilty first-grader. "My idea, Mama."

"Small wonder you have stomach problems." She propped her hands on her hips. "Well, as long as I'm up at chicken-thirty, I might as well start a pot of coffee."

"There's a lot to be said for food used to comfort. My friends have brought me dish after dish of their favorites over the years. Sadly, when I'm taking the chemo, everything tastes like mashed-up cardboard. It's just the thought that someone made their best feel-better food and bothered to bring it over. I know most of the recipes had to have been passed down from their own mothers."

Margaret Bronson

Chapter Twenty

The waiting area for the oncology practice of Doctors Alex Keegan and Whit Johnson was decorated in subtle tones of teal, pale peach, and a creamy beige that reminded Karen of cappuccino. Framed photographs by a locally renowned artist depicted tranquil North Florida seaside scenes. Lush green tropical plants and whitewashed rattan chairs upholstered in thick cushions created the illusion of a high-end beach rental house rather than an oncology office. Karen chose a recent copy of *Southern Living* and settled into a soft chair next to an older woman who looked like a combination of Aunt Bea from *Mayberry, RFD* and Mrs. Olson from a 1960s coffee commercial.

"Excuse me for bothering you, but you look so familiar," the woman said. "Are you from Tallahassee?"

"Chattahoochee originally—although I've been away for a number of years. Maybe you've seen me here before."

"That's probably it. Everyone starts to look familiar when a person reaches my age."

Her smile was genuine: the expression of a come-have-milk-and-cookies, next-door neighbor. The woman extended her hand, a soft grandmotherly sort of hand. Karen instantly thought of Piddie.

"Forgive my ill manners. I didn't introduce myself. I'm Margaret Bronson."

"Karen Fletcher. Pleased."

"How do you like Dr. Johnson? Or, do you see Dr. Keegan? They're both such angels."

"Dr. Keegan. He's fantastic. Of course, I would like to *not* know him, but . . ."

Margaret reached over and patted Karen's hand."I know exactly what you mean. He and I go way back. I was one of his first patients over twenty years ago when my breast cancer first showed up." She smiled. "Things surely have changed. You should have seen the carpet back then. Pea green—ugliest shade in the known universe—particularly if you were feeling a little nauseated. The chemo was given with you sitting in a hard-backed chair. They have big cushiony recliners now."

"Today's my last chemo before surgery. And I still have radiation treatments to go after that. Bet it feels good to be closer to the aftermath stage. I didn't realize they followed a person for so long."

Margaret's face darkened briefly. "Actually, I'm back in chemotherapy. The devil has reared his ugly head once more."

Karen could think of no reply.

"All I asked the good Lord for all those years back was to see my children grow up. I've been granted that and so much more. My first great-grandbaby was born two weeks ago. Here, I have a picture. Would you like to see her?"

"Sure."

Margaret fumbled in an oversized straw purse and removed a small bound leather brag book. "Here she is! Christina Hope Bronson. She's named after me—my second name is Christina—but my grandson and his wife are going to call her Hope."

"She's beautiful. Look at those big blue eyes!"

"Yes, and her great-grandmamma loves her to absolute death."

She thumbed through the remaining pages, pointing to snapshots of her three grown children and a host of grandchildren.

"Sorry to bother you with all that. My Charlie used to fuss at me about going on and on about my babies."

"Not at all. Your husband must be very proud, too."

"He was. He passed just last spring. Heart troubles. But he didn't know much by then. He had late stage Alzheimer's."

"Oh."

"I took care of him as long as I was able. Had to move him into a memory care facility for the last four months of his life. It just got too much for me to handle—and the kids, they have their own lives. All the stress was what made the monster rear his head and come after me again, I think. Not that I would have done a thing differently. Charlie was there with me every step of the way when I was sick, and I meant to be there for him."

"Your cancer came back after he died?"

"Not right away. It was six months, almost to the day. I felt a little odd, sore spot—kind of a lump—and mentioned it to my doctor. He ordered a chest x-ray, and there the beast was, his ugly mug smiling back at the radiologist. 'Course, they called it an 'area of concern.'" Margaret chuckled. "These medical types have so many ways of sugaring up the words. I knew before they actually said *cancer* that it had come back."

Karen frowned. "I thought a person was out of the woods pretty much after five years had passed."

"Oh no, honey. Just because you remove a breast and have chemotherapy and radiation, you're not assured it won't recur at some point. Mine came back in the chest bone—the sternum I should say—and now I'm dealing with it. Cancer is a disease that you always live with. You never really let your guard down, not for a second. Never let the monster know you believe in his power."

Karen felt her spirit sink to a new all-time low.

"Oh dear, I've upset you. Me and my big mouth. Let me put it another way. The secret to outlasting the threat of cancer is positive living."

Karen rolled her eyes. "That word again. I don't mean to sound like a terrible person here, Margaret. Heaven help me, I'm so tired of being told to think positively!"

Margaret waved her hands. "No, no. You've misunderstood me. I didn't mean to *think positive*; I meant to *live* in a positive way. There's a big difference."

"You lost me."

"Well . . . let me think of an example. Okay, say you're standing on the side of the street. You think to yourself, *I can cross this road.* Positive thinking. But you haven't bothered to see if there are any cars coming or looked around for a button to press to trip the light. You just strut out there and *wham!*—a truck smashes you flatter than a flitter. Now, there you are again. Same road—you still wanting to cross. You've studied the traffic flow and know when the signal will halt the cars. You hold your head up high, your legs carry you, and before you know it, you're safely on the other side. Positive living."

Karen regarded her with a bemused smile.

"Clear as mud? I can see by the way you're looking at me. You see, it's one thing to go around saying that you'll be healthy and live a long life. It's entirely another to really live each day as if it was the greatest gift in the universe. Love your family. Kiss babies. Play with abandon. Make a chocolate cake and lick the icing off your fingers one by one. Sit and watch a sunset." She leaned closer and smiled. "Cancer tries to rob a person of all that. Arm yourself with knowledge, but live positively so that it can't have the power to steal from right under your nose whatever amount of time you have been granted."

"Margaret, you are amazing."

She grinned. "You know what is amazing? You and me sitting here visiting like we're old friends. See? Positive living."

The oncology nurse opened the door. "Mrs. Bronson?"

Margaret gathered her purse and a worn paperback book. "I'll be sure to leave my number with the front desk lady on a slip of paper for you. You call me, Karen Fletcher. I do believe we will meet one day and have a cup of tea and some fancy pastries from France. And we'll talk about anything but cancer."

Karen sat alone for a moment before the clinic entrance door flew open. Jason "Simpy" Simpson, Georgia Metro's finest videographer, peered into the room. He tipped his head in Karen's direction, then hauled a camera and two cases of equipment into the foyer and shut the door with his foot.

"Sorry I'm late." He settled into the chair beside her. "I thought drivers in Atlanta were bad, but this place is insane! Someone forgot to instruct them on the location and use of the accelerator. It took two lights before I got out of the parking lot at the hotel. Some lady had pulled halfway into the median and was having a chat with a guy in his car." Simpy frowned. "That woman was completely oblivious to the pile-up of frustrated drivers in her wake!"

"Tallahassee is really an overgrown town, but it has its charm."

Simpy shrugged.

"Jake offered a room on the second floor of the Triple C, if you don't want to stay over here."

"That'll work for some of the background footage I need to shoot," Simpy said, "but I really need to stay closer until after your surgery. I can't imagine driving back and forth every day, not with as much as I need to be here. Did you talk things over with your doctor?"

"He's fine with it, as long as we are careful not to infringe on any of the other patients' privacy. I'll be in a room by myself on the seventh floor—that's the oncology unit—so no problems there. My chemo today is in a private room, too. We'll have to make sure to get written releases for the oncology nurse and Dr. Keegan, of course. Also, we'll need to contact the surgeon and speak with the charge nurse."

"I have all the necessary paperwork on hand." Simpy grinned. "You may have ditched the accent, but you're still the same old bossy lady I'm accustomed to kowtowing to."

"A character flaw Mary Elizabeth and I share, I suppose."

The chemotherapy treatment ended without fanfare, and the oncology nurse taped a small bandage over the port. Simpy packed his equipment, flirted shamelessly with the receptionist, and left to locate some lunch.

"I'm glad this is the final one," Karen commented. "I'm beginning to feel like a pincushion. Like on one of the old Looney Tunes cartoons where the bad guy is shot full of holes, then leaks out like a shower head when he takes a drink of water."

Jackie Shiver, R.N., smiled. "I've never heard it put quite like that. Of course, they'll have to start an IV on you for the surgery next week."

"And to draw yet another vial to test my blood."

Jackie scribbled in Karen's chart. "You'll get a break, at least, before radiation therapy begins, and there are no needles with that."

"I'm sure someone will find the need to stick me for something or the other. Needles don't really bother me that much, actually. Having this port in place for the chemo has helped, too."

Dr. Keegan entered the room. "Good morning to you, Ma'am. Looks like you bought us a pretty springtime day. We should really figure out a way to set up for the chemo outside underneath a tree, eh?" He smiled warmly. "Becky up front has you all set up for your ultrasound on Tuesday. I'll be interested to see what your tumor has been doing with itself."

"It's the size of a pea, I swear to you."

Dr. Keegan's face lit up. "I'd just as soon it was gone altogether, if I'm permitted to put my order in."

"Suppose the wondering will be over after the ultrasound."

"It will give us a pretty good idea on whether or not we can save your breast. Have you given any more thought to reconstruction if we are faced with a mastectomy?"

Karen sighed. "I just don't know. I've read every book I can on the subject. It would be easier to have the reconstruction done at the same time, but I'm concerned, still, about the future."

"It's your call. You can always have it done at a later date, if necessary. We can have you fitted with a prosthesis until then. Don't feel as if you're pressured into anything. Clear?"

"Absolutely."

"Good. Your surgeon, Dr. Strathmore, will meet with you on Tuesday to go over any last minute concerns about the surgery. It might be a good idea to jot down any questions that come to mind. If you're like me, I can't remember a doggone thing when I'm faced with important discussions about my own health."

Karen smiled. "That's one thing I like about you, Dr. Keegan. You actually admit to being human."

Jackie chuckled. "He has to. The position of God is already taken."

"I look pretty tacky in a Superman costume. My legs are too darn skinny for tights."

"My mother was a cold woman. Never saw her show much emotion, to speak of. So, when I think of comfort, she doesn't naturally fit the bill. Sad to say, but true. Thoughts of Piddie Longman, my dear departed friend, come to mind. There was always something good to eat in her little kitchen. She lived just two houses down from me for years. I was at her house near as much as mine. Either that or we'd be on the phone. You didn't sit down in Piddie's kitchen that she didn't fix up a plate of something or other for you to nibble on. When I was feeling a little blue, I'd head out my back door and aim for Piddie's house. Her back door was never locked, so I'd just holler out and walk on in. She never once acted like she was less than thrilled to see me. Her friendship was like a mother's love."

Elvina Houston

Chapter Twenty-one

Elvina Houston wiped fallen oak leaves from the garden bench and settled into position. A gray squirrel scampered down the pine tree beside her and paused, hanging upended and chattering wildly.

"I know you see what I've brought out here. It'll do you no good to cling to that tree fussing at me with all the blood rushing to your head. Come on down here like I showed you yesterday, and you'll get your reward."

She held a roasted peanut in her hand and waited.

"Lordy be! You're as ornery as my old tomcat Buster. Get your little fuzz-butt down that tree!"

As if he had understood the dressing-down, the squirrel leapt easily onto the end of the bench and twitched nervously. Elvina calmly placed the peanut in the space between them. He inched forward, grabbed the nut, and retreated to the pine tree.

"I don't for the life of me see why you have to drag it off way over there to eat it. It's not like I'm going to snatch it away!"

The old woman placed a mound of peanuts on the bench and brushed her hands. "I can't spend too much time fooling with you today, mister. I've got more important matters to attend to."

Elvina studied the garden patch. "Looky there! I do believe some of your daisies are starting to pop up, Piddie. I know this isn't my regular time to visit, but I guess you know there are plenty of goings-on in the family right now.

"You ought to see the magnolia tree by the back of the mansion. I don't believe I've ever seen it so full of blossoms. I can smell the sweet aroma as soon as I set foot out of the back door. Takes me back, that smell does." She smiled wistfully. "We planted that tree, remember? Me, you, and Betsy Witherspoon—in honor of our dear friend, Sissy Pridgeon. My, but it seems like it was just yesterday. Betsy wouldn't lower herself to work a shovel, so you and I had to dig the hole. And just look at that tree now. It must tower a good thirty feet tall!

"Jake and Jon are having a little get-together for Karen this afternoon. She goes in for her surgery tomorrow, early. Whole family will be there for the party, along with all of us from the Triple C; you might as well say we're family, too. Jake hopes it will take Karen's mind off things for a bit and let her know we're all pulling for her.

"Pinky and Wanda are engaged. Ain't that a hoot? Redhead from the North hitching up with a backwoods country boy from the Deep South. It should keep things interesting. Myself, I'll be glad when the new wears off between those two. If you get caught in the crosshairs of the steamy looks they shoot at each other, it'll make you have a pure hot flash.

"Ain't romance fun, though? Been so long for me, I've near 'bout forgotten what it felt like. Suppose that's why it does me good to see such as Pinky and Wanda making moon eyes at each other."

Elvina stuffed a stray gray hair into her tight bun. "Mandy's been giving me a hard time about my new hairstyle. Says I'm trying to look like you. Maybe I am. It sure is a sight cooler with it piled up on top of my head, I'll tell you. And you wouldn't mind if you were here sitting beside me, now would you?

"Reason I'm here this afternoon rather than in the morning, is that I'll be getting up and driving over with Joe and Evelyn to sit during Karen's surgery. She has to be over there so darn early, but I reckon I can put my tea in a to-go cup. Buster will just have to make do with dry food left on the porch. He doesn't usually drag in till I'm finished with my oatmeal, anyway. One day without his canned tuna won't kill him."

Elvina sat quietly for a moment, staring into the lush green garden behind her friend's memorial space. "If you could, Piddie, put in a good word with the Lord on Karen's behalf. I know we've all been praying to beat the band. But since you're staying in His neighborhood now, it might mean more coming from you."

She shook her head. "That poor girl has painted herself into a corner. Looks like her fellow has left her, she's got a terrible disease, and to top it all off, some floozy up and told the world about Karen's private affairs. Mandy showed me a copy of the trashy magazine. There was Karen on the front, in a blurry picture that looked like it had been taken in Joe and Evelyn's back yard. The picture didn't do a thing for her, either. She was standing there with her bald head shining, looking so thin and pale. And sad! Lordy be. If anyone who had seen her on the TV when she was healthy saw that picture, they'd be hard pressed to believe it was the same girl."

She exhaled. "We do have some powerful trials to contend with on this earth, don't we?"

Hattie Davis Lewis leaned over and deposited her squirming daughter on the ground. Sarah immediately spotted a beetle trailing through the soft sand and dropped on all fours to investigate, and Elvis exploited the opportunity to slather the toddler's face with dog kisses.

"When did you put up the fence?" Hattie glanced across Jake and Jon's shady back yard.

"Lonnie Adams finished it just yesterday," Jake said. "Jon and I could've done it ourselves, but I've been swamped with spring weddings, and Jon's so tired after his work week, I hate to make him do manual labor."

"I thought you wanted to leave the yard natural. Don't get me wrong, I love that you have a fence. I was dreading keeping up with the little princess here. She can disappear in the blink of an eye. Leigh says Josh is about as bad. No fear. No fear at all."

Jake frowned. "I've always thought chain link fencing looked rather prison-ish, but we really needed a place to let Elvis run outside without worrying about cars. Folks just fly by on Morgan Avenue. He slipped off from me a couple of weeks ago when I was down in the vegetable garden pulling weeds. The little dickens was clean to Elvina's back yard before I noticed he was gone. He's usually pretty good about staying right by me. Jon went ballistic. I thought he was going to stroke out. Luckily, Elvina was sitting on her back patio and spotted Elvis, or heaven knows how far he would've strayed. I would have just packed up and left the country."

Jake brushed his hand dismissively through the air. "Any-who, I'm going to take advantage of the fence—use it as a trellis for ivy and flowering vines. I just haven't had a second to run over to Native Nurseries. I may snip some cuttings off the climbers behind the Triple C. In my spare time, you know."

"Why don't you make a list of the plants you want, and I'll swing by on my way home from the hospital? Native Nurseries is right up Centerville Road, and I wouldn't mind. After Karen's up on the unit and settled in, Holston and I will come on back. She won't need a lot of folks hovering over her, not the first day after surgery."

"Okay, I'll jot a few things down. How long is she going to be in?"

"Couple of days, tops, unless there are complications. Maybe more if it turns into a mastectomy."

"I have two weddings and a funeral to do." Jake flipped one hand into the air. "I may not even get over to the hospital."

"So, see her when she gets home. It'll be okay. Elvina's on a mission to limit the barrage of visitors anyway, at Evelyn's request."

"Where's that handsome husband of yours?" Jake winked.

"Final edit due on his next book. You know what that means. He might make it. Might not."

Bobby Davis descended the steps carrying a worn guitar case. "Where's your guitar, Hattie? Don't tell me you're going to hose Pinky and me."

She rolled her eyes. "It's in the truck. But I can't imagine my limited talent will add much to the performance."

Bobby grinned. His blue eyes twinkled in his permanently tanned face. "It's all about richness and depth of sound, Sis. You'll hit the right chords most of the time. Like Piddie used to say, 'Even a blind hog finds an acorn every now and then.'"

Hattie smirked. "Thanks for the vote of confidence. I feel much better now."

Pinky and Wanda appeared at the screened door.

"Hey, all!" Pinky called. "Is this party out back?"

Jake waved them down. "I figured you musicians could set up over there under the magnolia. That way, everyone can hear you and you'll be center stage . . . or, center yard, as it were."

Elvina Houston was the next to arrive.

"Hey, Miz 'Vina. I was beginning to worry about you," Jake said.

Elvina huffed. "Take this thing." She shoved a platter containing a cherry cheesecake toward him. "This humidity! The darn cake split right down the middle! I just filled it in with fruit topping. You know I hate to come late to a party."

"Come over here and sit yourself down," Jake soothed. "You've worked yourself into a high rolling boil, sugar. Besides, you're not late. The guest of honor has yet to appear."

Elvina accepted a tall glass of iced tea offered by Hattie. "I guess my timing's not all bad, then."

By the time Evelyn, Joe, Byron, and Karen arrived in the Town Car, vehicles lined both sides of Morgan Avenue and wrapped around the side street behind Jake and Jon's house.

"I thought Jake said this was to be a small gathering," Karen fretted.

"Over the top, as usual," Evelyn said. "He told me he wanted to do something to take your mind off the surgery tomorrow."

"A mob of admirers ought to do the trick," Byron added.

Karen touched her temple. "Maybe I should have worn my wig."

Her mother sniffed. "Don't be silly. The humidity's too high. You would have a heat stroke in that thing."

Byron reached over and stroked her bald scalp. "I think you look kind of cute, Sissy. You've got a great head shape. Not too many people carry off the look like you do."

"You're just saying that to make me feel better."

Byron smirked. "Since when have I ever given you an unsolicited compliment?"

"Never."

"Rest my case. Let's go to your party, big girl."

The noisy chatter abated when the Fletcher family appeared at the top of the stairs. Jon initiated a round of applause for the guest of honor. Karen blushed and gave her best homecoming queen wave.

Jon and Jake flitted through the crowd offering tall glasses of iced tea and soft drinks. Along with Karen's extended family, the crew from the Triple C was in attendance, as well as Mr. Bill and Julie from the Homeplace Restaurant, Hattie's neighbors, John and Margie, and Chief of Police Rich Burns and his wife Carol.

"I know you can't eat or drink after midnight, so help yourself to the food, Karen. Jon made sure there are plenty of veggies and healthy stuff. He even convinced Elvina to make her cheesecake with sugar substitute." He lowered his voice to a whisper. "Brag on it, will you? Elvina's beside herself about it cracking down the middle. She wanted it to be perfect for you."

A bright flash startled Karen. "What the—?"

A strange man in dark sunglasses stood beyond the fence with an extended lens camera pointed in her direction. He snapped several frames before turning tail. Rich Burns hustled to the gate and took off in pursuit.

Karen scowled. "I was wondering when they would begin to show up."

Jake rested his arm across her shoulders. "They're like ants at a picnic. Nobody invites them, but they come anyway."

"I'm not even famous, Jake. I was a low profile personality at a public television station, for God's sake."

"I was a nobody, too, Karen, before my fifteen minutes of fame. All I did was get beaten up."

Rich appeared at the gate.

"You catch him?" Evelyn asked. Her voice quivered with rage.

"Nope. He's long gone. But you best believe I'll have deputies prowling around from this point forward. I've dealt with the media before. I can do it again."

"At least I'm wearing a new dress, thanks to Mama." Karen snickered. "And my hair's done."

The thought sent her into a frenzy of infectious laughter that spread like warm honey over the gathering.

"Whew!" Jake heaved a deep breath. "I haven't laughed like that in God knows how long." He squeezed Karen's shoulder. "I'm so sorry, sugar. Maybe we should've had this party inside somewhere."

"Nope. I'm not hiding for anyone. Not anymore. Actually, this has made me realize that I've made the right decision about allowing the station to film the documentary about my treatment. If anyone's going to tell my story, it will, by God, be me!"

Jake threw one hand into the air. "Well, amen Sister!"

Wanda leaned toward the white wicker chair where the guest of honor rested.

"I asked Pinky to play this first song especially for you, Karen. He loves James Taylor—knows just about all his songs by heart. This is the one that got me into trouble my first visit to the farm."

"Aw, Wanda." Pinky unlatched the leather case and removed a well-seasoned Martin six-string acoustic guitar.

"He has dozens of guitars," Wanda volunteered. "I think it's so he can reach one from anyplace he decides to sit down, including the bathroom!"

"I only have eight total, thank you." He smiled in Karen's direction. "Collecting guitars is my passion. I started buying them after my sister died. It was awfully lonely out there. The music kept me going."

Pinky fought his shyness and raised his voice loud enough to carry over the din of conversation. "Okay, folks. I'm going to play this first tune by myself. Bobby and Hattie are going to pitch in afterwards for some songs we can all sing along with, if you've a mind to.

"Most of y'all didn't get to know my sister, Alice Jo. She left home right after high school and wandered the planet. When she did return, she didn't get to town much.

"Anyway, this was her favorite song from the master, James Taylor. It's called 'Shower the People.'" His resonant voice enveloped the small audience. A few joined in for the chorus.

Pinky's cheeks burned fiery red as applause echoed under the sprawling arms of the old magnolia.

"Lord have mercy, Pinky. None of us knew you could sing, much less as good as all that," Rich Burns commented. "Maybe you ought to work up a couple of numbers for the Madhatter's Festival this fall."

"I'll have to think about that one."

Wanda patted him affectionately on the arm. "He's awfully shy."

"Just say the word," Jake said. "I'm starting to put together the entertainment now, so I can add you in, for sure."

Pinky nodded. "All righty! The three of us have practiced some old folk songs most of you probably know by heart. Be sure to join in.

Ain't nobody going to fault you if you can't sing very good."

Jake cut his eyes toward Hattie. Holston, a late arrival, stood behind her chair with a tall glass of iced tea in hand.

"I know what you're thinking," she mouthed silently. "Don't even start."

Jake wore an evil smile. As handsome and good-hearted as her husband was, anyone within earshot would soon know what Jake held out as her husband's single fault: Holston Lewis could not carry a tune in a bucket.

"Chicken and rice. Mom cooked it whenever there was a crisis. Some-one died? Chicken and rice. Bad day at the office, Dad? Chicken and rice. Lost the baseball game, Son? You got it—chicken and rice. Of course, they call it chicken pilau here in the Deep South. Guess it was soothing, all that starch. Every now and then, when one of the little country churches around Atlanta has a chicken pilau dinner, I go. I've driven over fifty miles to eat chicken and rice. Suppose that says some-thing about me?"

D. J. Peterson

Chapter Twenty-two

Other than once in early childhood when he lost a favorite ca-nine to old age, D. J. Peterson could not recall a time when he felt so desperately depressed. Even the loss of his parents had not affected him as profoundly. At the office, he toiled long after normal hours on projects slated far into the future. Everyone noticed his flat-line de-meanor. Will popped by on a regular basis, and Janice from account-ing plied him with homemade cakes and cookies. He took little note of his immediate surroundings. The entire female cast of *Baywatch* could have paraded by his desk in butt-floss bikinis, and D. J. would have offered the same bland expression.

His neighbors in upscale Buckhead, had they taken the time and effort to care, might have noted his absence. Since his return from Florida, he had lived at Mary Elizabeth Kensington's condominium: the only place he felt any respite. Getting in touch with his feelings was not a guy-thing, and he struggled to dig deep enough to reach the core of emotions that most females seemed to effortlessly access.

Who was this woman with whom he had been intimately involved for the past five years? In much the same way he had searched for clues to her identity, D. J. wandered from room to room, touching knick-knacks and pieces of art. He stood in her walk-in closet and brushed his hand along the rows of expensive outfits, trying somehow to un-earth the person behind the façade.

The sought-after answers came in memories—brief snippets of everyday life. A line from Shakespeare repeated like an old LP record with a skip, over and over: *What's in a name? That which we call a rose would by any other name smell as sweet.* What was a person other than the collective actions of daily existence? D. J. recalled the time Karen had asked him to stop while she purchased a hot meal in a Styrofoam take-out container, handing it to a prisoner-of-war thin vagrant who huddled against the wind in a downtown door jamb.

He remembered the way she cocked her head when she considered anything of beauty. Her gentleness when a child, animal, or elderly person came into her line of focus. The times when she had patiently nursed him back to health when he had been anything but loveable.

Weren't these the indications of a human's worth, rather than a name or place of origin? D. J. sleep-walked through daily routines as he tried to tease the irregular puzzle pieces into place to create a semblance of the woman he loved.

The doorbell rang three times before he reluctantly rose from the couch and stumbled to the front entrance. Though the peep hole, he recognized the distorted image of Trisha Truman.

D. J. swung the door open. "What the hell are you doing here?"

Trisha brushed past him and strode into the living room. She spun around and smiled seductively. "I've come to rescue you, D. J. I figured I'd find you here, wallowing in the remains of your shattered romance."

"I have nothing to say to you."

Trisha tilted her head to one side. "I'm sure you feel some vestige of emotion for Mary, Karen, whoever—but I can help you."

"How's that?" Being enclosed in a small space with the woman had the feel of lunching with a poisonous asp. Misstep and you wouldn't make it to the phone to dial 911.

"You need someone who appreciates you." She oozed closer and reached a taloned hand to brush an unkempt hank of hair from his forehead. "Poor baby, you look so untidy. That she-devil has soured your heart with her lies."

D. J. pulled back sharply. "Thanks to you, Karen has to not only fight for her life, but deal with the bullshit media, too."

"That's so sweet of you—defending someone who has clearly ruined your life."

"Why don't you leave, Trisha?"

"Is that any way to treat the woman who only has your best interests at heart?"

D. J. scowled. "My best interests?"

Trisha tilted her head and studied him. "Can't you see? I'm in a position to help you distance yourself from the mess she's created and dumped at your feet."

"I don't require your help. Besides, you're an unemployed secretary. Who's going to give you any credence about anything?"

Her heel tapped a staccato rhythm. "Really, D. J.! Nastiness doesn't become you at all. I'm not unemployed, as of yesterday."

"You land a hostess job at some backwoods truck stop?"

Trisha laughed. "No, silly. You're looking at the newest investigative reporter for the *National Informant.*"

"That suits you. Now you can swim with the rest of the bottom-feeders. I'll eagerly await your exposé on aliens raising baby chimps in the wild."

Trisha studied him for a moment, one fingernail tapping idly on her lower lip. "It's beginning to dawn on me now. Why didn't I see this before?"

D. J.'s temples pulsed as he clenched his teeth.

"You and Will. You were in on Karen's sham, all along. You knew she was deceiving the American public, didn't you?"

"I'm not answering a single one of your inane questions, Trisha. Leave my house!"

"Your house? Aren't we a bit presumptuous?"

D.J. took in a deep breath and tried to staunch his desire to grab and squeeze Trisha Truman's neck.

"I was the talent at Georgia Metro. If not for your slut girlfriend, I would've been in front of the cameras. Clearly, *I* have the face and body for it." She drew back slightly from the white-hot anger that flashed from his eyes. "Don't say I never offered to save you, D. J. Peterson. You and that lying bitch will rue the day you shunned Trisha Truman."

She whirled around and stomped from the room, slamming the front door in her wake. Tequila appeared from her hiding place beneath the couch and curled around his feet. D. J. picked up the rotund Persian and buried his nose in her fur.

"You okay, honey?" The unmasked concern in Evelyn's voice tore at Karen's heart.

"Yeah, Mama. I just couldn't sleep."

"I knew that party was a bad idea. I tried to tell Jon, but no! He was dead set on making a big hoo-hah right before your surgery. I—"

"It's okay, Mom. Really. The party was fantastic. It served to take my mind off things for a little while."

"Dr. Keegan prescribed you some light sleeping pills. I'll go get one for you."

"No, thank you."

"Some warm milk, then? It won't take me a minute to—"

"No. I don't need anything. Please."

"You have to get your rest, baby doll. Tomorrow's a big day."

"I'll be out of it from about seven in the morning on, and then, drugged up for the next twenty-four hours or so. Right now, right this very moment, I want to sit out here and enjoy the moonlight. Will you join me?"

Evelyn clutched the thin cotton summer robe to her chest. "I reckon I could. The breeze seems to be keeping the mosquitoes away."

She settled into a lawn chair. "It is beautiful, isn't it? Your father has worked so hard on this yard. I never understood why he was so obsessed with planting so many flowering trees and shrubs. When I walk out here and get a whiff of the magnolias, gardenias, and mimosas, I appreciate him for it. I surely do."

The expansive yard was lined with evergreen hedges. Tall Southern magnolia and live oak trees loomed overhead, surrounded with moats of flowering annuals and perennials. Brushed by the glow of the full moon, grapefruit-sized magnolia blossoms bobbed like ethereal birthday balloons in the gentle evening breeze. Tiny dots of flickering green light swirled at the edge of the thicket beyond the manicured grounds.

"Mama! Look!"

Karen's voice, innocent and childlike, caused her mother to smile.

"Don't y'all have fireflies in Atlanta?"

"I guess. I haven't taken notice."

"This is the best time of year to see them, when spring's easing toward summer. The males are the ones you see flitting around. The females stay close to the ground."

"You amaze me, Mama. Do you know everything?"

"Saw it on the Discovery Channel. Law, I remember you and Byron loved to catch fireflies in mason jars with holes punched in the lid. You would always insist on letting them go free as you couldn't abide the notion of anything dying all cooped up."

Her mother pivoted and pointed. "Remember what you used to call that tree right there?"

"No."

"The magic praying tree."

"The mimosa?"

Her mother nodded. "You held out it was magic on account of the way the little bitty leaves folded up at night like it was in prayer, and then opened back up, come the light of morning."

Karen hopped up and walked over to study a low-hanging branch. Feathery clumps of hot pink powder-puff flowers adorned the fern-like foliage.

"I remember now. Look how the little leaves tucked together to touch each other. Amazing."

"Your daddy threatened to cut that one down. It makes a heck of a mess on the patio when the blooms start dropping. I wouldn't hear of him killing it—on account of it was your magic tree. I reckon it's not such a bad thing, having a tree so full of prayers in your back yard."

Karen stared at the headset for a moment before dialing the cell phone number written on the back of a Dragonfly Florist business card.

Jake Witherspoon's voice answered after the second ring. "Hi, doll. What's wrong? Can't sleep?"

No matter how much she accepted technological advances such as caller ID, it still unnerved Karen when someone on the opposite end of the line knew her name before hello. "This a bad time?"

Jake chuckled. "You kidding? Two a.m. is never a bad time for a call from a friend. I told you I was available at all hours, and I meant it."

"Don't you ever sleep?"

"On my feet, I guess. Insomnia was the one gift of my unfortunate run-in with homo-hate that has kept on giving in the form of stabbing leg pain when I lay down. I rarely touch the sheets on my side of the bed."

"I'm sorry."

"Don't be. You didn't do it. Besides, I get a lot done in the wee hours when it's quiet enough to think. Does Evelyn know you're awake? If she does, I bet she's fit to be tied."

"I went to bed at the same time she turned in. It was useless to toss and turn, so I got up and read on the loveseat in the garden room. I dozed off for a little while."

"I'm familiar with that concept. Heaven forbid I should actually try to sleep on a mattress. I have to sneak up on slumber. Honestly, in the past three years, I've slept more on the recliner than in my own bed." He paused. "So, what's up? Want to sneak over and play some cards or something? I'm positively deadly at spades."

"No, just wanted to hear a friendly voice."

"You sound strange. Did you have that dream again?"

Karen released a long sigh. "Yeah."

"Why don't you tell Dr. Jake about it? Hell, it'll beat having to watch reruns and infomercials."

"It was different this time."

"Different how?"

Karen struggled to pull the dreamscape into focus. "It started the same. I was on the path climbing steadily upward. Except this time, someone was following me. Not like an ominous presence, more like I was hiking with a companion. Someone I liked."

"That's an improvement, at least."

"Soon, the path was so full of boulders; I had to get down on all fours to continue moving. I knew I couldn't help the person behind me. I was barely able to pull myself along."

"Freud would have a field day with this one."

"Then, I was at the same clearing—the one with the dark cave. I was paralyzed with fear. Even felt my chest was constricting so that my breathing was labored. It felt so incredibly real!" Karen took several deep breaths. "The thing was in the cave—only I got the feeling it was waiting right at the entrance, just beyond a bend in the rock wall. Then, I was so angry my body shook with a rage so deep it was boiling up inside. Whatever was inside the cave—it needed to come out!"

"Sounds like a B-rated science fiction flick: Godzilla and the Cave of Doom. What happened next?"

"I started to scream. I yelled and yelled for it to come out and let me see what it was!"

"Did it?"

"No. I woke up in a cold sweat."

"I hate to-be-continued episodes, Karen."

"You? What about me? It's getting to the point I dread falling asleep!"

"Let's look at this. You're doing something you enjoy, maybe, with a person, unknown, whom you like. Then, all of a sudden, the going gets rough, and you have to pull the hill on your own without any consideration for the other hiker. You are confronted with a scary monster, whatever, in the dark cave. You can't see it, but you know it's there. And it makes you mad that it won't come out and play."

"Sounds pretty simplistic when you say it."

"I don't have all the emotions to go along with the storyline. You do."

"So, what are you saying? The cancer is the dark thing in the cave?"

"Is it?"

"I'm asking you, Jake."

"It's your dream, for God's sake."

"Who is the person behind me? Donald? My former self?"

"I'm a florist. What do I know from dream analysis? You want my opinion on the proper fertilizer for African violets, or how to achieve balance and harmony in an asymmetrical arrangement, I'm your guy."

"No wonder you and Hattie are such tight friends. Neither of you will ever give me a straight answer."

"Ain't nothing straight about me, Karen. Or haven't you noticed?"

"Funny."

"It is good to have someone who can be funny at this hour, don't you agree?"

Karen laughed in spite of herself. The deep burn of anger at the dream monster eased a notch. "Know what's weird?"

"Besides the fact that we're chatting when most sane folks are peacefully dreaming of tropical islands and naked Nubians serving drinks with flowers and little umbrellas balanced on top?"

"When I lighten up, I don't feel so dismal."

Jake laughed. "You just broke my code, honey pot. I'll send you my bill."

"Everyone in this little town of mine knows my mama makes the best banana pudding. She brings it to all of the church socials, and the bowl empties like magic. She takes no shortcuts. Not my mama! Makes the egg custard from scratch instead of that instant stuff out of a box. She loads it up with layers of vanilla wafers and sliced bananas, topped off by a good three or four inches of tall, stiff, browned meringue. I can close my eyes and near about taste it!"

Officer Rich Burns

Chapter Twenty-three

Hattie caught her longtime friend, Mary Mathues, coming out of shift-change report in the Tallahassee Memorial emergency room. The petite R.N. enveloped her in a fierce bear hug.

"Gosh, it's good to see you!" Mary's expression became serious. "Oh, no. This means someone in your family is checking in. Since when do you drop by to see me at . . ." she checked the time on her watch, "seven fifteen a.m.?"

"My cousin's in for surgery this morning."

"Not Evelyn?"

Hattie shook her head. "No, no. She's fine. It's her daughter, Karen."

Mary smiled. "The weird cousin from Atlanta?"

"The same."

"But you guys haven't had any contact with her for years. Of course, it's been a while since you and I talked."

"It's a long, strange story—one that I'll tell you in exhausting detail when we can sit down over coffee."

"Sure. You want me to check in on her after the surgery? She'll probably be up on three."

"Actually, she'll be on seven."

Mary's expression darkened. "Oh. The oncology unit."

"Yeah. Hopefully," Hattie crossed her fingers, "she'll have a lumpectomy."

"Small wonder she came running home. I wouldn't want to face that alone, either." Mary pursed her lips. "I think Sue Connell's the day charge nurse on seven. I'll call and give her a head's up before I leave.

What's her full name? I know I should remember it. Heaven help me, I can't remember shit from shine-ola since I've reached my forties."

"Feel your pain. My cousin's original name was Karen Fletcher, but her legal name is Mary Elizabeth Kensington."

"Of course! She's the one I've heard so much about lately. Can you believe it? I didn't connect that whole story with your family. Am I a moron, or what?"

"It's not like you don't have a three-ring circus for a life, Mary. Give yourself a break."

"I can't fathom why everyone's so worked up over her story. I mean, what star in Hollywood hasn't changed names and invented herself? I don't get it."

"Who knows? One of her coworkers has helped to make it into this big hairy deal—like Karen's the devil with blue eyes."

"I never understand people who are that vindictive. I mean, my ex-husband's a pain in the ass, but I don't go out of my way to ruin his life."

"He still coming around?"

"Calls every now and then, begging for another chance. After ten years, can you believe it? I don't berate him in front of Lindy. I want her to have some semblance of a relationship with her father. Honestly, Derek is a lah-ooze-zer. He misses me waiting on his sorry butt."

"At least you woke up before your whole life passed you by."

Mary shrugged. "Did you bring your precious baby girl with you?"

"We left Sarah with my brother and his wife. Holston and I are hanging out with Evelyn and Joe for most of the day, and I didn't want to entertain her. You know how a toddler can be."

"Just wait till you have a teenager who borrows your clothes and thinks you have the IQ of an ice cube. Young children are a walk in the park by comparison." Mary rolled her eyes. "On a good note— I'm seeing the most delectable man."

"It's about time!"

"You know how it is out there, Hattie. By the time you reach our age, the good ones are taken or horribly flawed."

"So, tell me. Tell me."

Mary's lips curled upward at the edges. "He's an attorney."

"Ugh."

"One of the good ones. I know—I had the same reaction originally. I almost didn't go out with him."

"Y'all will have to come over to the Hill one weekend. Holston's discovered the barbeque grill."

"What is it about men? They don't like to cook unless there's an element of danger involved."

Hattie laughed. "Hey, I'm not complaining. It keeps me out of the kitchen."

"Who are you trying to fool, my friend? Your idea of cooking is ripping the cardboard wrapper off a microwave meal. It's me you're talking to, Hattie."

"You would be amazed at how much I've learned. I didn't cook much when I was single. Why bother? I find I actually enjoy it now, as long as I don't get too carried away and start doing it every day."

"Will wonders never cease." She grinned. "Look, I gotta run. Lindy's in a dance production at Leon High later this morning, and I don't want to miss it. I'll be sure to call and plan a weekend soon."

Mary gave her a quick hug.

"I'll phone Sue on seven and put the word out on your cousin. Don't worry. They're a great bunch up there. She'll be well taken care of."

Karen squinted in an unsuccessful effort to bring her mother's features into focus.

"I'm just going to step out for a second, honey. I need to make sure they've gotten my roll-away cot ordered for tonight."

"You don't have to stay with me, Mama. I'll be all right." Her tongue felt as heavy as wet shag carpeting.

"Nonsense. You'll need me to watch over you, at least for the first couple of nights." She leaned over and kissed Karen lightly on the cheek. "Back in the blink of an eye."

The preoperative sedative calmed the rising tide of fear and anticipation. Karen closed her eyes. Immediately, the dream appeared, unbidden. She stood at the threshold of the cave, desperately peering into the darkness. The thing loomed. One step closer . . . another . . .

"Karen?" A soft voice asked.

She fought the drug-induced drowsiness and opened one eye. A female nurse stood by the gurney.

"You better call me Mary Elizabeth." Her words emerged haphazardly, bumping into her thick tongue on the way out. "On my chart. My insurance won't pay if you put my real name, Karen Fletcher. S'long story."

The young nurse smiled. Karen opened both eyes to slits and peered at her name tag, but the letters smeared together. "Don't you want to ask my birth date?"

"No."

"Why not?" She swallowed in a vain attempt to moisten her scorched mouth. "Everybody else has. That's so you guys don't mix me up with some woman who needs her leg cut off."

Karen offered a loopy grin. The nurse lingered. "Oh, I see. You're here to wheel me to surgery, then."

"No."

"I've already given blood and peed. What more do you want? Is there something else?"

The nurse rested a warm hand on Karen's shoulder. A gentle peace flowed through her body.

"Umm. These drugs are great. I really don't care if you cut off my leg." The image of hopping around on a single high-heeled pump flashed in her mind and she giggled.

"Everything is going to be fine, Karen. Don't worry. We're watching over you."

The room swam in and out of focus, causing her to feel slightly dizzy. She closed her eyes. "That's nice. Thanks for stopping by to let me know."

Her mother's voice: "Honey?"

"Umm?"

"The man is here to take you to surgery now. I love you more than life itself."

Karen felt her mother's lips brush her forehead.

Her father's voice: "We'll be right here waiting on you when you come out of recovery, sugar plum."

"That nice nurse told me it's going to be okay."

Her mother's voice: "What nice nurse, honey?"

Karen tried to lift her head, but the effort was too great. "She was just in here."

"You must've dreamed it, sugar," Evelyn said. "I was right outside the door talking on the phone to the folks down in central registration. I didn't see anyone come and go from this room."

The hospital attendant flipped open the chart. "Your name?"

"Mary Elizabeth Kensington, at least for the time being."

"Date of birth?"

"September 29, 1946. I'm a Libra—sign of the scales. We like balance in our lives." She giggled.

"What procedure are you having today?"

"Boob! They're cutting out a piece of my boob!"

She heard her mother stifle a nervous chuckle.

He snapped the metal clipboard shut and laid it on the end of the bed. "Okay, then. Here we go."

Her father asked, "Surgical waiting area?"

"First floor, Sir."

"We'll see you real soon, baby!" her mother's voice rang out behind her.

Karen kept her eyes open long enough to watch a succession of fluorescent ceiling lights pass overhead before she slipped into oblivion.

"Some folks use the packaged vanilla pudding for the custard filling. Not my mama. She says it's not real banana pudding if you don't make the filling from scratch."

Rich Burns

Rich Burns's Mama's Nanner Pudding

3 ½ Tablespoons all-purpose flour
1 ½ cups white sugar
dash of salt
3 eggs, separated
3 cups milk
2 teaspoons vanilla extract
1, 12-ounce package of vanilla wafers
6 medium bananas
¼ cup plus 2 Tablespoons sugar

To make the custard: Combine the flour, 1 ½ cups white sugar, and salt in a heavy saucepan. Beat egg yolks. Mix the egg yolks and milk together, well. Stir into the dry ingredients. Cook over medium heat, stirring constantly, until smooth and thickened. Remove from heat and stir in one teaspoon of the vanilla.

Layer one-third of the vanilla wafers in a 4-quart baking dish. Slice two of the bananas and layer over the cookies. Pour 1/3 of the custard over bananas. Repeat the layers twice.

Meringue topping: Beat egg whites (at room temperature) until foamy. Gradually add remaining sugar, one tablespoon at a time, beating until stiff peaks form. Add one teaspoon of vanilla and beat until blended. Spread meringue over filling, sealing to the edges of the dish. Bake in a 425° oven for about 10 to 12 minutes, or until lightly browned on top.

Note: as a variation, I sometimes stir in about a ½ cup crushed, drained pineapple to the filling.

Chapter Twenty-four

The phrase *strength in numbers* could have served as the family motto. With the arrival of Pinky Green and Wanda Orenstein, the head count of the anxious gathering bivouacked in one corner of the surgical waiting area of Tallahassee Memorial numbered ten. Evelyn and Joe were flanked by Byron, Hattie, and Holston on one side, and the Reverend Thurston and Lucille Jackson on the other. Elvina Houston insisted on pacing back and forth in a path between the group and the reception desk manned by a woman in a pink jacket, fondly known as a Pink Lady volunteer.

"Elvina, I think you best leave the little Pink Lady alone," Evelyn commented. "She's beginning to regard us with an evil eye."

"Nonsense!" Elvina plopped reluctantly into a vinyl upholstered chair. "Don't let that blank look of empathy on her face fool you. She's got a finger on the pulse of most of what goes on in the O.R."

"She looks familiar," Hattie added.

"Of course she does." Elvina aimed a bony finger in the volunteer's direction. "She's been over here practically since the hospital opened its doors. She's older than Methuselah."

"Now that you mention it, I remember her from the time I spent in here during Jake's emergency surgery."

Elvina sniffed. "It's a control thing with these Pink Ladies, I tell you. They like to act like they're dumb as a stick, but believe you me, that one there has snooped enough to know if Karen's been moved to the recovery room."

"Oh come now, Miz Elvina," Lucille said. "Give the poor soul a break. She deals with families at the worst times of their lives, and seems to really care. I think these volunteers deserve a heap of credit."

"Well . . ." Elvina crossed her arms, sullen.

Joe checked his watch. "Been two hours now. Reckon we'll hear pretty soon anyway."

The double doors swung open and Dr. Strathmore, the surgeon, entered the room "Mr. and Mrs. Fletcher?" He approached the group. "Your daughter is in recovery. If you will step into the consulting room, I'll fill you in on the details."

Evelyn's face revealed her fear: the stunned expression of a night-prowling deer frozen in the headlights of an oncoming car. Joe rested his arm around his wife's shoulders and urged her to stand and follow the doctor.

Dr. Strathmore closed the windowed metal door and motioned for them sit at a round table. "I'm encouraged by my findings."

Evelyn expelled a large breath. "Oh, thank God."

"We saved the breast. Mary's tumor was much smaller than the first set of measurements prior to her chemotherapy treatments. It was two by three centimeters." He grabbed a pad of paper and a pen and sketched an irregular circle the size of a pea. "The tumor I removed today was less than six millimeters in diameter."

"Quite a difference," Joe commented.

"Only piece of bad news is that I found a micrometasasis in one of her lymph nodes—one of the sentinel nodes we excised. We took fifteen total, and we'll have the lab reports soon to see if it was the only one."

Joe frowned. "And that means?"

"More than likely, adjuvant chemotherapy along with radiation."

Evelyn felt tears gathering in her eyes. "What about her chances later on?"

"The cancer was a non-aggressive type, largely contained in a duct. Dr. Keegan will speak to her about follow-up care. Most routinely, a course of radiation is highly advised. The percentage of recurrence without it is roughly thirty percent, where the addition of post-operative radiation decreases it to five percent."

Evelyn picked at a hangnail until a small pearl of blood appeared. She grappled in her purse for a tissue. "She has to go through more of that dreadful chemotherapy."

Dr. Strathmore replied, "Dr. Keegan will be making that call, Mrs. Fletcher."

Evelyn wrung her hands together, whipping the blood-spotted tissue into a tight wad. "Can we see her?"

"She will be in recovery for about forty-five minutes to an hour.

As soon as she wakes up, I'll have the nurse come get you. We should be moving her up to seven soon afterwards. Barring any complications, I expect to release her in two or three days."

Joe stood and shook the doctor's hand rigorously. "We can't thank you enough, Dr. Strathmore."

He smiled. "You are very welcome. Your daughter's continued health will be my reward. Now, if you will excuse me, I'm due in surgery in twenty minutes."

"There's no rest for the weary, is there, Doc?" Evelyn said.

"Not most days."

Hattie lowered the day's copy of the *Tallahassee Democrat* to check on her cousin. Karen's eyes were open a slit.

"Hey, you." She leaned over and rested her hand on Karen's. "How's life in lah-lah land?"

Karen blinked her eyes and tried to focus on the wall clock next to the suspended television. "What time is it?"

"Just after three in the afternoon. Your mom and dad went to grab a late lunch. Joe couldn't take the hospital cafeteria food anymore. Simpy left to get some rest and eat. He was pretty wiped out after filming the surgery and hanging around in post-op. I think it got to him a bit, but don't tell him I said so." She smiled. "You want some ice chips? Or, maybe some juice? The nurse said you could have anything you want now that you're a day past the anesthesia."

"Some apple juice?"

Hattie jumped up. "Sure. I'll go raid the pantry. No need to call the R.N."

She appeared shortly with a plastic cup and straw. "Take it slowly, Karen. This whole surgery adventure does a number on your stomach, and you don't want to get nauseated."

She held the juice cup and helped her cousin drink.

"Whew!" Karen allowed her head to drop onto the stacked pillows. "Even that wears me out."

"How are you feeling in general?"

"All right."

"No pain?"

"A little stinging around the incisions, but the morphine pretty much nixes the pain. I'm a little itchy—like things are crawling on my skin." She rubbed her forearm vigorously. "I'll be glad to get these leg wrap things off. They're making me sweat."

"Those keep you from forming blood clots in your legs, Karen. Really important when you're flat and not moving around much. As soon as you are up and parading up and down the halls in your fancy open-air gown, they'll be history."

The three-to-eleven nurse, Dawn Ebert, knocked and entered the room, grabbing the flip-chart on her way. "Oh, I see you're awake. Good! Dr. Strathmore wants you up and walking some this afternoon."

Dawn went through the routine vital signs check, then emptied the urine collection bag and recorded the measurements. "You have a low grade temp—99.3°."

"That bad?"

"Pretty normal after surgery, as long as it doesn't start to spike. Actually, it's generally a bit higher in the afternoon. We'll keep an eye on it." She smiled warmly. "How's your pain level on a scale of one to ten, one being no pain, and ten being extreme pain?"

"The little I've had, maybe three?"

The nurse checked the PCA—patient controlled analgesia—monitor. "You haven't used much of your morphine. We'll probably take this away by tomorrow morning and use oral pain medications afterwards."

She flipped the chart shut. "How about lunch? Were you able to eat anything?"

"I had a little chicken soup and some lime Jell-O."

"I recall the lime Jell-O," Hattie said. "It's always lime Jell-O in a hospital. I can't fathom why they don't branch out into any of the other delightful flavors."

Dawn chuckled. "I think it's so the patient will hurry up and get well enough to go home. Keep on trying with the food and liquids, Mary. The sooner you eat and drink and move around, the sooner you can break out of this joint."

"You have to perform the three P's, too," Hattie added.

The nurse supplied the explanation: "Pee, poop, and pass gas." She glanced around the room. "Look at all your flowers and plants! I don't believe the Pink Ladies could stuff one more arrangement in here."

"This isn't all of them," Hattie said. "Our friend Jake Witherspoon is the main florist in Chattahoochee. He's holding orders at his shop until she gets home."

"Probably a good thing. Too many more obstacles and the IV monitor pole wouldn't fit in here. Is your mother going to stay tonight, Mary? If not, I can call to have the cot taken away to give you a bit more room. I'm going to remove the catheter in a bit, and you'll have to maneuver your way to the bathroom."

"Knowing Mama, she'll be here."

Hattie said, "Actually, I'm staying tonight. I'm sending Ev home. She wouldn't admit it in a million years, but she's dead on her feet. The only way she would agree to go home is if I stayed."

"I'm sorry, Hattie. This whole thing has been so disruptive for you and my whole family."

"They never left my side when I was in here. It really helps to have someone to get your wobbly self and that dang rolling pole contraption crammed into the bathroom. Trust me on this one."

"I'll leave you ladies for now. Mary, I'd like for you and Hattie to go for a little stroll this afternoon after I remove the catheter. You'll need to slip the leg sleeves off—they're held together with Velcro strips. Take it slow and don't feel like you have to go a mile. Just get up and stretch some, even try sitting up in the recliner instead of the bed. It will help everything wake up and start to move, if you catch my drift."

"One more thing," Karen added. "I'm really starting to itch."

"That would be the morphine. Itching is an unfortunate after-effect. I'll contact Dr. Strathmore. If you aren't experiencing a lot of pain and can switch to oral meds, I don't see why we can't get rid of the pump, or he may order Benadryl in your IV to help with the itching."

"Thanks, Dawn."

Hattie settled onto the side of the bed. "How big's your incision? Have you seen it yet?"

"There are three. The one on my breast is crescent-shaped, about three inches long. I have two railroad-track cuts under my armpit where they took the lymph nodes. I have a feeling those are going to be the sore ones. Also, the drains—pretty creepy. They are leaking mostly bloody-looking fluid now, but Dr. Strathmore said it'll run clear soon. I suppose a nurse will give me drain-care instructions before I leave here. I will have them in for a week or longer. In the meantime,

I suppose I'll just sit around and ooze."

"Nice visual, Karen. Thanks for that."

"You're most welcome." Karen glanced around the small private room. "Who are all these from? Mama was reading off the cards last night, but I was so groggy on the morphine I don't remember."

Hattie picked the florist cards from each arrangement, one by one, reading the typed inscriptions. "The peace lily plant is from the prayer circle at the Morningside AME church. African violet basket—the Chattahoochee Woman's Club. Elvina's the president. Assorted spring flower bouquet from . . . Wanda Orenstein and Pinky Green. That's sweet. Hanging fern, First Baptist Church Adult Women's Sunday School Class—your mama's friends. The basket of daisies is from your coworkers at GMPTV. They've all signed the card. See?"

Hattie held a small planter aloft. "Here's the plant Holston and I ordered—a miniature rose. I didn't know it had arrived. I thought Evelyn could transplant it for you later into a larger container. They work well indoors."

"It's beautiful, Hattie."

She plucked the Dragonfly Florist card from a plastic stake. "I'll bet even money this one came from Jake."

"Looks oriental."

"His specialty. Jake has this thing for asymmetrical arrangements. He says that since his leg was damaged from the assault, his body is not even. So, he's drawn to finding balance that's off-center. Does a great job, don't you think?"

Karen pointed to a glass vase containing a dozen long-stemmed red roses and fern. "Who sent those?"

Hattie carefully lifted the heavy vase from the top corner shelf and opened the card. "All my love and best wishes for a speedy recovery. Donald."

"Oh."

"Your mom said he's called twice since the surgery to check on you."

Karen's expression darkened. Tears appeared at the corners of her eyes.

"I'm sorry. I didn't mean to upset you by telling you that. I promise I won't mention him again."

Karen waved her hand dismissively. "It's not you, Hattie. It's me.

I don't really know what to do about Donald. The woman he thinks he loves doesn't exist anymore."

"Have you ever thought maybe he loves you, regardless of who you really are?"

She sighed. "That's just it. I don't know myself. How can I possibly have anything to offer another person?"

"You'll figure it out. The one thing I found out about my run-in with cancer, it whisks away the chaff in your life pretty quickly. The real you will come shining through."

"I'm going to set up with a counselor Daddy's found after I recover from surgery."

"Not a bad idea. You feel it will help?"

Karen shrugged, then winced at the tug of the stitches beneath her arm. "My thoughts are so muddled. I feel like if I just had someone who could direct me, I might have a better chance of unraveling this web I've created."

"Knowing when to ask for help is half the battle, my mama used to say."

"Baking was my mother's specialty. Cakes, pies, bread. She wasn't much for making big family dinners—save for Thanksgiving and Christmas, maybe. But she would get in one of her baking moods and there would be two or three cakes and pies before she wound down. Afterwards, she would always send me or one of my sisters to deliver one to a neighbor's house. Good baking is made better by sharing, she always said."

Dr. Joe Fletcher

Chapter Twenty-five

Less than a week after surgery, the cave dream returned in vivid detail. As soon as she drifted off to sleep, Karen's dream-self stood at the mouth of the earthen room. The mingled scent of magnolia and gardenia blooms permeated the misty mountain air. She looked behind for the mystery hiking companion. The series of sharp boulder-strewn switchbacks revealed no movement save the fleeting flash of a lizard scampering for shade.

A faint shuffling noise caused her to spin around. Karen squinted into the murky cool darkness. The scuttle was followed by periods of profound silence. An oversized insect head appeared in the dim light, and Karen inhaled sharply, inching slowly backwards toward the dirt clearing at the cave entrance.

Two multifaceted globe-shaped eyes gleamed in the reflected illumination, and a set of willowy feelers whipped the air. The creature moved steadily toward freedom. Karen tripped backward and fell onto her side, and then shifted to the protection of a granite boulder. The insect staggered fully into the daylight, all six legs carrying the body forward until the segmented tail cleared the cave opening. Four iridescent wings unfurled with a snap like sails committed to a stiff sea breeze. Sunlight reflected from the sequined wing panels in jewel shades of purple, blue, and green.

Karen gasped. The head swiveled in her direction. A sensation of benevolence exuded from the exquisite winged creature. Karen felt the tension ebb from her sore muscles.

No need to worry. The sentence came into her awareness, spoken from wordless lips. *We are watching over you.*

The five-foot double wings vibrated, and the creature lifted effortlessly from the ground. It hovered momentarily above the spot where Karen huddled before rising smoothly into the sky. She followed its departure until it was a darting speck above the tree line.

In moments, the clearing was awash with normal-sized dragonflies: legions of multi-colored winged creatures. Some rested on the tips of branches and overturned boulders, others sailed and danced on the mountain breezes.

Far away, the insistent jangle of a shrill bell shattered the peace. The mystical valley disintegrated into dim fragments as Karen fought to regain conscious thought.

Disoriented, she peered into the room. Tall plants and multiple clusters of fresh flowers decorated the low light.

"I'm in the garden room at Mama's," she said out loud.

She uncurled from one end of the wicker loveseat where the tortuous night had finally surrendered to sweet dream-laced sleep. The dual incisions in her armpit stung slightly as she sat upright. Someone was moving stealthily in the kitchen in the main part of the house.

"Mama? Daddy?"

Evelyn appeared at the doorway. "Oh, honey. I'm sorry I awakened you."

"Was that the phone?"

"Yes, I'm afraid so. I tried to catch it before it rang too long."

Karen glanced at the luminous dial on a miniature crystal clock on the wicker table in front of the loveseat. "It's two o'clock."

Her mother descended the steps down to the garden room, clutching her chenille robe to her throat. "It was your Aunt Diane up in Virginia. I'm afraid your Grandma Fletcher's suffered a stroke."

"Is it bad?"

Evelyn perched on the edge of the chair opposite of the loveseat and absently pushed a stray hank of sleep-tousled hair behind one ear. "I'm afraid so. Diane didn't know whether or not their mama would make it through the night. She tormented herself about calling so late, but wanted Joe to check with the airlines as soon as possible to see how quickly he could get home."

She fidgeted with her wedding band, twirling it around on her finger until the skin reddened. "Mama used to say things happen in clusters—good and bad. You just have to keep your head above the surface and tread like the dickens until the bad clusters pass you by."

Karen reached over and grasped her mother's hand. "We're in one heck of a cluster here lately."

"Sad thing is, we had planned on going up to Virginia sometime this year to spend a few days with Mildred. Joe was going to close up the shop." Her mother's eyes watered.

"I'm so sorry I ruined those plans."

Evelyn squeezed her daughter's hand. "Oh, no, honey. That wasn't aimed in your direction at all! Joe's mama wouldn't set foot on an airplane if she heard it went straight to glory. I can think of only one time she ever ventured farther south than the Virginia state line. That was when your daddy and I got married up at the church in Alabama."

Evelyn shook her head. "Joe and I have seen her a handful of times in the past ten years—all when he got a few days off from work and we could drive up. She was a dear sweet woman, your Grandmother Fletcher. She didn't take much to travel; she only saw you and Byron in person twice."

"Mama, you're talking about her like she's already dead. She could pull through this."

"No, honey. Not from what your Aunt Diane told me. Mildred's on life support now, just so your daddy can see her before . . ." Evelyn hung her head.

"You are going up with him, of course."

"Oh, no. I couldn't leave you alone."

"I'll be okay, Mom. It's not like this is a big unfriendly city. I have the follow-up with Dr. Strathmore early next week to remove the drains. But I'm sure I can drive myself over."

"You'll do no such! I'll call Elvina."

"Why don't you let me worry about that? It'll work out. Your place right now is with Daddy. You've gotten me out of immediate danger. Now, it's just a waiting game until I start radiation therapy."

Evelyn frowned. "I just don't know—"

"I do. If Grandma Fletcher is so near death, then you'll need to stay on for the arrangements and funeral, maybe longer. I assure you, I can't even so much as check the mailbox out by the road without someone spotting me and setting off the little-old-lady-hotline alert."

"That Elvina is a dear, isn't she? Those women all check in with her. So much like Mama used to be—so full of concern for other folks' well being."

Her mother smiled. "Mama used to say Elvina was a pea-shade shy of a busybody. I hated to point it out, her being my mother, but that sure was the pot calling the kettle black."

"You need me to help you and Daddy pack?"

"No. Your daddy's on the computer with the airlines right now seeing to a flight. I'll go tell him to reserve me a seat, too. I never flew until we all went on the cruise a couple of years back, but I surely love it. I just hate that it's under such conditions as this."

"Maybe you and Daddy can plan a fun vacation soon."

"Maybe so. We'll just have to see what fate sends our way. Do you need anything? I could brew you a cup of chamomile tea. Maybe that would help you regain sleep."

"No, Mama. You go be with Daddy. I can fend for myself."

Evelyn reached over and hugged her daughter gently before slipping back into the main part of the house.

Elvina Houston dabbed the beads of perspiration from her brow with an embroidered handkerchief.

"Lordy be! It's just now seven thirty and already the humidity's setting in! I swannee, the summers seem to get longer and longer every year."

She reached down and plucked a beggar weed from the edge of the Piddie Longman Memorial Daisy Garden.

"Piddie, I know you're looking down on your daughter, especially now. She and Joe have surely had a tough row to hoe here lately with Karen's cancer and now Mildred's passing. You always were fond of her, as I recall. Didn't see much of her over the years, but y'all wrote regular, and you were always commenting on some book she'd mailed you or one you were sending her way.

"She went peaceful; Evelyn told me when she called last night. Never regained her senses once the stroke came on her. Joe got to sit by her bed for a while afore she passed. Evelyn was glad of that.

"The graveside service is set for day after tomorrow to let any of the rest of the family come in. They're scattered all across the globe, save Joe's sister, Diane. One cousin is flying in from Germany!"

She patted the damp skin beneath her bodice and fanned furiously. "If I didn't know better, I'd swear I was having a hot flash." Elvina chuckled. "But that ship sailed many moons ago.

"We've all been taking turns checking in on Karen. She's doing all right rattling around in that big old house by herself. I offered to stay over with her at night, but she said she wasn't the least bit scared. Folks still bring food by to her, as they always do around here in times of trouble or need. It kindly blows Karen away that people have been so generous toward her. I explained that her mama and daddy are always among the first to come to someone's aid, and it's just our way to look out for one another. Reckon she forgot all that, living up in the big city."

Elvina watched two chickadees squabbling over a perch on one of the three bird feeders.

"Karen's took up drawing to pass the time. Said she used to do it a lot back in college, but fell out of the habit. The pictures are pretty fantastical. Gobs of dragonflies and mountains and such. Don't much understand it, but it seems to be helping her."

She pitched a peanut to her pet squirrel. "I didn't think you were coming this morning. Here, go on and take the rest I brought out for you. I can't sit out here too long this morning.

"I've volunteered to drive Karen over to have those drains removed first of the week. She wants to make a stop by the art supply shop and get some brushes and paints." Elvina smiled. "Remember when all our gang—Betsy Witherspoon, Sissy Pridgeon, you, and me—used to get together and paint by numbers? I still have that barn picture you did hanging right over my mantle in the living room. I cherish it like it was made out of pure gold.

"Anyway, I figure to pick up some fresh supplies, too. I think I'll try my hand at painting again. Since you been gone, I've been hard-pressed to fill time on the weekends and they just drag by. Me and Angelina talk on the phone regular, but it just ain't the same. You and me was always up to something or other."

Her voice grew low and conspiratorial, as if the shrubs and song birds had ears. "I talked to Karen's beau on the phone yesterday. He's been calling the Triple C to speak with Evelyn about Karen's progress. I told him about Evelyn and Joe being gone up to Virginia for the funeral.

"He's a nice young man, and I do believe he holds love in his heart of hearts for Karen. I gave him a little pep talk. Couldn't help it. The boy sounded so low he had to look up to see the bottom. I told him not to give up, that Karen was sorting herself out. He asked a pile of questions about the family, so I filled him in. Piddie, you don't reckon anyone will mind, do you?"

Elvina swatted the air with one hand. "Psshaw! It's like you always maintained, even Cupid needs a swift kick in the patootie on occasion."

"The Countess, Betsy Lou Witherspoon, barely knew where the kitchen was, much less how to actually pick up a pan. When I think of comfort food, it doesn't send me into spasms of homesickness like it does other folks."

Jake Witherspoon, owner of The Dragonfly Florist

Chapter Twenty-six

"Whenever there is a pause, it's your turn," Karen quipped.

Simpy grimaced. "Keep your panties on, sister. True cinematic genius takes time."

"Do you need me to move more to the side?" asked Heidi Parker, Dr. Strathmore's nurse practitioner.

Simpy looked pensive. "I'm trying to figure out—would it better to actually see the drain coming out? Or, would that be too graphic?"

"You only get one shot at this, Simpy. No way we're stuffing it back in for a second take."

"Okay, okay!" He knelt on one knee. "This angle will work without too much of a close-up."

"No need to creep anyone out. I'm already there," Karen stated.

Simpy pointed his index finger to indicate filming was underway.

Heidi focused her attention on her patient. "I've already snipped the stitches holding the drains in place. This will smart a bit, but it's important to do it quickly. It's easier on you that way. Direct your awareness to a spot at the far side of the room and take a deep breath."

With one swift yank, Heidi extracted the first drain.

"Yow! Oh, man! Boy, do I want to curse right now!" Karen clenched her teeth.

"I know it was uncomfortable, but it's like removing a bandage strip. When you go slowly, you feel the tug of every little trapped hair. Ready for the second one?"

"Unless I want a flaccid piece of rubber hanging permanently from my armpit, do I have a choice? Do it."

The nurse practitioner snatched the axillary drain.

Karen winced. "Are my eyes crossed? They should be." The sharp pain subsided to a dull throb after a few moments.

"Got it." Simpy grinned. "Good, Karen."

"Glad you enjoyed it. Imagine lassoing a kidney and pulling it out though your navel, and you'll have a good grip on the sensation."

Simpy and Heidi chuckled.

"Maybe that's what I'll tell patients from now on, instead of trying to get them to focus and deep breathe," Heidi said, removing her gloves with a snap.

While the nurse reviewed follow-up care with Karen, Simpy packed the video equipment.

"You leaving from here?" Karen buttoned her shirt.

"Thought I might grab an early lunch first, then I'll hit the trail. That'll put me in Atlanta before the worst part of evening rush."

He stuffed a coil of wire into the case. "I need to discuss things with Will, and start editing the first segment of the film. I'm not sure how we'll handle the radiation therapy four weeks from now. Maybe I'll swing down for the first couple of sessions, and then the last one. They're all basically the same, right?"

"More or less, with the exception of my skin. As I understand, by the time the final radiation session rolls around, I'll look like a bad day at the beach on the side undergoing treatment."

"Be good to show that. We can do the voice-overs when you return to the station."

Karen's expression darkened noticeably.

"Not looking forward to that? I can tell."

"I have to deal with the mess I've left behind, sooner or later."

"Suppose." He dug around for the keys to the rental van.

"Simpy?"

"Hum?"

"Will you be seeing Donald when you get back?"

He stood and adjusted the padded carry-all strap. "Some weeks, I don't see much of anyone when I'm working on a project, but I could. You need me to pass something along to D. J.?"

She shrugged. "Just . . . tell him I said hello. And to call me if he has any problems with the kitties or anything."

"Here's a thought. Call and talk to the man."

"I don't know if I'm ready yet."

He nodded. "Good enough. You and Elvina want to join me for

lunch? I'm terribly addicted to the wet burrito supreme at this little place off, I believe, Magnolia?"

"You must mean Cabos Tacos—one of Hattie's favorites. Sounds good to me."

Karen stood and tucked the shirttail into her shorts. "Just don't give up on us if we're not right behind you. Elvina took shortcuts through neighborhoods I've never seen before. We made at least ten turns after we left the interstate. It was like Mr. Toad's wild ride."

"I guess you and I should've ridden over together. I could've left later on from Chattahoochee."

"That's okay, Simpy. The way I have it figured—if I can survive chemo and cancer surgery, I can certainly live through Elvina Houston's driving."

Karen heard Wanda Orenstein's voice long before she spotted the bright red hairdo bobbing over the top of the hedges lining the patio.

"Yoo-hoo! KAY-REN! Yoo-hoo! Karen?"

"Over here!" Karen rested a fine-tipped brush on the corner of the palette and leaned back to stretch her shoulders.

"Whew!" Wanda plopped down into a cushioned wrought-iron chair. "I'm glad you're okay. I've been ringing the bell and framming on the front door for five minutes! I was ready to call the law."

"I'm fine, as you can see."

"You got some color back in your cheeks. That's good to see. This fresh air's bound to do you good." She smiled. "These last couple of days have been a Godsend, haven't they? I thought for certain we were heading dead into summer last week with the humidity so high, but it looks like spring may hold out a little longer."

"That's why I'm painting outside."

"Elvina mentioned you were taking up art again. Mind if I sneak a peek?"

"Sure."

Wanda jumped up and leaned over to study the painting. "I do believe that's about the prettiest thing I've seen in a good long while. I could nearly reach in and touch the dragonfly perched on that stem, it's so lifelike. And that magnolia blossom! It's so real I swear I can smell it!"

Karen motioned to the cut bloom on the side table by the easel. "Thanks for the compliments, Wanda. But the scent is coming from the real thing."

"Well, it's still perfect." She glanced at the glass resting on the side table. "Mind if I steal some tea from you?" The New Jersey girl affected a twangy southern accent. "I've been running around like mad already this morning, and I'm parched."

"Help yourself. Tea's in the refrigerator, and you know where Mama keeps the cups. Use the plastic tumblers. She frowns on glass out here on the brick."

Wanda disappeared into the house, returning shortly with a tall tumbler of peppermint tea. "What got you into painting dragonflies?"

"An inspiration from a dream I had following surgery."

"I've always loved them. I like damselflies, too. They're the smaller ones that fold their little wings way back when they light. Dragonflies' wings stay extended. Pinky told me that. He's a wealth of knowledge when it comes to nature."

"So, you two are going strong?"

"Thick as thieves. That's one of the reasons I stopped by, other than to see how you were feeling." She reached into a cloth drawstring bag and removed an envelope. "I wanted to bring your invitation by in person. I'll get Evelyn and Joe's to them as soon as they get home. Pinky and I are getting married in two weeks."

"Great!" Karen opened the plain white envelope. "It's A Party" was printed in bold rainbow colors across the front of the invitation.

"Pinky wanted to run off to a justice of the peace, but I wouldn't hear of it. Weddings are a time to be shared with your friends. It's not going to be anything fancy-pants-y, just a gathering of our closest friends. I've done the big hoo-hah with confections and lace, and can't be bothered with all that."

"Weddings are somewhat overdone, sometimes."

"Don't I know it? My first near to put my daddy in the poor house. The marriage barely lasted long enough to unwrap the fine china." Wanda laughed. "No, this one's going to be very, very casual. Wear your blue jeans. We are. If it's too warm, I may end up in hot pants. We're going to have a brief ceremony, then we'll feast. Pinky's a vegetarian, you know. He will eat some chicken or fish on occasion. He's ordered Pacific salmon fillets and free-range chicken to grill."

She chuckled. Her red hair shook slightly. "Whenever I hear him talking about free-range chickens, I always get a mental picture of little hens standing around in spurs with six-shooters laced around their bellies. Maybe even tiny white cowboy hats."

"Two weeks—that's not a lot of time to plan a wedding, is it?"

"Oh, we've been pulling it together for a while. We wanted to pick a time after your surgery before you started up with the radiation and chemotherapy so you would feel up to coming."

"I'm touched. That was very considerate of you, Wanda."

Wanda picked at a stray sprig of red hair that had escaped her heavily-sprayed hairdo. "Don't worry about a gift, now. That'd be downright silly at our ages. We both have more than we need as it is. Just come and help us celebrate, okay?"

"I'll be there."

"Good. When are Evelyn and Joe coming back?"

"End of the week, I think. Daddy wanted to stay to help my aunts clean out the house. My grandmother has a number of antiques, and all three of the children are taking a share. Mama and Daddy will drive a rental van back."

"That's a long trip for them. I'll be sure to check in with you and round up some food for when they arrive."

"I can cook."

"Didn't say you couldn't, hon. It'll be easier for you, though, and we all like to feel we're helping out in some small way." Wanda looked thoughtful. "You spoken with your fiancé?"

"No."

"Hmm. Elvina told me he's called most every day to check on you."

"She didn't mention it."

"Oh, Lord. Me and my big trap. Don't tell 'Vina I said anything. I didn't realize it was a secret."

"No harm's been done. Don't worry."

Wanda leaped up and air-pecked Karen on the cheek. "All-righty then. I have to scoot. I've got a million and one things on my honey-do list."

Halfway to the hedgerow, she spun around. "Hey! If you make

prints of that painting when it's finished, I'd love to buy one."

Karen had refreshed her tea and settled back into the chair in front of the easel when she heard the slam of a car door.

"Yoo-hoo!" A male voice called.

"Two yoo-hoo's in one afternoon. How lucky can a girl get?" Karen shook her head and smiled.

Jake Witherspoon rounded the corner of the yard, balancing a massive floral arrangement in his right hand while maneuvering the uneven ground with a red, white, and blue cane in his left hand.

"Miss Karen Fletcher?"

"Last time I checked. Depends on who you ask."

"If you are, these are for you." He made room and placed the glass container carefully on the side table next to her chair.

"Who are they from?"

"I could tell you, but I won't. Be a sport, and at least read the card."

She plucked the small envelope from its plastic support stake.
Thinking of you. With love, Donald.

"Oh."

"Man calls personally from Atlanta and all you can say is 'oh'? Not a wired floral order, mind you. He called the shop himself! He has a wonderful, deep voice, by the way. I almost dropped the phone, my hands got so sweaty."

"I'm sorry. I don't quite know what to do about him . . . just yet."

"If you're out of fresh ideas, I could provide a few."

Karen rolled her eyes. "He's straight, Jake. That might not stop you from ogling, though."

Jake turned his attention to the easel. "Interesting painting. Does it have to do with the dreams you and I have discussed in our late night phone marathons?"

She held up her hands and shrugged.

Jake tilted his head. "Somehow, the jewel-toned dragonfly doesn't seem as sinister as the evil cave-dwelling creature you hinted at."

"Since surgery, the dream has changed. Now, it's like a visit to Never Never Land, sans Captain Hook."

Jake studied the painting closely. "The magnolia bloom is perfectly rendered."

Karen frowned. "Wanda used the same word—perfect. I don't want it to appear perfect."

"Reason?"

She picked the live magnolia blossom from the table and passed it to Jake. "Look at it."

"Flawless. But then, I think all of Joe's flowers are required to be flawless."

"Look closer." She pointed to one petal. "See. It's beginning to turn brown around the edges. Compare the petal sizes. Nothing is truly symmetrical."

"A point? I suppose you have one in this enchanting little nature lesson?"

"The beauty lies in its imperfection."

"My, my. Profound, aren't we?"

Karen released a large sigh. "It's a metaphor for my life, Jake. I strived for perfection—the condo, designer clothes, best restaurants, pricey makeup. Perfect. And where has it gotten me? In a world of shit, that's where." A tear trickled down her cheek. Since the surgery, her emotions could switch from giddy to morose in the space of one breath.

"Hey, hey." Jake hugged her gently. "Aspiring to be all you can be isn't a crime, hon. It's not really fair to shun everything you've accomplished, now is it?"

"It didn't make me happy."

"Cut yourself a little slack, hon. Your body is trying so hard to heal, it exhausts you on all levels—emotional as well as physical. It's hard for you to feel very optimistic." Jake offered a folded tissue from his shirt pocket. "Here, wipe your nose. Don't worry, it's clean. I have allergies, so I always keep a tissue handy."

"Thanks." She blew loudly. "God, I'm a mess."

"Isn't everyone to some extent? Listen, hon. I feel for what you're going through—this series of jump-start-your-life epiphanies. I went through a similar time following my assault."

"Yeah?"

"Questioned everything I believed: about myself, about people. Drew in the things I thought rang true and discarded the ones that didn't—including people. Catch and release isn't just for fish. Sometimes you got to let go of the old to let the new come flooding in. Trust me, it's no picnic. It's the hardest work you'll ever do, and it hurts."

Jake smiled. "Piddie used to say, 'The more pain carves out your heart, the more joy you can hold.'"

He reached over and caressed her bald head. A fine dusting of new hair prickled his palm. "Have you given any thought to talking to a counselor?"

"Daddy thinks it would be a good idea."

"And you?"

"I have a list of names. I'll call soon, set up a time to coincide with one of my many doctor's appointments. Of course, when I start radiation, I'll be over in Tallahassee every weekday for almost two months."

She offered a weak smile. "Don't think I'm suicidal, Jake. I *do* have the occasional breakthrough. I just need help stringing them together to make sense."

"Oh, baby-doll, they will. They will."

"At least, I feel something. Finally, finally I feel something—even if it's raw and awful. I was so busy inventing a life and keeping it afloat, I had almost forgotten how." Karen frowned. "Shit!"

"What?"

"Turn and wave."

"Wha—?"

"Just turn to your right and wave." She pasted on a bright smile and threw a hand high into the air. Jake followed her lead.

"What the heck was that about?"

Karen pointed to the rear of the yard. "Paparazzi at three o'clock, behind the tea olive bush."

"I'll go call Rich Burns."

Karen rested her hand on his arm. "No, Jake. It's useless to fight them, so I strive to strike a pose."

"Suppose that guy is one of what's-her-name's minions?" Jake said, then flashed a toothy grin toward the bush where the cameraman lurked.

"Trisha Truman? Probably."

Karen glanced from the hedge to Jake.

"I haven't told anyone this."

"Eww, secrets. I love secrets."

"Promise me you won't share this with anyone. Seriously."

He leaned in. "Lips zipped. Tell."

Karen breathed in, then exhaled slowly. "I've received a couple of anonymous cards, mixed in with all of the sweet get-well cards. Borderline threats: 'The mighty will fall. You will, too'—in one. The second one—'Safety is an illusion meant to be shattered.'"

"Wow. Weird. Doesn't that scare the beejezus out of you? Should we tell the police? Maybe put some kind of guard on this place?"

She shook her head. "That would be giving in, wouldn't it?"

"After what happened to me, I never take threats lightly. There are a lot of nutcases roaming around." Jake's lips drew into a thin, hard line.

I won't buy into fear. Not anymore." She threw a dismissive hand into the air, then tipped her head toward the hedge. "As to this latest photo op, we'll know in a few days if Trisha was behind it. I'm sure it will make the front page of the *Informant*. You'll be identified, too. Local liar shares intimate moment with former gay-bashing victim, or something of the like."

"Maybe we should take out a subscription. Too bad we couldn't drag Hank Henderson out of his padded cell for a group photo. Notorious Chattahoochee celebs have tea."

"Lord help me, I've worked around food so many years, it's a stretch for me to say I find comfort in it. Fool with food and wait tables a few days, and you'll understand what I mean. Guess I have to say, my mama's potato soup comes the closest to comfort food. She would make a pot when any of us younguns were feeling poorly. Warm and thin, and not too hard on the tummy. Pretty soon, I'd be good as new. Sometimes, I cook up some myself."

Julie Nix, waitress, The Homeplace Restaurant

Chapter Twenty-seven

D. J. Peterson hovered just inside the threshold of the editing room. Sensing a foreign presence, Jason Simpson glanced up from the computer monitor.

"C'mon in, man. Don't just stand there like a first-grader without a hall pass." He shoved a wheeled chair backwards. "You might be interested in this. I'm working on the breast cancer piece."

D. J. ambled slowly across the room and slumped into the proffered chair.

"Damn, Deej. You look like hell, bud."

D. J. raked a hand through his hair. "Not much sleep."

Simpy smirked. "Who would've ever thought it? Atlanta's most eligible bachelor, conqueror of a long line of distinguished socialites, reduced to a quivering pile of yak."

D. J. stared at the image on the monitor. "How far along is she in treatment?"

"This segment was filmed a couple of days past surgery." He referenced a desk calendar. "I'll be heading back down next week before the first radiation therapy session. That'll go on for six weeks, I believe."

"She looks so small and frail."

Jason chuffed. "That woman's anything but frail. Thin—yes. Pale—sure. But who wouldn't be?"

"And she's facing it alone." The desolate expression on D. J.'s face was so complete, Simpy immediately regretted his cavalier tone.

"Deej, Karen's got an incredible family who has been by her side from the start. And if they aren't there for some reason, the whole dang community circles around her. Makes me believe I want to end up in a small town some day, instead of a city so big you hardly recognize your next-door neighbor."

"You liked it there?"

Simpy grinned. "What's not to like? I stayed in a refurbished Southern mansion with hot and cold running charm. Someone was always bringing me food, and Stephanie, a very attractive massage therapist, gave me discounted sessions. Mandy cut my hair for a third of what the salon here does, and this woman, Julie, up at the main restaurant made the best damn French dip sandwich I've ever tasted." He nodded emphatically. "Like it? I can't wait to go back. Wanda, the other stylist, has asked me to shoot her wedding. She and this character, Pinky Green, are throwing a big cookout shindig the weekend before Karen starts radiation. The food should be awesome."

Simpy reached over and slapped a hand on D. J.'s shoulder. "Karen's thinking of you, Deej. She told me to tell you hello."

"Really?"

"Do I look like freakin' Cupid? Of course she actually said it."

"I have spoken with her mother and Elvina Houston, but not to her."

"Ah, Elvina Houston. There's a small town icon for you. Knows everyone for miles and their lineage, plus all the accumulated dirt. She's like a gossip columnist with tons more class. Drives this massive boat of a car, and I've never seen her without a phone in her hand." He grinned. "Woman loves me. Pinches my cheek at least once a day. And I've sat on her patio drinking green tea till the wee hours."

"What could you possibly have in common with someone like her, enough to carry on a decent conversation?"

Simpy stretched backward in the chair. "You'd be surprised. Elvina keeps up on current international affairs. Reads three major newspapers on the Internet, each day. We hashed over the rising tide of unrest in the Middle East and the president's handling of terrorism following the 9-11 attacks." He shrugged. "You need to find out about all these folks for yourself, especially with you marrying into Karen's family. They come with the package."

"Remains to be seen."

Simpy clamped him on the back. "What you need is a grand gesture, my friend. Load up the dang cats and show up on her doorstep."

"You're kidding."

"Unless you've cooked up a better plan. She's missing you and her felines. I've been around the woman enough to see it. She's not going to turn her back on all three of you." Simpy studied him for a minute. "Karen's not the one facing this alone, Deej. You are. Get up off your mangy, depressed butt and do something about it."

Karen settled into the passenger's seat of Hattie's sport utility vehicle. "You going to tell me where we're going?"

"Nope. Surprise." Hattie shifted into reverse, then braked suddenly. "Your mom's yelling to us." She rolled the window down.

Evelyn ran to the driveway carrying a small jute bag. "Y'all almost forgot this, honey." She handed the tote through the open window. "SPF 30 plus and a special lotion just for faces. Be sure to keep covered up, now. You don't want to sunburn going into the radiation therapy next week."

"Don't worry, Ev." Hattie patted her older cousin's hand. "Holston packed so much sunscreen in my bag, we'll probably draw in clouds for fifty miles."

"You sure you have enough along to eat? There's some of Joe's chicken salad in the refrigerator. I could send it along with you."

"Actually, your wonderful husband brought a cooler filled with food by the house earlier this morning. There's no telling what we have in there."

"Well . . . all right. Y'all be careful. You keep the cell phone turned on, Karen, and call if you have any trouble."

"Yes, mommy dearest!" Karen blew her a kiss.

"Be home before dark!" Evelyn yelled in their wake.

Karen glanced at her mother's reflection in the side view mirror. "Do parents ever believe their children grow up?"

"No. Even when I visited the Hill long after I turned forty, Mom would send me off with half the contents of her refrigerator packed in the car. I understand the protectiveness, though. When Sarah gets old enough to leave for college, I'm moving, too."

"Oh, that will be fun for her."

Hattie tipped her head. "Not nearly as joyous as having her father and me along on her first date."

Karen laughed, enjoying the easy cousinly camaraderie. "I appreciate you taking off to spend the day with me, Hattie. And in the middle of the week, no less."

Hattie smiled. "One of the perks of self-employment—I'm a great boss who believes in mental health leave. Holston's between projects, so he didn't mind hanging with Sarah."

Karen dug in her purse, extracted a tube of lip balm, and peered into the sun visor vanity mirror. "Mama's trying to cram the furniture she and Daddy brought from Virginia into the house. I was starting to feel a bit claustrophobic. Where all that stuff is going to fit is beyond me. One piece in particular, a rustic jelly cupboard that belonged to my great-grandmother, doesn't match mother's formal style at all."

"Ev will figure it out, I'm sure."

Karen fiddled with the radio. "I thought originally we might be heading for the coast, but since we're going east toward Tallahassee, you have me stumped."

"Suffice it to say, I'm escorting you to my favorite outdoor Florida spot: one of the most beautiful places within an hour's drive."

When she reached the capital city, Hattie exited the interstate and turned south. A few miles from town, she veered onto a tree-canopied two lane highway. One more turn brought them to the entrance to Wakulla Springs State Park.

"All those years at FSU, and I never came here," Karen said.

"Really? I spent almost every weekend by the springs during warm weather. The Lodge is still one of my favorite places to eat."

"Guess I was too busy being weird, huh?"

Hattie raised one eyebrow. "You said it. I didn't. Anyway, that was then, and this is now."

Hattie parked the Ford Escape beneath the deep shade of a towering live oak tree and helped Karen with two folding chairs, a beach bag, and the wheeled cooler. A short walk brought them to the edge of a white-beached swimming area adjacent to the headwater spring feeding the Wakulla River. Though the temperature was climbing into the nineties, a slight breeze off the water provided natural air conditioning. Karen felt the fine hairs on her chilled forearms prickle.

The women commandeered a patch of soft grass beneath a stand of cypress trees. Karen settled into her chair with a sketch pad and a set of artist's pencils, and Hattie opened a dog-eared paperback.

"Help yourself to the cooler. Your dad packed all kinds of soft drinks, bottled water, and iced tea, in addition to the numerous plastic containers of mystery edibles."

Karen glanced to either side. Other than a young couple with a toddler and an elderly gentleman and his wife, they had the spring to themselves.

"Go ahead, Karen. Strip down to your bathing suit."

"I hate for anyone to see my body the way it looks right now. I can barely look at myself in the mirror when I dress. Too many craggy places where I once had curves."

Hattie lowered her novel and offered a smirk. "I didn't loan you the suit so you could perish in the heat, Karen. No one knows you here. Besides, " she grinned, "I'll charm them so thoroughly with my cellulite thighs, they won't even bother to notice you."

Karen conceded, removed her jeans and shirt, and slumped down in the beach chair with a sea grass hat pulled over her eyes.

Hattie rolled her eyes. "Now, isn't that much better?"

With the sketch pad opened in her lap, Karen held a charcoal pencil poised in mid-air. Fifty feet across the water on the spring's far shore, the graceful silhouette of a great blue heron blended into the tall marsh grass. Karen was mesmerized by the richness and variety of colors. The tree line was dappled with hues of spring green against a deep blue sky. High, air-brushed wispy clouds moved lazily overhead.

The crystalline water was a faint shade of celadon green, cleared and raked of vegetation within the swimming area. Beyond the floating ropes and buoys, ribbons of freshwater grass undulated in the gentle current.

Karen allowed her ears to attune to the subtle sounds of nature: the caw of a disgruntled crow, an occasional cricket call, and the cackle of coots and wood ducks skimming among the duckweed and lily pads. Periodically, the slap of a mullet landing after jumping skyward broke the glassine water surface. An anhinga skimmed low over the river, diving headfirst into the water and reappearing with a small fish clamped in its beak. The bird flipped its head back and swallowed the catch whole before emitting a raucous victory cackle.

Karen watched a pair of wetsuit-clad divers pass behind their chairs carrying air tanks and fins. "They allow diving here?"

Hattie shook her head. "Don't think so. Doesn't do much for business if a tourist spots an alligator toting off a human leg." She laughed at her cousin's mortified expression. "Just kidding, Karen. Actually, there are tons of gators in the waterways of Florida. Most folks mistake them for floating logs—until they wink. Those two guys are probably state employees. I think they do water quality studies, stuff like that."

"Oh."

Suddenly, the misty peace was broken by the loud chatter of children.

"Oh, no." Hattie whined. "An invasion! I thought we'd have it to ourselves today, with school still in session."

"They don't seem to be heading our way."

A long train of middle-school-aged youngsters intertwined with adult chaperones trailed to the cement loading dock. Uniformed state park employees herded the groups carefully onto long river boats. One by one, the jungle cruise boats left the dock and inched upriver, stopping at intervals to provide nature lessons over tinny speaker systems. After a slow circle around the deep mouth of the spring, the engines roared to life, sending a wake into the swimming area. By the time a half-hour had passed, Hattie and Karen had counted ten boat tours.

"That's the first time I've ever seen them move that fast," Hattie said. "The last boat could've pulled a skier."

An absurd picture formed in Karen's mind: a loaded tour boat crammed to capacity with loud children, arms and legs poking out at odd angles, with a pink-frocked Cypress Gardens-type fifties female skier holding the rope with a cocked foot while waving to the shore. She dissolved into a fit of giggles.

The bemused expression on her cousin's face caused her to laugh harder, to the point of snorts and gasps for air.

"You okay?" Hattie asked when Karen finally calmed.

"Yes. Better than okay."

The deserted tour boats were moored. The only sound was the distant call of an eagle in a roost high atop a cypress tree down river. The toddler laughed, digging holes in the wet sand with a yellow plastic shovel. A slight breeze pushed spring-cooled air across Karen's skin and sent miniature ripples across the mirrored surface of the water.

An iridescent fly, green with gold bands, landed on her arm. She studied it closely, marveling in the rich sparkle of sun-reflected color. Karen became aware of the infinite complexity and beauty surrounding them. For the first time in months, she moved outside of herself; she slipped away from the shame of harbored lies, physical pain, and the all-consuming world of cancer and sickness.

Karen closed her eyes. The faint scent of magnolia blooms mingled with the darker aroma of rich, wet river soil. "Thank you for today."

Hattie marked her place with one finger and looked over to where her cousin reclined, a peaceful smile playing across her features.

"You're welcome. There's more to come. We'll be having dinner, too. The chef here makes the most incredible pecan-encrusted grouper. Not to mention the twice-baked potatoes. My toes are curling just thinking of it."

"I think I may actually have an appetite."

"Good. One more thing—we're staying the night."

Karen's head jerked up. "Here?"

Hattie motioned to the grounds. "You think the spring is enchanting and peaceful now, wait until it's just the registered guests. The lodge is old, but very well kept—marble bathrooms, that sort of thing. Feels like the kind of place Clark Gable would have stayed."

"But . . . Mama?"

"Your daddy knows the plan. Evelyn would've had a cow and insisted on you coming home. I thought, perhaps, you would like a break from Chattahoochee. We can always pack up and leave after dinner if you'd rather."

"No. It's just—I don't have a change of clothes."

Hattie smiled. "Took care of that, too. Elvina and I went in when you and Ev were up at the spa. Packed your toiletries, underwear, some fresh clothes, and just about every thing else imaginable."

"What a sneak you've turned out to be!"

Hattie swatted the air with one hand. "Oh, honey, you don't know the half of it."

"What does that mean exactly?"

Hattie arched her eyebrows playfully. "Me to know, and you to find out."

"Oh, come on!"

Hattie opened the novel. "No use prying. You'll find out soon enough. By the way, what are you wearing to Wanda and Pinky's wedding on Saturday?"

"White Capri pants and a floral shirt. You're changing the subject."

Hattie's expression was unreadable behind the dark sunglasses. "So I am."

"Hattie! Hi!" The raven-haired male waiter flashed a row of even white teeth. "Where're the husband and baby?"

"Preston, I was hoping you were still here. Holston and Sarah are at home. This is girls' night out." She motioned across the table. "My cousin, Karen Fletcher."

Preston bowed slightly. "Enchanted. Glad you two could come over."

"Is the grouper fresh?"

"Not half as fresh as me." He winked. "It's been flying out of the kitchen tonight. Very popular."

"Good, save me a piece."

"Me, too," Karen added.

"So, how's school going?" Hattie asked. The restaurant was run by FSU's Hospitality Program, and most of the staffers were students in restaurant management training.

"Slowly. If only I didn't have to work, I could get more accomplished in a shorter space, you know?" He filled the water glasses.

Hattie smiled. "Been there—about twenty plus years ago. Hang tough, you'll get through."

"Ah, well. May I start you ladies off with an appetizer?"

"Some of your smoked salmon spread."

"Good choice." He smiled and disappeared through the heavy swinging double doors leading to the kitchen.

"Do you know everyone, Hattie?"

"Mainly at food establishments. Sad, huh? I came here a lot when I lived in Tallahassee. Holston and I have been a few times. Sarah loves Preston to death; lights up when he comes anywhere near her.

If she was eighteen years older, I'd worry."

By the time Preston delivered after-dinner coffee and cream, Karen and Hattie had pushed back in the cushioned chairs.

"Sure I can't interest you ladies in dessert? Ruby made Key Lime pie."

"That sounds great, but I don't know where I'd put it." Hattie rested a hand protectively over her belly.

"Me, either."

Preston nodded. "You two ladies driving back to the Hooch tonight?"

"Actually, we're staying over." Hattie pointed toward the ceiling.

"If you're in the room directly above us, you're adjacent to the honeymoon suite."

"Oh, Lord. I forgot about that when I called for reservations. I've certainly made that mistake before." She glanced toward Karen. "Little insulation and marble floors. Everything echoes." Then, back to Preston. "Any newlyweds on board tonight?"

A grin lit his face. "I don't know, but I bet you'll find out."

After dinner, they retired to a long, cavernous marble-parquet sitting hall decorated by three separate couch and chair groupings, a grand piano, three marble checkers tables, and a massive masonry fireplace. Following six games of checkers, the cousins strolled around the grounds beneath ancient Spanish moss-draped live oaks, sweet gum trees, and magnolias. Thick evening mist rolled over the springs.

"*The Creature from the Black Lagoon* was filmed here," Hattie commented.

"I can see why."

"They run a moonlight boat tour, usually in the fall. They take the boats across the spring into an inlet and cut the engine. It's so eerie and quiet. All you can see is the reflection of scores of beady little reptilian eyes shining in the light from the moon."

"Nice." Karen shuddered involuntarily.

"Then, everyone goes into the Lodge for dinner. Very romantic. Very old Florida. The best part—very *not* Disney."

Finally, they had talked themselves into exhaustion, and the soft queen-sized beds beckoned.

Karen had drifted into a dreamlike state when the sound of raucous sexual gymnastics resonated from the suite next door.

"Hattie?"

"I hear them."

A radio blared country music in the background, punctuated with loud grunts of male passion and female love chatter.

"I hope this doesn't go on all night," Karen remarked in a loud whisper.

The grunting escalated, accompanied by the screech of distressed bed springs. A rhythmic thumping echoed through the wall.

"What's that?"

Hattie snickered. "Headboard."

The louder the lovemaking grew, the more Karen and her cousin giggled: two adolescents watching their first R-rated movie, two bratty little sisters spying on their older brother and his date lip-locking on the family couch.

When the final frenzied cry calmed and the music was silenced, Karen and Hattie lay gasping for air.

"No one will believe this night." Karen released a huge after-belly-laugh breath.

"Worst part of it, we will probably have to face those two at breakfast in the morning."

"Good motivation to rise early and beat it the heck out of here."

"Amen.

"Hattie?"

"Hmm?"

"Thanks again."

"You're welcome, cuz."

"My Grandma May-May made tomato soup. She always said her teeth were store-boughten, so she strained out the seeds. Said they worked up underneath her plate. She had these big jars of tomatoes me and Moses—he's my brother—helped her can, lined up in the pantry. That's what she made the soup from. She would leave the pulpy stuff in. It was so good! Me and Moses would eat that soup up with soda crackers crumbled up in it."

Tameka Clark

Chapter Twenty-eight

The mental health counseling practice of Dr. Krystle Nakoa was located in a small wood frame house on a shady tree-lined section of East Park Avenue, five blocks south of downtown Tallahassee. Identical in style to the majority of structures lining the street, it contained two treatment rooms, a private office, a common waiting area, a kitchen lounge, one bathroom, and a screened porch off the lobby.

From the moment Karen entered the double French doors, she admired the distinctly non-clinical atmosphere. An embroidered-pillow-studded couch covered in soft dark blue denim and a matching chair welcomed clients. Healthy plants thick with new growth and quirky artwork decorated each wall and corner. A built-in bookshelf stretched the length of one wall, lined with reference volumes on cancer and nutrition with a sign-out sheet to allow clients to borrow reading materials.

The inscription on a terra cotta pottery plaque caught Karen's eye: "The Only Way Out Is Through." Two stained glass pieces in jewel tones cast purple, blue, and green refracted light across the highly-polished wood plank floor. The room's ambience stated: this is a place where a person can get to the core of things in a relaxed fashion.

A petite woman peeked around the corner of one of the rooms.

"You must be Karen Fletcher. I'm Dr. Nakoa. Krystle. I have to take this quick phone call, and then I'll be with you. There's tea steeping in the lounge. Coffee, too. First door to your left. Please help yourself to a cup. I'll only be a minute or two."

She smiled warmly and vanished into the private office.

"I have such a hard time staying inside on a morning like this. Why don't we have our session on the porch?" the therapist asked when she reappeared. "The purple finches are fighting over the sunflower seeds I just put out." Krystle flashed a white smile. "Must have been a colorblind person who named them purple finches. Orange, maybe. But purple? I've yet to see a dot of purple on a single one."

Karen followed the counselor to a cozy porch. Hanging ferns and wind chimes were suspended from the eaves, and the shade of a mature pecan tree blocked the direct sun. She chose one of two white wooden rocking chairs and placed her tea cup on a small glass side table.

The doctor settled into a cushioned wicker loveseat and reviewed the intake information Karen had faxed the day prior. Krystle Nakoa appeared to be in her mid-forties and of Native American descent. Her smooth skin was a creamy café latte shade, and a long braid of ribbon-trimmed glossy black hair trailed down her back.

Dr. Nakoa regarded Karen with gentle dark brown eyes. "First of all, welcome. I read your intake questionnaire last evening, but I wanted to review it quickly to make sure I didn't miss any pertinent details."

Long dangling silver rope earrings danced with her slightest movement. "Before we charge right in, allow me to tell you a bit about myself. I have been an R.N. for twenty-five years, a private practice psychologist for fifteen years, and a licensed massage therapist for the past three."

"Interesting combination."

"Yes, and I use it all. Often, touch therapy will open doors traditional venues cannot. As a nurse, I have full knowledge of the medical challenges you are undergoing. Initially, my focus was family counseling. My personal battle with breast cancer six years ago steered me in a different direction. Now, I primarily see cancer patients and sometimes their family members in relation to the client's treatment."

"I didn't know."

Krystle tipped her head to one side and raised one eyebrow. "But your father did. No doubt my name was on the top of your list, correct?"

Karen nodded.

The doctor kicked off her sandals and folded her legs underneath her. "I've known Dr. Joe for a number of years. At one time, I worked at the hospital in Chattahoochee. He's a fine man, and an excellent mental health worker."

Karen's gaze dropped. "But too close to help me."

"A certain amount of detachment is necessary, Karen. Above all, he is your father. It would be very hard for him to look past that." Krystle took a long sip from a glass of iced tea. "Credentials aside, let me tell you how I work. I'm not a namby-pamby, hold-your-hand type of therapist. Don't come in here expecting me to sit back with a pad, taking notes and muttering how do you feel about that?"

Karen smiled.

Krystle's dark gaze was unsettling. "I don't go for bullshit. If I sense you are hedging and trying to play me, I'll call you on it." She chuckled. "Now, you may be thinking, *Help me, I've come up on the female counterpart to Dr. Phil.* I'm not heartless. You have to bear in mind, I have experienced the pain and uncertainty of cancer treatment. When I say I've been there, I have. Now, I'm sitting here on the other side of it holding out a hand to help you across the abyss."

"It's not just the cancer, the reason I'm here," Karen said in a soft voice.

"It seldom is. It's been my experience that the illness is merely a symptom of layers of underlying muck ripe for raking." Krystle studied the intake questionnaire. "You are a few weeks past surgery, right?"

"Almost six."

The doctor scribbled a quick note on the edge of Karen's health history. "When do you start radiation therapy?"

"Next week."

"We should be able to coordinate our sessions to jibe with your appointments at the hospital. There may be a time toward the end when you don't feel like coming in. But it's essential that we establish a routine; it sends a distinct message to the universe that you are serious about solving the dilemma that has been sent your way. Clear?"

"Very. How do we begin?"

"Since I have your clinical diagnosis and pertinent physical data, why don't you start by telling me who you are?"

"That's the problem. I don't know. I've pretended to be someone else for so many years, I seem to have lost the real me."

Krystle tilted her head to one side. A gentle smile played across her regal features. "Sometimes, the best way to find out who you are is to start out by finding out who you are *not.*"

Lucille Jackson stuck her head through the threshold of the Triple C's stylist salon. "Here everyone is! Y'all are so quiet; I thought no one was here."

Mandy looked up from the booklet in her lap. "I'm trying to catch up on my continuing education. This course is as dull as dirt. Come on in. I surely welcome a break." She tossed the wire-bound papers on the counter.

"You all by your lonesome this morning?" Lucille asked.

"Wanda is off, preparing for the wedding festivities on Saturday. Evelyn is at home, and Stephanie is in with an early massage client. Melody never comes in this early."

"Is Elvina off sick?"

"No, she's around. She's probably out back having her morning talk with Piddie."

Lucille pulled up a director's chair and plopped down. "You reckon she's ever going to outgrow that?"

Mandy shrugged. "Doesn't look like it. No time soon, anyway. Guess it's not harming anyone."

"Reckon not." Lucille smiled.

"Do you need me to look at Wanda's book and make an appointment for you?"

"No, I already got my regular time set up on Thursday next. I really stopped by hoping to pick your brain."

"After reading that course, you'll be lucky I have any left to pick."

"The Reverend and I want to get something special for Wanda and Pinky's wedding. You know, Wanda has done my hair for a good long while now, and she was so good to little Tameka and Moses Clark last year during all that awful unpleasantness."

"How are the kids?"

"Growing like weeds. Their uncle sends us pictures now and then. Moses has gotten into the sciences, especially biology, like a house a'fire. He got that from all the work he did here in the gardens, I suppose. And little Tameka, she's turning out to be a real beauty. Seems her brush with the likes of Hank Henderson didn't mar the child's tender soul. We surely were worried there for a while."

Mandy pursed her lips. "I'm having a time coming up with ideas, myself. They're going to be living part time at the farm and part time in town. Wanda's dead set on keeping her house."

"She's been through a lot. I can see why she's so independent-minded. I want to do something that means something to just her. For the life of me, I can't come up with a notion."

"You said you had recent pictures of the children? I wonder if Wanda has any? Usually, she will read letters from Birmingham, but I haven't heard her mention any lately."

"You just gave me an idea!" Lucille jumped up and slung her purse on one arm.

"Well, if you have any bright insights for me, please feel free to call and share."

Elvina snapped the water hose to loosen a crimp and adjusted the nozzle to the gentle shower setting.

"Looks like we're going to have quite a show of daisies this season, Piddie."

She aimed an arc of spray high over the memorial flower garden.

"That is, if I can keep a certain ungrateful marauding rodent run off! You'd think with me laying feed and nuts out for him, he'd have the decency not to root around in this one patch of sacred earth." She glared up the tall pine adjacent to the garden.

"I'm talking about you, mister! I know you're up there listening in. I'd best not find any more of these delicate new shoots with their roots in the sunshine, or you'll not see another single peanut from me! You hear?"

A tooth-stripped pine cone bounced in the grass inches from her.

"Hey! It won't do you a dab of good to hurl things at me, you little devil! Sure as the world, you won't score any points that-a-way."

She watered and stewed for a few minutes before settling down on the bench.

"Piddie, I know how much you always loved to play Cupid. You helped Hattie and Holston hook up, and heaven knows how many others in this town owe their nuptials to you. Here's the deal. I do believe

D. J. Peterson is the one for your granddaughter. I've interviewed him countless times on our phone conversations, and I've come to respect him as a stand-up kind of fellow. He makes good money, though I know that's not all-important." She grinned. "Doesn't hurt."

Elvina brushed a piece of dried grass from the top of one sandal. "He's miserable without her. You can hear it in his voice. She misses him, too, though she doesn't admit it. Evelyn says Karen's closed herself off a bit since she's started in with the shrink in Tallahassee."

She sniffed. "Myself, I can't fathom why Joe couldn't help her find her way through it all. He's counseled a whole lot nuttier than his daughter."

She waved a hand dismissively through the air. "Evelyn says it's not prudent for a father to counsel his own child. I reckon I can see it—in a way."

The gold watch reminded her of the morning's obligations. "Time surely flies when I'm out here. Now I know why I never wore a time-piece all these years before you left this one for me in your will. If I don't have the time a-staring me in the face, I don't have to admit to how fast it passes me by.

"We're all heading out to Pinky Green's farm in Sycamore tomor-row afternoon for the wedding. Wanda says it'll just be a handful of us. She's not into the foolishness of a big fancy show. I do hope this one works out for her. Bless her heart, she's had more husbands than Carters has little pills."

Elvina laughed. "Don't let on I said that! It was a bit mean-spir-ited, wasn't it?

"Any-who, Donald's planning on popping into town to bring Karen's cats for a visit. Nobody's letting on he's coming. It's to be a surprise."

She glanced skyward. "Please, please, Piddie. If you're not too busy, look down on those two young people and help them see past their troubles. There's not near enough love to go around in this sad old world."

"My mother is the last of the great pre-hippies. Before her time, actually. Free spirit. Think she might have been raised with wolves, or something. We never knew what a meal would entail. Always something from nature. She studied up on all that kind of stuff. None of us ever ended up in the ER, at least. Experimental—that's the cuisine I grew up with. I can eat practically anything that's not moving. Even then—if it's seasoned right, maybe."

Jason "Simpy" Simpson

Chapter Twenty-nine

D. J. parked the Acura NSX in the circular driveway off Main Street and glanced in the rear view mirror. Simpy eased into place behind him in the Georgia Metro van.

"All yours, my man." Simpy handed the animal transport carrier over to him. "Pretty cool feline. Didn't cry out but a couple of times. I let her out for a while, and she curled up beside me on the bench seat."

"Good for you. I had the screamer in my car. Don't think he drew a single breath without meowing for the past five hours. My hearing is permanently impaired. I tried to turn the radio up to drown him out, but that only drove him to new heights."

"No one can say this isn't a grand gesture of love and goodwill." He clamped D. J. on the shoulder. "Good luck, Deej. Knock the woman's panty hose off."

"You're not coming in?"

"This is your gig. I'm heading to the Homeplace for a French dip sandwich, then to the Triple C to my reserved suite. I have a hot date tonight!"

"Yeah?"

"Stephanie is cooking for me. If she does everything as well as massage therapy, I may never leave this town again." Simpy turned toward the van. "See you tomorrow. You are going to the wedding, right?"

"Hattie and Holston asked me to come along. It remains to be seen, depending on how things go."

Evelyn opened the front door before D. J. rang the bell. "Karen's out back with her painting."

She peered into the carriers. "These her babies?"

One corner of his lips twitched. "I hope you don't come to hate me for this, Mrs. Fletcher."

"Nonsense. And if you don't call me Evelyn, I'll take offense. I bought a special self-cleaning electric litter box and set it up back in Mama's bathroom. Also, plenty of the kind of food you told me they like. I love animals. Joe didn't want me to take in any more strays on account of I get way too attached and nearly grieve myself to death when one passes on."

She shrugged. "Ah, well. I can't see any harm in having one, or two, as house guests for a while. I believe it will help Karen's spirits. She's been so low since the surgery."

Evelyn crouched down and made cooing noises though the wire doors. "Shall we let the cats out to explore?"

"It might be in everyone's best interests to confine them to the back part of the house for a bit until they become acclimated and know where the litter box is located. Especially the little male tabby, Taizer. He can be a holy terror."

"The other one is?"

"Tequila. You'll fall madly in love with her. She's sweet and cuddly like a fat rag doll. I didn't care too much for cats at first, but she's seen to it that I changed my mind."

"Sit the carriers down in the hall, and I'll take them one at a time to Mama's suite. You go on out and see Karen." Evelyn rested a hand gently on his arm. "Don't be put off if she seems a little distant. She and the counselor are having a go at things. It's been pretty rough on her trying to sort herself out."

"Maybe this visit isn't such a good idea. I should have sent the cats down with Simpy."

"Oh, no, son. I dearly believe she'll be pleased to see you, just don't expect too much too soon."

"Thank you, Evelyn."

"I wouldn't mind you staying here with us, but—"

"Hattie is prepared for me to use their guest room. I would rather not crowd Karen."

Evelyn nodded. "Joe left you some fresh macaroni salad and cheddar herbed biscuits with ham for lunch, in case you're hungry after the long drive. I'll fix you a plate and glass of tea when you're ready."

Karen studied the gilded left wing on the damselfly perched on a thin stalk of wild peppermint slightly off center on the canvas. The perspective was slightly skewed, enough to offend a trained artist's eye. She dabbed a fan-shaped brush into the background shade pre-mixed on the palette and obliterated the image. A presence in her peripheral vision gained her attention. A warm flush of recognition stirred deep inside.

"Donald!" She rose and rushed to the patio door, hesitating briefly a few feet in front of him. "Donald, it's good to see you."

"C'mere." He welcomed Karen into outstretched arms. They embraced, rocking slightly for a few moments.

She pulled back and studied her fiancé, a question lingering in her expression. He leaned over and kissed her gently on the lips, and then cradled her head close to his heart.

"I have someone, actually two someones, who want to see you." He grasped her by the hand and led her inside through the main house into her grandmother's suite.

Taizer spotted Karen immediately and emitted a series of piteous yowls, each ending in an exclamation. She scooped the tabby into her arms and nuzzled between his ears, cooing in a soothing tone.

"The big yellow one is under Mama's bed," Evelyn said from the doorway. She placed two china saucers filled with albacore tuna beside a crystal water bowl. Taizer struggled to gain freedom and Tequila peered from her position on the floor beneath the edge of the quilt.

"Okay, okay." Karen deposited Taizer in front of the proffered fish. After a quick nervous glance around the room, Tequila emerged and hunkered down to eat.

"Well! Don't that beat all! I thought they'd be glad to see you after such a long time," Evelyn commented, her hands propped on her hips.

"Not cats, Mama. They're not the same as dogs. There will be a customary period of guilt-tripping before I'm allowed anywhere near their good graces."

She turned to Donald. "Certainly, you didn't bring both of them down in your car. You poor thing!"

"Tequila rode with Simpy in the station van. I had the extreme pleasure of Taizer's company for five hundred miles. I may never be the same."

"Why don't we let the little darlings settle in while we have some lunch?" Evelyn suggested. "Donald, the guest bathroom down the hall to the right has clean towels if you want to freshen up."

"Did you know about this?" Karen asked her mother after D. J. left the room.

"Don't go getting upset, honey. Donald called with the idea, and I thought it might lift your spirits having your pets here. He checked with me first to make sure I'd allow them in the house."

Karen smiled. "So, this is what Hattie had up her sleeve. Wait until I get a'hold of her."

"I called her. Donald was going to stay in a motel uptown, and I wouldn't hear of it. I tried to talk him into staying here, but he didn't want to make you feel he was edging in on you. Hattie and Holston have the spare bedroom and bath. There was no need of Donald being cooped up in some dingy motel room."

Evelyn studied her daughter for a moment. "That young man worships the ground at your feet, Karen. No matter how you feel about yourself right now, you can at least thank him for coming all this way to see you." Her brows knit in concern. "Aren't you the least bit glad to see him?"

"Yes, but—" Karen caught a glimpse of her reflection in the antique oak mirror above the bureau. "Look at me!"

Her mother's face set in a determined expression Karen had seen often during her torturous adolescence. "Let me tell you one thing I know to be perfectly true, young lady. If you plan on ever marrying, he is going to have to see you at your best as well as your worst. It's all about thick and thin, standing by each other no matter what life throws your way. Who do you think is going to bring you a cup of chicken broth when you get the stomach flu and have been hanging over the toilet for hours? Who's going to see you first thing of a morning with your hair all matted down, night-fuzz on your teeth, and no makeup on? Huh?"

"Well. "

"That's right! Mama had a saying. Of course, she had a saying for just about any situation. 'Life really is a bed of roses. You just have to learn to work around the thorns.'"

Krystle Nakoa settled into an overstuffed geometric-print chair. "Why don't you take the wicker love seat? It's perfect for meditation."

Karen perched on the edge of a striped cushion. "I've never done this before, unless you count the visualization exercises Hattie's been teaching me."

Krystle shrugged. "About the same, really. Sit back and get comfortable. You look like you're ready to bolt out of here. My hair that scary?" She pointed to the massive swirl of raven braids and multicolored cloth strips hanging like clusters of overripe grapes. "I was in a Carmen Miranda mood this morning when I got up."

The print of the therapist's sweeping sundress was equally tropical: vivid red hibiscus, deep green palm fronds, and rainbow-hued macaws. Karen smiled and eased into the soft cushions. "I like the look." She ran her hand across her scalp. "I'll be happy to have hair again so I can wear some kind of funky 'do."

The counselor reached over and rested a hand on Karen's shoulder. "All of this will pass. In the meantime, collect a load of wild printed bandanas. The way I figured it when I was bald—people notice anyway, so why not stand out and really give them something to focus on?"

"It was just beginning to grow back. Now, with starting chemo . . ." Karen frowned. "I had really hoped and prayed I wouldn't have to go through that again." She closed her eyes and shook her head. "Six more rounds. Six more freaking rounds."

"That's the reason I want to introduce you to this particular meditation." She sipped from a tall pottery mug. "I used it a lot when I was trudging through the tough spots." She hesitated. "It's difficult not to feel like a victim. At least, it was for me."

"I feel like I'm not safe, and will never be safe again."

"Exactly. You willing to give this a go?"

Karen shrugged. "What do I do?"

Krystle hit the power switch on a compact disc player. Soft ethereal harp and flute music filled the cozy, plant-furnished room. "Close your eyes. Become aware of your breathing, in and out."

Led by the counselor's even-timbred voice, Karen followed a series of suggestions to relax her scalp and facial muscles, moving slowly down to her toes. Her body felt leaden, sinking into the thick cushions.

"In your mind's eye, see a house. This is your dream home, your perfect place. A safe haven to be at one with your spirit."

A log cabin with a long covered front porch appeared in Karen's vision. Flower beds with tall stands of Black-eyed Susans and trailing purple passion flower vine trellises bordered a slate walkway. Two split cedar rocking chairs with ivy-printed cushions awaited. The surrounding woods were a thick, lush green, but friendly—unlike the deep dark forests of the cave dream.

"You are walking up to the front door. It is unlocked, so you step inside." Krystle's voice coaxed her forward.

The room she entered was bright and open, filled with filtered sunlight from four tall windows. Gleaming wooden floors shone at her feet. An oval woven rag rug filled the sitting area in front of a ceiling-to-floor stone fireplace.

"In this room, you can place things that bring you joy."

Karen noticed the cats. Taizer crouched beside the hearth holding a stuffed mouse in his paws. Tequila slept curled into a tight ball atop a crocheted afghan on one end of a pillow-filled couch. Throughout the room, plants were suspended from wooden split-log beams, and pots of wildflowers were nestled between rows of books.

"This room is your safe place, and you can visit any time to rest and feel at peace."

Donald's face appeared in Karen's vision. A slight smile curled the edges of his mouth. His eyes—soft brown, filled with love and compassion. She free-floated for a time, comforted by his presence.

"When you are ready, gently allow your awareness to come back to this room. The sofa beneath you, the feel of your body healthy and calm," Krystle's voice said.

Karen opened her eyes.

The counselor smiled. "Have a nice visit?"

"Very."

Krystle tipped her head. Several braids swung in time. "Anything you want to share?"

"Donald was there."

"My mother's middle name was comfort. She used food, especially sweets, to mend every bruised knee and broken heart. I must've needed a whole lot of comforting growing up. Trouble is, I still head for the kitchen when I'm feeling down. Doesn't take a shrink to tell me what that's all about. Not that I'm blaming my mother for my weight issues. Not at all. Love and food just go hand-in-hand in my world."

Big Will Cooke

Chapter Thirty

Simpy rapped on Will Cooke's door and stuck his head into the executive director's office. "I'm outta here, boss man!"

"Step in here a minute, Simpy. I've got something to show you." Will plopped the morning edition of the *Atlanta Journal-Constitution* on the desk. "You seen the paper?"

Simpy shook his head. "Been holed up working on the first half of Karen's cancer video. Haven't seen outside in—" he checked his watch, "—eighteen hours."

"Take a gander at the headline." Will jabbed a finger at the bold print on the first page.

"Terrorist attack suspected at *National Informant* offices," Simpy read. "Jeez!"

"Yeah. Take a close look at the center photo. Recognize the bubble-headed blonde?"

Simpy squinted. "Trisha Truman? I'll be damned." He jerked his head to flip the long ponytail back over his shoulder. "Finally, she's made the headlines."

"She was on the early news, too. Came out of the building supported by two paramedics. Practically swooned when she noticed the camera crews."

"What happened? Bomb?"

Will shook his head. "Nope. Seems an envelope was mailed to Trisha containing white powder and a threat of some sort. They immediately evacuated the offices and called in a HAZMAT team."

Simpy's thick eyebrows shot up. "Anthrax?"

Will shrugged. "Remains to be seen. They're processing the scene. It's live on CNN."

Simpy frowned. "Why the hell would terrorists target a smut rag like the *Informant*? The post office, federal buildings, IRS, I can see but—"

"My thoughts exactly." The springs on his leather chair complained loudly as he leaned back. "Maybe Trisha has finally bumbled onto a real news story."

Simpy dismissed the absurd idea with a wave of his thin hand. "Whatever. You need me to do anything before I leave for Florida?"

Will shook his head. "Just send my regards to Karen. I sure hate it, her having such a time with this."

"Me, too. D. J.'s with her. Don't know if it'll make it any easier on her, but he seems more content. Karen's another story. She's all over the place—up one minute, down the next. If he can hang in there through this, it'll be a miracle."

An idea came to Elvina as she sat stewing on the meditation bench. A bolt of white-hot summer lightning inspiration struck her right between the eyes: the perfect gift for Wanda's wedding.

She glanced heavenward. "I know that came from you, Piddie Longman, and I thank you for it."

Wanda Orenstein had everything a body could need. And if she didn't, Pinky Green did. Elvina was galled at the thought of wasting money on worthless gee-gaws and dust-catchers. Her gift would have a deeper meaning.

Elvina reached into the pocket of her denim skirt for a small cell phone. "Wish you'd'a lived to see the likes of this, Piddie. A telephone the size of my palm. Wonders never cease."

She jabbed a shell-pink fingernail to access the stored memory, then dialed a number in Birmingham, Alabama.

"I need the rest of the day off," Elvina said. She stood with her feet firmly planted, hands on her broad hips.

Mandy glanced up from the shampoo basin where Sue Ellen Sales's soap-lathered head rested. "Hot date?"

"I got somewheres to be at two."

Mandy massaged Sue Ellen's hair into a frenzy of foam. "Where you off to in such a hurry?"

Elvina sniffed. "None of your bees-wax."

Mandy tilted her head. "Dang, 'Vina. No need to go getting snippy. I really don't give a hoot if you need to leave. The voicemail can pick up."

Elvina's lips drew into a pout. "If you must know, I'm going to the airport over in Tallahassee."

Sue Ellen squeezed her eyes shut. "Hey, careful Mandy! You done got soap in my eyes."

"Sorry hon." Mandy dabbed her patron's face with a white hand towel. "That's what comes from being interrupted from my work."

"Well! Excuse me for living!" Elvina turned to leave.

"Oh, come on, 'Vina!" Mandy called. "I didn't mean nothing by it." Elvina spun around.

"Seriously, why the airport? You flying off into the wild blue yonder?" Mandy grinned wickedly. "Why don't you just take your broom?"

Sue Ellen chuckled beneath the stream of warm water Mandy aimed at her hair.

"Miss Smarty Pants, very funny. For your information, I'm working on my gift for Wanda, one me and Lucille came up with about the same exact time."

"Count me in, then. I can't figure for the life of me what to get her. Let me know what you spend, and I'll go in half."

Elvina shook her head. "This is mine, and mine alone, Mandy Andrews. You'll have to have your own brainstorm." She tucked her straw purse under one arm and left the hair salon.

Mandy wrapped a thick dry towel around Sue Ellen's wet hair and sat the chair upright.

"What was she all het up about?" Sue Ellen asked.

Mandy shrugged. "Beats heck out of me. Elvina's always got something going. Lord knows what she's having imported. Heaven help poor Wanda."

"I don't remember my mama cooking anything for me and Tameka. Maybe she did, when she was around. I mostly took care of us until we came to live with Grandma May-May. She made teacakes. They were these little puffed-up cookie kinda things, and the whole house smelled good when she baked them. May-May passed last year. Now, me and Tameka stay with my uncle and auntie. Auntie Alicia knows how to make teacakes, too. I think my uncle taught her. She made them a lot when we first moved up to Birmingham after May-May passed. I liked Auntie Alicia right off because of her teacakes. It was like a little part of May-May was watching over all of us."

Moses Clark

Chapter Thirty-one

Wanda Orenstein peeked from the front window of the farmhouse. The dappled shade cast by the widespread branches of a live oak tree provided cool respite for the gathering crowd. Her stomach rolled. "What the hell am I getting ready to do?" She took several deep breaths.

Mandy tapped her foot. "I don't know, Wanda'loo. If you don't sit your butt down and let me finish your hair, you're going to be doing it looking like a wet poodle." She jabbed the rat tail comb toward a mirrored vanity. "Sit!"

Wanda perched on the velvet-cushioned seat. "Is this the right thing, Mandy? Me getting married again? God knows, I haven't had such a good track record."

Mandy sectioned off a hank of hair and curled it around a brush. "You just picked the other fellas from Loser-ville." She spoke in a loud voice to compensate for the drone of the blow dryer. "Pinky's the charm, hon."

A slight smile tugged at the corners of Wanda's hot pink lips. "He is a good guy."

"And sweet, to boot. I'll bet you've lost track of how many roses he's sent you. And cook! A man who can cook! You are lucky beyond all belief. You could be marrying my Bull. His idea of hot romance is sweaty sex after spending the afternoon down the river fishing." Mandy chuckled. "Sometimes, the very smell of bait makes me hotter than a three-peckered billy goat."

They giggled like teenagers.

"You seen Elvina Houston today?" Mandy asked.

Wanda shrugged. "Not yet. I can't believe she's not here. She usually shows up an hour ahead of time."

"She's up to something big. I couldn't wedge a word out of her."

Lucille Jackson grasped Karen's hands. "Don't you look pretty, Miz Karen. Your mama make your dress?"

Karen nodded.

"And that bandana to match. Believe that's even better than a hat."

Evelyn stepped up beside the two women. "You like it?" She reached over and adjusted the lace-trimmed band. "I'm thinking of starting a line of ELF-wear head wraps. I sent one to Glenda Nelson over at the American Cancer Society in Tallahassee. She liked it so well, I plan to sew up a few to donate for women who are going through chemotherapy."

"A wonderful tithe, Miz Evelyn." The Reverend Thurston Jackson smiled and shook her hand. "The Lord finds ways to use our talents if we take a moment to heed the call." His ebony skin glistened with a sheen of perspiration beneath close-cropped white hair.

A horn blasted three times. Elvina Houston slid the Oldsmobile to a dust-raising halt. "Am I late?" she yelled from the car's lowered window.

"Near to it, Elvina," Evelyn called back.

Elvina swung her long bony arm from the window. "C'mere!"

Evelyn walked over and peered into the back seat. "Lord A'Mercy! Look who's here!" A broad smile spread across her face.

"Help me. I need to hide them out of sight till Wanda comes down." Elvina jumped from the car and slammed the door.

Evelyn propped her hands on her hips. "What do you want I should do, 'Vina? Poke 'em under my slip?"

"No, no. Of course not. Just check to see Wanda's not near a window, and we'll run up and stand on the other end of the porch till she comes out."

Evelyn motioned to Karen. "Get up there and peek in the front door. See where Wanda and Mandy are at, then wave if the coast is clear."

They waited on Karen's signal before Elvina and her two young charges, Moses and Tameka Clark, high-tailed it to the porch.

"Wanda's gonna fall out when she sees these two younguns." Evelyn gathered the black children to her and smashed them to her breast. "How y'all doing up there in Birmingham?"

Tameka, the nine-year-old, said, "Fine, I'm going to be taking jazz dance classes next year."

"Well, ain't you a big girl!"

Moses said, "Aunt 'Licia's letting me start football, too."

"I'm just so proud of you both, I could bust wide open." Evelyn gave them another squeeze and turned to motion behind her. "This here is my daughter, Miz Karen."

Tameka studied Karen. "Why you don't have no hair?"

Evelyn frowned. "Now, honey."

"That's okay, Mama." Karen knelt down in front of the petite child. "I've been sick and the medicine made my hair all fall out. Made most of my eyebrows and eyelashes disappear, too."

The child's almond-shaped brown eyes echoed kindness. "It gone come back?"

Karen smiled. "I do believe it will. If not, I'll just polish up my head till it shines."

Tameka giggled. Her long beaded braids danced and tapped together.

Elvina gathered the children and herded them toward the corner of the front porch. "Y'all stand right over here, now. When Miz Wanda comes out, we'll be ready to give her a big surprise."

Hattie and Holston's gold SUV pulled into the driveway, closely followed by Bobby, Leigh, and Tank in Bobby's faded blue pick-up. When Karen saw D. J. emerge from the back seat of Hattie's automobile, her throat constricted slightly.

" 'Bout time y'all got here!" Evelyn called.

Hattie plopped Sarah on one hip and grabbed a bulging diaper bag. "We were on time until Sarah and Spackle decided to play in a puddle by the front faucet."

Sarah clapped her pudgy little hands.

"Come to your Auntie Evelyn, little Chinaberry." She plucked the toddler from her mother's arms. "Glad you could come, Donald."

"Pleasure's all mine." His intense gaze rested on his fiancée.

Jake and Jon pulled up in the 4Runner. Melody and J. T. slid from the back seat. Simpy and Stephanie arrived in the GMPTV van.

"Okay! Party can start now. The fun crew has arrived." Jake wore pinstriped jeans with a chambray shirt and leaned on a coordinating denim-printed cane. Not to outshine his partner, Jon had opted for blue jeans and a white Polo shirt.

"I feel kind of underdressed for a wedding," Stephanie said, brushing the wrinkles from a simple sundress.

"You look just fine. I know Wanda Orenstein. If she said she'd belt anyone who dressed up fancy, she meant it," Evelyn said. "I wish more weddings were this way."

"Isn't that the truth," Holston said. "The thought of putting on a tie in this heat—"

The front screened door slammed. Pinky Green stepped onto the porch wearing faded jeans and a white T-shirt. "Everyone here? Wanda's about ready to come out!"

Evelyn glanced around. "Joe? Anybody seen Joe? Now, where is that husband of mine?"

Pinky pointed toward the barn. "Think I saw him and Bull walking off that way."

Evelyn snorted off in search of her husband while the Reverend took his place underneath the oak tree.

"There wasn't a thing my mama couldn't cook. If it could be fried, baked, or broiled, it best stay away from Piddie Longman's kitchen. Give her an iron skillet and a couple of bowls, and she could cook up a storm. My favorite? Her chicken 'n' dumplin's. Absolutely heaven on earth! I can't tell you how many pots of dumplin's I've eaten in my lifetime. Used to be, back when I was a little girl up in Alabama, Mama would have to go out and wring a chicken's neck in the back yard, then scald the feathers off and clean its insides out. That part always made me a little queasy. Much better now that we can get chicken parts already cleaned and cut-up."

Evelyn Longman Fletcher

Chapter Thirty-two

"Watch, Auntie 'Vina!" Tameka took several running steps and executed a perfect somersault followed by flip twist. Her yellow sun dress flounced over her head.

Elvina and the others sitting underneath the oak tree clapped. She motioned for the child. "That was mighty good, sugar-pot. You're as cute as a bug's ear. But maybe you should wait till you have on the special little bloomers so your underpanties don't shine."

Tameka's gaze dropped to the ground. "Yes'm. Can me and Moses go see the goats?"

Elvina glanced toward the gathering of men around the brick grill. "Go ask Mr. Pinky if it's okay. Don't go getting in the pen. You'll soil your pretty dress."

"Yes 'um." Tameka skipped off.

"Amazing how happy she is now," Evelyn said. "I'm so glad Hank Henderson's evil didn't taint that child."

Elvina's gaze followed Tameka and her brother as they walked hand-in-hand toward the barn. "I was most concerned about Moses, but it seems he's put the unpleasantness behind him, too."

Wanda jumped up and hugged Elvina. "You bringing those kids to my wedding was the best present of all." She planted a kiss on the old woman's wrinkled cheek.

Elvina smiled in spite of herself. "I can't take all the credit. Lucille was struck by the same notion. Do believe Piddie tapped both of us so we'd be sure to get the message."

Wanda shook her head. "I just wish Pinky and I were going to be around to spend more time with them."

Elvina adjusted her straw sun hat. "Y'all need to get on off on your honeymoon. Me and Lucille have plans for the younguns, anyhow."

"How long are they staying?" Hattie asked.

"I take them to the airport a week from today." Elvina smiled. "My old tomcat Buster's took to Tameka like nobody's business. And Moses, he's gonna help me set out a butterfly garden by the back steps."

Stephanie raised her eyebrows. "Why, Elvina, I never took you for a person who liked children."

Elvina sniffed. "Just 'cause I never birthed any, don't mean I don't like having them around sometimes."

Lucille joined in. "We're taking a busload from the church up to that adventure park near Valdosta on Wednesday."

Mandy clapped her hands. "I wanna go! I wanna go! I love that place."

Lucille nodded. "We could always use an extra chaperone."

"Means I'll have to reschedule a day's worth of clients now, Mandy." Elvina shook her bony finger.

"I hardly ever take a day off during the week," Mandy said. "Bull's home off the road for the week. I'll get him to go, too. It'll be a blast!"

Elvina dragged a pen from behind her ear and a notepad from her pocket. "I'll get to work on the books tomorrow."

Lucille turned to Karen. "When you starting back on your treatments?"

Karen's smile faded. "Monday at one. First, chemo, then on to radiation."

"Your young man, is he staying down right on?" Lucille motioned toward the barbeque grill. The scent of sizzling chicken wafted through the air.

Karen glanced at D. J. "Maybe so." He looked her way and smiled.

Elvina clapped her hands. "Whoop! I almost forgot! Hattie, tell everybody the story about your glasses. This is a good one!"

Hattie rolled her eyes. "I really don't—"

Jake leaned forward. "C'mon, Sister-girl. I never get to hear your adventures anymore, now that you're all happily married."

Holston jiggled Sarah on his lap. "It *is* pretty amusing, hon."

"All right." Hattie sighed. "Well, you know I'm more and more like Mama every day. She used to put her foot in her mouth on a regular basis."

Elvina frowned. "Spare them the build-up, Hattie. You give way too much detail sometimes."

"Ain't that the truth," Jake said. "If we were all lost, she'd take charge and lead us around in circles for hours."

"You want me to tell the story, or what?" Hattie said.

Jake blew a make-up kiss her way.

"Okay, like I was saying before I was so rudely interrupted—I was over in Tallahassee last week for a doctor's appointment—"

Jon asked. "You okay? Nothing we need to worry about?"

Hattie shook her head. "Oh, no. Just a routine follow-up with the oncologist. I'm fine."

"Quit interrupting her, for Heaven's sake," Elvina said.

Hattie continued. "I had a bunch of errands to run and right in the middle of it all, my glasses fell apart."

"That's a pain," Evelyn agreed.

"Yeah, well. I stopped by my regular doctor's office, and he was out of town. So, I decided to go to that vision place in the Governor's Mall. See if they could do a quick repair. I was having a late lunch with one of my friends on that side of town."

Hattie took a deep breath. "By the time I walked in, it was around noon, and the place was packed—mostly with men. The lady behind the counter spotted me and asked in a loud voice, 'Are you here for an appointment in the back, or are you picking up a pair of glasses?' I answered in a loud voice to carry over the din of conversation, 'No, I just stopped by for a quick screw!'"

The group howled with laughter. Jake stamped his cane on the ground. Tank and Sarah clapped and giggled because the adults were acting so strangely.

"Lord help, Hattie," Evelyn said when she could finally speak. "You didn't just put your foot in your mouth. You swallowed the whole dang leg."

Hattie smiled. "Every man in the room stopped dead and stared at me. It was surreal—like a scene out of a sitcom. My face got all red and hot. I said, 'Perhaps I should rephrase that.' That statement brought the house down. I heard them laughing all the way to the rear of the store. The fellow who took me back for the repair couldn't stop snickering. His shoulders shook the whole time he was replacing the missing screw. Then, he handed them back all fixed and cleaned up. When I asked how much, he said, 'Honey, you don't owe me a dime.'"

A second wave of laughter and knee-slapping resounded. Mandy wiped the joy-tears from her eyes. "Maybe you ought to stay away from the mall for a while."

Jake howled. "They probably have your picture up in the office!"

Elvina dabbed at her eyes. "I got one to tell on my dear friend, Piddie, God rest her soul. Few years back—oh, maybe fifteen or so— me 'n' Piddie were at the K-mart in Tallahassee, the old one used to be acrosst from Lake Ella. We were in a hurry, and trying to find the snack aisle. Betsy Witherspoon was having a tea, and we were supposed to bring the mixed nuts."

She smiled, remembering. "We hunted and hunted all over that store. Piddie finally said, 'We ain't never gonna find them. I'm gonna ask.' You know Piddie, not a shy bone in her body. She spotted this young fella up on a tall ladder stocking shelves and stood beneath him looking up. She yelled up to him, 'Young man, where are your nuts?' Lawsy, the look on that boy's face! I can still see it! I walked off and left her standing there."

The revelry continued through the elaborate picnic dinner and afterwards, between sessions of guitar-picking and singing. Simpy slipped silently among the gathering, video camera in hand.

Karen studied the group. Jake with his maimed leg. Hattie—both parents deceased, with colon cancer behind her. Evelyn still grieving Piddie's death. Pinky with a beloved sister gone to cancer. Moses and Tameka—victims of a porn money-making scheme. How could so much joviality spring from a group riddled with pain and tragedy?

Later she asked her mother.

"It's just our way, sugar," Evelyn said. "Always has been. There's a'plenty in this old world to be depressed over. If you haven't had personal tragedy touch your life, all you have to do is pick up a paper or watch TV. Pain is all around. Laughter is good. Helps us forget for a few moments all the suffering humanity puts itself through. Without it, a person's spirit would be squashed like a bug, sure as I'm standing here."

"When I was a little girl, my mama made this plain, thin, starchy soup when I was sick. I made it for my own kids when they were sick or just having a bad day. They're grown now, but still ask for it sometimes."
Julie Nix, server at The Homeplace Restaurant

Julie's Mama's Potato Soup

3 Yukon Gold potatoes, washed, peeled, and diced.
3 cups water
salt and pepper to taste
pat of butter

Place the potatoes in a small saucepan and cover with the cold water. Add salt and pepper, if desired. Bring to a boil and reduce heat to simmer potatoes for 15-20 minutes. You want the potatoes to cook until they're very soft and fall apart.

Remove from heat and lightly mash with a fork to break up large pieces of potato. Add a pat of butter. Adjust salt and pepper to taste. Serve while hot.

You want this soup to be thin and watery if you are serving it to a sick person, especially if they have a fever. The idea is to give them nourishment they can keep down.

Some good variations, if you aren't running a fever—a cup of chopped, cooked broccoli, ½ cup shredded cheddar cheese, ½ cup cream (reduce water), or add all three.

Chapter Thirty-three

The Nucletron Simulux HP reminded Karen of an oversized praying mantis. The radiation machine looked benign enough, dominating the cavernous barren room. Hard to believe, a machine just like it would fire invisible killer devil-rays at her from its gaping maw.

"Imagine you're on a massage table," Hattie had suggested. "I'll give you some of my relaxation CDs, and you can drift off to a sunny beach or green mountain glen. Before you know it, the session will be over."

Quite a stretch for Karen's budding visualization skills—from a paint-stenciled, bald, skinny body to a voluptuous beauty queen on a balmy Caribbean beach.

"Welcome to the simulator room," Dr. McDowell said. "This machine is just a plain x-ray machine, possibly a bit intimidating, but the one you will receive your treatments on—the Linear Accelerator, LINAC—is larger."

Karen liked everything about the radiation oncologist: freckles, carrot-red hair, eyebrows, and lashes, open-faced expression, and kind blue eyes that smiled even when his mouth didn't.

Her first appointment had been for a two-hour visit dedicated to the nurses and Dr. McDowell performing an initial consultation: a thorough history and physical examination followed by a lengthy counseling session where the radiation oncologist explained the rationale for radiation and the typical side effects. The second session included a CAT scan and a walk-through of the facility punctuated by Dr. McDowell's commentary. Karen met two of the RTT's, radiation therapy therapists, who would guide her though the procedures. Dr. McDowell explained the computer-generated radiation plan and fabrication of the custom-tooled lead shielding used inside of the unit to direct the powerful beam. Paint pens were used to mark her skin to help the therapists aim the machine.

"No radiation this time. Just a test run." The doctor smiled.

Happy Days—he would fit in with the family on the old sitcom perfectly. *Dating yourself again, dear,* Karen chided herself. Only one of the two therapists was old enough to recall the show.

"Go ahead and recline, Karen," the doctor said.

She eased onto the cushioned table.

"Now, your arm will rest above your head on these pads so that we can aim here." He pointed to the area adjacent to the scar underneath her armpit. "We'll be treating from several angles—to treat the breast and the area where your lymph nodes were. Usually one to two minutes per field. You won't feel anything. Just hear a series of beeping and buzzing noises. The therapists will be monitoring you from the control room."

He pointed upward toward the corners of the room. "See the video cameras? If you get scared or need help, all you have to do is wave. Any problems, they will be right on it. There are microphones so you and the therapists can talk if there is an issue. Important thing—don't move unless you truly have a problem. Let the technicians position you and then stay perfectly still." Dr. McDowell smiled. "They will scold you, if you start shifting around. I know it's tempting at first to rise up and try to see what the heck is going on, but it is absolutely imperative that you remain still. You'll learn not to move your head unconsciously when the therapist is talking to you. Even talking or lifting the other arm to scratch an itch is a no-no. Any questions?"

"These . . . " she pointed to the lines drawn on her chest, "will they wash off?"

"Not much. We may have to redraw here and there. They're not permanent tattoos, but they will last for a while. We can use pin-point permanent tattoos at the centers and corners of the radiation fields if you would like. That way, you don't have to try to keep the lines in place day after day, especially if your skin is oily." Dr. McDowell said.

"Think I'd rather deal with the wash-off kind, if you don't mind. I never have been one, much, for body art."

"Radiation therapy for breast cancer is a breeze compared to chemo. Some other radiation therapies for other body areas are far worse than chemo." He hesitated. "Just to review what we covered in the consultation session, after a few weeks, usually two to three, you may have what amounts to a bad sunburn. Your skin may be itchy and red. We have special lotions to soothe the irritated skin. Some patients use aloe—up to you—just nothing with any zinc oxide or aluminum. Remember, no deodorants or perfumes."

Karen rolled her eyes. "I know. I have to go natural for the next six weeks. And in the dead of the summer, no less." She smiled. "I'll be lucky to have any friends left who'll get anywhere near me—bush woman."

"If it's any consolation, most deodorants lose potency in our kind of heat and humidity, anyway. I must have five different brands at home." Dr. McDowell's freckled nose wrinkled as he grinned. He clapped his hands together. "So, Monday morning, we start out. Park in the front lot. We have several spaces reserved for radiation patients. By the time you come in, slip into one of our delightful designer gowns, have your treatment, and dress—you're looking at fifteen to twenty minutes, tops. Monday through Friday, with weekends off for good behavior."

Karen smiled wistfully. "If only chemo was that easy."

The Borrowed Thyme Bakery and Eatery bustled with the typical morning rush. Joe Fletcher moved expertly between the griddle and tables, delivering heaping plates of eggs, waffles, pancakes, and hot biscuits. He passed by D. J. and said, "Let me finish up this last order, and I'll have a cup of coffee with you before you leave."

D. J. leaned back and patted the pooch at his waistline. Good thing he was going home. Joe's homemade breakfasts were becoming too much of a habit. That, and no workouts for three weeks—D. J. groaned, thinking of the glee on his personal trainer's face when he finally faced the flab-earned music.

Joe slipped a plate in front of a customer, then drew up a chair beside D. J. "Whew! This ole stallion ain't what he used to be. That's for sure. Either life is speeding up, or I'm slowing down."

"Lack of sleep isn't doing you or your wife any favors."

Joe shrugged and took a noisy swill of coffee. "Can't be helped. Reckon Karen would like a decent night, too. When you planning on taking off?"

D. J. glanced at his Rolex. "Pretty soon. I'd like to hit Atlanta mid-afternoon, well before the evening rush."

Joe dabbed the sweat from his brow with a napkin. "Don't see it as a setback, son—Karen sending you packing. She's trying to prepare herself for the last round of chemo treatments. She's weak and I think this one will be much harder for her."

"We had a long talk last night. I understand why she needs some space. She's dealing with a lot." He took a deep breath. "Besides, it'll do me good to get back to work and focus on something else for a while."

Joe pointed to D. J.'s empty mug. "Refill?"

"How about a to-go cup? I need all the caffeine I can get this morning."

"You too tired to drive? Maybe you ought to go on back to the house and lay down for a few hours before hitting the road."

"I'll be all right." He stretched his arms overhead and yawned.

Joe packed a Styrofoam cup in a white paper bag and added sugar and creamer packets. "Want a cathead for the road?"

D. J. rolled his eyes. "Oh, what the hell? Sure."

Joe handed the bags over. "I put some butter pats and jelly in there, too. Maybe you can pull over halfway and have a bite or two."

"Thanks, Joe." D. J. shook the older man's hand. "You have my numbers. Don't hesitate to call me. I can hop a flight and be here in less than two hours."

"And D. J.? Try not to be down-hearted about my daughter. She's riding this thing out. I—we—think the world of you, and I know Karen does, too."

The phone rang once before Jake answered. "Insomniacs Hotline, Jake speaking."

Karen laughed.

"What's the matter, sweetie-poots? Can't sleep again?"

"Same ole."

"Hang on a sec."

She heard him shifting around before he came back on the line.

"Moved to the porch so I could catch a little night air. You taking any drugs to help you?"

"Falling to sleep's not the issue," Karen said.

"Hmm. The cave dream's back. Tell Jakey all about it."

"Wish I could. It's a nightmare. Or something. I wake up yelling."

"No wonder Evelyn's under-eye circles are down to her chin."

"And I've been so edgy."

Jake sniffed. "Sorry, my allergies are dealing me a fit. You being a brat? Break anything?"

"I stabbed a canvas until it looked like Swiss cheese. Threw a mug across Mama's kitchen. Snapped at my brother when he called from Ohio to check on me."

She heard Jake whispering. "I didn't wake Jon, did I?"

"Huh? No. Elvis is up pattering around. Jon is dead out. Snoring like nobody's business. I could storm naked through the bedroom with cymbals and a snare drum and he wouldn't budge. Damn him. Maybe you should come live with me, and I could ship Jon to your Mama's."

Karen huffed. "Way I'm acting, you wouldn't want me."

"Poor baby. Is lover boy still planning on sticking around for your treatments?"

Karen paused. "I sent him back to Atlanta this morning."

"What'd you do that for? He hasn't done anything to upset you, has he? I'll thrash him about the head and ears!"

"No, not at all. Donald's been . . . exceptional. I just couldn't deal with him, with us, right now. It's all I can do to get out of bed and drag to the hospital. Not to mention right after chemo."

"Wretched?"

"Right."

"Can I reassure you that, at least, where I was concerned, the temper tantrums are normal? I pitched my share of falling-out fits when I came home from the hospital after the assault. Broke three of my favorite canes during one particularly memorable one."

Karen smiled. "Any words of wisdom about dealing with the anger?"

Jake chuckled. "Better pissed off than pissed on."

"It's not actually food I remember from childhood. It's hot tea. My mother was from the UK, and tea was her lifeblood. A cup of tea was the answer to all of life's ills. If I was feeling low, physically or emotionally, my mother would appear with the tea set. We would sit together, two civilized women, sipping our tea. What could possibly be so wrong about the world that a fresh spot of tea couldn't heal?"

Dr. Krystle Nakoa

Chapter Thirty-four

Dr. Krystle Nakoa breezed into the reception room in black palazzo pants and a flowing deep purple batik-print tunic. Long silver earrings dangled from her earlobes. "C'mon back, Karen."

"Thanks for seeing me. I know my appointment's not until Friday," Karen said.

"My schedule hardly ever flows in a predictable line. What's up?"

Karen settled into the wicker loveseat and drew her legs underneath her. "I'm having a rough go of it lately."

"I can take one look at your eyes and tell that. Not sleeping? Or is it the chemo?"

"Both." Karen shifted her weight and the wicker creaked in reply. "I knew what was in store with the chemo. Certainly I didn't look forward to it, but at least I knew what to expect." Karen pointed to her head. "Hair's history, again."

Krystle smiled. "At least it's not cold outside. My scalp actually chapped."

"Small favors. Guess I should be grateful for those."

"Sometimes they're all we get." Krystle tilted her head. "I get the sense that's not all."

Karen rubbed her burning eyes. "I'm having nightmares again, only this time I can't recall them. I wake up shouting with sweat pouring off me. Scares my parents half to death."

"You tried painting? That brought the cave dream images into clearer focus."

"All I could see was blackness. Sometimes, I feel like a bratty child. I actually threw a temper tantrum when I couldn't get through to whatever crap's buried inside of me."

"Really? Tell me." The counselor pitched gently back and forth in the wicker rocker.

"I attacked a canvas I was attempting to paint on. Jabbed it full of holes with the pointy end of a brush. Slammed it to the ground and literally ripped it to shreds."

Krystle chuckled. "Nothing like a little anger venting to purge the soul. I kicked a door in."

"You're kidding."

"Nope. Broke my big toe. Can't splint toes, I found out. It swelled to three times its normal size. Turned purple and blue. Had to be taped to its neighbors for a few weeks. Felt like a big hunk of meat. I couldn't wear any cute shoes for nearly two months."

Karen smiled. "Thanks, Krystle. Just when I feel like I'm some kind of nut case, you make me feel normal."

Krystle's eyebrows shot up. "Don't go there, Karen. Normal people worry me." She stood. "Want some tea? It's Red Zinger. I have tupelo honey."

"Sure."

She returned with two pottery mugs. "Shall we delve into this recurring nightmare?"

Karen shrugged. "How?"

"Hypnosis."

Karen sipped the rich, flavored tea. "You think it will work on me?"

"Don't see why not. You can visualize easily. You can go to your safe place, then I'll guide you to the memory. Sometimes you can access things not available on a conscious level with hypnosis. By my suggesting you view the memory as a detached onlooker, you can usually experience it without the trauma of feeling the corresponding emotions."

Karen ran her hand over her bald head. "At this point, I'm willing to try just about anything to get some sleep."

Krystle led her through a practiced series of relaxation suggestions. Karen's breathing became deep and even and her head dropped forward.

The log cabin great room appeared in Karen's vision. She crossed the wooden plank floor to a marshmallow-soft chair covered in worn denim. The cats hovered nearby. Tequila crouched on one arm rest, purring contentedly. Taizer flopped across her feet.

Krystle's soft voice blended with low-volume soothing music. "You are calm and relaxed. The dream images from previous nights come to you. Images that can do no harm. Simply allow yourself to observe from a safe distance, as if you were watching a movie. Your breathing is deep and even. Your body—totally relaxed. When you are ready, tell me what you see."

"I'm walking. A little uphill—not much. There's no light. Anywhere." Karen squeezed her eyelids tightly shut. "Are my eyes open? Feels like they are, but still I can't see."

Karen breathed deeply, then said, "I'm not alone. Something, or someone, is ahead of me. Menacing." Her voice grew stern. "I know you're there! I can sense you!" She was silent for a moment. "A dim flicker of light up ahead. Like a candle or lantern. I move faster now. My skin tingles." Karen wrapped her arms around her midsection.

Krystle's voice: "Allow the images to play back for you to view. No need to feel the emotions they evoke. You are safe. You are safe."

"Safe," Karen echoed. "A room, a rock cavern . . . cold." She shivered and hugged her arms tighter around her chest. "A scent in the air. Perfume?" She sniffed, her chin tilted upward. "Where are you? Let me see you!"

"From deep within, anger—pure white and hot. It's bubbling to the surface." Karen's hands curled into fists. She clenched her teeth together so hard, the muscles of her face trembled with the strain.

"Detach from the images, Karen. Deep breaths," Krystle's calm voice urged.

"The perfume. Familiar, but faint. Tropical flowers with a spicy undertone. Stronger now, more pungent. Almost choking." Karen rocked back and forth.

"Talk to me, Karen. What do you see?"

Karen focused on a spot in the deep darkness—the origin of the scent. A figure stood in the shadows. "Come out! Let me see you!" She suppressed a rising wave of fear and anger. "Please—come out."

A tall woman stepped into the dim circle of yellow light. Beautiful, her chin held at a haughty angle, blue eyes glinting. Long blonde hair drawn severely into a single tight ponytail. Tailored clothes, diamond studs on her ear lobes.

Karen drew a sharp intake of breath. The emotion bubbling from the figure was a toxic mixture of fear, anger, and pain: the jilted lover, the one left behind. Karen began to weep, tears rolling down her cheeks in a steady stream.

"As I count backward from five to one, you will emerge. Five, four . . . breathing deeply . . . three, two . . . your awareness returning to this safe place . . . one. Open your eyes." Krystle handed her a tissue. "When you're ready, you can share with me if you would like."

Karen opened her eyes and took a shaky breath. "Mary Elizabeth. The person in the dream was Mary Elizabeth Kensington. I've dealt with the dragon of cancer. Now it seems she's stepped up for a turn."

"When I'm down with a bad chest cold, Lucille does something my own dear mother used to do for me. First, she makes up a little warm tonic water and makes me drink it all—that's sipping whiskey, watered down, with just a bit of honey and lemon: comfort in a cup. Then she smears great big gobs of Vicks VapoRub on my chest and covers it with a warmed mammy cloth. Whew! The scent of that warm camphor drifts from my chest and opens my head up. Course, Mama didn't use Vicks—that came along a few years later. She made up some other concoction, but it had much the same scent and effect. As for Lucille's liquor mix, it puts me right to sleep. Don't believe the Good Lord minds it used for medicinal purposes."

Reverend Thurston Jackson

Chapter Thirty-five

Will Cooke snoozed through the national evening news in a La-Z-Boy leather recliner, his bare feet propped up.

His wife, Sharon, jostled his arm. "Honey, wake up. Look!"

He grunted and yawned. Sharon pointed to the big screen plasma high definition television.

"Isn't that the Truman woman who used to work for you?"

Will snapped the recliner upright and stared unblinking at the monitor.

"Turn it up!"

"An arrest has been made in the suspected terrorist mail attack at *National Informant's* offices," the announcer said.

Will whistled. "I'll be damned."

Two armed officers led the hand-cuffed, bubble-headed blonde down the front steps of the duplex office building to an awaiting cruiser. The final frame showed a frowning, tearful Trisha Truman peering through the rear window.

" . . . evidence linking Miss Patricia Truman to the suspected mail tampering plot. She will be held without bail. In other news . . . "

Sharon shook her head. "I'm certainly glad she's not working for the station anymore."

Will grabbed the phone headset. "Looks like she's really stepped in it this time. I'd best call my people."

He knew it wouldn't be too long before the press came sniffing around Georgia Metro.

In the dream, Karen's safe room looked the same: inviting furniture, sleeping cats, gleaming polished wood, and the muffled trill of birds outside the tall windows. Except for Mary Elizabeth Kensington, who paced the woven rag rug in front of the hearth.

"What are you doing here?" Karen asked.

Mary Elizabeth stopped and cocked her head. "You invited me, remember?"

Karen shook her head. Had she really sounded so irritatingly arrogant? Small wonder she had so few close friends in Atlanta. She plopped into the denim chair and propped her feet on the matching ottoman. "Take a load off, Mary. Obviously, you and I need to hash a few things out. That *is* why you're here."

Mary Elizabeth glared at her double, then chose a wooden rocking chair. "You can't just pretend I never existed, Karen." She spat Karen's name out, a hard edge to her voice.

Mary Elizabeth glanced around the spacious room. "A bit too earthy for my tastes, this place. Looks like you're expecting Elly Mae Clampett to drop by."

Karen smiled. "I like it. Suits me perfectly. Your taste in furnishings is too patrician for me."

"*Refined.* Suppose this means you'll be ditching the antiques at the townhouse, then?"

Karen shrugged. "Haven't really given it much thought. Now that you mention it—"

Mary Elizabeth snatched a throw pillow from the couch and hurled it toward her, missing by inches. "You bitch!" She ducked her head and began to cry. The sound ripped through Karen's soul. She awakened in a sticky, cold sweat.

Joe Fletcher peered into the darkness. He reached over and brushed his sleeping wife's shoulder, then eased from his side of the bed. The nights had taken on a predictable pattern: exhaustion by nine thirty and wide-eyed at three a.m. When was the last time he had slept the night through without chemical help? As he slipped down the hall, the sound of muffled weeping emanated from behind his daughter's closed door. Joe rapped softly. "Karen? Honey?" He opened the door a crack. Karen was huddled on the bed cradling a pillow. "Baby? What is it? You feeling sick at your stomach?"

Karen reached for her father and curled into his embrace. "Oh Daddy, I'm such a mess."

Joe rocked back and forth, patting her on the back, much as he had when she was a wounded little girl. "You want to talk about it?" His voice was soft.

Karen's nose dripped. She snuffled and grabbed a tissue. "Not really."

"I was on my way to the kitchen. Why don't we go find some of that tea Pinky made for you? Unless your mother's eaten them, there should be a few ginger cookies left." He kissed the top of her bald head.

Arm in arm, they walked quietly down the hallway.

"Daddy," Karen said when she was seated with her cup. "I'm so sorry for everything."

"Oh, honey. I hope you'll get past feeling guilty for all of this. That's what families are for. You've just hit a bad spot. We'll make it through."

The Jacksons' modest brick ranch-style house on Wire Road was surrounded by a thick well-manicured lawn. A row of clipped boxwood hedges lined the gravel circular driveway and property lines. Patches of seasonal flowers stood beneath the windows. Karen parked and sat for a moment before leaving the car.

"Hi, Karen. Come on in." Lucille Jackson welcomed her into a cozy living room furnished with a pastel floral-upholstered sofa and matching chairs.

"I've made a fresh pitcher of tea. Will you join me?"

"That would be nice." Karen glanced around the comfortable room. Except for a handful of religious icons, little pointed to the occupation of the owners. She walked over to a wall filled with framed family photos.

"Only three of those children are mine and Thurston's," Lucille said as she placed a silver tray on a glass table. "That's the blessing of being in the Lord's service. Many, many children in our lives. Of course, now we get to enjoy their children." She smiled. "No time to get lonely."

Karen accepted a tall glass of iced tea. "Must be a good feeling, that sense of community."

Lucille crossed her hands on her lap. "You said you needed to talk. Wouldn't you be more comfortable speaking with the Reverend? He is the trained counselor, after all." She raised one hand. "Not that I mind, understand."

Karen perched on the edge of a high-backed chair. "Somehow, it was you I was drawn toward."

Lucille's white eyebrows arched. "Oh?"

"If I can find a way to explain." Karen sighed. "I'm already seeing a professional counselor, and she's helping a great deal—with some things." She stood and paced. "My grandmother, from what I can recall, was always so . . . content . . . about everything. She seemed to just rise above problems. Had such a grip on things—how she felt, what she believed." She turned to face Lucille. "I don't know you well, Mrs. Jackson—"

"Please, call me Lucille."

"Lucille. You seem to possess the same quality Piddie did. A quiet spirituality. And I know you were her friend."

Lucille smiled. She absently tugged a stray sprig of white hair and secured it with a tortoise-shell comb. "Piddie Longman was one of the best people I have ever known."

Karen frowned. "I'm having a lot of trouble. Not just with the chemotherapy. It's like . . . there's a big hole inside of me. I feel so empty."

"You're having what Thurston calls a spiritual crisis," Lucille said. "Very stressful life situations can bring one on—make you doubt yourself, your choices." She paused briefly. "I've been in your shoes, Karen."

"Cancer?"

"No, no. I've been blessed with good health for the most part. Thurston, too. Other than a tinge of rheumatism when the weather's bad, we do passingly well."

Karen sat down. "What happened, if you don't mind me asking?"

"It was such a long time ago." Lucille gazed into space, remembering. "I was thirty-seven, pregnant with my fourth baby. Oh, I was so excited. I do so love children! There were a number of years between my third and that final pregnancy. Almost ten."

Lucille's brown eyes watered. "I knew it was a girl. That was before all the tests they have now. I just felt her little spirit filling me up inside." She fished a small handkerchief from her dress pocket and dabbed the corners of her eyes. "Look at me. I'm sorry to well up over it. You'd think after all these years . . . "

Karen leaned over and rested her hand on Lucille's wrinkled arm. "Please, don't apologize. I cry at the drop of a hat these days."

"I was about two weeks out from delivering. Had her little bed all ready. Had sewed up a passel of little dresses." She gave a short laugh. "Heaven knows what I'd of done if the baby had been a boy—and he lived."

The tip-tap of a walnut wall clock punctuated the silence.

"What happened?"

"She stopped moving. I wasn't too worried at first. Babies quit shuffling around so much toward the last few days. Reckon it's too crowded for them. But soon, I knew. Something terrible had happened. She left me. Went straight up to Heaven and back to God's arms before I ever held her in mine."

"I'm so sorry."

Lucille's gaze met hers. "That's when I lost my faith, Karen. I was so mad at God for stealing my baby girl. Here I was, a preacher's wife—expected to minister to the flock right along with my husband, care for the folks who looked to us for strength—and all I felt inside was a deep, abiding anger. I had a hole big as the universe in my soul."

Karen asked in a soft voice, "How did you—?"

"Get past it? One second at a time. One foot in front of the other, day after day. I still had a family to take care of. Thank goodness for that. Your grandmother helped me a lot during that black time. She had a lot of hardship in her life, too. Lost two babies. She knew what hell I was fighting my way through. Piddie would listen to my ranting hour upon hour—holding my shaking hands, urging me to keep on." Lucille nodded. "Your grandmother was one of the most deeply spiritual people I have ever known. My Thurston often says she had him beat, hands down, and that he'll be lucky to clean the floors in her mansion when he gets to Heaven."

"I've never been one to go to church, much," Karen said.

Lucille shook her finger. "It's not church that makes a person spiritual, Karen. Big difference between being religious and being spiritual. Lots of folks can thump the Bible and quote scriptures till they're red in the face. Doesn't amount to much." She placed one hand over her heart. "True spirituality comes from here: in the way a person treats other folks, watches out for the weak—children, animals, the elderly, the afflicted. How he or she treats people on a daily basis, not just on Sundays."

Lucille spread her arms wide. "God's house is the whole wide world—not a building with cushioned pews and fancy stained glass windows. He lives in every rock, plant, animal, sunrise and sunset. And there are many, many ways to Him—not just one."

Karen sat, mesmerized by the gentle words of the diminutive black woman with the compassionate countenance.

Lucille smiled. "The trick is: not being too proud to ask Him for help." She shook her head. "And that doesn't mean polishing the front pew every time the church opens its doors."

"Piddie never measured anything. When I finally managed to write the recipe down, I had to stop her every time she added a handful of this or that, and figure out how much she'd put in. Still, mine never tastes quite the same. She added love to her cooking. Suppose that doesn't come from a box."

Elvina Houston

Piddie Longman's Chicken 'n' Dumplin's

1 (2 ½ to 3 pound) whole chicken
4 cups water
salt and pepper to taste

2 cups all-purpose white flour
3 Tablespoons shortening
1 teaspoon salt
¼ cup water

In a soup pot with a lid, place the chicken, salt, pepper and water. Bring to a boil, then reduce heat to simmer. Cook until the meat is tender, about an hour.

Let cooked chicken cool, then take the meat off the bones and cut up into bite-size chunks. Discard the skin and bones. Skim the excess fat off the broth. Return the chicken pieces to the pot. Simmer over low heat while you make the dumplings.

In a medium mixing bowl, cut shortening into the flour and salt. Stir in ¼ cup water (more if needed) and mix well with your hands to form soft dough. Roll dough out on a floured surface. Dust the ball with flour to keep from sticking to your rolling pin. With the rolling pin, flatten dough until very thin. Using a knife, slice flattened dough into long strips, then cut crossways so that each dumpling is about three or four inches long. Drop the strips, one at a time, into the simmering broth. (Other than to create a spot for the next dumpling, Piddie told me it was important not to stir the mixture. This will make the dumplings fall apart, and you'll end up with a lumpy mess.) Simmer for ten minutes with the lid off. Then, put the lid on and simmer for about ten minutes more. Serve warm. Sometimes, Piddie would hard-boil a couple of eggs and cut them up to add to the dumplings after they had simmered. Either way, it is the best of Southern cooking you will find!

Chapter Thirty-six

The small gray squirrel perched at the end of the Piddie Longman memorial bench, twitching.

"Don't shake your dang nervous self to death, now. I ain't gonna do you no harm." Elvina rolled a couple of shelled peanuts away from her. The squirrel nibbled cautiously, keeping a careful eye trained her way. "I'm sorry I don't have any of the kind with shells. You like those best, I do believe. I'll get you some at the Walmart tomorrow. Meantime, make yourself satisfied with these." She rested her index finger against her chin. "Salt don't hurt squirrels, does it? 'Cause these are lightly salted."

The squirrel stared at her, unblinking.

"What would you know about salt, anyways? You better be glad you're living here behind the day spa. If you were at my house, Buster would run you clean off the porch!"

Elvina dumped a handful of peanuts on the bench. "Here, I ain't got time to fool with you this morning. I haven't even talked to my friend yet."

She folded her hands in her lap after she brushed away the papery peanut coatings and salt dust.

"Morning, Piddie. I know I'm starting to come near to chicken-thirty every day, but the heat's starting to build earlier and earlier. I just can't tolerate it like I used to. Remember when we didn't have air conditioning? Lawsy, I don't know how we made it through the long, hot summers back then. Lots of fanning and iced lemonade, I reckon.

"Angelina Palazzolo's younguns have all piled in on her this week. All six with the grandyounguns to boot! Brings the total to sixteen. Law, how she keeps a sane head amidst it all, I'll never know. All of them, nice as can be, though. She invited me over for lasagna dinner a couple of nights ago; I forgot to tell you. Had homemade garlic rolls, too. I ate till I near about popped. And they all talk at oncest, each one louder and louder trying to be heard over the rest. Eat and pass food, and the red wine was flowing freely. I learned real fast to get right in there and carry on with the best of them. Angelina fixed these little pastries for dessert—cannoli." Elvina whistled. "G-double-O-D, good! I was full as a tick from dinner, but I managed to eat one with a cup of coffee."

She glanced heavenward. "Let's see . . . Pinky and Wanda got back from Pennsylvania. Wanda is all a-buzz about visiting Hershey. Said it was a chocolate-lover's paradise, and that even the street lamps were shaped like Kisses. They rode on up to Niagara Falls, it being their honeymoon and all. Stopped at vineyards along the way and tasted all kinds of wine. Brought us a few bottles back to try. Now, I'm not much to drink, except for the hard lemonade you and me used to have during football games, but I do like a little glass of wine on occasion. Hear it's good for your heart."

Elvina smiled. "Wedding must've inspired Bull. That's Mandy's beau, remember? He gave Mandy an engagement ring a couple of days after, and she's been a'shoving that little diamond-dust band in front of everybody's face. Melody is hoping that J. T. will get bit by the bug, too."

She shook her head. "Your granddaughter is still battling through her chemo and radiation. Evelyn says Karen went to see Lucille and seems to be a little more contented since. Lucille has that way about her. Karen sent D. J. on back to Atlanta, but there's still a flame to be fanned there. I hope it all works out.

"That Simpy fella is keeping regular company with Stephanie whenever he's in town. I didn't take much to him at first—thought he was one of them rock 'n' roll long-hair types. Into drugs and all. But oncest I got to know him a bit, I got past the ponytail. He's okay, and funny as they come. He's back up in Atlanta, too, for now. He comes and films for a few days, then goes home. Steph mopes around with her bottom lip hanging clean to her waist when he leaves. What will happen there?

"Hattie's giving a beginner's class on how to do that Reiki stuff. I signed up. What the heck? If I can use it to help my arthritis aches and pains, I'm willing to give it a go."

Elvina scratched her head. "Reckon that's about all the local news worth telling. I ain't gonna report what goes on in the rest of the world. Too dang depressing. Besides, we got our own to worry over. And that's a full-time job, I'll tell you!"

Karen stared at the canvas. The background sketch was complete, but she couldn't call up an appropriate image for the focal point. "Great. The one thing I can do to calm my brain, and now I'm blocked."

She squared her shoulders, picked up a charcoal pencil, and allowed her hand to draw without consciously controlling the strokes. The silhouette of a woman appeared. "What the—?"

She sat back and took a long sip of herbal tea. Two chickadees dipped and dove at the feeder by the patio, fighting for dominance.

"Okay," she said. "Show me."

She picked up the pencil. A mirror image of the first silhouette took form. The women stood nose to nose, one slightly thinner, but otherwise identical in features.

Karen continued to sketch. The women's hands were entwined. A slight smile played on the thinner twin's mouth. The other's eyes were downcast, looking at something held in their joined hands.

Karen rolled her eyes and laughed. "An olive branch? How corny is that!"

Radiant heat boiled from the asphalt in shimming waves. Except for a few temperature-tolerant workers, people scurried from one air-conditioned cubicle to the next. Angry motorists blasted horns and tempers flared with little provocation. Summer had arrived in the Deep South.

D. J. maneuvered the NSX around a fender-bender cluster and accelerated sharply, anxious to escape downtown Atlanta. He drove toward Lake Lanier, a peaceful respite in the rolling hills north of the city. Just to get away. Stare at his navel, slack-jawed, for a few hours. Find peace.

He felt the grip of two powerful emotions: intense, giddy, new love and profound guilt. Ridiculous, really, since both were tied to the same woman.

As if an imaginary boundary existed between the urban heat and the countryside, the air temperature dropped noticeably as soon as he reached the lake. D. J. pulled the Acura into the shade of a thick stand of tulip poplars. A well-marked trail led to the edge of the water and a small grassy clearing with a wooden bench. He gathered a handful of smooth flat stones and skipped them one by one across the mirrored surface of the lake.

To have such a bizarre problem—in love with two different women, yet only one in reality. The day before, as he tended the potted plants at his fiancée's upscale townhouse, D. J. pondered the strange love triangle in which he had become entangled. He missed Mary Elizabeth Kensington—aloof, prim and proper, just shy of complete bitch status. But this new woman, Karen Fletcher, she had stolen his affections in ways his British fiancée never could.

Would Mary E. spend endless hours talking about feelings, childhood dreams, and fears? No. Would she possess the gentle self-effacing Southern humor? Hardly. The free-spirited, piss-and-vinegar attitude? Not Mary Elizabeth's style. Still, when he thought back on their relationship, Donald noted glimpses of Karen Fletcher beneath Mary Elizabeth's frosty veneer. Kindness to animals, the elderly, the disenfranchised: gestures of empathy when she thought no one noticed. In truth, Karen Fletcher wasn't a stranger.

How did this happen to him? Love-sick, love-struck, slobbering devotion. Willing to crawl miles thorough any kind of crap just to be near her.

"You just thought you were a hopeless idiot, D. J.," he said. "There's no telling what depths you'll sink to."

So, where was the guilt coming from? He felt as if he was sidestepping out the back door under cover of darkness, the sleaze-bag boyfriend who would chase any skirt, any time.

D. J. shook his head. "This is ridiculous!" He pitched a stone with such force, it skipped six times before landing with a loud plop. "Mary E.'s gone, and she's not coming back." He stared at the concentric circles of ripples radiating from the stone's last hit. "And I love Karen Fletcher."

There. He had said it aloud. Sad thing, he would never be able to say goodbye to Mary Elizabeth. D. J. chuckled. "Karen, hon. What say you turn into Mary E. one last time so I can dump her properly, and you and I can live happily forever after?"

He closed his eyes. The drama of the past few months read like a plot line from a daytime soap opera. No, in a soap opera, Karen would turn out to be his long-lost first cousin; no need to go that far.

D. J. sat on the park bench and stared at the water until the first fingers of sunset air-brushed the horizon peach and orange. Inside, something important shifted. When he returned to his car, a skip returned to his step.

A few houses down, he spotted a *For Sale by Owner* sign and slowed to a crawl. A farmhouse-style log home stood by the lake's edge. He whipped a U-turn and pulled into the tree-lined gravel driveway.

"My mama was an angel dropped down from Heaven. Really. Everything she cooked, she poured love into. Can't think of one dish I could single out. All of her cooking gave me comfort. Just sitting in her little kitchen with all of us kids swarming around her feet, listening to her hum underneath her breath while she was stirring a pot of stew or soup—I can see it in my mind's eye. A feeling of being held in her warm arms cloaks over me."

Jon "Shug" Presley

Chapter Thirty-seven

Jon Presley wiped his sneakers on the Triple C's back door mat. "Morning glory," he called out to Wanda, "got the coffee on?"

"I'm here, aren't I? Of course it's on."

He scowled at the mud clinging to the sole of his shoes, removed them, and left them beside the door.

Wanda smiled as she watched her fastidious friend tiptoe across the kitchen in his stocking feet. "Floor's clean, Shug, Don't think you'll muss those white-beyond-belief socks."

Jon rolled his eyes and poured a cup of hot coffee. He topped it off with cream and a packet of artificial sweetener.

"No java at your house this morning?"

Jon shook his head. "Jake's sleeping in. I didn't want to wake him. He gets so little rest." He smiled. "Besides, I haven't seen you in forever, happily-married girl. I hoped you'd be here."

"I'm always here."

"Work builds character, Wanda'loo."

"Right. I'm already a character. I should need this, too?"

Jon settled into the oak chair across the table from her. "You're not your usual effervescent self this morning. You all right?"

Wanda shrugged. "I guess so."

"Tsk, tsk. Honeymoon over, doll? Pinky leave his stinky socks on the floor? What?"

"You kidding? He'd probably be the one to complain about me." She smiled. "I swear to you, if I get up to pee in the middle of the night—which happens more and more the closer I get to fifty—he makes up my side of the bed while I'm gone."

Jon laughed. "The queen of neat has met her match." He tilted his head and studied her. "Really, what is up with you?"

The genuine compassion shining in his gentle brown eyes brought tears to her eyes. "I don't know, Shug. Life is so unfair sometimes." She took a sip of coffee. "Karen was in the spa yesterday afternoon. Melody was going to give her a manicure. Help her feel a little more normal. She can't wear any perfume because of the radiation treatments, and her hair's gone again."

"Anything that helps her feel more feminine is welcome, I'm sure. I see it in my hospice patients all the time. Even if a person is nearing death, she still wants to feel attractive."

Wanda nodded. "Exactly. Melody had just started to work on Karen's nails when Karen turned ten shades of pale and jumped up to run to the bathroom."

"The fumes?"

"I guess. She had to go home." Wanda shook her head. "I feel so bad for her. I don't know her real well, not like Hattie and Mandy do. She's come out a few times with Evelyn to talk over herbal treatments with Pinky. She seems like a pretty decent person."

Jon walked to the kitchen counter and refilled his cup. "Warm-up for you?"

"No. I've had three cups already, thanks."

Jon stood by the bay window. "One thing I've learned over the years, Wanda'loo. Cancer is an equal-opportunity disease. Takes young and old, rich or poor, and doesn't bypass good people for bad." His gaze rested on the hummingbird feeder where two whirring iridescent male birds fought for dominance. "Too bad, really. It would be nice if it would cull out some of the nasty, hateful people—serial killers, child molesters, rapists."

Wanda nodded. "Hmm."

Stephanie breezed into the break room and grabbed the empty coffee urn. "Jeez-o-pete! Y'all could've saved me a cup!"

"Morning to you too, Steph," Jon said. "My fault. I mooched a mug. I'll start a fresh pot just for you."

"You're here awfully early," Wanda said.

"Ain't it the dang truth?" Stephanie said. "I'm giving prenuptial massages to Michael King and Jessie Kahn. They're getting married at three this afternoon." She turned to leave, calling over her shoulder. "Let me know when the coffee's done. I sure could use a cup. Either that, or I'm crawling on the massage table myself for a nap."

"Know what would be good for both of us?" Jon asked Wanda after Stephanie left.

She grinned. "It is legal?"

"In most countries. Why don't I call up Julie at the Homeplace and order up a couple of her gut-bomb killer cheeseburgers, couple of orders of fries, and we'll take ourselves out to the lake for a little picnic at lunch?"

Wanda smiled. "I'd really like that. Talk some trash. Eat some fat. My kind of afternoon delight."

Jon washed out the mug and deposited it in the dishwasher. "Great. I have a few errands to run. Pick you up around, say, eleven-thirty?"

Wanda winked. "As long as you don't plan on taking advantage of me. I'm a married woman now."

Jon kissed her on the top of the head on his way to the door. "Can't fathom anyone, straight or gay, has ever taken advantage of you, Wanda'loo."

"You idiot!" Hattie braked suddenly and cursed under her breath as she negotiated the snarled traffic in front of Tallahassee Memorial Hospital. The Mercedes driver who nearly sideswiped her SUV whipped into the drive-in teller line of the corner bank. Hattie glanced at her passenger. "Sorry, Karen."

"You didn't do anything wrong. That butt hole did. Too bad I'm not my usual nauseated self this morning. I could've followed him and barfed on his precious black sedan."

Hattie focused her attention on traffic. "At the risk of sounding like everyone else who asks you this, how are the radiation treatments going?"

Karen shrugged. "The sessions themselves are not an issue. The therapists are fabulous, even when I'm being a complete and total bitch. And believe me, there have been many mornings I have been. I just lay there a few minutes and it's done." She pulled her blouse slightly to one side to reveal the top edge of the radiation site. "This is what hurts."

The skin was a deep red: the hue of fresh-cut sirloin, the color of fire-hot anger. Hattie glanced over quickly. "Jeez-o-Pete! That looks awful!"

Karen buttoned her blouse. "Like the worst sunburn I ever had. Like I've been char-broiled over hot coals on a spit they forgot to rotate often enough."

"Don't you have anything to put on it?"

"Some cream the doctors gave me. The aloe Pinky sent me works best though, especially if I keep it in the fridge."

At the intersection of Magnolia Drive and Park Avenue, Hattie and Karen watched as an elderly couple maneuvered the crosswalk. The gentleman steered a wheelchair-scooter. His bent, white-haired companion hitched a ride on the back, standing with her hands resting on his shoulders.

Hattie smiled. "That's about the sweetest thing I've seen in a while."

Karen swallowed hard. The pressure of intense emotion pressed on her chest, squeezing, making her breathing difficult and labored.

Hattie's brows knit together as she entered the driveway to Dr. Nakoa's office. "You okay? You look a little pale."

"Sure." Karen opened the door as the SUV rolled to a stop and hurried toward the double doors.

"Karen?" Hattie called from the opened window. "I'll be back in an hour to pick you up." Before backing away, she watched her cousin slip quickly into the clinic.

Karen knocked once, then burst into Krystle's private office. The counselor looked up from the stack of papers on her desk. "What—?"

No words came to Karen. The pain boiled from her in dry heaves, shaking her body. Krystle wrapped her arms around the sobbing woman's shoulders and guided her gently to a soft chair and knelt by her until the crying subsided.

"Rough morning?" Krystle offered a box of tissues.

Karen blew her nose and snuffled. "God, this is so ridiculous." She closed her eyes and heaved a shuddering sigh.

Krystle patted her on the shoulder. "Let me grab a couple of cups of chamomile tea, and we'll talk."

By the time the counselor returned, Karen felt more composed.

"Here? Or on the porch? It's not too hot just yet, and I can turn on the overhead fan."

Karen rose. "Outside. I'd like that."

On the porch, Karen pitched back and forth in a rocker, describing the simple scene she had witnessed. "Just two old people, taking care of each other. I don't know, it set me off. Hell, I cry over McDonald's commercials anymore."

"Why do you think it bothered you?" Krystle's loose hair fell in dark waves as she leaned forward to listen.

"I want that. I want to grow old with the man I love, with Donald. I want to be able to be the old lady hanging onto his shoulders. I want to live, damn it, to be incredibly old and full of memories." With each statement, Karen pounded a clenched fist on the rocker's armrest.

Krystle smiled, her eyes glistening. "This is wonderful, Karen."

"I'm sobbing my eyes out and ranting and raving like a complete lunatic, and you think it's wonderful? Who's crazier here, you or me?"

Krystle shook her head. "I've been seeing you for, what, a month and a half now?"

Karen nodded.

"This is the first time I've heard you say what you want. Not what your mother and father, your boss, Donald, or the rest of your family want, but what *Karen* wants. Don't you see? You're on the way out of this. Now you're clear on what you're fighting for."

"I want to live," Karen said in a soft voice.

"I'm so proud of you." Krystle jumped up, sending the rocker into motion. "This calls for a celebration! I have a pecan pie in the break room. One of my friends brought it by. Can your stomach take it?"

"Bring it on. I'll sure give it a try." She held up two fingers an inch apart. "A small piece."

The flavors of sweet, dark cane syrup and toasted pecans filled Karen's mouth. She closed her eyes and moaned. "This is so good. Mama would just die if she knew I was eating this."

"Devil sugar?" Krystle grinned. "Feeding the hungry little cancer cells."

"Right." Karen cocked her head. "You know, I would hate for my epitaph to read: she never did a thing bad to herself. "

"And still died anyway," Krystle added.

They laughed. For a moment, friends more than counselor and client. Krystle wiped the flaky crust crumbs from the corners of her mouth. "Coming up on your last week of radiation treatments, right?"

"This time next week, I'll be a free woman. Well, except for two more chemo treatments. At least I can lose the permanent one-sided sunburn."

Karen smiled. "It's kind of funny, you know. I've made friends with some of the other patients coming in for radiation. I see the same faces, day after day. At first, I was pretty freaked out at the side effects some of them had—the nausea, feeding tubes, really severe skin burns. But I had to remember that not everyone was being treated for the same kind of cancer. Even so, we were all in it together, and I've made a few friends that I hope to keep up with."

"Comrades in arms, as it were," The counselor said. "Have you given any thought to your job and Atlanta?"

"A little." Karen frowned and watched the squirrels darting back and forth to the birdfeeders. "Have to face returning to the townhouse at some point."

"To live?"

Karen shook her head. "Absolutely not. I have no desire to return to that place. Donald and I have discussed listing with a realtor. I just need to decide what to do with the furnishings."

"Out with the old?"

"For the most part, yes." Karen chewed absently on her lower lip. "Guess I'll see how I feel when I'm standing at the door."

"Ah," Krystle said, "yet another threshold."

"My mama was a fine Southern cook, but when I think of comfort food, my thoughts stray to my granny. Every year at Christmas, she would make me my very own pecan pie. Just for me! She gave the family divinity or fudge, and of course, she made other pies for after dinner, but she always made one whole pie as her special gift to me. I've been in the restaurant business for many more years than I care to count, and I don't know too many foods I don't like. But my granny's pecan pie holds a place in my heart."

Mr. Bill, owner of The Homeplace Restaurant

Chapter Thirty-eight

Ghostly mists of morning moisture curled in pools around the flower beds in Joe Fletcher's backyard garden. Two scarlet cardinals quarreled over the hanging birdfeeder, and a family of fox squirrels rooted for buried acorns beneath the live oak tree.

"Morning, honey." Joe leaned down and kissed his daughter on the cheek. "Brought you a fresh sweet potato biscuit. Don't tell your mama. This one is made with real sugar."

Karen glanced up from her canvas and smiled. "Thanks, Daddy."

"You're up and at it awfully early." He settled onto a patio chair and sipped from a tall pottery mug.

Karen sketched as she talked. "I had a dream last night. Not a new thing, they seem to come most every time I fall asleep anymore. This one was so vivid. Exhilarating."

Joe leaned over and studied the charcoal rendering. "Looks like some kind of boat?"

Karen nodded. "I finally got around to reading that book you told me about—the one on dragon boat racing. Must've made an impression on me."

"I see." He gestured with his index finger. "This end . . . I can make out the bow of the boat." He leaned back. "You got all this from that book? I don't recall seeing any pictures with the text."

"They were well described." She shrugged. "The actual boats may not come close to this, but it's how I envision them."

The sketch showed two long rowboats. The lead craft was clearly defined. The bow was fashioned as a fierce dragon head with a flowing mane, lips curled back to reveal rows of jagged teeth. The stern resembled a spiked tail tipped with a dagger-like point. Ten rows of indistinct figures pulled at the oars. The woman who sat at the bow facing backward held a drum, her long hair curled over her face. The woman at the stern was her mirror-image—a rudder in hand, intently focused on the waters ahead. A second boat of similar design loomed in the shadows, slightly behind the first.

"The colors and sensations were so striking," Karen said. "I could feel the bite of the wind, feel the moisture on my lips. I was at once the woman at the bow and the steersman on the stern, watching for the clearest path to victory."

"Suppose that signifies you and Mary Elizabeth?"

"Once a counselor always a counselor, huh Daddy?" Karen smiled. "You're probably right. She seems to sneak into my dreams and paintings more and more."

"You talk this over with Dr. Nakoa?"

"In exhausting detail. Trust me." She pinched off a section of buttered biscuit and popped it into her mouth. "Umm. I wasn't hungry, but this tastes good."

"I'm glad. Your mother—she worries when you don't eat."

Karen sighed. "I know. I'm trying. I just don't have much of an appetite."

Joe allowed the silence to fill the space for a few moments before he spoke. "I heard you mention to Jake that you were planning on going back to Atlanta soon."

"Yes. Before the next round of chemo. Donald's picking me up at the airport on Tuesday."

"Sure you're ready?"

"To move back? No. I won't do that until after all my treatments are over. But I need—I want—to go to the townhouse and start to somehow figure out what goes and what stays."

"You're going to sell it?"

"Definitely. I don't want to live there anymore. It's going on the market as soon as possible."

"You know what's best for you, sugar. You'll always have a place here with us." He stood. "Do you want to go to church with your mama and me this morning?"

Karen picked up the charcoal pencil and resumed the sketch. "Elvina's picking me up at ten-thirty for the Morningside AME service. Some kind of special music, I think."

Joe smiled. "Your grandmother would be proud. She always maintained they had a direct line to God."

In the dream, Karen stood barefoot in the townhouse foyer, her feet chilled by the cool Italian tile.

"Well, let's do it." Donald's voice sounded behind her.

"Don't rush me." She turned around. No one stood behind her.

Karen ducked her chin and clenched her fists into hard white balls. "Fine, I'll do this alone then."

She walked into the kitchen and began to open and close cabinets, making notes on the contents on a small yellow lined pad. Next, the dining room with the rich mahogany table and chairs glistening in the reflected light of a crystal chandelier.

"This all goes. Too formal. Too prissy." She added the furniture to the sell column. The living room furnishings she noted as well, along with listing the framed artwork and sculptures. When Karen stepped into the master bedroom, she met the fierce glare of Mary Elizabeth Kensington. "What are you doing here?"

Mary Elizabeth stood with her feet firmly planted, arms crossed over her chest, her hair drawn back into a tight ball at the nape of her neck. "I live here. How dare you come barging in with your damn note pad!" She picked up a Waterford vase. "How about this? Remember it? Five hundred dollars of precious, hard-earned cash."

Mary Elizabeth swung her arm in a high arc. The crystal vase hit the wall to Karen's right and shattered, sending a spray of glass across the hardwood floor.

"Or this?" She grabbed a Ming Dynasty reproduction vase from its stone pedestal and hoisted it overhead before sending it crashing to the floor beneath her feet.

Karen held up one hand and stepped closer. "Wait!"

"Stay away from me, you bitch! How dare you decide what goes forward with us!"

Karen stood, speechless. She watched Mary Elizabeth rip oil paintings from the walls, break an antique mirror, and rip the flocked sheers from the windows. "No! Don't!" Karen called out as her double picked up a jewelry armoire and pitched it toward the window. The panes shattered in slow motion as the chest sailed through. Next, Mary Elizabeth snatched open the door to the closet and began to rip the designer clothing from the racks, heaving armfuls out the broken window. A silk scarf of rainbow colors hung like a limp linguine noodle, speared by a pointed shard of glass.

Then the lights blinked off. Total darkness. Karen strained to detect any hint of illumination. The sounds of glass breaking, heavy furniture slamming into walls, and screamed obscenities emanated from every direction.

When Karen awakened, the sweat-soaked sheets were churned into a strangling body cast. For a moment, she fought rising panic. She forced her breathing to slow and gradually inched from the linen sarcophagus. A wave of nausea washed over her and she dashed to the bathroom.

"Hello, Karen."

"Jake."

"Good thing you're a woman, or Jon would have reason to suspect our nightly clandestine conversations."

"You're getting tired of me calling?"

Jake chuckled. "Absolutely not. Bad night?"

"Another weird dream." She shared the details of the nightmare. "This thing with Mary Elizabeth is really beginning to send me over the edge."

"Thought you went there awhile ago."

Jake heard Karen snort on the other end.

"Funny."

Jake grabbed his cane and walked to the back porch. "I'm not trying to make light of what you're going through, doll. Lord only knows, I've had my share of identity crises. You remind me of something I heard in a class I took one time on romance novel writing."

"You write? I didn't know that."

"Not anymore. That was a few years back. I was god-awful at it. Anyway, the instructor told us that, when we hit a point in the story where we didn't know how to proceed, that we should torture the heroine."

"And that reminds you of me?"

"In a fashion. Just when I think you're making progress, some ethereal author writes a new element of torment into your life story."

"What can I do to shake my past, Jake? I'm seeing a shrink, for God's sake. We've picked my life to pieces twice over. Still, there must be a part of me that's deeply disturbed."

"Otherwise, the dreams would stop, eh?"

"Uh-huh."

Jake sipped from a mug of herbal tea. "You ever think about allowing Mary Elizabeth to be a part of it all? From what you've told me, most of her antics sound like a spoiled child trying to get attention."

"I'm not sure I get you."

Jake cleared his throat. "Sorry. Allergies. Okay, this British lady's pissed at you for coming along and ripping the expensive Persian rug right out from underneath her feet. You have just, overnight, become someone else—a log-cabin, southern-drawling hick from North Florida, to boot."

The hiss of dead air met his comment.

Jake continued. "Work with me on this, will you? Here's an example. Say, you are in love with this wonderful man, have a home with him, blah, blah, blah, and you die. Your ghost hovers around to check on how your beloved is taking the whole thing. To your surprise, he throws all of your gee-gaws out in the next morning's trash and moves a blonde floozy into his house. Nothing of you remains in his life. Now, if you could stick around and be a thorn in the man's side, wouldn't you?"

"Wait. You're implying Mary Elizabeth is jealous?"

"Perhaps. In a manner of speaking."

"What do you suggest, oh great swami?"

Jake chuckled. "I would try making peace with her. She ruled your life for twenty or so years. Maybe she doesn't think she deserves to be thrown out on her British bum. Be considerate with the part of your life she shared. Perhaps, if you don't keep all of the material things she was attached to, you can make sure they go to good homes."

"She did have incredible taste."

"*You* have incredible taste. Remember, she *is* you, when you come right down to it. Maybe if you stop trying to see her as separate, the two of you can bury the hatchet once and for all. If not, I suggest you stock up on prescription sleeping pills."

Maizie Clark's Tea Cakes (Grandma May-May)

½ cup butter, softened
1 cup white sugar
1 egg
1 teaspoon vanilla extract
2 cups all-purpose flour
1 teaspoon baking powder
½ teaspoon baking soda
¼ cup milk or buttermilk

In a medium mixing bowl, cream together butter and sugar until smooth. Beat in egg and vanilla. In a separate bowl, combine flour, baking powder, and baking soda. Beat into the creamed mixture a little at a time, alternating with the milk.

On a greased cookie sheet, drop by rounded spoonfuls, allowing a little room between the dough balls. Bake for 8 to 10 minutes in a preheated 350° oven.

Chapter Thirty-nine

Karen listened for the familiar series of mechanical clicks and beeps overhead. Soothing finger-style guitar sounded through her earpieces. The room: semi-dark. Not a place to fear or hate now. Just a space she had visited Monday through Friday for six weeks. Same routine: undress, cotton gown, being positioned carefully by experienced hands, the radiation session, redress.

On some days, when energy levels approached normal, she visited the local bookstores before returning to Chattahoochee. One of the few places she felt welcome—meandering between rows of fiction—a haven with thousands of opportunities to lose herself in someone else's drama for a few precious moments.

She closed her eyes, savoring the final minutes of solitude. In the reception area, her mother, father, and Simpy waited to share and document the last radiation treatment. Karen imagined her mother's filmed interview. Evelyn would comment on her relief that one phase of follow-up treatment was coming to a close. Life could return to normal. Her father would nod, holding his wife's hand as she wiped a tear.

The door opened. "That's it, Karen." The radiation therapist: Lisa of the soft voice and kind, warm hands. "You're done with us."

Karen swung her legs around to one side and slipped from the table. "I'd love to say it's been fun, but—"

Lisa rolled her eyes. "I know. Nothing personal, right?"

Karen hugged the therapist. "You, Stephen, and Dr. McDowell have made it bearable. Don't think for a second I don't realize that. Thank you. And please tell them for me too, will you?"

The therapist nodded. "I always wish—well, with some patients, anyway—that we could meet under less stressful circumstances." She shrugged. "Best of luck to you, Karen. I hope I get to see you again, just not in here, except for the occasional follow-up visit, of course."

Karen smiled. "Amen, sister."

She took her time getting dressed, relishing the finish line at the end of one set of hurdles. When she stepped into the brightly-lit waiting room, her mother and father stood to greet her. Simpy grabbed the video camera and jockeyed for a good angle. The three Fletchers hugged, only vaguely aware of the nods of approval and smiles around them.

Evelyn Fletcher rummaged in her purse. "Oh, where did I put that list?"

"What list, Mama?" Karen handed her e-ticket confirmation and driver's license to the Delta representative.

"I wrote all the phone numbers down for you in case you need to find me or your father in a hurry." She snapped the purse closed. "I must've left it on the kitchen counter. I swannee! I'd lose my head if it wasn't tied on." Evelyn grabbed a blank baggage identification tag and scribbled. "Here. The spa, your daddy's place, Elvina's, Jake's, Hattie's, and—you can remember the house number?"

"I have most of these programmed into my cell phone already, but if you insist." Karen folded the tag and stuck it into the carry-on bag. "I'll be okay. I wish you'd stop worrying."

"You're just so weak. I should be going with you."

Karen envisioned her mother tearing through the Atlanta townhouse, questioning her every move. "No, no. Please, Mama. Donald will be with me."

Joe rested his hands on his wife's shoulders. "It's okay, Ev. That boy would take a bullet for her, I do believe." He leaned over and kissed Karen on the cheek. "We'll be here to pick you up next week."

"Guess it's just gonna be you and me again, Joe," Evelyn said.

He gathered his wife in his arms and ran one hand across her hair. "I'm all you started with, Mrs. Fletcher."

Evelyn glanced toward the security gate where ticketed passengers stood in line. "Used to be, we could go all the way to the gate with you. I just hate it, all this high-alert business! What it's done to our country."

"I'd strip naked for them if it meant not being blown to bits by some terrorist," Joe said.

Evelyn reached over and smoothed a wrinkle on her daughter's collar. "Don't forget to call us now, the minute you get there."

"I will. I will." Karen extended the handle on the rolling carry-on case. "Bye. Love you."

Evelyn enveloped her in a suffocating embrace and kissed both cheeks. Her father bussed the top of her scarf-wrapped head. Her parents watched until she passed through the security area, waved, and disappeared around the corner in the direction of Gate A-7.

When Karen emerged at the gate, the first person she spotted was her fiancé standing behind an airport wheelchair. Tears formed at the corners of her eyes.

D. J. smiled. "Your chariot, Madam."

"How'd you manage this?" she asked, taking a seat. "They usually don't allow anyone past security without a ticket."

Donald pointed to the clip-on badge. "Special permission. I knew you wouldn't ask for assistance, and it's a long way to baggage claim, even with the people-movers."

"I'm okay, Donald, really." Karen felt irritation budding and forced it down. "You're right, I don't have a lot of excess energy. I feel a bit foolish, but this is probably a good idea."

"You check any luggage?" he asked as he maneuvered the concourse.

"All I have is this carry-on."

On countless occasions, Karen had frequented the Hartsfield International Airport. The rush of humanity never ceased to fascinate her. A steady stream of harried travelers moved in myriad directions: a freeway at rush hour with no rules. Frazzled mothers dragged screaming toddlers and suited businessmen darted between eddies of loiterers at bathroom entrances, food retailers, and departure/arrival monitors. Expressions ranged from bored to bewildered. Snippets of conversations in a dozen languages filled the air, overridden in spots by terse loudspeaker announcements. Karen smiled, recalling the observation her grandmother Piddie had made about the Atlanta airport after the family's trip to Alaska, the place looked for all the world like a kicked-over fire ant hill.

Karen stood on the cold Italian tile. The first thing she noticed was a lingering scent—tropical flowers with a spicy undertone. Mary

Elizabeth's cologne. Something brushed against her cheek and she shivered.

"Man, it's cold in here!" D. J. checked the thermostat in the foyer. "No wonder. I left it on seventy. Sorry. Want me to find a sweater for you?"

Karen shook her head. She walked past the kitchen into the living room. In the dim light, a shadow appeared in one corner. Her same size, same height. She caught her breath and froze in place. The shadow mimicked her stance.

"Mary Elizabeth?" she whispered.

D. J. flipped on the light. The shadow disappeared. "Who you talking to, hon?"

Karen shrugged. "No one."

D. J. clapped his hands together. "Okay if I leave you here and go pick up some boxes? I have a few in the trunk, but the guy at the liquor store has some of those heavy lidded ones he's holding for me."

"Sure, go ahead." Karen offered a weak smile. "I'll be fine, D. J."

Donald kissed her quickly on the lips and started for the door. "Hey, what say I pick up some Chinese take-out on the way back?"

The townhouse was eerily silent after he left. An antique wall clock in the dining room ticked off the seconds. She wandered through the elegantly decorated rooms like a wary intruder.

"This is silly, Karen." She shook her head. "It's your own damn place. You have every right to be here."

She touched a brocade high-back chair, ran her fingers across the buttery leather couch and loveseat. Stopped to admire an original Japanese-inspired watercolor painting in the living room. She stepped onto the porch. The décor—straight from an issue of *Southern Living*—featured cool beach-house shades of sherbet and white with airy rattan furniture and billowy ferns. Music of splashing water tinkled from a nearby fountain.

Karen took a shaky breath. The most intimate part of her town home loomed—the master bedroom. A queen-sized, pillow-top mattress beckoned with layers of coordinating pillows. Rich mahogany shone in the muted light: an armoire, dressing table, two end-tables, and a sleigh-bed frame. Beautiful thick fabrics in jewel tones adorned several pieces, drapes of semi-sheer flocked voile hung at tall windows, and a wool area rug floated atop shining wood floors.

The walk-in closet held organized rows of designer clothing—the trappings of a successful businesswoman: a cedar shelf loaded with shoes in every shade, heavy plastic-wrapped coats and cashmere wraps. Karen hugged a pair of worn running shoes to her chest. The rest belonged to a woman who no longer existed.

Next, she turned her attention to the jewelry armoire. The double doors swung open to a series of small drawers, laden with rows of gold earrings, bracelets, and lapel pins. The bottom drawer held a selection of diamond and gemstone rings in various sizes. Karen slipped one of Mary Elizabeth's favorite bands on her finger and admired her hand.

"This is going to be a little like cleaning out a house after a death," she said aloud. "Help me, Mary. I can't see me wearing your clothing." She glanced down at her thin body. "Wouldn't fit me, anyway. I'll give them away to a good charity. Maybe one of those places where underprivileged women go to find career clothes. You always liked the idea of helping people in need."

Karen looked upward, as if the spirit of the house loomed in the air just above her head. "I want to keep reminders of you, Mary Elizabeth. I think that would be good, don't you? Personal things." She glanced down. "Like this ring. Things you would want to stay with me. Things that have some meaning."

Karen sat on the edge of the soft bedding. "I can't take all of this with me. It wouldn't be healthy. Don't you see? I have to make a new life just for me. But I want to remember you, the person I became when you existed."

She sat for a few minutes, allowing her thoughts to drift back to the hectic mornings when she donned Mary Elizabeth's persona like an expensive theatrical wrap. Up at five a.m. Running two miles in the park. Karen then, thinking her own clandestine thoughts as if in a foreign language. Mary Elizabeth hated exercise. Karen was the one in charge of keeping the physical body in fashion-model shape.

Coming home to freshly-brewed strong coffee. Two cups, black. The morning paper, sprawled on the couch, or outside on the rattan porch swing in pleasant weather. Thinking thoughts of home. Wondering what her parents, her grandmother, her brother, were doing at that very moment.

Then, back inside. Showering. Shaving her legs. Going through the elaborate beauty ritual to transform her girl-next-door features into something more exotic and refined. Putting on the make-up. The clothes. The expensive pumps. Looking in the mirror as her alter-ego emerged. Feeling the Karen-self sink into the background so that the woman she had created could take over and run her life. Pursing her lips to apply a tasteful shade of lipstick. Staring in the mirror at a person so unlike Karen in every way. Finally, the cologne. A strong personalized blend of exotic scents made especially for Mary Elizabeth Kensington.

Her thoughts were interrupted by the buzz of the door bell. She hurried to the front door, peered through the peep-hole, and opened the door.

"Will! Sharon!" She hugged her boss and his wife.

"Hope we're not interrupting," Sharon Cooke said. "We came to help you and D. J. pack. I know how exhausting moving can be."

Karen smiled. In the years she had known her boss's spouse, she had never noticed how kind and motherly her features were, or how the gray-tinged hair soft around her face made her appear worthy of complete trust. "Oh, that would be great." She gestured them inside. "I haven't even begun yet. D. J. went to round up some boxes."

Will jangled his car keys. "We brought a few, too."

Sharon smiled. "How was your trip?"

"Fine. Tiring."

"You just leave the packing up to us," Sharon said, "All you have to do is sit back and motion as to what you want to keep, and what goes. Between the three of us, we should be able to at least put a dent in things this afternoon."

"Talked to D. J. on his cell. Told him to pick up some extra Cashew Chicken and as many egg rolls as he could tote." Will grinned and dropped a stack of folded cardboard boxes on the kitchen floor. "Packing up takes a lot out of a person of my girth."

"I love surprises, Donald. But won't you give me any idea where we're going? I mean, am I dressed appropriately for this place?" She glanced down at the faded blue jeans and plain cotton T-shirt.

D. J. smiled. "You could wear a toga and feel dressed for the spot

I'm taking you, Karen, my love. I promise you—you will feel perfectly at home."

D. J. negotiated the multi-lane Atlanta bypass until he reached the exit for Interstate 85 heading north away from the city.

"Wait." Karen poked him playfully in the shoulder. "Are we going up to the foothills? Kind of late in the day, isn't it?"

D. J. winked. "You'll see. You'll see."

After a few miles, D. J. exited the four-lane expressway on State Road 20 leading toward Lake Lanier.

"You found a new restaurant up here, didn't you? Boy, I leave for a few months and everything changes."

Donald didn't answer. He followed the familiar route to the small park he had frequented many times. Two houses down, he turned into the driveway of a large cypress log home and shut off the engine.

Karen's brows knit together. "What a beautiful house. Looks a lot like the one I want to have one of these days—well, no need to go there. What gives? Do you know these people? Are they expecting us or something?"

"There's a basket in the back. Will you get it for me?" He flipped the trunk release.

Karen shrugged, grabbed the wicker picnic basket, and followed him to the front porch. Donald pulled a set of keys from his pocket.

"Oh, now I get it! You rented this place for a couple of days. How sweet!"

Donald swung the heavy wooden door open wide and flipped the light switch. The massive great room was barren except for a red and white checkered cloth spread in front of the granite fireplace.

"Certainly sparse. Hope there's a bed." Karen walked into the room. "Look at the beams in this room! Can you imagine living in a house like this?" She sat the picnic basket down and wandered into the gourmet kitchen. "My mother would absolutely die to see this kitchen." She opened the cabinets. "Nothing's in here. Donald, is this some kind of wilderness-camping-weekend joke?" She stood like a petulant five-year-old with her lips pushed out in a pout and hands propped on her hips.

"Won't be much here until we move in," he said.

Karen's mouth dropped open.

"Close your mouth. You'll catch flies." D. J. laughed. "Got that one from your mom."

Karen walked over and threw her arms around his neck. "What are you saying, exactly, Donald Peterson?"

"House belongs to a lovely engaged couple from Atlanta. Nice folks, really. She's had a pretty tough go of things here lately. They'll be moving in, shortly."

Karen kissed D. J. hard. "I can't believe you bought this!"

"Hope you're not mad. I had to move fast. It wouldn't have lasted long on the market. I closed on it last Friday. I know I should have consulted you, Karen. Hell, you haven't even said you'd still marry me." He shrugged. "I may be rambling around in this place all alone."

"Not on your life, Donald."

"I'd have to say my Mama's greens were my favorite. Sometimes, turnips with plump purple and white bottoms cooked in. Other times, mustard greens—slightly bitter until she added just a pinch of sugar. Always cooked up with a ham hock to add flavor. She would spoon up a mug of the juice, the pot-liquor, for me to sip on before dinner. That dark green juice held the very essence of the greens. I'd close my eyes as it warmed all the way down to my stomach."

Lucille Jackson

Chapter Forty

"Brought you a hot cinnamon roll. One of your daddy's, but made with Splenda, no sugar." Evelyn leaned over and peeked at the sketch on Karen's canvas. "What are you painting this morning?" She sipped coffee from a delicate porcelain cup.

"Our new cabin on Lake Sidney Lanier. Well, I guess I shouldn't call it a cabin. It has four bedrooms. Log home."

Evelyn settled into a rocker. "That was a big surprise, Donald buying that place. Bit of a piece for you and him to drive to work and back."

Karen studied the canvas, her head tilted sideways. She picked up a fine-tipped brush. "I'm not so sure I'll be going back to the station, at least not full time. Donald's keeping his townhouse in the city for the times when he has to work late."

Evelyn frowned. "I hate to hear you're dropping out of TV. You're so good at it."

"Mary Elizabeth was good at it." She glanced at her mother. "I don't know what I'm good at . . . yet."

Evelyn rocked back and forth gently. "Tell you what I did. I latched onto what gave me the greatest joy. Found something that lit me up inside. Oh, I was happy enough being a homemaker till you kids left out. Then it just seemed so . . . pointless."

Karen lay the palette and brush down and grabbed the warm cinnamon roll. "I can't imagine just staying home all the time. You must have been bored silly."

"Wasn't bad when I had you children underfoot. Lord knows, those years passed in the blink of an eye. And you can only redecorate a house so many times. I was beginning to get a reputation, or so Jake Witherspoon tells it."

"And the sewing? It makes you feel good?"

"Better than good. I'm creating something with these." She held her hands up and wiggled her fingers. "Folks look proud when they wear my fashions. I just can't get enough of it! Just about the time I think—well, I've reached the end of my limits—a fresh idea pops to mind, and boom! I'm tearing off in a new direction."

Taizer jumped onto the chair with Karen and trilled.

"I fed the kitties, by the way," Evelyn said.

Karen shook her head and smiled. "So did I, close to an hour ago before I came out here to start painting."

"Well, well. That little devil there came twirling around my feet acting like he hadn't eaten in a month of Sundays. And Tequila didn't object to being fed again, either." She wiggled her finger in the kitten's direction. "Fooled me again, you little dickens."

"Maybe we should start leaving each other notes on the fridge."

"I'll make some kind of check-off list. I'm certain Joe's been feeding them, too." She dismissed the subject. "What do you have on your agenda for today, missy?"

"I'm heading out to Pinky and Wanda's around lunchtime. She has the afternoon off, and Pinky wants to show me some tinctures to help rebuild my immune system."

"Be careful driving, and do try to get home before good dark. Lots of critters lurk beside those country roads come dusk."

Karen paused a moment before speaking. "Would you consider designing my wedding gown, Mama?"

Evelyn abruptly stopped rocking. Her eyes opened wide. "Would I? That would only be the dream of a lifetime, me designing your dress."

"I don't want anything too elaborate. No lace or seed pearls. Simple. Tea length."

Her mother clasped her hands. "I can do anything you have your heart set on." Her brows knit together. "How soon are we talking about, exactly?"

"Late spring. May, early June. By that time, I should have some hair again."

"That gives us—" she counted on her fingers, "ten months. Doable. We should sit down and let me do some sketches so I can figure a design." Evelyn smiled as she resumed rocking. "I just love weddings. You gonna have it here at the First Baptist?"

Karen shook her head. "Nope. I made a decision while I was in Atlanta last week. Donald agreed. We want an outside ceremony. Very small, at our place on Lake Lanier."

"That ought to be pretty. I've always wanted to visit there. Maybe your daddy and I can plan a little vacation afterwards. Go up into the mountains." Her eyes sparkled.

"There are rental houses nearby. We can put everyone up for the weekend."

Evelyn glanced at her watch and hopped up. "Look at the time! I have to get on up to the workshop. I have five baby ensembles and blankets to finish before Sue Ellen Sales's shower on Saturday. They're certainly not going to sew themselves. Although your daddy seems to think the new-fangled machine he bought me could." She smiled. "You sure you're going to be okay here alone?"

"I'm fine, Mama. Now that I don't have to dash off to Tallahassee every morning, it's a break for me. Until the next round of chemo."

Evelyn's expression darkened. "I know you'll be glad to have all this behind you, honey. Two more of those dreadful treatments." She leaned over and kissed Karen on the cheek. "You call me if you need anything, or Elvina. She can drop and run on a moment's notice."

"I. Will. Be. Fine. Go to work!"

"I left the *Democrat* on the kitchen counter if you want to read it later on," Evelyn called over her shoulder.

Wanda handed a tall glass of iced tea to Karen. "You and the witch doctor get your potions mixed?" She reached over and tousled Pinky's red curly hair.

"You don't quit calling me that, I'm going to run a bone through my nose and wear a grass skirt."

Wanda's eyebrows shot up. "That, I have to see." She wiggled her hips. "I'd like to know, do witch doctors go natural under those little skirts like the Scots do underneath their kilts?"

"Wanda Jean." Pinky blushed brilliant red and picked up the battered guitar beside his chair. "You beat all, sometimes."

Karen listened to his finger-picking. "That sounds familiar."

"James Taylor. Who else?" Wanda plopped down on the porch swing. "Good thing I love all the man's songs, or I'd lose what's left of my mind."

Pinky shrugged. "Guess I'm a creature of habit."

"It's 'You've Got a Friend,' right?" Karen asked.

"You got it!" Wanda threw her hand in the air like a game show hostess. "You win a goat!"

Karen laughed. "That would send poor Evelyn over the edge, for sure. I'm still amazed at her and my cats. She bought a two-hundred dollar kitty condo for them to play in."

"I would have never thought it, with Evelyn being such a clean freak and all. The hair must send her up the wall."

Karen shook her head. "She brushes both of them twice a day. You should see it. They line up like tourists at a cruise ship buffet. I'll be lucky to tear them away from her when I move back to Atlanta."

"You anxious to get home?" Pinky asked. His long nimble fingers darted across the fret board.

"Yes and no." Karen reached down and petted Annie, the hound/shepherd mix, curled up beneath her feet. "Sing for us, Pinky. Please?"

Midway through Pinky's soulful rendition of the folk song, Karen burst into tears, sending Wanda scampering into the house for tissues.

"Maybe I should've picked something a bit more upbeat." Pinky returned the guitar to its stand.

Karen wiped her nose and eyes. "No, it's not you. I'm so sorry for crying like this."

Wanda rested a hand on Karen's shoulder. "You need to unload, hon? Me and Pinky are good listeners. He's had tons of practice since I moved in."

"It's just—this lady I met once at the doctor's office—I read her obituary in the paper this morning."

Pinky and Wanda exchanged puzzled glances.

"I didn't even know her well, just one brief conversation while we were waiting to go back." Karen's voice quivered. "I wanted to get together with her for coffee, or lunch after the surgery. Then, I had to go through radiation and chemo. I thought about her often and almost called a couple of times."

"Must've been a nice person, to have made such an impression on you," Pinky said.

"She was."

"You know any of her folks?" Wanda asked.

Karen shook her head. "There is some sort of memorial service in a couple of days. I wouldn't feel right about showing up there. It would feel like I was intruding on their grief. Not like we were close friends."

"Maybe you could make a donation in her name," Wanda said.

Karen nodded. "I probably will."

Pinky tilted his head. "It's a bitter pill to swallow. I know. After I lost Alice Jo, I found the most comfort in doing things that, in my mind, honored her spirit." He motioned toward the garden. "Keeping up with the herbs is one of them."

Karen offered a weak smile and dabbed the remaining moisture from her cheeks. "You two have been such good friends. I don't know how I would've gotten through all this without you." She reached over and squeezed first Wanda's, then Pinky's hands.

They sat for a moment, wrapped in the comforting cloak of closeness.

Wanda said, "Pinky made some carrot-tofu cupcakes. That ought to make you feel a little better. Want one with a cup of coffee?"

Karen smiled. "Ah, food. The balm to ease all sorrows. Sure, why the heck not?"

Karen wasn't certain, exactly, how she ended up in the Morningside AME sanctuary, three pews from the pulpit with the late afternoon sun streaming through the tall windows. Some kind of spiritual distress homing device? She studied the wooden carving of Jesus on the cross. What was it about this simple, no-frills room that exuded tranquility? Even filled to the brim on Sunday morning, with children darting up and down the aisles and neighbors exchanging small talk, the diminutive church was surrounded by an aura of protection and peace.

She bowed her head and murmured a brief prayer for Margaret Bronson and her family. Just shy of *amen,* she began to cry.

"Miz Karen?" A gentle voice asked.

She glanced up to see Lucille Jackson, arms filled with a stack of booklets.

"I'm sorry." Karen rose to leave. "The door was unlocked, so I—"

Lucille rested a hand on Karen's shoulder. "Church's doors are always open during daylight hours. No telling when a person might need to feel God's presence. Used to be, we didn't lock them at night either, but times are what they are." She motioned for Karen to be seated, then eased onto the pew beside her. "I just stopped in to leave the new music for the choir practice tonight—for the new Christmas cantata. Never too soon to start practicing."

Karen wiped her eyes with a tissue. "I should go."

"You sit here long as you like. I've come in here right by myself many a time. Lord doesn't mind you visiting his house on days other than Sundays." The skin around her soft brown eyes crinkled when she smiled. "Used to find your Grandmama Piddie here on occasion. She loved to come and sit in the peace and pray."

Karen's gaze fell downward. "I wish Piddie was here."

"Oh, but she is, child. Not so you can touch her. But her love goes right on and on. Every time I think of her, I get a warm feeling in my heart, and I know she's hovering close-by, watching out over all of us she loved while she was here on this earth." She cocked her head. "Something weighing heavy on you today?"

"Nothing, and everything, Miz Lucille." Karen offered a weak smile. "Sometimes, fear overwhelms me and—this woman I met a few months back—she died." Karen paused. "She was a breast cancer patient, too." Karen wrung her hands. "If she couldn't make it, how will I? She was just so alive."

Lucille chuckled. "Brings to mind something Piddie said to me one time. I made that same comment about someone: that he was so alive, and it was hard to believe he could just up and die." She waved a hand through the air. "I'll never forget what your grandmama said to me: 'Lucille, that's the silliest thing I've ever heard. Why is it folks say such a thing, you reckon? We're all alive till we're not. Just some people don't remember to act like it.'"

"That's it! Margaret seemed like she was the kind of person who lived every single minute." She shrugged. "I didn't really know her all that well. She just kind of radiated."

"Some folks do that. No matter how life beats them into the ground, they pop right up. Believe they're put here on this good earth to remind all of the rest of us what a gift every day is."

Karen smiled.

"Well," Lucille slapped her thighs with her palms. "I've got to scoot along. The Reverend and I visit the shut-ins on Wednesday afternoons. You sit here just as long as you want. If you're still here by the time choir practice commences, why, just join in. Lord won't object to one more voice lifted up."

"Mama told me I loved her fried chicken so much, I would beg her to make it. Once, I fell asleep underneath the kitchen table with a fried chicken leg in my mouth. I come from a line of good Southern cooks. Suppose that's why it feels so natural for me to putter around in the kitchen. There's an art to frying chicken so the skin's all brown and crispy. Your grease has to be fresh, and just the right temperature. Too hot, and you'll get a scalded flavor to the meat. Not hot enough, and the flour will soak up the grease too much and make the skin gummy."

Leigh Andrews Davis

Chapter Forty-one

"Patsy Hornsby and her daughter Ruth are over for the weekend," Hattie said to Karen. "Little Ruth is the artist who painted the abstracts at the Triple C and the one in Sarah's bedroom. Remember? She overheard Patsy and me talking about your paintings and really wants to meet you."

"Oh?"

"We're going to hang out around the pool this afternoon. Probably throw some burgers on the grill. Will you join us?"

Karen hesitated. "I don't know, Hattie. I don't look very good in a swimsuit right now. And I shouldn't get too wet; I have the port to consider. I just don't—"

"Oh, c'mon cuz! It's not like it'll be a big crowd. Just the family out here on the Hill. Jake may join us, but Jon has to work. Usually the neighbors come up, but they're in the mountains for a couple of weeks. We'll set you up in a lounger in the shade and ply you with tall glasses of iced tea. What d'ya say?"

The prospect of another long day wandering around the empty house loomed. "Okay, okay. You talked me into it."

"Great! Come on out whenever you like. We'll eat around noon. And Karen?"

"Hmm?"

"Bring one of your paintings, will you? Ruth has been bugging us to death about seeing some of your work. I don't think she'll calm down till she does."

Children. Karen shook her head. For the most part, they were loud, unruly, and brutally honest, the latter being the main reason she had avoided them in the past. Until the teenaged years when anyone over eighteen was ignored like last year's fashion fad, the children she had contact with seemed to possess the eerie ability to look directly through to her innermost secrets. Since her soul now lay open and ragged, would a child be more or less of a threat?

Karen flipped thorough the stack of canvases for a few moments, unable to choose. Finally, she settled on the dragonfly meadow painting for its mystical quality. Also, it was less dark and revealing than much of her later work.

When she pulled her sports car under the shade of an aging pecan tree, the pool yard was bustling with activity. Hattie glanced up from the food-laden picnic table and waved. Karen leaned down to pet Spackle and Elvis, the canine greeting committee.

Clad in vivid hibiscus-print swim shorts with a matching tropical-hued cane, Jake shuffled toward her car. "Need any help?"

"Nope. I can handle it." She shouldered a small canvas beach bag and grabbed the cake carrier.

"Ew! Did you bake?" Jake's blue eyes twinkled.

"Hardly. My idea of baking is Sara Lee. This is a hummingbird cake Daddy sent along."

Jake patted his flat stomach. "My, my. I'll have to live on Slim-Fast shakes after today. Leigh and Hattie already have enough carbs on the table to put a full-blown Michelin tire around my waist."

Elvis pranced at Karen's feet. A floral sun visor bobbed atop his head. "I've yet to see this dog without an outfit." Karen knelt and ruffled the Pomeranian's fur.

"He has little flip-flops, too. They come off when he runs around too much. Your mama made my swim trunks to match his visor."

"Simply amazing."

Karen realized one simple fact each time she attended a family function: she came from a body-slamming, hugging group of Southerners. Since her surgery, they had graciously modified the breath-smothering embraces to a gentler A-frame squeeze and back-pat.

After a round of good mornings, Hattie introduced Karen to the Tallahassee guests. Patsy Hornsby's emerald green eyes and impish grin brought her Irish freckled face to life. "So pleased to finally meet you! Hattie has told Rainey and me so much about you and your work. All good, naturally. And my adopted daughter, Ruth— " she glanced toward the pool where a small Chinese girl reclined on a beach float, dark over-sized red sunglasses propped on the end of her nose, "—has been positively frantic to meet you. Ruthie?" she called. "Miss Karen is here, sweetie."

Ruth hand-paddled the raft to the steps and managed to emerge with only her feet wet. She bowed slightly when her mother introduced her. Ruth removed the sunglasses, and her ebony eyes studied Karen. For a brief instant, the child's spirit merged with hers, and she was left with a warm afterglow, as if caressed by a balmy tropical trade wind.

"I would like to see your paintings," Ruth said politely. "If you please, ma'am."

"Oh, honey," Patsy said. "Let Miss Karen enjoy being here for a bit, shall we? There'll be plenty of time after lunch."

The child shrugged and returned to her position on the float.

"Sorry, Karen." Patsy shook her head. "When that one gets something on her mind, she's a broken record, or maybe I should say cracked CD. I'm dating myself."

"That's okay." Karen watched as Ruth floated to the deep end of the pool away from the frantic splashing of the younger Josh and Sarah. Bobby pinched his son's nostrils together and they went underwater. The toddler emerged, giggling and wiping his chubby face with one hand. Sarah, more tentative than her cousin, clung to Holston and winced each time her aggressive, Chattahoochee-born male cousin splashed water in her direction.

"Look at these adorable little refrigerator magnets Ruth made for us." Hattie pointed to a series of miniature pieces of wood painted with splashes of abstract colors.

Jake smirked. "Like you need just one more magnet on that fridge." He propped one hand on his hip. "The joke is, Karen, that when one of the Davis women dies, they bury them in the refrigerator. That way, they get rid of the body and the magnets at the same time."

Everyone laughed except Hattie. "You leave me and my magnets alone, Jakey. Everyone has a collection of some sort."

Jake snorted. "None nearly as gaudy, Sister-girl. The tiny plastic flush toilet with the teeny novel open on top positively slays me every time I open your freezer door."

Hattie waved her hands in the air. "This, coming from the man with—let's see, is it fifty or sixty canes at this point?" She tapped her chin with one finger. "My favorite is the brilliant red one with the hot pink fake fur on the handle and the Gypsy Rose Lee signature down one side. So, don't even lecture me about taste."

Leigh rolled her eyes. "You two. Always going at each other. I swannee."

Jake hobbled over and planted a loud lip-smacking kiss on Hattie's cheek. "It's love, pure and simple. Right, Sister-girl? I'm all she had before Holston came and pushed me to the curb."

Holston laughed and bounced Sarah up and down in the water. "I'm keeping clear of this one!"

By the time thick Angus beef burgers and hot dogs were shoveled from the grill, the picnic table was laden with food: cabbage cole slaw, potato salad, three-bean salad, buttered corn on the cob, baked beans topped with country bacon, and sliced homegrown beefsteak tomatoes. Joe Fletcher's hummingbird cake, Hattie's best damned chocolate cake from Piddie's age-old recipe, and Leigh's huckleberry cobbler stood ready on a separate folding table reserved for desserts and drinks.

Everyone talked at once until Jake called out, "Who wants to say the blessing?"

The family joined hands, heads bowed, as Bobby offered a short prayer.

"God, we thank you for our food. For rest and home and all things good. For wind and rain and sun above. But most of all, for those we love. Amen."

Immediately, a scrabble ensued. The toddlers were settled into highchairs with paper plates of food to wear and eat. The dogs took up sentry positions at their feet, awaiting the inevitable spoonfuls of dropped chow.

Holston leaned back and exhaled a few minutes later. "Man! I couldn't eat another bite."

"Until cake and ice cream." Hattie pointed to the churn, packed down in rock salt and ice to allow the homemade dessert to firm.

Jake grinned. "What flavor?"

"Plain old vanilla," Leigh said. "We thought it might go better with any kind of cake."

Jake stuck his lower lip out. "I was hoping for double chocolate fudge with walnuts."

Hattie rolled her eyes. "You'll have to call your friends Ben and Jerry."

Ruth loitered beside Karen's chair, a faint sheen of melted butter on her lips. "Can I see your painting now?"

Patsy grabbed a napkin, wet it with saliva, and wiped her daughter's mouth. "*May* I?"

"*May* I?" Ruth asked.

Karen stood. "It's in my car. I'll get it." She returned shortly with the paper-wrapped canvas.

Ruth stood back from the painting, one hand on her hip, the other propped beneath her chin. She narrowed her eyes and tilted her head slightly from one side to the other. "I like it." She smiled at Karen. Then, to her mother, "May I go back in the pool now?"

Patsy reached over and smoothed back a hank of hair from Ruth's eyes. "I'd rather you wait a few more minutes, honey. It's not good to go in right after you eat a big meal."

Bobby added, "You'd sink clean to the bottom if you tried to swim right now."

Ruth studied both adults as if she knew their logic was loaded with holes. "I can go swing?" Patsy granted permission. Ruth skipped from the pool yard to the swing set underneath the pecan tree.

"She didn't have a lot to say," Karen said as she wrapped the painting.

Patsy shrugged. "That's just her way. She'll mull over it a bit, then tell the world. She's not quick to let go of an art opinion."

By mid-afternoon, the toddlers were cranky and water-logged. Hattie and Leigh put them down for naps in a playpen in the shade while the adults visited. Laughter flowed like a gentle tide around the circle of folding chairs.

Ruth danced and skipped to Karen's car. She smiled down at the petite child. "It certainly was good to meet you, Miss Ruth. Maybe next time I'm in Tallahassee, I can stop by and see your studio."

Ruth crooked her index finger for Karen to bend to her level. "Everything is going to be okay," she whispered into Karen's ear. "The shadow won't hurt you. They are watching over you."

Karen drew back and stared at the little Chinese girl with the shiny black hair and dark eyes. "They?"

Ruth held a hand slightly over her mouth and spoke in a soft voice. "The angels," a smile transformed her serious expression, "over your shoulders."

Patsy approached the car. "C'mon, Ruthie. Time to go inside out of the sun for a while." She rested her hands on her adoptive daughter's shoulders. "She'd stay outside all day if I allowed it." Patsy patted Ruth on the back. "Run on inside, honey."

Patsy grasped Karen's hand and gave a gentle squeeze. "Please come visit any time. I'd love for Rainey to meet you."

Karen smiled. "Hattie has your number. I'll call."

"When will you be heading back to Atlanta?"

"I have one final chemotherapy treatment next week. I'll probably stay on until after the worst of the side effects wear off. Then, I need to go to Georgia Metro for a few days to help with the final edit and voice-over on the documentary." Karen's gaze dropped slightly. "After that, who knows?"

"Best of luck—whatever you decide to do. I'm sure things will turn out for the best."

As Karen drove the country highway towards town, she contemplated Ruth's comments. The last time she had heard those comforting words, she had been facing surgery.

"For heaven's sake. What next?"

"I can tell you, sure as the world, what floats my man Bull's boat. Fish. You ought to see my freezer! I can barely get to the field peas for all the dang frozen fish. I don't think it has a lot to do with his mama, though. More, his daddy. He adored his daddy. Come the weekend, he and Bull would light out for the river and stay all day of a Saturday until it was so dark they had to train a flashlight on the cork to see it. Whenever Bull acts like the world is getting him down, I thaw a mess of bream and fry them up with some hushpuppies and maybe some home fries. I can see it in his face, how the comfort comes over him. Come to think of it, I suppose his mama cooked fish all the time, too. If she had the overload Bull provides for us, I reckon they had fish once or twice a week."

Mandy Andrews

Chapter Forty-two

"Your problem," Mandy's nostrils flared slightly, "is that you can never leave well enough alone!"

Elvina huffed. "Had to do something. You certainly weren't taking up the reins."

"You two!" Evelyn sat a tray of filled coffee mugs and biscotti cookies on a small table. "I swannee, Elvina, if you and Mandy don't carry on with each other just like you and Mama used to."

Elvina swatted the air with a bony hand. "Leave Piddie out of this. Besides, if she was here, she'd back me up on this one!"

"What are you going on at each other about, anyway?" Melody asked. She took a seat in one of Hattie's dining room chairs that had been moved against the wall to make room for the massage tables.

Elvina snorted. "That dang little disgrace of an engagement ring Bull gave her, that's what. Mandy's mad as a wet hen over me talking to him about sizing it up a few carats."

Melody arched one eyebrow, glanced down at her own marquee-cut diamond band, and took a noisy sip of coffee.

Mandy twisted the delicate gold ring around on her finger. "Not a thing wrong with this ring. Bull put a lot of love and consideration behind it."

"And my patootie is bright blue!" Elvina said. "That man drives a brand spanking new Dodge Hemi Ram pick-up truck with every contraption known to man built in—it hitched to a matching seventeen-foot Bass Pro boat worth twice the truck a-pulling it, and that," she jabbed a finger at Mandy's ring, "is all he could cough up for the woman he wants to marry? Really!"

Mandy frowned. "It's the thought that counts, after all."

"That's the case, you've not only promised yourself to a tightwad, but an ignoramus to boot—the quality of thought he gave it!"

Hattie held up her hands to form a time-out symbol. "Could we, perhaps, cool it down a notch or two, ladies? This is, after all, a time for quiet, calm, and loving instruction in an ancient healing art."

Mandy and Elvina threw a final glare at each other before moving to opposite corners of the massage table.

"Thank you." Hattie held out her hands. "Now, do you all have the little booklets I handed out last week? Has everyone had a chance to read over them?"

"I read it," Melody said. "Didn't make a lot of sense, Hattie, to be honest."

"Was as clear as mud to me, too," Elvina said. "Still, Christ did healings by laying on hands, so I can sort of grasp the notion behind it all."

Leigh smiled. "I've had one of your sessions, and it was very relaxing, Hattie."

Wanda spoke up. "Pinky should've been the one coming today. He's all into natural healing. I don't see where I can be any good at it."

"That's just it," Hattie said. "You don't need to have a talent for Reiki. The energy flows through your body into the person receiving. You are merely a conduit."

"If you con-du-it, then I con-du-it," Elvina said, proud of herself for the quip.

Karen laughed. The circle of women around her reacted in various ways, but the underlying impression was of camaraderie and mutual trust. Following a brief history of Reiki, Hattie demonstrated the series of hand placements over energy centers of the body, using Karen as a volunteer.

"What's it feel like to you?" Melody asked.

"Warm. Just like someone is holding a heating element over the spot. Not a burning heat," Karen said. "Sometimes, during our sessions in the past, I've felt a tingle shoot down from my head to my toes."

"Sounds scary," Wanda said. "Kind of like the first time I kissed Pinky Green."

Elvina propped her hands on her hips. "Get your mind out of the gutter, Wanda."

"Okay." Hattie clasped her hands together. "I'm going to take each one of you into the kitchen and pass a level one attunement. Nothing to be anxious over. I'll be placing four Reiki symbols into your aura—the energy field we all have around our bodies. They will aid you in channeling the energy more effectively. It only takes a few minutes per person."

Following the attunements, the group took a quick break for a snack and tall glasses of ice water with lemon.

"One thing I worry over," Evelyn said, "is about someone blaming me for not being healed afterwards. You ever run up against that, Hattie?"

"Good question, Ev. And it leads me to an important point: never, never, say you are going to heal a person. You are not doing the work. The energy of the universe—God, the great collective consciousness, spirit, whatever you choose to call it—is in charge."

Hattie frowned slightly. "I've searched for years for an explanation of why sickness happens. Why do good-hearted, loving people fall prey to cancer, strokes, and the like? And why am I powerless to heal them?"

She hesitated before continuing. "This is what rings true for me; you may all find your own answers. Sometimes, the disease or condition brings to that individual great gifts: understanding, peace, perhaps a resolution of long-standing issues. If the person needs those lessons to grow in spirit, then no amount of Reiki will dissolve the disease."

Hattie stood and paced the kitchen. "It really frustrated me at first. Here I had this wonderful tool at my disposal, and I could not stop pain and suffering."

Elvina rested a hand on Hattie's shoulder. "No one expects you to be God, sugar."

"I guess that's my point, Elvina. You hit the nail square on the head." She rested her gaze briefly on each woman. "None of us are God. But we can provide relaxation and an atmosphere where healing can occur, if that is what the universe intends."

"Makes good sense to me," Wanda said. "All of Alice Jo, Pinky's sister's, herbal concoctions didn't save her life. In the end, they surely helped her passing to be less traumatic, from what he told me."

Evelyn said. "And after all, aren't we put here to help each other get by?"

"Till we leave for the great by and by?" Elvina's lips twitched with the start of a grin.

" 'Vina," Mandy slapped the old woman playfully on the back. "You do have a way with words, old gal."

"Don't know who you're calling *old*, less you've caught sight of your own self in the mirror." Elvina snorted. "And I still think that diamond's too small."

Hattie motioned the group to the center of the room. "The last thing I would like all of us to take part in, is a Reiki circle."

"Sounds kinky," Mandy said. Elvina jabbed her in the ribs with a bony elbow.

Hattie smiled. Without a doubt, this had proven the most enjoyable class she had ever taught. "We'll take turns on the table with everyone else performing Reiki. I'll ground the energy at the feet, with the rest of you around the table. It doesn't matter much about hand positions for this, as long as one person is at the crown chakra at the top of the head. And because each session lasts only a few minutes per person, we will all be able to experience the power of a group healing circle."

Karen was the final recipient. Soft harp music played in the background. She felt the intense warmth at her feet as Hattie took her position. Elvina's hands rested on Karen's head, with the rest of the women in a circle around her body.

As Karen relaxed into the session, allowing her breathing to become deep and even, she envisioned the people she held close to heart. One by one, their faces appeared in her mind's eye, each leaving a lingering impression of love and concern. Then, a steady white-golden light filtered through, obliterating all images. Her skin tingled and the base of her spine burned.

The intense heat climbed steadily higher until it reached the base of her skull. Her body felt as if it was pulsating—not only on the surface, but deep within—every cell dancing in the white light's infinite energy.

After a few moments, the heat crept higher and stopped at the top of her head. The colors of the spectrum flashed by: red, orange, yellow, green, blue, indigo, violet. Her spirit bubbled with limitless peace and joy. A rush of emotion washed over her: pain, happiness, love, anger. Karen began to cry.

"What's wrong?" Melody asked.

Hattie's voice was gentle and reassuring. "Be with her. Don't be afraid."

Karen sobbed for what seemed an eternity. The fear, the doubts, all the negativity held for a lifetime, surged to the surface and shattered into iridescent bubbles, washed away in the glow of white light.

Karen heaved a shuddering breath and opened her eyes, smiling.

"Have mercy on my soul," Elvina said. "Was all that inside of you, gal?"

"It was. Not anymore." She turned her head slowly to rest her gaze on each of the women. "Thank you, all of you."

Melody shrugged. "We didn't do anything, Karen, except hold our hands over you."

Karen's face glowed.

"Take your time getting up, now." Hattie motioned for the group to remove their hands. "We can let you have some time alone if you need it."

"That's not necessary. I just realized something. I've spent my entire life to this point, isolated, even when I was surrounded by people. I don't intend for that to happen again. Not ever."

"Food is just something to keep you alive. Nothing my mother did ever impressed me. She was just this mousy little powerless blob. Never stood up to my father—not even until the day she died. When I need comfort, I shop. Certainly, I can take care of myself. And I never want to think of my wimpy mother when I think of comfort. That's for certain."

Trisha Truman

Chapter Forty-three

The transformation from emotional hermit to valued confidant was so gradual, Karen couldn't pinpoint the exact beginning. At first, conversations with Chattahoochee's women were confined to their gentle inquiries about her health and the progress of therapy. Later, recipes were discussed and exchanged. Karen realized she had become privy to many aspects of the area families' lives: children, grandchildren, births and deaths, and the endless stream of daily minutiae. Tentative initially, she soon shared details of her wishes and dreams. The excitement of starting a new painting. The joy of noting the abundance of flowering plants and shrubs—capturing just the right shade of deep coral for the crape myrtle blooms or the creamy beige of magnolia blossoms. The women listened intently, as if they, too, struggled with the best shade of cerulean blue to express the depth of a cloudless summer sky. The concept of subtlety was not lost on them, for each strived for perfection in one form or another.

Epiphanies came to Karen as often as she allowed her stagnant spirit to stretch and unfold to envelop the people around her. At first, she feared the newfound sense of community existed only in her hometown. Soon, she noticed the same ease with strangers she met in Tallahassee. Could it be that she might be able to foster the novel talent and form close bonds wherever she and Donald chose to make a home?

More and more, Karen understood that it was she, not the rest of humanity, who had sent her into isolation, to hide behind the mask of fake identity.

Elvina Houston's philosophy stated the obvious in plain words: "If a troubling situation keeps popping up over and over, playing itself out in much the same fashion time after time, and you are the common thread; then, perhaps, you are the root of the problem, not everyone else you've been trying to lay the blame on."

For early August, the morning temperature was unseasonably comfortable. Following a week of mid-nineties and one hundred percent humidity, a cool air mass from the north muscled into the Florida Panhandle bringing welcomed relief. Karen moved her easel to the corner of the patio beside the mimosa tree. The outline of a magic praying tree took form in the center of the canvas as she sketched with charcoal. Below, in the wispy shadows cast by its lacy fern-like foliage, two indistinct figures faced each other.

"You again, Mary Elizabeth?" Karen leaned back, smiled, and took a sip of black coffee. The last four paintings featured her mirror image alter-ego in various settings. Two distinct themes were clear in the series of paintings: Karen vs. cancer and the cave, and Karen vs. Mary Elizabeth Kensington.

A stealthy movement caught her attention. She rolled her eyes. "Don't you people ever give up?" she yelled. "Might as well step out from behind the hedge so you can get a better shot!"

Trisha Truman stood and pushed through the row of wax-leaf ligustrum. A glint of metal flashed in her right hand. Definitely not a camera.

Karen felt the thud of her pulse in her throat as Trisha edged closer.

"Don't you move, you bitch!" Trisha's voice, thick with hatred.

Karen stood slowly, her hands held in front of her. "Wait, Trisha. Calm down. What are you doing here?"

Trisha's temples pulsed as she clenched her teeth. "Like you don't know."

Karen willed her voice to remain calm and even. "I've been out of the loop for a long time, Trisha. I'm afraid I don't understand. Why don't you put the gun down, and we'll sit and talk."

"No!" The blonde's trigger finger twitched.

Karen closed her eyes and forced a deep, even breath. "Can you at least tell me why you are standing there with a gun pointed at me?"

Trisha laughed, a high-pitched demented sound like shattering glass. "You stupid bitch! You've ruined my life." She began to sob; her shoulders curled forward. "Donald was supposed to be mine. We would've been happy. D. J.'s smile. My looks and talent. Our children would've been beautiful and amazing. You were the only reason he didn't come to me. He wanted to. I could see it in his eyes every time he looked at me. You destroyed everything! My job. My love. My life!"

Karen took a tentative step toward her.

"No! Get back!" Trisha snapped the gun barrel level. "I mean it!"

Both women jumped when the phone trilled. After three rings, Karen said softly, "That'll be my mother. If I don't answer, she'll be here to check on me in less than five minutes."

Trisha motioned with the gun barrel. "Go ahead. But you say one word about me, I swear I'll blow your damn head clean off." Her glassy red-rimmed glare reinforced the warning.

"Oh, hello Mother." Karen spoke deliberately, emphasizing each word. "Yes, I'm fine . . . uh-huh . . . "

Karen heard Elvina Houston's voice on the other end: "This isn't your mama, honey. Don't you know who I am? You hitting the pain medication this morning? Or did I just wake you up?"

"That's right, Mo-*ther*. I'm fine. You shouldn't come over right now. But I think you're right about Rich Burns. I'd feel *much* better if you called him *right away*. Okay, mother? Love you! Bye!" Karen smiled as she slowly replaced the phone on a table beside the easel. "My mom—such a worry-wart. She doesn't talk to me once an hour, she gets nervous."

"Who's that Rich person?" Trisha's eyes narrowed.

"Oh." Karen waved one hand dismissively. "Mother's business affairs. He's some guy she buys wholesale fabric from over in Tallahassee. They had a bit of a misunderstanding. Mama was up fretting about it most of last night. You'd have to know my mother to understand—"

"Shut up!" Trisha rubbed her temple with the fingers of her left hand. "I don't need all the damn details of your dull interbred family!"

"Your head hurt?" Karen forced concern into her voice. "I have just about any kind of pain reliever in the house. I could go get you—"

"You're not going anywhere."

Karen felt the fear slip from her shoulders like a shed snakeskin. A sense of calm cloaked her. "You know what, Trisha? I just don't feel well enough to stand here in my parents' garden looking down the barrel of a handgun." She plopped down on a lawn chair. "You came to say something to me, obviously. Spit it out, or go ahead and shoot." She laughed. "I've felt so rotten after this last round of chemo, it might actually be a relief."

"You have D. J. snowed, and Will. You never fooled me. I knew you were plastic from the minute we met."

Karen shrugged.

"I should be the one." Trisha sniffed. "Should've been me! You've ruined my life." The gun shook in her hands. "You made me do things—bad things."

"Let me get this straight. I'm responsible for you perpetrating the terrorist hoax that ended you in jail? *That* is rich. How'd you manage to get out, by the way?"

Trisha's expression oozed into a tight grin. "Judge decided to set bail."

"Fortunate for you . . . less so for me, so it seems." Karen cast about for words to fill the time. "Did you offer to sleep with him, Trish? How'd you work that out?"

Behind Trisha, Rich Burns stepped stealthily around the edge of the house and nodded to Karen.

"Just like you to try to take over, Mary Elizabeth, uh, Karen! Make me say and do things to your liking! I'm famous. Did you know that? Oh, I forgot. You probably don't get the national news way down here in Cretin-ville. My picture's been on all the major networks. You can't say the same."

"Not unless you count the footage a few months back when you exposed me to the world. Thanks, by the way."

"Well yeah. But I've still made the news more than you."

Rich crept up slowly behind Trisha and pointed his 9 mm directly at the base of her skull. "Put the gun down, Miss. And no one will get hurt," he said, his order reinforced by the metallic click of the pistol being cocked.

Trisha closed her eyes and released a loud breath. She lowered the weapon. Hung her head. Hanks of matted bleached-blonde hair clung to her face. As Rich stepped forward, Trisha snapped the gun level, took aim and fired. Karen dove to one side as the bullet whizzed past and ricocheted off the mimosa's trunk.

Rich tackled Trisha, sending her face down in the grass. He slammed her wrist twice before dislodging the handgun, then gathered her arms behind her back. In a few seconds, she was secured in handcuffs.

Another officer finally arrived. "Sorry, Rich. I was clean up at Lake Seminole when I got the call."

Rich helped Trisha to her feet. Her demented gaze fell briefly on Karen before the second officer led her away.

"You okay?" Rich asked as he helped Karen to her feet.

Karen brushed the dried grass from her shorts. "Yeah. Obviously, Elvina figured out my cloaked call for help. I don't know what would've happened had you not gotten here." She gave the police chief a gentle hug. "I'd better ride on up to the Triple C and tell Elvina and Mama what happened in person. Let them see me with their own eyes. Lord help us both if someone calls up there first." She shook her head. "All my years in journalism and broadcasting, and I can certainly say, that was the only time I've ever been shot at."

"I'm not much of an eater. My mom used to blast me for just picking at my food. I go in spells. I won't eat much for several days, then I'll kill for a cheeseburger. My mother could always get me to eat a toasted cheese sandwich. No matter what. If I went several meals without eating to her satisfaction, she'd break out the hoop cheese, cut a thick slice, and melt it slowly between two pieces of toasted white bread. She knew how to do it just right so the cheese was all gooey and the bread was soaked through with butter and browned to perfection."

Stephanie Peters, massage therapist

Chapter Forty-four

Karen stood at the water's edge. A fine mist hung over Lake Lanier and curled at the bases of the pines and hardwoods along the shore. Fallen leaves in scarlet, lemon yellow, and burgundy floated by, framing the mirror image of the trees they had once adorned. October: her favorite month. In North Georgia, it signaled the start of crisp evenings laced with the scent of wood fires, foliage so brilliant it stung her eyes, and cable-knit-sweater mornings spent hugging a steaming mug of black coffee.

Her hair was back—curly, thick, and a shade darker—with a mind of its own. Some of her weight had returned, also. Her face, no longer gaunt, wore the blush of renewed health and vigor. Every morning, she walked the streets around the lake with Sugar-Britches, their newly-adopted two-year-old rescue Springer Spaniel, loping by her side. The cats were blissfully happy with the spacious new digs, especially the screened-in back porch facing the lake. Taizer no longer ruined D. J.'s shoes, and Tequila had found a new lease on life with the abundance of squirrels and birds to watch. After the first few days of spitting and hissing, both cats ceased to pay any mind to the dog.

The immediate neighbors Karen already knew by first names, and many others she acknowledged on the daily outings. Anne McGaffey, the retired hairdresser two houses down, immediately befriended her. Because of the budding relationship, Karen was privy to the heartbeat of the small lakeside community. Anne was to Lake Sidney Lanier what Elvina Houston was to Chattahoochee: a good woman to count as an ally.

The loft study provided a perfect space for her art studio. Thanks to little Ruth Hornsby's praise and promotion, Karen's paintings, a series entitled *Journey Through*, now hung in a prestigious Atlanta gallery. Three pieces had been purchased for a respectable amount by a west coast collector. The inspirations kept flowing from her dreams, and she took full advantage of her muses.

Donald slipped his arms around her waist from behind. "Thought I'd find you out here. You're up early." He kissed her lightly on the hair. "You okay?"

"Uh-hmm. Just enjoying the view. I was thinking back to this time last year. I don't know if I even noticed the leaves, or anything else for that matter."

"We all get too busy with work sometimes."

Karen shook her head. "It was more than that, Donald. It's like I was dead inside. Just going through the motions. Now, " she gazed out over the water, "I can't wait to get up in the mornings to see if anything's changed during the night. I've come alive, finally, and I'm nearly half-way through my life."

"Some folks never wake up," Donald said. "Hey, speaking of enjoying life, I'm taking the day off."

Karen turned and hugged him tightly. "Wonderful! Is Will okay with that? I think he'd be over both of us by now, since I decided to retire."

"He'll get past it. Will's a good guy. He's just a little too caught up in the station. Actually, he told me he envied you."

"Why?"

"For making a change, I suppose. The freedom, the adventure of starting something new." Donald shrugged. "He'll be the sort of guy who'll have a mid-life crisis some day and show up in a fancy new red sports car or, God forbid, on a Harley."

The image of her ex-boss clad in black leather festooned with silver studs atop a chrome-trimmed motorcycle made Karen laugh. "That would be rich!"

"Why don't we throw a picnic lunch and the hound in the car and take a drive in the mountains? Shouldn't be quite as crowded on a weekday."

As they strolled arm-in-arm toward the cabin, Donald said, "Got an email from your mother, by the way. Obviously, she's finally learned to work the fancy new computer your dad bought for her. She's worried about your dress. Says she needs you to keep her up to date on any changes in your measurements so she can nip and tuck here and there as needed before the wedding."

"They're coming up for Thanksgiving. I can model for her then. Besides, if I keep going like I am now, I doubt nipping and tucking will be an issue. I'll need a muumuu."

The mountain laurel bushes bloomed in baby-pink clouds, contrasted by dark green waxy leaves. The effects of the recent warm days were apparent in the woods surrounding Lake Sidney Lanier. Barren trees sprouted new growth in brilliant tones of lime green. Squirrels scuttled in the overhead arbor, and songbirds auditioned for mates.

The day of D. J. and Karen's wedding dawned with a chill in the flower-scented air, but warmed by mid-afternoon. The simple ceremony was held lakeside underneath an ivy-trimmed arbor. Hattie was matron of honor, and Will Cooke stood up for Donald. In the audience were the people they held dear: a small gathering of Chattahoochee friends, her family, coworkers from Georgia Metro, and a handful of neighbors.

Evelyn stood at the garden's edge. Laughter and conversation from the reception filtered across the lawn.

"Mama? You okay? Why are you down here by yourself?" Karen held a half-filled champagne flute.

Evelyn swatted the air with one hand. "I'm perfectly fine, honey." She smiled and pointed to a small woody bush bearing the signs of new life. "I just noticed you have a magic tree—a mimosa—on your property."

Karen offered a slightly-intoxicated grin. "Well, what d'ya know! I hadn't noticed it before. Must be a good sign. The one at home took a bullet for me."

Her mother huffed. "That crazy Truman woman! Glad they locked her up and threw away the key. Your father nursed that poor tree back to health. Mimosas lose their foliage during the cold weather, you know. So it was hard to say whether or not the hole she blasted in the trunk was going to be its undoing. Your daddy painted some concoction on the wound—same he uses when he prunes limbs so the bugs won't set in. But come warm weather, your magic tree sent out new shoots. Reckon it'll survive after all. Nature is a miracle of God, it is."

"You and Daddy leaving tomorrow?"

Evelyn tucked a stray sprig of brown hair into the ribbon-trimmed bun at the nape of her neck. "Might as well. You and Donald'll be heading off for your honeymoon. Most everyone else will be going on back home. Byron and Linda are taking the boys back down to Six Flags Over Georgia. Your daddy and I have been looking forward to driving up the Blue Ridge Parkway. We haven't been on a real car trip for as long as I can recall."

"We're just taking a few days to wander the hills, too. We'll save our big vacation until June when we go to Canada for the Alcan Dragon Boat Festival."

Evelyn said, "I'm glad to hear you're taking time to travel while you're young. Gets harder as you get a few years on you."

Karen pointed to the lakeside bench where Simpy and Stephanie sat. "What do you think will happen with those two?"

Evelyn cocked her head to one side. "Hard to say. Stephanie's eat up with him, and he seems to feel about the same. Long distance love affairs are a chore, though. She loves a small town, and his work's in the city." She shrugged. "Who's to say how they'll figure that out."

They watched the party for a moment.

"Elvina and your neighbor lady sure hit it off. Don't imagine you could drop a bomb between them and they'd stop blabbing," Evelyn said.

Karen chuckled. "Anne's sweet, but she is a bit of a busybody. Heaven help, don't tell her I said so. She has a computer, so I imagine she and Elvina will burn up the Internet back and forth."

"That's a good thing for Elvina. She's been a lost soul since Mama died. Used to talk to her on the phone several times a day when they weren't eye to eye." Evelyn turned to face her daughter. Fine lines formed around her eyes as she smiled. "You can't grasp how very proud I am of you, honey."

Karen's eyes filled with tears. "Oh, Mama."

"Don't tune up and cry, now. You'll ruin your mascara." She handed Karen a delicate embroidered handkerchief. "I'm just so blessed to be able to come up here to share this wedding with you and Donald."

"Mama, just because we live in another state, doesn't mean we can't stay in touch. There's email, and we'll visit, and you and Daddy are always welcome here, any time. I'll not be a stranger to you and daddy, not ever again."

Careful not to crush the corsage of miniature white sweetheart roses pinned on her linen jacket, Evelyn hugged her daughter. "My sweet girl, you never were a stranger."

"This is the most important thing I have to tell you, gal. In the end, all that matters is love. Be sure to surround yourself with folks you love, and who love you. All the rest is just so much fool's gold. Looks pretty on the outside, but it ain't the real thing."

Excerpt from audiotape,
the late Piddie Davis Longman,
made for Karen Fletcher

Postlude

Karen watched the pink-shirted Women's Abreast dragon boat team file past. Most she now knew by name, if not by story. Following the success of the *Journey Through* documentary, she and Simpy had once again embarked on a fact-finding mission to record the intricacies of dragon boat racing, with emphasis on the women's cancer survivor crews. D. J. and Karen's Canadian trip had evolved into a working vacation, and the four friends had made the best of it.

"You ready?" Jason asked. Stephanie smiled from behind him, holding a heavy equipment bag.

Karen nodded and released a single pink carnation. The bloom floated on the surface, soon joining others cast into the water in memory of the ones who had fought the brave fight.

"Love to you, Margaret Bronson . . . and Godspeed."

About the Author

Rhett DeVane is the author of two published mainstream southern fiction novels: *The Madhatter's Guide to Chocolate* (Rabid Press, November 2003) and Up the Devil's Belly (Rabid Press, November 2005). She co-authored a vampire parody, *Evenings on Dark Island* (Infinity Publishing, March 2010) with Larry Rock. The political thriller, *Accidental Ambition* (Infinity Publishing, July 2010) co-authored with Senator Robert W. McKnight, was honored with one of the Premier Book Awards for 2010.

Two short fiction pieces appear in the anthologies *Forever Friends* (Mandinam Press, 2008) and *Forever Travels* (Mandinam Press, 2010)

Rhett is an active member of the Tallahassee Writers Association. She was a presenter in the 2004 Newbie Authors panel at the Harriette Austin Writers Conference (HAWC) at University of Georgia, and a session presenter for the 2007 HAWC. She presented a session at the 2010 Tallahassee Writers Conference. Rhett was the featured speaker for the 2008 Women Making Magic Awards in Tallahassee, guest author for the 2006 Gadsden County Author's Dinner, and speaker at the 2004 Florida Professional Business Women's Association convention in Orlando, Florida.

Rhett DeVane is a true Southerner—born and raised in the deep, muggy, bug-infested pine and oak forests of the Florida Panhandle. For the past thirty-plus years, Rhett has made her home in Tallahassee, Florida, located in Florida's Big Bend area, where she is a practicing dental hygienist. Rhett donates a portion of her royalties to a local Tallahassee breast cancer support group.

A Few Words from Rhett . . .

"As I create a novel, I am often reminded of my mama's homemade chicken vegetable soup. Each pot was unique, depending on the ingredients handy to the cook and her mood. Stories come to me from different sources—a humorous line here, a poignant tale there—and I blend them into the plot, mold them to the characters. Reality peeks through the pages, as it should, and breathes life into the narrative.

"*Mama's Comfort Food* is the third book in a series of Southern fiction novels set in my hometown of Chattahoochee, Florida. Though the characters and plot are fictional, the setting is real—the lovely, tree-lined small southern town where my two siblings and I spent our formative years.

"When I first had the idea for this series, I considered using a fabricated setting. Then it occurred to me: what better place to play out a series of humorous and heartfelt Southern stories than a close-knit town with only two stoplights and a state mental institution on the main drag, a place where my parents lived, laughed and loved for over fifty years? Perfect!

"To the townspeople of Chattahoochee: you have always held, and continue to hold, a special place in my heart."

Please visit Rhett's website: www.rhettdevane.com. The door's always open, the tea is sweet, and there's a porch rocker waiting for you.

Discussion points

1. What provides you with insights into Mary Elizabeth/Karen's true character?

2. The characters add tidbits about ties between food and comfort. What foods do you associate with comfort? Have these been passed down in your family?

3. The issue of facing cancer with the support of family and friends occurs many times. If faced with grave illness, how would you handle it, privately or with widespread knowledge and support?

4. Cousin Hattie gives Karen a daisy pendant, a talisman of sorts. Can you think of a time when a physical object took on special meaning for you?

5. Evelyn draws part of her strength from memories of her deceased mother, Piddie Longman. Are there times when recalling your mother's words of wisdom helped you?

6. Life-altering events often cause a shift in a person's perception of the world. How did cancer change Karen? Donald? The family?

7. More and more, the connection between the mind and body is accepted as a powerful tool in health and the treatment of disease. What experiences have you had to reinforce this theory?

8. Karen's father Joe says, "When you have children, you keep right on loving them. Always hoping for the best" (p. 101). Does this resonate in your family members' lives?

9. Karen tells her father that the cancer diagnosis was "almost a relief" (p. 122). How could an illness possibly be positive?

10 Fellow cancer patient Margaret Bronson appears briefly as a comrade. When have strangers played important roles in your life? Margaret talks to Karen about the difference between positive thinking and positive living (p. 129). Do you think this helped Karen?

11. The cave dream recurs for Karen as she progresses in her identity search. What role have dreams played for you during stressful times?

12. Jake says, "Catch and release is not just for fish." What ideas have you discarded because of a life or health challenge?

13. Elvina received motherly love from her friend Piddie Longman. What nurturing roles have other women occupied in your life, or you in theirs?

14. The characters often lean on their spiritual connections. Do you feel this belief in a higher power helps? How?

15. Cancer or any grave illness can become all-consuming. When Hattie takes her cousin to Wakulla Springs, Karen seems to find solace in nature. Have there been times in your life when you found sources of

respite?

16. Karen's counselor states, "Sometimes, the best way to find out who you are is to start out by finding out who you are not" (p. 188). What does this mean to you?

17. Evelyn remarks to Karen on humor and how it helps to overcome pain and hardship. Has humor ever helped you through a difficult time?

18. Lucille Jackson delivers her thoughts on religion vs. true spirituality (p. 222-224). Do you agree or disagree with her?

19. Through Trisha Truman's words, you get a glimpse into her upbringing (p. 270). Do you feel lack of a positive, strong maternal figure negatively influences a person?

20. One passage states, "True freedom comes from relinquishing control" (p. 124). How does this resonate with you?

Recipe Index

CPSIA information can be obtained at www.ICGtesting.com
Printed in the USA
241495LV00002B/2/P